Praise for the novels of
STELLA CAMERON

"If you haven't read Stella Cameron, you haven't read romance."

—Elizabeth Lowell

"Stella Cameron is sensational!"

—Jayne Ann Krentz

"Don't miss a word!"

—Catherine Coulter

Praise for the novels of
LISA JACKSON

"No one tells a story like Lisa Jackson. She's headed straight for the top!"

—Debbie Macomber

"Lisa Jackson is a real treat. She writes the kind of books I like to read!"

—Kat Martin

"Lisa Jackson takes my breath away."

—Linda Lael Miller

Praise for the novels of
JILL MARIE LANDIS

"Jill Marie Landis creates characters of great dimension, compassion and strength."

—*Publishers Weekly*

"A must read for anyone who loves a good book."

—*Rocky Mountain News*

BOOK YOUR PLACE ON OUR WEBSITE AND MAKE THE READING CONNECTION!

We've created a customized website just for our very special readers, where you can get the inside scoop on everything that's going on with Zebra, Pinnacle and Kensington books.

When you come online, you'll have the exciting opportunity to:

- View covers of upcoming books
- Read sample chapters
- Learn about our future publishing schedule (listed by publication month *and author*)
- Find out when your favorite authors will be visiting a city near you
- Search for and order backlist books from our online catalog
- Check out author bios and background information
- Send e-mail to your favorite authors
- Meet the Kensington staff online
- Join us in weekly chats with authors, readers and other guests
- Get writing guidelines
- AND MUCH MORE!

**Visit our website at
http://www.zebrabooks.com**

SLOW HEAT

Stella Cameron
Lisa Jackson
Jill Marie Landis

ZEBRA BOOKS
Kensington Publishing Corp.
http://www.zebrabooks.com

CONTENTS

Early in the Morning

Stella Cameron

A Friday evening in July

"What do you think about sex therapists?" Chloe Dunn held her breath and frowned at the ten of clubs she'd just picked up.

But for the tap of Steven Early's short, clean fingernails on the kitchen table, silence was absolute.

Chloe pulled nervously at the neck of her tank top. A sultry Seattle evening, the kind they weren't supposed to have, stuck the cotton to her skin. "Steven?" She smiled so brilliantly her jaw hurt. "Tell me what you think."

"About what?"

He hadn't even heard her. "I'm discarding the ten of clubs," she said irritably, and glanced at him. He glanced back. The bluest eyes in the world, they had to be.

Chloe sighed. She loved him. He loved her. But if they couldn't deal with their differences they'd lose each other.

Steven retrieved her discarded card, but didn't appear particularly triumphant.

He was every woman's dream—most women's dream. Sensitive, kind, strong, and a slightly crooked nose short of being handsome. Dreamy. Steven was the kind of man a woman looked at, then started dreaming about.

And that was the problem. In the ten months since Chloe had met Steven she'd done a great deal of dreaming—but very little else. In the physical sense, that was. In other words: sexually.

Tonight was the night.

She'd made up her mind. Tonight they would find a way to confront this problem.

Tomorrow was their wedding day.

Supposed to be their wedding day.

It would be their wedding day. Chloe jutted her bottom lip and puffed at a strand of hair around her warm face. "It's my fault," she blurted out. "I make mistakes. I'm not good at thinking enough before I act."

Steven turned sideways in his chair and stretched out his legs. "You couldn't be sure I needed the ten of clubs," he said, and he studied her quickly from eyes to mouth, and then not so quickly all the way to her shorts and bare legs.

Chloe's skin prickled.

"I can be pretty sneaky," Steven said.

Now he'd decided she was apologizing over a game of rummy! "You sure can be sneaky." And infuriating.

He was a tall, lean man. Lithe, economical of movement.

Great body.

She'd never actually seen him naked—completely naked. Chloe shuddered.

"Hey, sweetheart." Steven reached across the table and covered her hand. "You're not getting sick on me, are you? I'd hate to have to carry you to the wedding."

Chloe shuddered again. "I'm not sick." He could carry her anywhere. "Not really. Just jumpy about tomorrow. I want it to be the most special day of our lives."

"Me, too." He patted her fingers and withdrew his hand. "And it will be. I'd better get that garbage out for you, and go home. We both need our beauty sleep before tomorrow." His laugh did fabulous things for a wide, clever mouth.

Steven's mouth was very clever.

He could kiss—and kiss, and kiss.

Chloe took a deep breath. Kisses pretty much accounted for the romantic diet Steven had offered her—before, and after their engagement of three months. Not that she didn't turn completely weak when he kissed her. Yeah, she did. Weak, and hot, and shaky, and then hotter, and weaker, and more shaky—and then she couldn't breathe too well, and couldn't find enough of him to touch, and she ached and burned in places that definitely felt good when they ached and burned. But aching and burning demanded more, they wanted much, much more. Sweet, over-the-top pain, and warm, throbbing satisfaction would be good. Uh huh, that would be very good.

Whew, so good. Must be all those days she spent whispering in the Seattle public library. Made a woman need some escape, some release. People thought librarians were automatons, book machines. Well, librarians were librarians because they loved books, and book people's minds were highly tuned to exploring and experiencing. Not just in pages, but in life.

She was wandering. Felt like her brain was fevered. Probably caused by feeling hot so often, and getting to stay that way for too long.

Chloe really did adore Steven.

He was the funniest, most honorable, generous man she'd ever met. She couldn't walk away from him just because . . .

Sex wasn't everything.

But why didn't he show any interest in making love to her? She'd tried to make herself talk about it, and tried, and tried, but chickened out every time. How did you ask your fiancé why he didn't want to have sex?

She wasn't the type men lusted after. Never had been. *You can tell Chloe anything.* How many times had friends said that of her? *Chloe's wonderful—she makes you feel so safe. You can trust Chloe with anything.* Everyone's confidante, everyone's shoulder to cry on—no one's one-and-only. Never the girl who got the boy. Never the woman who got the man—until Steven, and Steven had been the first, the only man she'd ever truly loved. But maybe he was just looking for a confidante, a buddy, someone to trust.

Chloe pressed her temples. Having him as a lover and a best friend was her dream, but if best friends were as much as they were destined to be, then she'd take that.

But she had to know what to expect.

"You look tired, Chloe."

"I'm not," she said. "We need to talk."

Steven smiled again and his blue eyes crinkled at the corners. "After tonight we're going to be able to talk all we want to." His dark, curly hair touched the collar of his navy blue polo shirt. "Last night alone, partner—for either of us. I'll be relieved to move out of the apartment. I'm glad we settled on this house, aren't you?"

"Yes."

He tilted his head and studied her. "No second thoughts about buying so far out in the boonies?"

Woods surrounded the single-story, hilltop house. Their closest neighbors were five miles away on the opposite side of Cougar Valley.

"I like being isolated," Chloe said. "I'm going to love being isolated with you."

Steven gathered the playing cards into a heap, stacked them, shuffled them, set them down in the middle of the table. She was almost sure he'd broken into a sweat. His brow glistened.

He didn't say, "Me, too, honey."

Some people would find an old-fashioned approach

to a relationship charming. Most of the time Chloe found it charming. She wasn't exactly a woman of vast sexual experience anyway. But her friend, Barbara, who also worked at the library, but who was going to school at night to become a psychologist, said Steven's behavior was suspicious.

"Tomorrow, the wedding," he said. "Then two weeks alone right here in our own home, sweet home."

Chloe watched his lips form the words.

"Are you looking forward to home, sweet home as much as I am, Chloe?"

She whistled silently and said, "Uh huh. But I think we should talk now."

"Sweetheart"—he took a deep, deep breath—"you mean everything to me. I couldn't face life without you."

His sudden, naked expression disarmed her. She said, "You won't have to face life without me. But, Steven . . . Steven, I want to make love." She felt her blood stand still.

Steven rubbed a hand over his face. "Tomorrow, Chloe."

"Tomorrow, Chloe? Chloe isn't always the sweet, well-behaved little Ms. Dunn. I breathe, Steven. I *feel.* I *want.* I *long,* Steven, I *absolutely long."* She rose to her feet. "I *desire.* I am a *passionate* woman, Steven. *Passionate."*

His eyes widened a fraction, then narrowed. He crossed his arms and muscles flexed. Steven had very nice muscles.

"So?" Chloe said. "What do you think of that?"

"This is tough, sweetheart. Getting married is stressful."

God! "You'd never know it by your behavior. But then, you've done it before, and—" Shoot, she hadn't meant to sound like a shrew.

There was the faintly troubled expression again, the expression she'd seen on the few occasions when the subject of his ex-wife had been raised.

"Garbage out," he said, standing. He was so much taller than Chloe—something that made her feel like a silly, spiteful kid at this moment. He continued, "Why don't you go to bed, honey? Take Merlin with you. He'll cheer you up."

Chloe looked at her white puffball of a Persian cat and felt something within her grow very strained. That was the instant before the "something" snapped. A breath, two breaths. She mustn't shout, or say something she would absolutely regret in the morning. "What will it take to get through to you? I don't think Merlin's quite going to do it for me tonight," she murmured. "If you know what I mean."

She would absolutely regret that in the morning.

"I do take you seriously," Steven said. "Will you just trust me? Go on and get some sleep, Chloe."

He had cold feet. That was it. He didn't really want to marry her. "I asked you what you thought about sex therapy."

Merlin leaped onto the kitchen counter and strolled, high-stepped delicately among a group of canisters. Playing like a naughty toddler . . .

"It's very common for couples to see sex therapists nowadays," Chloe said. There would be no turning back now.

Steven studied her without blinking—or speaking.

"Don't think I'm being critical. Sometimes people have hang-ups about sex."

"Do they?" That clever mouth could thin to an exceedingly straight line. "I don't."

"I wouldn't want you to think sex is all I think about."

"No, you probably wouldn't want me to think that."

"But it does cross people's minds. In situations. Certain situations. People *think* about it."

Steven worked his jaw before saying, "You mean some people are obsessed by it, don't you?"

"I'm not obsessed by sex," she told him, incensed. "But it is an important thing in marriage."

"Yes, it is."

"I'm really not preoccupied with sex."

Steven picked up Merlin and placed him on the floor. The cat promptly jumped up on the counter again.

"Are you listening to me, Steven?"

"You're not preoccupied with sex—just unable to think about anything else."

Her face flamed. "That's nasty. You're trying to shut me up."

"Please go to bed. You'll feel fine in the morning. We'll feel fine in the morning."

This was a side of him she'd never seen before. A cutting, put-you-down side. "We're getting married tomorrow."

He pulled the garbage bin from the cupboard beside the sink. "Yes." And he didn't turn to look at her. "It's just as important to me as it is to you."

"We've never had sex."

"I'm traditional."

Chloe sat down again. Hard. "You're thirty-five."

"Can't I be thirty-five and traditional?"

She had a horrible thought. "Is that why . . . ?" Could Barbara's wild suggestion be true?

"Why what?"

"Didn't you . . . ?"

He set down the can. *"What?"*

"Barbara says it's possible."

"I've never met your friend, Barbara, but I don't think I'd like her."

"Even though you were married . . . Are you a virgin, Steven?"

Hurt transformed into disbelief. "Good grief."

She did love him, and she couldn't bear to lose him. "Sex doesn't matter," she told him hurriedly. "Really. I can live without it."

"But not without talking about it." His teeth set between slightly parted lips.

"Well," Chloe said, feeling weak. "You're avoiding the issue here."

"You know what they say?"

"No. Are you afraid of sex?"

"Do you know what they say you should do if you're in a hole?"

"No!"

"Stop digging."

"Steven, this is important."

"If your horse dies, get off."

"I don't have a horse."

He opened a drawer, pulled out a plastic bag, and headed toward the hall.

It was now or never. Either they found a way to be open with each other or it was over. "You're walking away from an argument."

"I'm going to deal with the wastepaper baskets. I've got to take the goddamn garbage out."

He shut the kitchen door firmly and closed his eyes. Damn, this was hell. Sex was all she would talk about tonight, and sex was all he could think about tonight.

What would she say if he just opened up and told her what was on his mind?

Sex.

Oh, terrific. And his thoughts on the topic played right into what she'd just suggested—sort of.

Emptying the wastepaper baskets didn't take long. One in the bathroom off the master bedroom and one in the bedroom itself. He stared at the bed, then went back into the black-and-white bathroom. The shower had two gold heads. "A his and hers," the real estate woman had said coyly.

Chloe had moved into the house three weeks earlier.

Her shampoo rested on a ledge, and a bar of soap and a razor. He picked up the soap. *Slick skin to slick skin. Water pounding down on them. Steam. Sliding, sliding.*

Steven took a deep breath.

She wanted him.

He wanted her. He didn't want to disappoint her.

Searching hands on his body—touching, testing, holding. Soapy breasts and thighs. Laughter. So easy to lift her, to enter her . . .

Hell, he had to control his mind, then make sure he got everything right when the time came.

He went back into the kitchen and stuffed the bag into the trash bin.

"Steven, please don't do this. We can't base a marriage on avoidance."

He was scared, dammit. His palms sweated. He'd been so sure they'd make it through the wedding without having this discussion. Then everything would be okay—he was sure of it. Almost.

There was no one like Chloe. He hesitated and looked at her, and smiled.

Curly red hair, big, deceptively sleepy-looking gray eyes, pointed chin, a definite upward tilt at the corners of her mouth. A lovely face made more interesting by the way her moods changed the set of her eyes and lips. The mood of the moment was all watchful irritation.

He widened his grin.

She didn't grin back. Her yellow tank top rested on her pale, smooth skin the way he'd like to rest on it—like warm butter applied with a brush. He tried not to linger too long at the level of her pointed breasts. Her cutoff shorts rode low on her round hips and clipped the tops of bare, well-shaped legs. When she moved just so, her smooth middle showed between the tank top and the shorts.

He was dying.

Death by repressed sex drive.

"What are you thinking?" she demanded.

That he'd like to grab her, kiss her silly, and not stop kissing her until they were both naked and he was so deep inside her he'd forget every hang-up he'd ever had.

"I'm a lucky guy," he said quickly, and swallowed.

He would forget his hang-ups eventually. They weren't worth clinging to. He didn't want to cling to them. Faye had been wrong—she'd cast around for some excuse to hurl at him and suggesting he was a failure sexually had been what she'd found. *"Selfish to the bone. Get what you want and to hell with my needs. Don't ever change your last name, Steven. It suits you perfectly. Early. Always early."* Her voice had risen with each word until she'd shrieked, *"Early."*

"Oh, Steven." Chloe's mouth quivered. She came to him and wrapped her arms around his neck, pressed her face into his chest. "Please talk to me about this."

Beautiful Faye had wanted out of their marriage. When they'd met, she'd known all about his very wealthy family—she hadn't expected to find herself the wife of a high school physics teacher who'd become estranged from that moneyed family.

He was a perfectly competent lover.

Wasn't he?

"Chloe, darling, you're overwrought."

"I am not *overwrought!*"

And now she was crying. "Maybe we shouldn't have decided to make this wedding such a private event after all." He brushed at the tears, kissed her lightly—and felt the expected jolt. "You'd be more secure if your mother was here."

"I don't want my mother," she wailed, hugging him tighter. "I'm thirty years old and I don't want my mother. I want you."

"And I want you," he told her, his heart beating too hard, too fast. "I want you so damn much." She believed marriage was forever. Steven had decided to concentrate on that and trust that once they were married, if there were any . . . adjustment problems, they'd work them out. He couldn't risk losing her on the eve of their wedding just because he finally surrendered in a battle with his zipper.

"You say you want me," Chloe said. Her eyes were anything but sleepy now. "But you're deliberately avoiding what it means for a man and woman to want each other and I need to know why. Do you realize we've never even seen each other undressed—completely undressed?"

Oh, God.

She played the backs of her fingers along his jaw. "I've never been a forward person."

"No. You're just you. Look, I don't want to brush you off on this, but—"

"But you're going to anyway." Chloe stepped back and yanked her tank top over her head. Her skin was very white. She sucked in her bottom lip. "Only I'm not going to let you. Take something off."

He grabbed her wrists as she reached back for the fastening on her bra. "What are you doing?"

"Getting naked. Now it's your turn. Start with your shirt—that would be fair."

Heat followed chill in a race over his body. "This isn't like you."

"No, it isn't. At least, I don't think it is."

Gently, but firmly, he trapped her hands against his chest. "Sweetheart, I'll be by for you around nine in the morning. Tomorrow's going to be a wonderful day."

"Okay, I've got it. I've got the answer. Let's elope."

Steven's mind went into free fall.

"We could get into your car right now and drive to . . . No. What am I saying? That would take longer . . . Oooh, this is awful. I started talking and now I can't seem to stop." She made a sound Steven was afraid might be a choked-down sob. "Why did I say anything?"

"Because you're confused. My fault. I guess I've been sending mixed messages." She had to know how much he loved her, and wanted her, yet every time the signal had been clearly declared, "go for it," he'd said, "back off," without giving Chloe as much as a vote.

"But why, Steven?" She was crying, really crying.

"Chloe—"

"I'm sorry. I lost it for a few minutes." She sniffed and swiped at her cheeks. Her forced laugh made him feel like shit. "I was going to suggest we play strip poker. Can you believe that?"

Steven swallowed. He didn't trust himself to say anything.

Lace trim along the top of her skimpy bra didn't cover the hardened tips of nipples the color of warm honey.

He couldn't look away from her breasts. They'd fill his hands, weigh softly in his palms—and they'd taste sweeter than honey. And he was torturing himself.

"Most men would be having a stag party tonight, Steven."

In other words, most men not only thought about sex at times like this, they acted on the thought. "And you wish I were?"

"No. I hate the thought of those things. But I would like to play strip poker with you. There! Now I've told the truth."

"Chloe!"

"I wish you wouldn't say *Chloe* like that. I've never played strip poker."

"But you think your education's incomplete without the experience?"

"No! But I want . . . Oh, this is horrible and it shouldn't be."

He should tell her, just tell her what was on his mind

and trust her to understand. "You aren't ready for this marriage." *Nice job of coming clean.* "I've rushed you."

"We've known each other for months," she told him.

"Not long enough."

She spun away. "You want to call the wedding off?"

"Chloe, I do not want to call the wedding off. What man would want to call off a marriage to you?" He was being so unfair.

The slump of her shoulders smote at him. She said, "I'm so embarrassed."

"You don't have anything to be embarrassed about. You're lovely, and natural, and I need you, Chloe. I can hardly wait for our wedding."

"Then don't." When she faced him again, her cheeks were flushed—and her breasts. "Kiss me, please."

Steven lost the battle to control his breathing, and his heart rate—and other bodily elevations. Her fingers, slipping beneath his shirt, were cool and very, very determined. Chloe wasn't tall. She rose to her toes to seek his mouth and as she rose, she pushed up his shirt and pressed her breasts to his chest. Her lacy bra scratched just the slightest, most infuriatingly sexy bit.

Her breath played over his lips, a soft, warm, sweet puff that sucked him down, sucked him in.

Kissing Chloe was torture of the best kind, but still torture. For months, he'd been kissing her, feeling her, yet not feeling her.

The tip of her tongue sought out his.

He passed his palms up and down her sides. "I love you," he told her. "I always will."

Chloe kissed him hard, closed her eyes and rocked their mouths together, and rubbed her all-but-naked breasts against his chest until he thought he'd explode. "Keep touching me," she said.

The tremor that hit him tightened his grip on her waist.

She sighed, and her fingers roamed down his spine, inside the waistband of his shorts as far as she could reach, then out again and down to the tensed muscles of his thighs.

He *would* explode.

"I love the feel of your body," she murmured.

The next sound she made was a cry, part surprise, part excitement—all pleasure. Chloe fastened on Steven's penis and she had to know the effect she was having on him.

Getting it up had never been a problem.

Even Faye had said that much. It was what he did with it, and other things afterward, that his beloved ex-wife had insisted left her unsatisfied and frustrated to near-suicide.

"Oh, Steven," Chloe whispered. "You do want me as much as I want you."

"Wrong," he said through his teeth. "I want you more."

"I don't think so."

Gently, but firmly—and not without the pain of loss—he took her hands from his crotch.

"What is it?" Chloe crossed her arms over her breasts. "Tell me what's wrong."

"Nothing." He picked up the garbage bin and went outside into a hot, dark night. He throbbed. His legs didn't want to support him. Even the wind through tall evergreens didn't cool him.

Concentrate on the small stuff and get the hell out of here.

Clouds spun a drape across the moon. The skitter and scrape of invisible, living things seemed louder than it could possibly be.

Small stuff.

They were fortunate to have garbage pickup at all out here. The truck passed on its way between two developments near the town of Issaquah, and Chloe had managed to arrange for it to stop each week.

He heard her footsteps behind him and kept walking down the gravel drive toward the road. The trees rustled and whined on either side of him.

Something white shot past his ankles. Merlin's unexpectedly deep yowl jarred Steven.

Chloe caught up and stood beside him. "I've made up my mind."

For an instant he paused, then carried on. "We made up our minds some time ago, my love."

He dumped the bin into a larger one stashed in a wooden shelter beside the road.

"I've made up my mind to tell you exactly what's really worrying me. We're going to be man and wife. I owe it to my husband to explain what I'm thinking, don't I?"

The cat meowed again, more loudly this time. The sound went on and on. Steven tried to shut the noise out. "You don't have to say anything else," he told Chloe. "You are honest. I'm the one who's been holding out. What's the matter with the cat?"

Chloe shushed the animal and took one of Steven's hands in both of hers. "Never mind Merlin. What do you mean, you've been holding out?"

He drew in a breath so deep it made him cough. "Hell, Chloe, there's something wrong with me." That hadn't been what he'd intended to say, but he couldn't form sentences like, *Faye complained of premature ejaculation.* "I may have a . . . problem."

"Steven! Oh, darling. You should have told me. What is it?" She'd put her tank top back on but her breasts felt just as inspiring when she pressed his hand between them. "What's wrong with you?"

If there was an Idiot of the Year award, he had it in the bag. "I didn't put that very well. It's this possible loss of—or maybe gradual loss of function."

She gasped and whispered, "Paralysis?"

"No, not exactly. Although it could be something like that because I'm not even aware of it happening."

"I don't understand."

No kidding. "Things may sort of . . . *fall off* without my noticing."

Chloe gave a small scream.

Merlin set up a wail and kept on wailing.

A shudder climbed over Steven's back. He was murdering this confession.

"My poor darling," Chloe said, wrapping him in a hug so tight his breath shot from his lungs. "Don't worry about me. I don't care what drops off. You'll always have me here holding things together."

"Chloe—"

"I've always been told that the harder things get, the better I perform. And I'm Jennie-on-the-spot. If there's an emergency, I come through fast."

According to Faye, coming through fast had been Steven's downfall.

The damned cat shrieked for attention.

"Shush, Merlin. Steven's got enough problems without that racket. Sweetheart, lean on me, please. And promise me you'll never try to hide anything from me again. For richer, for poorer. In sickness and in health. Remember."

"I'm not sick."

"Don't give me that brave stuff. Whatever happens, you'll never be alone. If you—if you lose things, we'll find a way to have just as full a life without them. There are always ways to compensate for these things."

Think. Backpedal fast. "Things don't fall off. Not the way I made it sound. It's more that they apparently don't always do what they're supposed to do and I'm not even aware of it."

"Don't give it another thought. From now on I'm in charge. You can put yourself in my hands."

Oh, yes, yesss!

Chloe grew still. She looked past him and said, "Sweetheart, what time is it?"

"I don't know. Ten, maybe."

"Huh. I could have sworn I saw light coming up

through the trees. Anyway, as I was saying, I'm in charge. I'll make sure you know if something's not working quite right."

Oh, joy—history about to repeat itself.

"And I'll work with you, my love," Chloe told him, smiling adorably. "If something's not performing up to expectations, I'll just work on it until it does. And I'll enjoy doing it."

If you're in a hole, stop digging. "Thanks, Chloe darling. I don't know about you, but I'm suddenly exhausted."

Merlin, landing on his shoulder—with all claws extended—made Steven shout.

"It's okay," Chloe said, threading her arm through his. "Come on, I'm getting you back into the house. We've got a lot to talk about."

She was gentle and caring, and so special. He owed her complete honesty, and he owed it to her now. "Okay. You've got it, sweetheart. We're going to get everything in the open. Then I'm just going to have to hope you'll still want me."

"There's nothing that could make me not want you," Chloe said.

He started to leave, but held back, turned around. "It is getting light out."

Chloe's grip on his arm stiffened. "Not light," she whispered. "Not really. It's getting bigger. Glowing. Steven!"

The cat's cry died, but the animal placed its feet close together on Steven's shoulder and arched its body.

"Geez. Do you think the real estate woman forgot to tell us there was another house over there?"

"That doesn't have anything to do with a house," Chloe muttered.

"No." She was right. Steven said, "No. Get behind me. And if I say run, do it. Get back to the house and call 911."

"And say what? Excuse me but there's a glow in our woods?"

"Shit," Steven said under his breath. "If I didn't think I was seeing things, I'd say there's a blue light coming this way."

"Make that two of us seeing things," Chloe said. Waves of shivers shook her arms. "A bubble of blue light with green fog coming out of it."

"You see it, too. Maybe it's some sort of atmospheric reaction. Warm air. Cold ground, and . . . Hell, I don't know."

"Nothing's cold right now," Chloe said. "I'm so hot I may melt. Is there something in the middle of the light? Steven! Is it a UFO?"

He laughed. "What happened to your sensible side? I thought you didn't believe in that kind of stuff, anymore than I do."

"Two somethings, Steven," she said in a small voice. "I see two . . . There are two people inside that, that whatever-it-is. And they're coming this way."

Two people. Two tall, slim people wearing silver. Steven closed his eyes for a few seconds, squeezed them tightly shut, and opened them again. His heart made a flying leap into his throat. "Run, Chloe! Now. I'm right with you."

Chloe didn't move. Neither did Steven. He couldn't. He couldn't move his arms and legs at all.

"Run, Chloe!"

"I can't," she said, her words coming in pants. "Steven, I'm scared."

"That's because you're smart," he told her. "I don't believe this."

"Hello," a male voice said, a voice both far away yet so close it might have come from the very air Steven breathed. "How fortuitous. The exact people we'd hoped to encounter"

"I'd faint," Chloe murmured. "Only I can't move, so I can't fall down."

The luminous bubble drew to a halt several yards away.

"A man and a woman," Steven said. "I don't get this."

"We must ensure that we speak most slowly and clearly or they will not understand," the woman said to her companion. Almost as tall as the man, close to six feet at least, the light revealed her black eyes and hair, and pale skin—a thin, sharply intelligent face. "We are so very pleased to meet you. You are lovers, yes?"

Steven tried, without success, to move his legs. "Don't be scared," he whispered to Chloe. His mouth was all that would move. "This is just . . . it's . . ."

"Weird," Chloe finished for him.

"They are lovers," the man said. He bowed slightly. "We're honored to be in the company of lovers. This has been our hope, that we might be granted the extreme good fortune to select precisely the right subjects for our needs. How blessed we are. We are most grateful."

"I want to scream," Chloe said, her voice suddenly loud. "Steven, help me scream. I can't move. I'm glued here."

"Well-favored," the woman said, and the bubble bobbed a little closer. "Are they not well-favored, designated mate?"

The man leaned forward a little. "Quite, I believe. The clothing is primitive, but has a certain antique charm. I've seen pictures of such garments. And their forms are very pleasing."

"I collect they will suit quite well," the woman said. "Clearly we made an accurate interpretation of the messages we harvested from their minds. They are topping."

"Oh, *shit*," Steven said, then added, "Sorry, Chloe. Slipped out."

"Shit seems about right to me," Chloe said. "This is really happening, isn't it?"

"Yup." The man's eyes were pale, as silvery as the one-piece, body-hugging suit he wore. His short, blond hair took on some of the light's bluish hue. Elegantly handsome, and haughty rather than arrogant. "It's happening," Steven said. "Two aliens just floated out of those woods. They're inside a bubble that gives off green vapor. And they sound like a cross between characters from an English period film and a bad sci-fi flick."

"I couldn't have described them better," Chloe said. "They're beautiful, aren't they? Who are you?" she asked the woman.

The man looked at the woman. "Perhaps we should have done more work on decoding their verbal strings."

"Too primitive," was her response. "And unnecessary. We have identified and isolated those thought topics that are of interest to us. That will be adequate for our purposes. There is no doubt that they have what we require. I do believe they may be afraid—at a purely primal level, of course. They are gentle, I feel that."

"As do I."

"And we have made contact with what was lost by the ones who have gone long ago," the woman said. "It is here in these two simple creatures."

"Simple creatures," Chloe echoed. "Who is she calling simple?"

"Remember, our data tells us that they can hear us and that they will understand uncomplicated sentences." The man smiled at Steven as an adult might at a young child. "We are friends," he said. "We have need of you for a short time. You will come with us. You will help us. We will not hurt you."

"Fuck off!"

"Steven!"

"Sorry. I'm . . . This is wild. We've got to get out of here."

The woman clapped her hands together and laughed. "Why, listen to their enthusiastic, youthful sounds."

"This could be serious," Steven said.

Chloe snorted. "This *is* serious."

"We would be most happy if you would listen to us carefully," the man said. "You will not be hurt."

"I'm so comforted," Steven muttered. "Don't panic, sweetheart, I'll get us out of this."

"Sure. And I'm the man-in-the-moon."

Steven laughed, and laughed harder when Chloe joined in. She sputtered, "Make that the woman-in-the-moon."

"I am Orchis," the woman told them when they'd subsided to spasms of chuckles. "This is my designated mate, Vigar."

"Let me get this straight," Steven said. "We can understand when you talk—in simple sentences, of course. You can't understand a word we say. And you can read our minds?"

"They do jabber rather, don't they," Orchis commented. "The male is . . . well, he is, rather, isn't he?"

Vigar, or whatever he was called, glanced down the high bridge of his nose at Steven. "Possibly. Some females might find him so, I suppose. Apparently overt sexuality used to be common."

"Precisely," Orchis agreed. "And we must be vigilant. We must grasp this sexuality and make the best of it."

"Over my dead body," Chloe muttered.

Steven managed to grin and it felt good. "Jealous, Chloe?"

"The female is also sexually obvious," Vigar said.

"Gee, thanks," Chloe said.

Orchis and Vigar skimmed even closer in their bubble. Orchis studied Chloe. "One of the old ones told of how the women used to reveal their breasts. I didn't believe her."

"Oh!" Chloe's voice rose. "I want to cross my arms and I can't."

Vigar turned to Orchis. "We should take them to the caposphere at once. It is essential that they be comfortable or they may not be as useful as we require. We agreed that we should ensure their quiescence without restraint before embarkation."

"Caposphere?" Chloe said. "Quiescence? *Embarkation?*"

Steven longed to hold her hand, to draw her close and convince her, even though it would be a lie, that everything was okay.

"I agree," Orchis said. "I am concerned that the required thought patterns have ceased."

"Indeed. Fear—possibly of us, of the unknown—may be the cause."

"Ooh, they're quick," Chloe said.

Vigar laced his long fingers together. "Let us gather them quickly. There is a great deal to be accomplished."

"The thoughts have utterly ceased," Orchis said, also lacing her fingers. "Perhaps we should endeavor to calm them."

"The bubble doesn't touch the ground," Steven said, more to himself than Chloe. "It's floating. They're floating."

"I'm glad I'm not doing this alone," Chloe told Steven. "I'd think I'd lost it if I were."

"Nice to feel needed," Steven said. "Sorry, love. Didn't mean to sound flip. I'm rattled too, I guess. So far all we've got on our side is that they don't understand our speech. We should be grateful for that, I suppose."

"Here it is warm," Orchis said, extending her joined hands. "Come to us."

Vigar echoed her words and actions.

Only when Steven discovered his eyes several inches

above the level of the bubble did he realize he'd moved.

"Steven!" Chloe shouted suddenly. "I can move again. Look at me. I'm moving. You're moving!"

He did look at her—an instant before she shrieked and flailed her arms. Steven still held Merlin. The cat made a scrambling leap and left more tracks on his master's back before Steven could draw the cat into his arms.

"We're flying, Steven! I'm going to throw up."

Chloe didn't throw up. Softly, with a sensation similar to sweeping velvet over one's skin, Steven was drawn inside the vaporous globe. With Chloe at his side he touched gently down.

"It is warm," Chloe said, pushing a hand beneath Steven's arm. "But this thing's solid, isn't it?"

He gave the globe a poke. "Ouch! You bet it's hard. And I can't see out—but they could. They could see us." If this was someone's idea of a pre-wedding gag, he wasn't laughing.

"Soothing words, Orchis" Vigar said. "We should try simple, soothing words to ensure comfort, and cooperation. I think we will work on their verbal strings after all, but there will be plenty of time for that after embarkation."

"Just so. These sounds they make are annoying, especially in the absence of readable mind messages."

"If our research is entirely accurate and there are indeed as many of them as we think, then they must be driven to couple."

Chloe's nails dug into Steven's arm. "Driven to *couple,*" she repeated. "Do they mean . . . ?"

"Reproduction is their entire purpose." Vigar reached out, brought a single forefinger within an inch of Chloe, and made an outline from the top of her head, down her profile, beneath her chin, to the tip of a breast . . . and to the tip of the other breast. "Exactly as the old ones described. See how she links to him—evidently without thought. So primitive."

"So necessary for our research," Orchis said. "I shall try to communicate with them, then we'll take them to the caposphere."

"Listen carefully," Steven said to Chloe. "I want you to make a lot of noise. They don't like it because they don't understand what we say. Shout and scream and fling your arms about."

"That should accomplish a lot."

"Save the acid tongue, my love. You create the diversion and I'll give our evolved friend an old-fashioned fist. Maybe we'll get lucky and catch him off guard."

"We need you," Orchis said, sounding out her words slowly, carefully. "Our people are dying."

Steven settled a hand on the back of Chloe's neck. "I'm a teacher," he said. "Chloe's a librarian. Not a medical bone between us." He turned to Chloe. "Maybe reason will work."

Orchis continued. "Not dying really. Becoming extinct."

"So much for reason," Chloe muttered. "They don't get a word we say, remember?"

Vigar watched Orchis intently. She raised her finely sculpted chin. "Once, many generations ago, there were young ones—many young ones. Vigar, how will we know if they comprehend us?"

"We will know. Trust, Orchis, we will know."

"Over hundreds of what you call years, the numbers of young have decreased. Now there are still young, but they are rare and must be carefully guarded."

"The patterns are returning!" Vigar's triumph brought an unexpected smile to his lips. "Do you see them, Orchis?"

"I must continue very rapidly." Orchis brought her face close to Steven's. "This is why we had to return to the roots of Sardo. Sardo is the place we come from. It is very far from here, but you will like it."

"I fucking-well won't," Steven said, and felt every word snap from his lips.

"You are to help us save the planet that grew from the most innovative minds your people ever produced, minds that probed the greatness and founded a better place."

Chloe made a scoffing sound. "She sounds like a deranged evangelist."

"Excuse me," Steven said, with great care. "But you need medical help. We'll be glad to help you find what you need."

"We chose you because your . . . *minds* tell us you will be able to teach us all about what we have lost, what is essential now." The depths of Orchis's eyes shone gold and intense. "If you understand, please move your heads up and down."

"Now what?" Chloe said. "Where are the police when you need them?"

"Pretending we don't understand isn't going to help," Steven said. He nodded up and down. "Maybe if we draw them onto our side, they'll get sloppy and we can make a run for it."

Chloe grabbed his shoulder. "Mushrooms! I put mushrooms in the casserole."

He looked at her.

"This is a hallucination. Oh, thank God, that's it. We're having a hallucination. Whew, I've never been so scared in my life. That'll teach me to think I'm a whiz at picking good, edible mushrooms."

"I think the male understands," Vigar said. "Continue and we'll be certain."

"The *same* hallucination?" Steven said, wishing he didn't have to snatch away her straw. "The same hallucination at the same time?"

Orchis closed in on Chloe. "You must show me how you do it."

"What does she mean?"

"Let her finish," Steven said, and jumped violently. "Get your hands off me!" Orchis didn't actually touch him, but his penis rose in the wake of her undulating fingers as if she'd used a tire pump.

"*Steven!*"

He dropped his hands in front of him.

Orchis said, "The ability to produce this protrusion is no longer enough. That is functional but has ceased to be effective since none of our people spend time in such shallow pursuits anymore. But you must show me how to want this to happen, and then how to make my designated mate want this to happen. You must both show us the steps. We would learn what we have forgotten."

"Exactly," Vigar said. "We would learn how to begin the repopulation of our planet."

Orchis spread her arms, closed her eyes, and executed something akin to a slow-motion backward dive. Vigar moved gracefully beside her.

"We're going," Chloe squeaked. "Hold my hand. We're going!"

"Like Mary Poppins," Steven said through his teeth while they all sailed along. He couldn't see beyond the green gas. "Or Peter Pan. I love you, Chloe, so much."

"And I love you, Steven. We can't lose each other now."

"If we get out of this alive, we're never getting out of bed again."

"What?"

"Never getting out of bed," he shouted over a roaring sound that grew and grew. "We'll hold each other forever. Sex, sex, and more sex. Morning, noon and night. Wall-to-wall sex. I'll only come out of you to—"

"Yes," Chloe sang out. "If we live, we'll be naked all the time and never—"

"Perfect," Vigar announced loudly. "You have done

perfectly, Orchis. They understand. They can hardly wait to begin."

"Indeed, Vigar. Two rudimentary minds, but with a single thought. Remarkable."

"A single thought," Vigar agreed. "Coupling."

"Yes, coupling. What one of them seems to catalog as *fucking their brains out*."

The same Friday evening in July—but later

Just because they'd never heard of two people having the same hallucination at the same time didn't mean it couldn't happen.

"Steven?"

"What?"

"Nothing. I was just checking."

"Checking what?"

"Oh, this doesn't prove it one way or the other. Us—talking, or me thinking we're talking. For all I know, I'm the only one having a hallucination. If I am, then I'm passed out somewhere imagining we've just been captured by two aliens who look like spectacular humans—"

"Chloe."

"And I'm so delirious I think they've floated us to their spaceship and taken us aboard, and left us—"

"Chloe."

"And left us in a room—or whatever this is—that looks like something in a movie about a Roman orgy, and smells of incense. The mushrooms were so strong they're making me think you're with me and talking to me. And I'm only imagining there are two silver weirdos who want us to show them . . . No, the mushrooms were so strong I've dreamed up some craziness about these creatures knowing all about how sex works, but nothing about wanting it in the first place."

"Chloe!"

"Yes!"

"You've just described exactly what's really happening to us."

"I was afraid of that." She stepped between two green satin-covered divans, peered at a multitiered golden centerpiece dripping too-brightly colored fruit, and stood shoulder to shoulder with Steven. They faced a sliding panel in the wall—also silk-covered, but in deep blue—of the semi-circular chamber. Vigar and Orchis had left through that panel.

"Their people originally came from earth." Steven picked up Merlin and stroked the cat absently. "But they don't understand what we say. They're so damned smart, or *evolved,* they think they don't have to know what we say—that seems dangerously arrogant to me."

"I'm glad they don't understand us." Chloe stared at the place where Vigar and Orchis had last stood. "They just drifted away, didn't they? But they said they'd be back?"

"Probably before we're ready for them," Steven said. "As soon as they've dealt with 'necessary tasks.' They are so cold."

Chloe surveyed the silk- and satin-lined chamber. "We've got to try to think up a way out of here."

"Yeah, and before this thing takes off." Steven arranged Merlin around his neck. "From what I gathered, the ship, or sphere, is less visible to any interested parties by day, so they'll wait for morning light. That gives us a few hours. Did I imagine it, or do they lose contact with our so-called mind patterns if we're not thinking about sex?"

For a man who'd been avoiding the subject of sex for months, Steven Early was showing very little reticence now. "That's what I understood. So don't think about it."

Chloe slipped a hand into his. He laced their fingers together and squeezed. "They picked us because we're always thinking about sex. That's what they said."

A faint smile flitted over his features.

"That means you, too." She tapped his arm until he looked at her. "Were you really thinking that?"

"What exactly?"

"What they said. You know."

His lips parted. He watched hers.

"Steven?"

"They say people under stress want sex for various reasons."

"Spare me the scientific discussion. We're about to be whisked into space, probably never to return."

He shook his head. "We're not going to let that happen."

"How will we stop it?"

"By giving them what they want before morning." Chloe frowned.

"Can you sum up what you think their problem is?"

She thought a moment. "They've become all brain and no heart."

"Uh huh. In other words, no emotion. And they've become remote from their bodies."

Chloe felt suddenly exhausted. She dropped to sit on the nearest divan and pulled Steven down beside her. Merlin complained, but didn't budge from Steven's neck.

"Maybe you were the one thinking it—what they said," Steven suggested.

"Thinking"—Chloe turned to him—"I've never even *thought* that word. You even said it tonight. Several times."

"Extreme circumstances," he said, avoiding her eyes. "Anyway, it's a guy thing."

She dug an elbow into his side. "I don't believe you just said that. But you actually thought it, huh? What they said?" He still avoided looking at her. Chloe poked him again. "*It.* You know. *That?*"

"I seem to remember telling you pretty clearly what I intend to do if we ever get out of here—as long as you don't mind, that is."

"Fuck my brains out?" She clapped a hand over her mouth and felt herself turn red.

Steven laughed. He tipped back his head and laughed and laughed.

"Stop it. I'm embarrassed."

"So you should be." He choked, and cleared his throat—and looked at her very closely now. "I can't believe you said a thing like that, either. But I forgive you. Excessive stress causes inappropriate behavior."

"Gee, thanks."

He stopped laughing. "They've forgotten how to love, Chloe."

Her heart seemed to stop beating. She should be too scared for such things, but she wanted to hold Steven. "Poor souls," she murmured.

"I love you, Chloe."

"I know. I love you, too—so much."

"We've got to make it to the church on time." His great grin made another fleeting appearance. "As the song goes.

"And we're going to show these—no, we're going to convince them we've given them all the information they need before sunrise, and then they'll let us go.

"Do you have a better idea?"

She felt hot all over—yet again. "Sounds like a fantastic idea. I just wish it didn't have to be here." A new thought struck. "This doesn't mean we have to . . ."

Steven raised his eyebrows.

"Well, you know what I mean. In front of them?"

He grimaced.

"It does?"

" 'Fraid so."

She eyed him suspiciously. "You wouldn't."

"Wouldn't I? Outrageous circumstances call for outrageous measures. Isn't that what they say?"

"But . . . We're going to . . . in front of *them*?"

"Not exactly."

The surge of disappointment Chloe felt shocked her. "Oh."

"We're going to think about it—in detail." He rubbed her thigh and Chloe jumped. Steven really grinned this time, and said, "Sorry, love. But it could work. I don't think they'd respond to a visual demonstration. It would probably be purely clinical to them. They've already let us know they view sex that way, and that's why their people aren't interested enough to . . . Geez, this is bizarre. We've got to teach them to *feel*. They'll only do that if we get at their minds. At least, that's my take on this."

"I'd rather work on the mushroom theory. I think I feel sick."

"Could I kiss you, sweetheart?"

The tenderness she heard in his voice overwhelmed Chloe. He lifted her to sit on his lap, chafed her bare arm, stroked her neck, settled the tip of a thumb beneath her chin, and covered her lips with his own.

Merlin yowled and flew to perch on the back of a sumptuous amethyst-colored chair.

Steven's kiss was gentle, but desperate. She let the pressure of his mouth tip her head back.

He slipped a hand inside her tank top, inside her bra. Chloe drew in a sharp breath but kept on kissing him. The sensation of his big hand supporting and lifting her breast, caressing seared skin, made her press against him. Beneath her bottom she felt his solid erection.

"We ought to be looking for the door out," she murmured between brief, hard, urgent kisses. "I wonder what time it is."

"Mmm." Steven kissed her to silence. "This is going to be tough."

She slipped a hand down to fondle the outline of his penis through his shorts.

Steven groaned. "So tough."

"Explain."

"I'm only human. It's going to be murder to stop."

"You never found it murder before."

"Didn't I?" He raised his head enough to see her eyes. "Take it from me, I've been dying from the moment I set eyes on you."

Chloe gripped his shoulders. "You've been *dying* since you set eyes on me? What are we talking about here? You wanting to make love to me? Or the falling-off things? You should have told me about that. I don't know how you could have thought it would change my mind. Why would you think I wouldn't want to just because you thought you were about to lose something?"

"I've been dying to make love to you," he said with no hint of a smile. "And I've been terrified I'd disappoint you."

She sat absolutely still. "Disappoint me?"

He exposed her breast.

Chloe followed his long look at her flesh, caught the flicker of his tensed jaw. With his thumb he circled her nipple, drew closer to the center until she panted with need. "Steven? Please don't stop."

"I'd better until we know exactly what we're doing."

"Oh, we know exactly what we're doing. I can tell we do."

"We've got to"—he bent to lick the soft rise of her breast—"We've got to plan how we're going to do this." His breath wafted over her peaked nipple.

"We're doing fine." Chloe wiggled.

"Don't do that, honey," Steven groaned. "I should have explained something to you a long time ago. I haven't been fair."

"We could find a way to convince them we need absolute privacy to . . . *do* this." They had to do it or she would faint. If Steven didn't take her in his mouth she'd probably faint anyway—but she would faint with ecstasy if he did.

Fainting might be a fabulous thing about now.

"That's what I thought, too," Steven said. He moved to the top of her other breast.

Chloe moaned. "Does that mean we have to try to get them back in here now?"

"Given what's happening here, I'm surprised they haven't come rushing in already." The stubble on his chin grazed her skin. Wonderful. "We've got to be sure what we intend to do. Then we'll attract their attention. And we can accomplish that pretty simply, I think."

"How?"

"Concentrate really hard on—you know."

At another time and in another place, this might be funny as well as incredibly arousing. "Are you sure we aren't already doing that?"

"We're going to organize the process. Make them think we'll give them some sort of step-by-step blueprint. That's the kind of thing they'll understand. They're short in the emotion department, remember."

"Short in the basic sex drive department, too," Chloe said brusquely, and thought that, until now, she'd been fearing Steven might suffer from the same condition.

"We'd better hope we can do something about that. If we can get them . . . Well, ideally we want them to . . ."

"I know what you mean," Chloe finished for him. "We want them making mad, passionate love and too busy enjoying making mad, passionate love to think about either flying this thing to Sourdough—"

"Sardo."

"Whatever. And we also want them to forget we even exist, at least for long enough to let us escape."

Steven said, "You've got it. But we start by getting

them here, then we concentrate on wanting—no, needing to be alone to, to make love? We rudimentary beings can only make love alone."

He still bent over her breasts, still tasted them with lips and tongue. His hair was very black against her pale skin. Other hair on his body would be black against her pale skin. Chloe's belly jerked tight. She felt herself grow wet.

"We've got to excite them," he murmured. "Then hope we can get out while they're too busy with other things."

"If I can still think at all," Chloe said.

"That'll make two of us. You've got beautiful breasts."

She filled her hands with his hair. "You've got a beautiful mouth. I've always thought how clever your mouth is."

"You make it clever." He skimmed the very edge of one of her areolas. "Chloe, I'm already self-destructing here. Let's get this show on the road."

She avoided considering the possibility of their love-making becoming a show. "An audio," she said vaguely.

Steven barked a laugh. "You're quick, love. Yeah, let's get the audio on the road." He straightened her top and shifted her beside him. "Concentrate on the first step."

Chloe closed her eyes, waited, opened them again. "The same first step as you?"

"Hell, yes, the same . . . Sorry. Okay. Think very hard about . . . about us holding a baby."

"A baby!"

"That's the end result they want," he told her with enough pained care to let her know this was costing him as much as it was costing her. "So we visualize what they want first. Then back up to the natural start-ing point."

"Holding the baby wouldn't have been my idea of

the first . . ." She let the sentence trail off. "Okay. Babies. Then what?"

"We keep on thinking about babies until they show up."

"The babies?"

"Chloe! You know I mean Vigar and Orchis."

"What if they don't show?"

"They will."

"Then what?"

He sat straighter. "Think about starting to make love, then stop."

Chloe giggled and said, "Coitus interruptus."

"We're not getting that far," Steven growled. "Don't be difficult."

"Be grateful I'm not screaming and throwing myself at the walls."

He smiled faintly. "That may come later. Close your eyes and see babies."

The incense-like scent that loaded the air made Chloe's nose itch. She squeezed her eyes shut and thought.

How ironic. They'd never as much as discussed having children—probably because they thought, without comparing notes, that they were marrying too late to start a family.

"You're thirty and I'm thirty-five," Steven said suddenly. "This would be a great time for us to have children. We'd make good parents, too. I know we would."

She stared at him. "Stay out of my mind."

"Huh?"

"You read my mind about being too old to start a family."

"I didn't. It's just that we haven't discussed having children and I don't know why. I'd like some, wouldn't you?"

Chloe hunched her shoulders and hugged herself. "Yes. Yes, of course." She felt soft inside, and very in love. "Our children."

"Think about them."

"I was."

"Good."

"Steven."

"Yes."

"What color is their hair?"

"How would I know?" A faint hiss preceded the entrance of Vigar and Orchis. "They've got red hair like you."

"The timing is inconvenient" Orchis said. "I would prefer to complete flight preparations. But they're actually relaxed—and sexually oriented. Amazing, but probably a function of their simplicity."

Chloe gritted her teeth.

"Exactly," Vigar agreed. "As we assumed, they have an extraordinary drive to procreate. We will proceed as we planned, only somewhat earlier."

Steven wanted children. In the midst of madness, Chloe savored that one crystalline, one charming thought. What more could she ask for than a man who loved her enough to want children with her?

"Think," Steven said under his breath. "Visualize."

Chloe did as she was told. Not red, but black hair. She smiled to herself. Lots of black hair.

"This process is not as we envisioned." Vigar sounded peeved. "Seated one beside the other. Thinking only. A more physical, less mindful approach would have seemed in character. On the other hand, doubtless this will make our job of instructing the others easier."

Steven's fingers, stealing over hers, broadened Chloe's smile. With him she could do anything, be anything. He wanted her for herself—and for himself. She was first with Steven, not someone who made a good distraction until he could have someone else.

He pressed her hand. "Are you thinking of the other now?"

"The other?" Her voice emerged as a hoarse croak.

"The *other.* About starting to make love. Then stop when I press again. Go blank then."

She concentrated. Sometimes sensation was everything. In the months since she and Steven had met, she'd spent more time than she should admit just imagining sensations. After they'd been together, the memory of how his lips felt on hers lingered, and how they felt on her neck, her ears, her closed eyes.

Steven always took his time. He could take forever just kissing her hands, nipping them in unexpectedly sensitive places. She'd never guessed that a nibble between finger and thumb could pull tight all the little muscles between her legs, or that the tip of his tongue on her knuckles might tense her nipples.

"So," Vigar remarked. "Do we agree that stripping away all clothing is the first step?"

Chloe's eyes opened instantly.

Steven squeezed her hand and she closed her eyes once more, but with difficulty.

"This is the male's perception?" Orchis said. "Interesting. With the female I saw only hands—but that does not mean the premise is not identical. However, there was a certain . . . something. No matter."

"Stripping off clothes?" Chloe muttered. "You animal."

Steven cleared his throat. "Think of nothing."

"I can't."

His sigh was audible. "Music then. Play something to shut out anything else."

"Good idea. Beethoven's Ninth."

" 'Masquerade' from *Phantom,* " Steven said. "Great music."

"Beethoven's Ninth," Chloe insisted.

" 'Masquerade' is—"

"The sexual progression has ceased."

Chloe heard Vigar, but schooled herself not to look at him.

"No." Orchis sounded different, less certain. "There

was some sound in the female. Very primitive music. One of the little-known composers preserved on the history disks."

"I told you to think of nothing," Steven said.

Chloe moved her hand to rest on top of his wrist. "You told me to hear music. I did, and so did Orchis."

A noise caught Chloe's attention and she did open her eyes—to glance at Orchis. The beautiful creature returned the look steadily, but with a frown puckering her smooth brow. Chloe had the disquieting notion that the woman might have recognized her own name on one of her "rudimentary" captives' lips. She'd definitely heard the Beethoven.

"Leave this to me," Steven said shortly. "Count backward or something."

Obediently, Chloe began counting backward from a hundred.

"Ah," Vigar said at last. "Once more he has removed her clothes."

"Not even a kiss?" Chloe murmured. "No finesse."

"Please don't say that."

The hard edge in Steven's voice held something more—anger? She bowed her head and remained silent this time.

"Anger," Vigar told Orchis. "Fading anger, but he's taking off his own clothes. How very outmoded."

These people had outsmarted themselves. They'd lost the best parts of being human, and being men and women in love, men and women loving.

"Gone again," Vigar said with more than a touch of annoyance. "They approach each other and stop. Then nothing but meaningless shapes. He is thinking of us."

"She is thinking of him."

Chloe looked at Orchis again. The other woman stared back intently.

"He sees us leaving and they're alone again," Vigar reported flatly. "Once more he is removing her clothes."

"Into undressing me, huh?" Chloe asked.

"Can't think of anything I'd rather do."

"He sees us leaving again. He waits for us to be gone. And he undresses her again. And she begins removing his clothes. He plans for them to produce a child."

"She feels something very deep for him."

"Feels?" Vigar's tone was sharp. "These creatures are not capable of feeling. They are too primal. They are not evolved enough to feel."

"Evolved," Steven muttered. "I think I hate the stupid, cold-blooded bastard. His kind have forgotten how to feel and he doesn't even know it. He's looking for some sort of technique to solve his problems."

"Surely they'd have sex manuals among all the data they boast about." Chloe recalled her own reading of the volumes Barbara had so generously picked out.

"Vigar," Orchis said. "If it were as simple as what goes where, we should not require help. The manuscripts would have provided the instruction we seek. Our difficulties are deeper—perhaps even older."

"Naturally I consider your opinions of the utmost value," Vigar said. "However, it occurs to me that you may be fatigued from the intensity of our recent efforts. We did not have sufficient time to make complete preparations for this mission and I know your passion for detail."

"You are generous, Vigar. But I declare that our inability to converse—"

"We would gain nothing from conversing with inferior minds."

Chloe stopped Steven's fingers from curling into a fist. "I think we're getting somewhere," she whispered. "Be patient."

"I should still find it interesting to attempt communication. There is something in her that is familiar—something that stirs a recollection in me. One of the old ones spoke of certain *sensations.*"

Chloe's spine stiffened.

"You must rest, Orchis. After we embark for Sardo you shall leave matters to me until you are recovered."

"His images of our leaving them," Orchis said as if she hadn't heard Vigar. "Could it be that our physical presence inhibits their coupling?"

"Hardly. The requirement for privacy at such times is not documented at their primitive stage of—"

"Evolution," Steven said explosively.

"At their primitive stage," Vigar continued. "Their communication is rough. I doubt we could decode the strings without some years of study. He is imagining us leaving again. And again. Taking off her clothes. No, we're leaving."

"Come, Vigar, we are going to the outer chamber."

"But we've known there was no certainty of getting the help we must have. If we fail to grasp this opportunity for knowledge—at this very moment—they may pass out of season."

Season? Like dogs and cats? Chloe wondered.

"We will not miss the opportunity. I believe that they are ripe to couple and that they will do so, but not unless they are physically alone."

"But—"

"But what, Vigar?"

Chloe squinted at them through slitted eyes. Orchis inclined her lovely face to watch Vigar. Unlikely color rose in his cheeks. "I merely thought that as reproduction specialists and designated mate counsellors it might be instructive for us to observe them coupling."

"Since we have never experienced spontaneous coupling ourselves?" Orchis walked past Vigar. "Open your mind and come with me. This is the moment we have dreamed of throughout our studies. We may hope that we are about to learn what our people need to know."

Vigar followed her in silence.

Orchis said, "We must be receptive to their mind

images. I believe I fully understand what we must do to optimize this extraordinary opportunity."

"As you say," Vigar said neutrally.

"I'm glad you agree." Orchis preceded him through the open panel. "I assure you that we shall increase our teaching potential immeasurably by engaging in a practical application."

"I fear your meaning is obscure, Orchis."

"Trust me, Vigar. I have always been considered a remarkable instructor. Allow me to demonstrate. We shall begin with your removing my clothing."

Even later on that Friday night in July

Moments of truth.

The moments that punctuated every life, and this was one of those moments, probably the biggest Steven had ever faced.

As the panel closed behind Orchis and Vigar, Chloe remained seated beside him.

A diffuse glow washed the room with multicolored beams, which shone through a border of glass floor tiles. The beams gradually dimmed.

"I thought they didn't know anything about creating moods," Chloe said.

Steven glanced at her long-fingered hands where they rested on her thighs—he glanced at her thighs, as far as the knee, and back to the hem of her shorts.

"Steven?"

"Hmm?"

"Did you hear what I said?"

"Moody people?"

"I said I thought Vigar and Orchis didn't know anything about creating moods."

Chloe wasn't very tall, but her legs were long and well shaped. She clasped them just above the knee.

"Steven?"

"Yes." He met her eyes. "No, I'm sure they don't know anything about the kind of moods we're used to."

"You aren't concentrating—on anything but my legs."

Her smile brought a matching one to his mouth. "I like looking at your legs."

The faintest blush stole over her cheeks. "Good. That's very good. But what about the dimmed lights? They left us alone, then they dimmed the lights in here. That's mood-setting stuff."

"It sure is. You're observant. Just a minute." He bowed his head and concentrated.

"What are you doing?"

"Making sure they don't pop back in here to see what's holding up *the sexual progression.*"

"Do you really think they're somewhere out there waiting for us to lead them to . . . *It?*"

"Uh huh. The lady definitely is."

A large table, low to the floor and made of a transparent medium shot through with gold flecks, claimed Chloe's attention. As if suspended, the contents of drawers in each side were clearly visible: shimmering crystals artfully arranged.

Chloe attempted to push her springy red curls away from her face. She anchored some of them behind her ears, managing to produce an appealingly fragile, elfin appearance. "They know what goes where but they can't be bothered to put it there," she said, scowling. "How do they think we can change that?"

"Not how, why. Because they figure we can be bothered, that we want to be bothered. They touched that truth when they touched our minds, and now they expect us to make them care, too."

"She's much more open than he is."

Steven propped his elbows and massaged his temples. "She seems to be."

"Or smarter, maybe."

"Possibly."

"Only to be expected, though."

"I'll let that pass—this time. I need to concentrate here."

"Women are more into some things."

He turned to see her. "Like sex? Dream on, Chloe."

"Because you're so into sex, you mean?" she asked sweetly.

"Let me deal with this, then I'll let you know what I mean."

Chloe hummed the melody to "Masquerade" from *Phantom of the Opera*. Her voice became gradually louder until she stood up and spread her arms with a flourish.

Steven sighed. "What's that all about?"

"Orchis reacts to music. She heard mine before. And I think she's the one who dimmed the lights because she's more evolved than he is."

"Chloe," Steven said, striving for a patient tone. "Would you mind avoiding that word?"

"Which . . . Oh, evolved." She sniggered. "Sure. But since you voted for 'Masquerade' I'll assume it's some sort of guy take on a sensual trigger. Maybe Orchis will hum it for Vigar and it'll turn him on."

"Good luck, Orchis," Steven said. "I wonder what's in Vigar's mind about now?"

"Taking off Orchis's clothes if you've been doing your job."

He thought about that, then tried not to think about it. "Lucky Orchis. That should be a thrill a minute with the ice man."

"Vigar is quite a man," Chloe said. "To look at, anyway."

"Is that right? I wouldn't have pegged him as your type."

"He isn't. I prefer darker, more obvious men."

"More obvious?"

She plucked a handful of red-blue grapes from the top tier of the golden centerpiece. "Much more obvious. The kind with primal instincts. Preferably down-right primitive."

Just the sight of her, more than slightly mussed and rumpled, excited him. "Anyone in mind?"

"Yes."

An amusing, intelligent, red-haired dynamo. "Want to share his identity with me?" Her breasts had tasted slightly salty and totally intoxicating.

"Not yet. At this point I have to check him out to see if he really fits all my criteria."

He studied her. "What made a woman like you fall for a man like me? Seriously?"

"Seriously?" She dropped her arms to her sides. "Wow, you mean it, don't you? You're actually asking the question, and you aren't even fishing. That's amazing."

"What does that mean?"

"Let me tell you—later." Chloe dropped to sit on the silk-carpeted floor at his feet. She wrapped her arms around her knees and rested her chin. "You may have bought us the time we need to escape. At least I hope so. But they are out there waiting for us to re-populate their planet."

"Yeah. Big job. We'd better move ahead. They could be getting chilly by now."

Her big gray eyes sought his.

"Without those silver suits, I mean." He grinned. "You aren't scared, are you?"

"Sure I am. But we're going to pull this off, or croak in the attempt."

There was something so magnetic about her, about everything about her. "You're something, Chloe Dunn. You're fabulous. Seeing your smile every day. Talking and laughing and being with you every day. Lying with you every night—and any other time I can tempt you— I want those things. I haven't thought about much else since we met."

"Neither have I. I'm forever going into the stacks

in the library and forgetting why I'm there. Goodness knows how many people I've left standing at the desk until they gave up and went away."

"You're kidding."

She scooted closer, propped her cheek against his thigh. "It's tough to concentrate on *A Guide to Potty Training Your Iguana* when I'm imagining you naked."

Even to him his laugh sounded self-conscious. "Women don't do that."

Her open mouth on his leg, the edges of her sharp little teeth against his skin, made him jump. She pulled back her lips in a mock snarl, then grinned up at him. "Men are backward. Have I ever told you that? Well, they are. Backward and pigheaded. Bad combination. They think they're still hunters for the poor little woman back in the cave—which would be fine with me from time to time. They also think sex wouldn't exist if they didn't spend their lives thinking about getting it, trying to get it, and getting it. Now that's really a laugh."

"It is?"

She did bite him then, lightly—and ran her fingers up the inside of his thigh and beneath his shorts.

"Hey!" He jumped and jackknifed forward. "Unhand me."

"Sure you want me to?"

"No."

"Neither is Vigar."

"So now you're reading their minds?" His shifting on the divan only allowed Chloe to slip her hand farther inside his shorts. He said, "Have pity on a man who needs to concentrate."

"Concentrate. Think of this as the next step to getting out of here."

"And I thought you were feeling me up because you're obsessed with getting inside my pants."

"I am obsessed. But I'm already inside your pants and you feel so good, Steven." She rose to her knees and contrived to work her nimble-fingered way to his bare, throbbing flesh. "I'd like to have you in my mouth. Does that shock you?"

The jolt she caused snapped him. "It's going to make me lose it—right now if I'm not very careful." He covered her hand at his crotch. "You're killing me—but don't stop."

"Okay," she breathed, and undid the waist of his shorts. "I want to watch what I'm doing. I've seen you like this in my mind. Now I want to really see you."

"You aren't joking, are you?"

"No more than you would be if you said you'd imagined me naked."

Heat flashed, in his body, and in his brain. "We both know I've done enough of that."

She lifted his shirt and blew softly on his belly. "I do now." Again she blew, and kissed the rim of his navel, blew—and kissed.

Steven fell against the back of the divan. "It's about time I let you hear the ways you get to me. Hear me count them. Didn't someone write about counting the ways?"

"Elizabeth Barrett Browning. How do I love thee? Let me count the ways," she said against his tensed stomach. "Hear us, Vigar and Orchis. Think about love. Show each other how you love."

"Every man should love at least one librarian. They know important stuff."

"Uh huh. One librarian. You only get to love one, Steven Early. Me."

Why had it taken an outrageous probable disaster to make him open up to this woman? "Faye said she was divorcing me because I was a lousy lover." He averted his face and held his breath.

"Shows what she knew." The splayed fingers of one of Chloe's hands skimmed each of his ribs, each muscle she could reach without raising her head.

Slowly, Steven turned back and looked down at her

tangle of red curls. "Is that it? All you've got to say? You don't have any questions about why she might have said that?"

"I may sometime—but not now. I'm busy."

"Chloe, I couldn't bear it if I lost you."

"You aren't going to lose me." The calculated adjustment of her grip on his most sensitive parts brought a groan to his lips—and a smile to Chloe's. "I've got you, my love, and I'm not letting you go. Not ever. Not that we aren't in imminent danger of getting lost together."

"Not funny. Chloe, I've been afraid to try to make love to you in case I disappointed you."

She hesitated, her drowsy expression clearing. "How could you disappoint me? Did you think I was going to rate your performance or something?"

"Or something. I didn't exactly do a great job of explaining, but when I said something stupid about *falling off*, I meant . . . Hell, some things are hard to say."

"So don't say them."

He had to, for both of their sakes. "Look, let me just tell you, okay? What I meant to say was that I'm not sure how my performance is—if it's frustrating enough to drive a woman mad."

Chloe regarded him solemnly. "When you kissed my breasts I thought I'd faint. Then I thought I'd faint if you didn't . . . well, if you didn't finish."

"I'd rather never finish. Not entirely."

"You are one sexy man." Swiftly, she parted his thighs and scooted on her knees until she could rest her head where he sure wasn't going to forget it. "You're so masculine."

"Thanks, but—"

"Hush, I'm counting the ways. You're elegantly powerful. The way you move. I've seen women watch you, and I want to tear their hearts out."

He heard his own, not very convincing laugh.

"You've got fabulous hands."

"So have you. And you're very good with them. God, are you good with your hands."

With her pointy chin resting on the underside of his erect penis, she hooked her fingers inside the waistband of his undershorts.

Steven quit breathing altogether.

"Your hair drives me crazy," she told him. "All of it. The way it looks against my breasts. Thinking about how the hair here"—she squeezed him—"how this hair will look—and feel—on my thighs."

His hips came off the divan.

Chloe laughed and edged his pants down another inch. "Your watch on your wrist. Against the bones in the back of your hand. The fine black hairs there, too. I watch your hands when you drive. And when you stroke Merlin—who is besotted with you, y'know. But I bet you never guessed that looking at your hands makes me feel heavy inside, did you?"

"Uh uh." He squirmed. "Have mercy."

"Never. You've got long, long muscles. Everywhere. I imagine the ones in your thighs holding me down, and I think of them heavy on me when I wake up."

"Chloe."

"No man ever had bluer eyes than you. Sometimes, when you're thinking about something else, and you turn your head just so—and look at me—I'm jelly inside."

Every word she spoke packed a one, two punch. What she said destroyed him and made him want to stay destroyed, and the jut of her chin pumped his already stretched male parts even tighter. He risked a downward glance and saw that the head of his penis was free of his pants and only a couple of inches from her mouth.

"Our two neophyte lovebirds had better be getting this out there," Steven said. "I can't go on much longer."

"Sure you can. The first time I saw you was at that new library dedication. You were looking at the mayor. Every woman in sight was looking at you—watching you."

"No they weren't."

"You kept running your fingers under your collar. Your hair was long—it still is."

"You'd like me to cut it?"

"Don't you dare."

"The first thing I remember about you is how you could make me laugh," Steven said. "You do that, you make me laugh. And you make me feel important. You listen to me, Chloe."

"Now I ought to feel shallow." His pants, with Chloe's help, worked even lower on his hips. "I do feel shallow. You were thinking about how I made you laugh while I was thinking about things like this. Just call me Sidewalk Puddle Chloe—the shallow one."

"You aren't shallow. You're—" His breath jammed.

Chloe extended her tongue and delicately rested the very tip on the distended head of his penis.

"Aaah." He blinked several times, slowly, and worked his jaw. "Chloe, sweetheart."

Her response was the slow curling of her tongue around him. She freed him entirely of his pants and supported him with both hands while she took him into her mouth.

Steven turned fiery hot, then cold. Sweat broke on his brow, his back. His hips surged upward and he was helpless to control the violence of the thrust.

Panting, he sank down. "Stop." He clamped his hands on her shoulders. "I don't care what our evolved friends are getting from this, I know what I'm getting. It's got to be a two-way street. You and me together. You want that, don't you?"

The curls around her face were damp. She drew her lower lip between her teeth and pressed her eyes shut.

He hadn't noticed how heavily she was breathing until now.

"Chloe?"

"I do want everything to be a two-way street, but that doesn't have to mean I can't do things for you sometimes. Don't you think I'm enjoying this?"

He'd never known a woman who showed pleasure simply at giving him pleasure. "I think you're enjoying it. Can I tell you what I want?"

For a moment she looked into his eyes, then she gently rested her face where her mouth had been and slid her arms around his waist. "Tell me. Everything." A faint shudder went through her.

Steven brought a hand within inches of her hair and hesitated. "You're pretending, aren't you? Faking it because you're feeling sorry for me. Tell me. Be honest, for god's sake."

Her skin drew tight over fine bones. "I wouldn't know enough to fake it. And I'm not pretending about this—this with you. But I'm scared. We're helpless."

"No, we—"

"What time is it?"

He checked his watch. "Midnight. Chloe—"

"What if they're getting the caposphere ready for takeoff? What if they're not paying any attention to us at all?"

"They're missing some great mind pictures."

She didn't laugh. "As soon as it starts to get light they intend to start their journey. Under early cloud cover, they said."

"Yeah, I know. General galactic concern about Earthies' preoccupation with UFOs. An agreement to eliminate as many sightings as possible. They called us Earthies! This is so off-the-wall. I heard everything they said to each other. They talk like machines—antiquated machines."

"They aren't machines, just people who've lost their way because their society put too much emphasis on—

well, not on wrong things, I guess. But they ignored important things until they went away."

"Kind of like the sign in Harwick's office."

She nuzzled deeper in his lap. "Who's Harwick?"

"My dentist. Great dentist. Great guy—if you like being made to laugh with a mouthful of cotton rolls. The sign says, 'Ignore Your Teeth. They'll Go Away.' That's what these people from Sardo have done with their emotions. But they aren't happy."

"No. And it isn't just because they're afraid of their race dying out. There's a wistfulness in them. Obviously they've got at least a notion of what's missing. They call it drive because they're dedicated to their science, but they selected us to help them because they felt something powerful in us."

Steven sighed. "Yeah. Frustration run amok. Two people ready to chew doorjambs if they don't get some sexual satisfaction—with each other."

"You were thinking about making love," Chloe said, sounding smug. "All that time when you were acting superior because I was trying to get some sort of re-action out of you—you were, well, you were doing it in your head. When you watched me, you thought about . . . Well, you did."

"Spit it out, love. You really turn me on when you say the words."

"Do I?" She pulled his shorts down to his ankles. "You were thinking of sliding your unbelievably sexy penis inside me."

"Hey!" He attempted to cover himself with his shirt. "And I always thought you were such a nice girl. What if our host and hostess decide to pay a visit?"

"He'll be jealous. So will she. And I am a nice girl."

Steven closed his eyes. "Nutty, but the nicest." He bent over her and kissed the back of her neck. "Your hair reminds me of red silk in the sun. You smell like sun, sun on warm, windswept grass. Hell, now I'm turning into a bad poet."

"Were you a good one once?" she asked innocently, and kissed that other area of dark hair she'd mentioned.

"Witch. You know how to make a man feel ten feet tall."

"And bulletproof?"

"That, too." The shudder coursed her spine again. He stroked her hair and rubbed the nape of her neck. "We're going to get out of this. Give it another hour and we'll find a way to get their attention."

Chloe sat up abruptly. Her eyes had widened and become too bright. "Why would we do that? I think we should work hard to distract them, then try to sneak away."

"And if we do that, and fail, they'll probably be able to find a way to keep us restrained until they get off the ground."

"Off Earth, you mean." Chloe's voice rose. "We don't even know if their time frames match ours. What if it takes two hundred of our years to get to Sourdough?"

"Sardo. You're right. We don't know a thing about their reality. If you can use a word like reality for any of this. The way I see it we've got one chance—to follow through with what we started. I can do it if you can." Even with the end of their world knocking at the door.

"We're just beginning our life together," she told him, and he felt her tears hit his legs. "I'm not ready for it to be all over."

"Sweetheart." Steven kissed her neck again. "I'm never going to be ready for it to be all over. But it's not going to be yet. A few more strong mind images and we'll raise enough ruckus to get them in here. Then we find a way to plead our way out."

"They don't understand a word we say."

"We'll make them understand. One way or the other."

"But what if we can't?"

"Leave it to me." The jaunty grin he assumed even felt good to him. "They can let us go quietly, or I'll knock the shit out of good old Vigar."

"Steven!"

"Sorry. Didn't mean to be sexist. We'll knock the shit out of both of them."

She actually giggled, and sat up to show him her flexed muscles. He peered at her slim arms and wrinkled his nose.

Chloe examined her muscles. "No fat there," she said.

"No muscle either. You're a wimp."

Without warning, she launched herself from the floor and landed, sprawled, on top of him. Steven grappled with her squirming, quicksilver body. She was all over him.

"No fair tickling," he gasped. "Stop it, No, not that." His struggle pulled his feet free of his pants. Chloe sat astride his hips, hauled his face toward her, and instantly took advantage of the opportunity to yank his shirt over his shoulders until it cleared his head.

She yipped, and bounced, and squealed—and tickled each vulnerable spot he exposed in his attempt to keep hold of his shirt.

The shirt hit the floor.

"This isn't the way it's supposed to go," he said, breathless. "You're ravishing me."

"Uh huh. Your turn to ravish me next. When we get out of here. This is important. Orchis is obviously going to have to take the lead with our snow king, so this is the way for now."

"Oh, don't give me excuses. You're aggressive. You're a sex fiend."

"True. True. Steven Early, I'm crazy for you. I'm going to have my way with you, so you might as well give up."

"Give up and what? I'm sitting on a silk divan, in a spaceship in the middle of some woods on the top of a hill. In the buff. With a beautiful woman on my lap. What am I giving up, anyway?"

"Choices. I'm in charge. I'm a ball-breaker." Her lips drew back in a sharklike leer. "Lie down."

"The hell I will."

"We've got one hour. Less than an hour now."

"Yeah. What does that mean to you?"

"Ooh, I'm going to experiment. And while I experiment I'm going to think of every little nuance I can come up with."

He grasped a tasseled cushion and batted her lightly with it. "You're going to do this for an hour? And I'm going to lie still for it?"

"Not still." The toothy grin grew wider. "No, I'd much rather you didn't lie still."

"Enough," he told her, and felt the tensing of his features. "You've forgotten one detail, ma'am. I'm a hell of a lot bigger than you. So now it's your turn."

He lifted her and swung her to lie stretched out between him and the back of the divan. "An hour can be a long time, Chloe, a very long time."

Her bravado faded. She touched his lips with trembling fingertips. "Then we beat the shit out of them?" she whispered.

"If we have to—only I still say we won't. I've got a plan."

"Another plan?"

"Yup. Another one."

"What?"

"This part is going to have to be a surprise." To both of them, since he didn't have the vaguest idea what he'd do. "It'll be important for you to behave as if you're shocked, too. Let me see. What shall I do to you first?"

"Steven—"

He swallowed whatever she'd meant to say with his

lips. Rolling half on top of her, pressing her into the divan, he closed his mouth over hers, surrounded her slight body, and ran his hands the length of her spine, over her round bottom, beneath the legs of her shorts to her warm cleft—and he smirked when she wriggled and squealed. He worked a single forefinger farther forward between her legs until he found what he wanted to find. Touching the hot, slick little nub of flesh made her gasp, and forget to press her legs together.

He slipped back and forth, back and forth, still kissing her even when she forgot to kiss him back. "That first night we met," he said, clicking his jaw in concentration, "you took such pride in showing me around that library. I couldn't believe my luck that you were the one appointed to me."

Sweating, he rolled to his back, pulled her on top of him.

"Er—Steven. Oh, Steven, oh—God." Her hips rode his thigh. She used her knees to lift herself enough to make his job easy. "Oh. I—wasn't. I wasn't appointed to you. I—oh—yes—yesss."

She was so wet, so ready. A little maneuvering and he unzipped her shorts to plunge inside the front of her panties. Chloe bucked. Her eyes glazed.

"You weren't appointed?"

"I—erased the name of the person who was supposed to show you around."

"You didn't."

Her body closed tightly around the two fingers he inserted, then the three. "Don't stop," she demanded. "Please, don't stop now."

"You wouldn't erase someone's name just to walk me around a library." He wanted her damn clothes off. He wanted inside her, and her breasts where he could fill his mouth, his hands, where he could slide them over his chest, his belly.

"I'm not stupid," she murmured. "I'd have shown

you around the silly library twice if I could have got away with it. Just standing close—Steven, don't stop! Just standing close to you made me shake."

"Funny. Standing close to you gave me some interesting feelings. But I didn't shake."

"Tell me about the feelings." Her urgent pressure against him sent the message that she wanted more, much more.

Steven clamped her to his thigh with one hand and eased her tank top over her head with the other. "Geez, Chloe. If we can stand up after this it'll be a miracle. Walking's probably going to be out of the question."

Through her teeth she said, "Because you're going to fuck my brains out?"

"Don't say that."

"Not ladylike, huh?"

"Not ladylike. Rub your breasts against me, against . . . Yeah, move down. Rub them there. And think about me coming into you till you think you're going to burst."

"Oh, burst me. Come on. Now."

"Not yet."

Her breasts spilled from the cups of her tantalizing lace bra. Slowly, she rubbed them back and forth over his penis. She lifted it and rubbed again, on top of his balls. And he imagined what he and Chloe looked like, or would look like to someone watching. He made the fucking mind images and didn't have to do a thing to add all the sensations that went with them.

Take that Vigar, brother. Do something about it. Your lady's ready.

"What were you feeling in the library?" Chloe asked.

A prize, a damned prize for self-control, that's what he had coming. "I was glad I was wearing a dark suit—with the jacket buttoned—and that I had a book to hold in front of me."

"No!" Her face came up. "Steven, no! That first time we met you . . . you know?"

"Uh huh. But all you felt was cold. A pity." The bra straps were easy to pull from her shoulders. He lifted her breasts from their accommodating pieces of nothingness and flattened them to his belly—and held her there.

Chloe scooted rapidly up his body until she could take him in her very capable hands. She said, "What I felt was that I had a more or less tamed wild creature at my side. You were all male energy hiding in that business suit and I wanted to unwrap you."

He laughed, undid the bra, and contrived to toss it aside. "You'd better watch what you do down there. I'm hanging onto control, barely."

"You won't be."

"Oh, don't—"

"Don't tell me what to do. Just be guided for once. We're working here, remember? Weren't you in the middle of something?"

"Oh, I haven't forgotten. Let's change positions—Chloe, stop."

Ignoring him, she took the tip of one of his flat nipples between her teeth while she used her closed hand to stimulate him.

Seconds. A second and it would be over. "Chloe, sweets. Please." Up and down, up and down. And her hard nipples dug into his skin—her thighs spread wide over his.

"I can't," he groaned. "No. Let me do this for you. I can wait."

"Sure you can."

He didn't know when she shed her own shorts and panties. He did know when she slid his aching penis between her legs and squeezed.

"Chloe."

"Just think."

"Are you just—thinking? Nothing but thinking?"

"Hmm—mmm?" She used him to bring her own pulse thundering on top of his own. "Mmmm. All those months of not letting ourselves go. Not even talking about—this. What a waste."

He intended to more than make up for the waste, Steven decided.

Music, blasting from every side of the room, battered his eardrums.

Chloe covered her ears and kept on moving.

"Masquerade" grew louder.

Steven winced and turned his head aside. "God, what the hell is that?"

"It's your—your 'Masquerade.' You created a monster."

Voices rose, crescendoed, fell, rose again. Voices throbbed. Steven felt nothing but Chloe—and the pain in his ears.

"Ooh!" She rose to her hands and knees. "How could they do that? They wouldn't know a piece like this and they couldn't just scare it up."

"That's exactly what they've done—they've just scared it up."

Chloe climbed off him. She breathed heavily, her breasts rising and falling. When he reached to cover one of them she placed a hand on top of his and ground it closer.

"Do you suppose they're watching after all?" Steven said, speaking his thoughts aloud. "And trying to help us along with the music, maybe?"

"Don't say that." Shooting to her feet, Chloe grabbed up her clothes. With quick motions, she stepped into her panties.

Steven rose to an elbow to watch her breasts swing with each move. "Lovely, my love."

She glared at him, grabbed up what appeared to be a plum, and stuffed it into his mouth.

He bit into very sweet flesh and wiped juice from his chin—and didn't take his eyes off Chloe's next hopping-from-foot-to-foot routine as she put on her shorts.

"Where's my bra?" She spun around, searching the floor. "What did you do with it?"

He waved a hand airily and pointed toward a ledge high on the curving, silk-covered wall. "Is that it up there? I threw it aside, I'm afraid."

Chloe backed away to look, then went close and jumped, reaching for the shelf. She jumped, and jumped, feeling along the edge of the shelf.

"You have a fantastic little body, my love," he said, taking another bite of the plum. "You have no idea what it does to me when you show it off like that. What legs. What buns. What a sweet waist. And your breasts." He kissed his sticky fingers. "Bring them here and I'll see if they like plum juice."

"I'm going to ignore that," she yelled. "How can you stand that music blaring?"

He knew the moment when she sighted the bra— beneath the cushion he'd also dropped. She glowered at him and strode to retrieve it.

Steven whipped up the bra and tucked it behind his back.

"Give it to me. They're watching us, I know they are. I'm so embarrassed."

"Come and get it, Chloe. Come on. I won't eat you. Not much of you, anyway."

The attempt she made to grab the bra landed her on top of him again. "Please," she said, gasping as he tweaked her nipples, one by one. "You promised we'd only give them so long before we caught their attention."

"I thought you said we'd already caught their attention."

Her peaked nipples made him long to take them in his teeth.

"You are completely horrible, Steven Early." Chloe

captured her bra and leaped away from him. "A badly behaved, immature, tormenting . . ."

"Go on." He frowned his disappointment as her breasts were covered—sort of.

"Why pretend? You're wonderful. This has been the most frustratingly fabulous experience of my life—and it's probably the best experience I'm ever going to get in my life." She donned the yellow tank top and tried, pointlessly, to smooth out wrinkles. "Get dressed. I don't want her looking at you like that."

Steven laughed aloud, and grimaced again at the deafening volume of the music. "I never thought you were selfish. Wanting me all for yourself."

"Put your clothes on," she shouted.

He did, not hurriedly, but leisurely—starting with his thongs. Next, his shirt.

"Be quick," Chloe begged, glancing toward the panel and twining her fingers together. In her agitation, she rose to her toes and jiggled. "Steven! Put on your pants. *Now.*"

"Well, I would, but they're in such a twist." They hadn't been, but by the time he wound them together, and half inside-out, they sure were.

Chloe marched in front of him and snatched the shorts away. "You're impossible. Steven!"

"Yes?" he asked innocently, gripping her hips while he backed her across the chamber. "What is it you want to say? We hadn't finished what we were doing, y'know."

She flapped his shorts, slapped his hands away. "Here. Put them on and let's see if we can get out of here before we're launched into space. Now I know where some of those so-called missing persons who were never found went. They were stolen by aliens and never returned."

Seemed very logical. Steven sighed and put on his pants. He knew he must be as wildly mussed as she was.

"Now we've got to make them let us go," Chloe said. She cradled her arms across her middle and paced. "How are we going to do that?"

"Shout?" Steven said tentatively.

The pacing ceased. Chloe stared at him with huge, accusing gray eyes. "You said you had a plan."

"I said . . . Yes, I did say that. I lied."

The next breath she exhaled seemed to drain her. "I see. All right. We'll shout. *Let us out!*"

"Masquerade" drowned her words.

"Come on, Steven. Help me." She climbed on the table and jumped up and down. Her bare feet made scarcely a sound. "This is useless."

"Completely," he agreed, studying the door panel. "I vote we try to figure a way through that."

He helped Chloe down and they approached the panel. She said, "They obviously have some sort of device they use to open it. Do you see a control pad or something?"

"No. And we'd better be careful. We haven't seen any sign of force—not conventional force—but I haven't forgotten that they can physically stun us without lifting a finger."

"They did lift their fingers—I think." Chloe drew close to his side and they took another step forward. "But they might be able to knock us unconscious the same way they stopped us from moving. Then we'd wake up somewhere out there." She raised her eyebrows at a ceiling draped with swags of blue and gold silk.

With a chirrup, Merlin strolled past them and went to the panel. He pressed his nose against the edge and waited while it slid open.

He walked out and disappeared.

Speechless, Steven looked at Chloe, and back through the opening to a space where colored shadows hovered and shifted. He saw the sheets of illuminated buttons he'd been too apprehensive to study when they'd been brought aboard the circular ship. Some of the buttons blinked. The shadows coalesced into wisps of vapor tinged with green, purple, magenta, silver. The wisps passed like flags born by invisible runners.

"Will you look at that? All we had to do was walk out."

He felt Chloe back away. "I think I'll sit down and think a bit first," she said.

"I think I'll just walk out," he said. "I'm going to find our hosts and figure out a way to let them know keeping us is a lousy idea."

"We ought to decide what we're going to say first."

His reassuring smile went unnoticed. Steven bowed his head. "Stay there, honey. There's no point trying to plan anything. I'm going to go on instinct. Anyway, I've got to find Merlin."

"I'm not letting you go alone." Chloe scrambled to her feet and followed him into a very cool gallery.

Once they'd walked past several banks of controls, the gallery became a catwalk over chambers that opened to the top of the vehicle.

"Weird," Chloe whispered. "Like a big, plush, divided bowl."

At the center of the bridge span, the soaring notes of the music became eerily sibilant and rose to echo between the curved, shining struts overhead.

Silently, Steven pointed to the outer shell of the caposphere. Here it assumed the quality of glass. Beyond they saw the night sky with clouds still skimming the moon, and the faint outlines of tall, wind-pressed evergreens in the woods so close to their house. These were the woods that shielded the ship from Sardo.

"And if we do get out, we'll never be able to talk about it," Chloe said, her voice filled with wonder. "They'd say we'd lost our minds."

Steven didn't mention that he wasn't sure he hadn't lost his mind. "The music's softer here."

"More open space . . . Steven"—her voice dropped again—"look. Over there."

He followed the direction of her pointing finger, and edged forward. Suspended across the open dome was a huge and definitely swinging hammock. Made of black gauze studded with gleaming specks, and loaded inside with gold satin pillows, the hammock wasn't empty.

"Those silver suits ought to be burned," Steven commented. "What a waste to cover that."

Orchis had the kind of body movie stars went under the knife to achieve. Supple, full, firm—talented. Showing the effects of a lot of activity, her black hair curled. And she could move—God, could she move.

She moved suddenly, differently, breaking the steady rhythm she'd employed on top of Vigar's matching nakedness. In fact it was Vigar, drawing her rapidly beside him and sitting in front of her, that caused the change in action.

Vigar reached to put a large pillow on top of Orchis. "Stay, my dearest," he said. "I will deal with this. Do not overset yourself."

"Oh, my," Chloe murmured.

Steven snorted. "They never got past English 1700 or whatever that is."

"Oh, my," Chloe repeated breathily.

Steven frowned at her, and discovered she was staring, open mouthed, at Vigar.

"Sorry to interrupt," Steven called. They shouldn't be standing here like a couple of voyeurs. "Excuse us. We had no idea. Come along, Chloe."

Chloe gripped the spun-glass ropes at the side of the catwalk. "He doesn't understand. But he is gorgeous."

"Don't look! Come on, let's get out of here."

A laugh, husky and suggestive, grabbed Steven in sensitive places. Orchis laughed and sat up, holding the pillow to her. "Listen to them, Vigar, my beloved.

Their language is distorted, but they do converse in an ugly form of English. He is as jealous of her as you are of me. How quaint."

Chloe planted her fists on her hips. "Our English is ugly?"

"Oh, indeed," Orchis told her. "Quite vulgar in fact. But if I am most patient, I can take your meaning."

Vigar made no attempt to cover himself. He did appear to concentrate intently.

"Look," Steven said. "We're glad to see the two of you having such a—stimulating time. If it's okay with you, we'd like to get home now."

"Egad," Vigar said slowly. "I do not understand each word, but I believe they wish to leave us."

"Gorgeous, and quick, too," Chloe muttered.

Steven chuckled, but sobered instantly. "You've got it, Vigar, old buddy. We'd like to blow. The lady and I are tying the knot in a few hours."

A blank stare was his reward.

"We shall need time to . . . to consider those comments," Orchis said. Her tone became petulant. "Tell them we'll join them when we're finished, Vigar."

"Good grief," Chloe said. "Does she mean what I think she means?"

Vigar's smile, the heavy-lidded expression that softened his features, made Steven turn away. "That's what she means."

"We shall not detain you long," Orchis called. "We're becoming most adept at these matters." She snaked an arm around Vigar and engaged in an activity too fresh in Steven's mind for comfort.

Vigar tore the pillow aside and rolled over Orchis.

The strains of "Masquerade" rose to pummel the onlookers' ears.

With Chloe's hand in his, Steven hurried back the way they'd come. At least the two overachievers weren't preparing the caposphere for departure. Cooperation and reason seemed as good an approach as any to diverting them from their plans.

The chamber where Vigar and Orchis had left them remained open. Chloe dashed ahead and threw herself down on the green divan. She drew up her legs and crossed them.

"They said they won't be long," Steven told her awkwardly.

"Adept at these matters," Chloe commented. "Incredible. I've heard of quick studies, but those two are something else."

Steven cleared his throat.

"Something else," she said again. "Did you see him?"

"I saw him." There were things a man shouldn't have to swallow. "Here's Merlin."

Chloe showed no sign of hearing—or listening. "What a body."

"Orchis isn't so bad either," he said, and didn't regret the jab.

Evidently Chloe still wasn't hearing a word he said. "I'd say they've put it all together, wouldn't you?"

Striving to flatten his own possessive urges, he said, "I guess."

"Oh, they have." Her little frown was the most endearing, the sexiest thing. "Steven, we did it. They not only know where to put what—and how. They want to!"

Saturday morning, not early enough

He was sulking!

In a darkly brooding, tummy-knottingly fascinating way—but sulking nevertheless. "What time is it?" Chloe asked.

"Almost six." Steven set out on another measured circuit of the chamber. "How long can it take, for crying out loud?"

She snickered, and sniffed, and managed to cough.

"Did I say something funny?" The full force of his blue eyes turned on her. "I'm glad your sense of humor is still intact. If I wasn't angry enough to eat aliens I'd be unconscious. I'm exhausted."

"Maybe I'm too hysterical to be exhausted."

"You aren't the hysterical type."

"No, I'm not," she agreed. "You just amused me when you asked how long making love could take. That's funny, Steven. Think about it."

He stopped pacing and came to sit on the edge of the table with its suspended store of brilliant crystals. Jutting his beard-darkened jaw close to her face he said, very softly, "I am thinking about it. I haven't stopped thinking about it—making love. Making love to you."

"Neither have I." Chloe poked his knee. "It was wonderful, wasn't it?"

"What there was of it was wonderful."

She couldn't look at him. "I thought there was a great deal of it."

"You didn't think we sort of missed the main point?"

"Nope." Chloe shook her head. "We got the main point, Steven."

He rubbed the back of her hand. "Are we talking about two different main points here?"

"I'm talking about how we learned that we're very good for each other. That we really are meant to be together. That each of us is going to bring an entire person to our marriage so it's two hundred percent of everything it can be."

His sigh moved her hair. "Yes," he agreed. "We did learn that. You just said it better than I would have."

"You weren't talking about the same thing. You were talking about sexual intercourse."

"Oh, *Chloe.*"

"*Oh, Chloe,*" she mimicked.

"Do you have to be so blunt?"

"Fucking our brains out is blunt. Sexual intercourse is clinical."

"And they're both inappropriate," he said shortly. "On your lips, anyway. I was talking about making love—really making love."

Softly, without a sound, Vigar and Orchis entered the chamber. Vigar hung back. Orchis, her arms crossed, stepped forward and stood, swaying slightly, with her eyes averted from Chloe.

Chloe cleared her throat and when Steven glanced at her she inclined her head. He turned around.

The silver suits were securely in place again.

Vigar clasped his hands behind his back and studied his silver boots from all angles.

"You do understand our speech?" Orchis asked, and when Chloe nodded, she added, "We owe you our apologies."

She and Vigar flushed faintly and lowered their heads as if they were bashful teenagers.

"Most certainly," Vigar added. "Sincere apologies. Most inappropriate."

Steven filled his lean cheeks with air.

"Think nothing of it," Chloe said. "I mean you certainly don't owe us any apologies. Whatever for?"

"How about snatching us away from our own garbage cans and taking us prisoner in this box of tricks?" Steven said as if he were remarking on an unremarkable wine. "Not giving us any choice but to give them lessons in how to make love?"

"Shush," Chloe told him. "You didn't enjoy that, huh?"

"Oh, but I did." A smile flickered, but quickly died. "But we have to keep things in perspective here. Don't apologize for a thing, folks. Just let us go home."

Orchis looked at Vigar. "I know our dear helpers will want to come to Sardo when they fully understand the importance of what they are to do there."

Steven shot to his feet. "The hell we will," he said explosively. "From what we saw out there you don't need any more help from us."

"No," Chloe said quickly, trying to send him signals to tame his comments. "You will be more than capable of teaching your people about emotion."

"Emotion." Orchis's dark eyes became intent. "Explain yourself, if you please."

"What you felt when you were together in that hammock. Emotion and passion—and plain old physical lust. And love. Great foursome. Feelings. The elements you were missing in your sexuality and your behavior together until tonight. They go together perfectly. You can build on them. First as a couple, then as a family when you have children."

"There will have to be practical examples of these things to share," Orchis said. "We certainly are not in a position to do more than facilitate your lectures on the subject."

"Oh, shit," Steven muttered.

Chloe glared at him, and asked Orchis, "Why would we be in a better position than you?"

Vigar came forward. The blush on his face intensified his fairness. "You have achieved this coupling. You have sealed your agreement to mate. Therefore you are ready for the next phase."

"We damn well haven't achieved this coupling," Steven said fiercely. "So we aren't ready for the next phase. But you've achieved this coupling. A number of times, or my name isn't Steven Early."

"We have a dilemma," Orchis said. She extended a hand to Vigar and he hesitated only a moment before lacing his fingers through hers. "All that you have said is true. Your unselfish sharing accomplished exactly what we had hoped it would accomplish. We have achieved a remarkable ability to create and enjoy satisfaction together, but we were precipitate."

"You mean you've only just met?" Steven suggested helpfully.

Vigar raised his handsome jaw. "We met as exceedingly young Sardines. Our parents approved our designated match whilst we yet suckled."

Sardines? "I see." Chloe didn't dare look at Steven. "How fascinating. An arranged designation."

"Naturally."

"But now you've discovered you don't dislike each other after all."

"We never did," Orchis said, haughty once more. "We are well matched."

"Exceedingly well matched," Vigar said.

Steven slid out a drawer in the table and selected a hunk of dark red crystal to examine.

"Then why would it be . . . be . . . precipitate?" Chloe asked. "For you to do the job you told us you have to do? Because you're these coupling experts?"

Vigar and Orchis swung their joined hands and studied the carpet.

"Yeah," Steven said, looking up sharply. "Why would you need us to do your job?"

Chloe saw the dangerous set of his jaw and her stomach turned. He was barely holding his temper.

"We have already told you we may have been very hasty in succumbing to our impetuous urges."

Steven rose to his feet and squared his considerable shoulders. "Spit it out."

"Pardon me?" Vigar's blank expression mirrored that of Orchis's.

"Speak plainly," Steven said. "How could you possibly have been hasty?"

"It is my season," Orchis announced.

Silence followed, then Vigar gathered her awkwardly into his arms and kissed her eyes shut.

Chloe murmured, "Aah."

"It is not unreasonable to suspect that we may have propagated. A slip may have been fertilized."

"Only one?" asked Steven.

The innocence in his voice made Chloe grin.

"This would be inconvenient," Orchis said, and sniffed. "We should not have succumbed to primitive drives. My fault. I incited—*lust.*"

"By no means, my love," Vigar said, his back even straighter. "If to be yourself is to incite lust, then it is so. But you are simply a female of great attraction. This is to be celebrated. There is no fault—certainly not on your part."

"I thought all this was exactly why you were here," Steven thundered, flexing his hands. "You've lost touch with your damn primitive urges and your people are dying out. Now you've got the urge again. So go home and multiply. And teach all the other—whatever you are, to multiply. *Sardines.* Young Sardines in every home—that should be your aim."

"We do not as yet have the dwelling we require."

Vigar held Orchis's face against his shoulder. "Or all the accoutrements appropriate to our station and the comfort we desire. The exceptional quality of instruction our young would require has not yet been provided for. Naturally the fund has been initiated, but it is by no means adequate.

"And we have yet to visit all the more desirable aspects of our planet. Then there is the diversionary dwelling on the sand flats to be secured. Diversionary equipment also, of course, and we should certainly require vehicles suitable to our changed state. We had planned to accomplish these things prior to attempting fertilization."

Assimilating this long speech took time. At last Chloe said, "Some things aren't so different on Sardo."

"But the two of you are this—designated mate thing?" asked Steven.

Orchis nodded.

"Then why can't you have your young while you work together for these things you want?"

Orchis wrinkled her perfect nose. "Once it was done that way. The old ones have spoken of reading about these things." She considered. "It does hold a certain appeal."

"Perhaps," Vigar said thoughtfully. "A most daring appeal, and we are daring people. However, we are designated, but not sealed."

With her eyes downcast, Orchis stepped away from him. "I would never compromise you."

Steven made owl eyes.

"You are not compromising me, my dear one," Vigar insisted. "You never would. But, if you should agree, I would like to embark upon this course the earthies have suggested. At once."

"What does your sealing involve?" Steven asked casually, not casually enough to fool Chloe. She'd noted his frequent glances at his watch. "Anything we can help with?"

Ignoring Steven, Vigar lowered himself to one knee before Orchis. "I would seal the agreement of our parents, Orchis." He took her hand in both of his. "If you would seal it also, if you would accept their wishes—and mine—as your own."

"Gives hokey a whole new slant, don't it?" Steven said under his breath.

Chloe shushed him softly. "It's sweet."

"I would seal the agreement of our parents," Orchis said to Vigar. She pressed her lips to the top of his head, to his brow, to their joined hands, and, finally, to his mouth in a chaste kiss.

"Let it be so, then," the man at her feet said. "We are sealed."

"And that's it?" Chloe's groom-to-be put his glittering red rock back in the table's drawer. "What happened to good old you-may-now-kiss-the-bride? Excuse us folks, but we've got a sealing of our own coming up."

The kiss ceased to be chaste.

"Excuse us," Steven repeated. "Hey, don't forget to breathe."

When the happy couple turned toward them, Chloe smiled and hunched her shoulders. "That was beautiful. So simple, and special. Congratulations."

"Yeah," Steven said. "Congratulations. You two need to be alone now. So, if you'll excuse us?"

The kiss resumed.

The still-open panel revealed the faintest shimmer of rising sunshine through the sphere's outer skin.

"Okay," Steven said to Chloe. "There's nothing for it. We're not going to Sardo to meet the rest of the Sardines, or any other place we don't want to go. We're getting married. This morning. This is it. Stand back. I'm going to beat the crap out of him.

"And you stand back, too, Orchis. This is going to be ugly. I'm going to have to fight your new mate."

Rather than move away from Vigar, Orchis drew him up and held him tightly. "Fight with Vigar?" Lines of confusion crumpled her face. "Why would you fight?"

"Because you two won't let us out of this thing. We don't want to go with you to your planet."

"But such missions bring honor. Our brother and sister Sardines will delight in honoring you."

"Honor we don't want," Steven said, advancing with raised fists. "Honor we won't have. Honor we'll fight rather than accept. This is going to hurt you more than it'll hurt me, but you asked for it."

"Oh, Steven, I can't let you do this for me," Chloe said. "You don't know what he can do to you."

"It doesn't matter what he does to me. I want you safely back in our house and I'm not letting them take you anywhere."

Vigar shook his head and smiled. "Such devotion. You are an inspiration."

"I am pissed!" Steven said. "We want out. Do you understand? Out. We want to go."

"Then go with peace," Vigar said, as he led Orchis to a divan. "You have our gratitude and the gratitude of all Sardines. All who wait there now, and all who are to come. You will be renowned among our future generations."

"The fruit of our first couplings shall bear your names," Orchis said. "Steven-the-generous. Chloe-the-wise. Never to be forgotten."

Vigar bowed and made a humble gesture. "We shall always remember you." He watched Merlin run his neck against the scarlet crystal and said, "We have no knowledge of such creatures as this one, but, since it appears of importance to you, our third slip shall be named Merlin-the-magnificent."

There were no words!

Sunlight burst across the chamber. "It's getting

late," Chloe said, visualizing the dress she'd planned to wear to her wedding—visualizing the dozens of tiny buttons she'd have to fasten. "It's going to be a terrible rush making it to Bellevue. How on earth are we going to get there on time?"

"Vigar, I fear they are very anxious to depart."

"So it would seem." Vigar led the way to the catwalk. "Proceed across. On the other side lies the way of passage to the outer places. The way will open to you."

Grabbing Chloe's hand, Steven broke into a run. "We've got to hurry."

"Orchis, my love," Vigar said. "They are generous, but they lack logic. Why didn't they tell us at once that they did not wish to leave their home?"

Early Saturday morning

Steven slammed Chloe's car door. Rather than go into the house, she walked slowly down the driveway toward the road.

"Hey!" He flexed his arms within the confines of his suitcoat sleeves. "I'm ready to carry my wife across the threshold."

With her ankle-length white gauze skirts billowing, she turned and smiled at him, but continued walking backward.

"Come on," Steven said, wiggling his fingers. "Champagne and strawberries in bed? Or plums, if we've got some?"

Moving as easily as if she wore tennis shoes rather than low-heeled white pumps, Chloe spun around and ran. She ran, and reached the road before Steven gave up expecting her to come back.

Rubbing the back of his neck, he started after her. Women could drive men slowly mad. Chloe was more woman than most. She might accomplish the task quickly.

"Chloe!"

He knew his shout reached her.

She ran faster.

Steven ran too. "Chloe! Hold up, dammit. What's with you?"

By the time she stumbled awkwardly down the dip on the opposite side of the road, Steven was right behind her. Her outstretched arms wobbled as she struggled to keep her balance.

"Could we talk about this?"

"No. Go back. You're tired. You should sleep."

Very quickly mad.

She reached the bottom of the slope and started up toward the woods. He'd as soon never go near those trees again but he wanted his bride. He wanted her now.

With each short gasp of breath Chloe made a raw, rasping sound. She entered the trees and surged ahead, dodging trunks, her white shoes flashing with each awkward leap over an obstacle.

They both knew where she was going.

The surprisingly small clearing lay several hundred yards from the perimeter of the woods. Surrounding Douglas firs had cut out light for a hundred years. Not grass, but springy moss covered uneven ground. Fallen branches hosted tender ferns, the same type of ferns reflected in a single shallow dew pond captured by an age-smoothed hollow rock.

"It seemed much bigger," Steven remarked quietly of the caposphere. "Too big to fit here."

Chloe tipped her face up toward the distant circle of sky.

"I suppose it could have been much bigger really," he said. "It could have been anything. Our perception wouldn't necessarily hold true for them."

"You sound like a confused physics teacher."

He smiled and nodded. "I am a confused physics teacher. And you're a confused librarian. You're also my wife."

"It wasn't a hallucination."

"No. It all happened."

"And we'll never be able to convince anyone else it did."

Her stiff posture warned him not to approach. "I don't think I want to. I like the idea of sharing something like that with you and no one else."

She glanced at him, and instantly lowered her gaze to the ground.

Very softly he asked, "What is it? Regrets?"

Her wedding band shone. A random scatter of little flowers were very white in her red hair. The simple lace-trimmed cotton dress she wore made of her a picture reminiscent of a Regency girl in a morning gown.

"Chloe?"

She shook her head.

"You've been through too much, love. Too much in too short a space of time. You need to rest."

"I don't." The shortness of her reply surprised him.

"But you do. Go and get some sleep. We'll talk when you wake up."

"Sleeping alone isn't what I've got in mind."

"You're honorable."

"Where did that come from?" He attempted to put an arm around her, but she stepped away. "Are you already wishing you'd never married me?"

"No," she flashed at him. "Are you?"

"*No.* What's the matter with you?"

"I'm embarrassed."

Whatever he might have expected her to say, that she felt embarrassed wasn't it.

Plucking at handmade lace around the cuff of one long sleeve she said, "That wasn't me. Not really."

Steven sensed he should wait rather than respond.

"I'm not like that. Barbara used to say I was sexually repressed and that's why men always saw me as a buddy rather than a potential lover."

"Barbara's a pain in the ass," he told her explosively. "I knew I wouldn't like her and I was right." Cold-eyed Barbara—the psychology hopeful—had been Chloe's witness at the brief wedding and she hadn't hidden her disapproval of Steven and Chloe's choice of a simple ceremony, no reception, and a honeymoon at their new home rather than in some exotic locale.

Chloe didn't defend Barbara.

"What do you mean by 'not like that?' " Steven asked.

"I don't want to talk about it. They've gone as if they were never here."

He looked around the clearing. "Not a trace left behind."

"I wonder where they are now."

"On their way back to the rest of the Sardines." He chuckled. "I thought they were joking about that at first."

Chloe didn't laugh. "So did I. I hope they'll have lots of children."

"If they don't, it won't be because they haven't tried."

Still Chloe didn't laugh. Instead she turned pink and fiddled with her hair. "I was so forward."

Stunned, he took a moment to respond. "Forward? I haven't heard that term in years."

Chloe rocked back and forth and her filmy skirts swayed about her slim ankles.

"Please tell me what this is all about. You were quiet at the wedding but I thought that was good, old-fashioned jitters. I had them, too."

"I don't blame you."

Steven frowned and grasped her arm. She tried to pull away but he wouldn't let go.

"You're a man with normal urges, but you're traditional."

Not so traditional. Very normal urges. "What's your point?"

"You're too kind to admit I horrified you."

"Horrified me! You couldn't horrify me if you tried. You're wonderful. Natural, sweet, passionate."

"And pushy."

He narrowed his eyes and considered. "I am tired.

I concede that much. But the rest of this is garbage. Could we cut to the chase and talk about your hang-ups? And get on with our lives?"

"I don't have any hang-ups."

"No? You believed a would-be psychologist when she tried to line you up as a future client."

"She didn't."

"Is she going to specialize?"

"Yes," Chloe said slowly.

"Please say she isn't planning to be a sex therapist."

Chloe turned a shade more pink.

"Uh huh. I rest my case on that. But what's all this stuff about you being forward, and my being horrified?"

"I don't want to talk about it."

Steven took off his jacket and trailed it over one shoulder. "I like thinking of you as my buddy."

Hurt flashed in her eyes.

"My buddy, and my lover—my everything. That's what this was all about. But I'm an honest guy. I thought about the loving before I considered how fascinating your mind might be."

"Did you?"

"Sure did. You must have been right when you called me an animal."

She smiled faintly. "I was way off base."

"Even though you found out I fantasize about taking your clothes off."

"You were doing that for Vigar and Orchis's benefit."

Steven laughed. "Sure I was." The flowers in her hair made him itch to push his fingers into her curls.

"I can't believe I was so aggressive. And I said all those things to you."

This really bothered her. "You were assertive and you said some sexy stuff."

"And I . . ." She turned up a palm and made *v*. . airy gestures toward him. "I . . . *touched* you "

If she wanted to call that just *touching*, he'd go along. Steven closed his eyes and murmured, "Oh, yeah."

"I took your clothes off."

"Terrible ordeal."

"You didn't invite me to do that."

Hadn't he? "I should have."

"I was the animal. You must have been too shocked to react."

She thought he hadn't reacted? "It was pretty shocking."

The region of his belt claimed her attention—and lower. She fashioned another, more descriptive gesture. "I never did that before."

"No?" Steven sucked in the corners of his mouth, where the smile threatened. "Don't worry. No one would ever know."

"Uh, Steven, I know you wouldn't share any of this." The earnest pucker of her brow all but undid him. "I just don't want you to think I'm going to make excessive demands on . . . well, you know. *Demands?*"

"I'm not sure I understand." He shouldn't be enjoying this so much. He shouldn't be enjoying it at all.

He was only human, and she did look so lovely when she was earnest.

"Okay, I'm going to stop tiptoeing around and just come right out and say what needs to be said."

"If that's what you want to do, that's what you should do."

"You're too generous, Steven."

"I believe in allowing people to exercise free will."

She nibbled at the light-colored lipstick she wore. "But I can't be weak. I can't let you allow me to abuse you the way I did, then not insist that I explain myself."

"No. No, I see that."

"I'm surprised you still married me."

He'd pushed her far enough. "I love you."

"Yes." When she inclined her head a single white

flower drifted to the ground. "I know you do and that makes it all even worse. I took advantage of your love."

Despite his best resolve his curiosity went on overload. "How do you feel you did that, Chloe?"

Her gray eyes shifted away, then back to his. "You're right to make me look closely at my behavior. Last night—before—I felt as if I were going to blow up from frustration. I wanted you to want to make love to me."

"I did," he said, with more force than he'd intended. "I did, and I do."

"You told me you're a traditional man. You meant you wanted to wait until after we were married and I should have honored your wishes."

He shrugged but didn't point out that the actual deed had yet to be done.

"I've had such a time of it keeping my hands off you, Steven."

Men dreamed of having a beautiful woman say those words.

"Every time I look at you"—her mouth remained open before she went on—"Every time I look at you it happens. It doesn't matter what you're wearing. Most of the time I couldn't tell you afterward. But every time I look at you I see you naked."

"Really?" Conveniently, the rock containing the pond was big enough for him to perch on an edge. He did so and crossed his legs. "That's really something."

"I imagine what you look like. Without anything on. At all."

He recrossed his legs in the other direction and gave her an encouraging smile.

"Men are supposed to say they're leg-men, or . . . whatever."

"Boob men?" he suggested helpfully.

"I guess. Among other things."

"Hmm." Where she was concerned, he was an everything man.

"When you wear shorts, I'm a leg-woman." Her nervous giggle softened the tension in her eyes. "But when I see your shoulders—in my mind—then I'm a shoulder-woman. Then there's your chest. Steven, you've got a fabulous chest. And shoulders, of course. And your back. Oh, Steven, even when you've got a shirt on I look at your back and my legs go all jellyfied. And I get this feeling inside." Her hand went to press low down on her belly.

Steven clasped his hands in his lap.

"And I used to visualize your *buns.*" She covered her mouth. "I feel *awful.* Like a dirty old lady."

"You can't be a dirty old lady at thirty."

"You know what I mean."

"I don't want you to give this another thought."

"I know—but I don't think I can stop myself."

In other words, his wife lusted after him? "There are times when we need to accept things the way they are and be grateful for our blessings."

"I'm sorry," Chloe said. "I will never, ever, say fuck your brains out again."

He all but swallowed his tongue.

"And I'll make sure you never have to tolerate my losing control of my appetites the way I did. But when I actually saw your"—once more she drew a hand picture—"Well, I'd sort of seen the outline. And I'd felt you get hard. But you always controlled yourself because of your principles."

"What I told you about being afraid of disappointing you was true," he said with complete honesty. "I wanted you as much as you wanted me. I'm a lucky guy."

"You told me our lovemaking had to be a two-way street. What I did stopped you from participating as fully as you wanted to—as you needed to. I could blame that on the stress of what happened last night, but it would be a lie."

"Really?"

"Yes." Chloe turned her back on him. "A complete lie. I used extraordinary circumstances to serve my own purpose. I exploited you and it was so wrong. I took away your right to make up your mind how far you wanted to go."

"We didn't have much choice, sweetheart," he reminded her, while he admired the straight line of her back, her narrow waist, inside her lace bodice. Dozens of minute buttons closed the back of her sweetly informal wedding dress. "We either had to convince Vigar and Orchis we'd taught them all they wanted to know or they were going to blast us into space with them."

"I still took advantage of the situation."

"You don't think I did, too?"

"Not the way I did. I . . . It's so hard to say it, but I've got to be brutally honest with myself. I pulled down your shorts and, and, and I took you in my mouth."

Steven barely bit back his moan.

"I forced you to get physically aroused."

"Chloe, I don't think—"

"I'm sorry. I know this must be horribly embarrassing to listen to. But this is why I'm not going to allow you to cater to my whims anymore."

If his belly sucked in much more it would scrape his backbone. "You're not?"

"Absolutely not. We love each other and that's a great start. It's more than most couples have to build on. But I obviously have to bring myself under control. You'll have to help me, Steven. You'll have to take me in hand."

"It'll be a pleasure." He cleared his throat. "I'll give it my best shot. Why don't we go back to the house now? If we move it, we can be in bed by eleven." That was not the way he'd intended to put the suggestion.

"Still trying to make me happy. Oh, Steven, I'm afraid that if you allow my lust for you to run wild I'll eat you up—I'll use you all up. I never thought I'd say such a thing, but now I don't have to imagine what you look like without clothes anymore, and just the memory of you makes me all hot and sweaty. Isn't that disgusting?"

"No."

"Yes, it is. I'm addicted. Addicted to you—to you and sex. I've read about people like me. There are support groups for sex addicts."

"Yeah. And I'm sure they do a great job. You won't need one."

Her shoulders hunched. He didn't dare think what that made him think of. Her pointed breasts pressed together were a sight he'd better not dwell on just yet.

"Let's make love, Chloe."

"Just to make me happy?"

The joke was over. "I want to make you happy. I also want to make me happy."

"You won't have to lie awake at night worrying I'll attack you," she told him. "I won't give in to it."

"Would you like to undress me again?"

She looked at him over her shoulder and whispered, "Yes. I can't lie. I would like to, but I won't. This has been a hard time for both of us. Would you mind leaving me alone to think? I won't be long."

This was his fault. His insecurities had led to her insecurities. And he'd also deprived them both of a whole lot of great lovemaking. No more.

Steven undid his shoes and slipped them off. He tossed his socks aside, and loosened his tie to pull it off and drop it on top of the shoes.

Chloe wandered a few yards away. She crossed her arms on the trunk of a tree and rested her face.

A beat, an insistent thrum began in Steven's chest and reverberated to his gut. His thighs tensed rock hard. So did his penis.

Sweat broke on his brow and ran down his temples. His shirt buttons defeated him and he wrenched them open. White linen hit mossy ground and would never be the same. His new belt resisted his efforts but finally fell apart. The zipper was easy.

"Sweetheart," he said, his throat so dry it ached. "Sweetheart, I want you."

"I'll always want you."

"Chloe, look at me, please."

Rather than face him, she turned her head just enough to see him. She blanched, then flushed. "Oh, you dear man."

Dear man hadn't been quite what he'd hoped for.

"What will it take to prove to you that you don't have to do this for me unless you're in the mood?" she asked.

He pushed his slacks down. "I'm in the mood."

"Oh, sure you are. You didn't sleep all night and you're standing outside in the woods." She hid her eyes once more.

The slacks went the way of his shirt, and his underpants followed. "Take another look, Mrs. Early, and tell me whether or not I'm in the mood."

After what felt like a very long pause, Chloe peeked at him with one eye. Starting at his face, that eye made a downward visual—then widened.

"Well?"

"You're cold."

"I am not cold!" Shouting was completely out of line. "I'm sorry, love."

"You want to make love with me?"

"This isn't a mirage." He planted his feet apart and waited until he had her attention. He pointed. "Thinking about you, about your body, and about making love to you did this."

"It's lovely."

Steven blushed.

"Barbara says a lot of women think they're ugly. Those things. I think they're beautiful."

He wasn't sure how he felt about the group classification.

"Not that I've seen too . . . well, not in the flesh, anyway. Barbara gets a magazine with pictures."

"You're kidding! And the two of you look?"

"I sort of glance." She remained where she was, the side of her face nestled on her crossed arms against the tree. "After all, men have always had their girlie magazines."

"I haven't."

"Barbara says—"

"I don't really want to hear what Barbara says."

"No. Steven, none of those men look as good as you do—without clothes."

A breeze wafted around his rear quarters. The same breeze flattened Chloe's skirt to her derriere. As impossible as it seemed, he grew even harder. "We can use my clothes as a blanket if you like."

"You're doing this to try to make me feel better."

"I'm doing this to make"—he swallowed the retort that he was the one most in need of feeling better— "I'm doing it for both of us."

"I put you between my legs. I used you."

The next shudder all but brought him to his knees. "It was wonderful," he told her, "and this time's going to be better."

"What if someone comes."

"Who's going to come?"

"The garbage people?"

"Into the woods? Come on, Chloe. Loosen up."

She dropped her hands to her sides but stayed by the tree.

"That dress has so many buttons."

"I know."

"They're going to take a long time to undo."

"I know."

He considered, then said, "I'm not going to undo them."

The breeze sharpened, whipped her skirts sideways. Her long legs curved from thigh to knee. The soft cotton wrapped over her calves, tucked closer yet to her bottom.

"Did you hear what I said?" Steven asked, drawing close enough to smell the light lily-of-the-valley perfume she wore.

"You aren't going to undo my buttons," she said clearly and reached behind her neck to fumble with them. "I'll do it."

"It'd take too long."

Steven knelt on the ground behind her. Slowly, he smoothed her dress upward, smoothed his way over her calves, made circles behind her knees with his thumbs.

Her sigh thrilled him.

Lacy white stockings ended halfway up her elegant thighs. Satin garters, each one trimmed with coy pink bows, secured the scalloped tops of the stockings. The skin between was soft. Steven kissed that skin and smiled when he felt Chloe brace herself against the tree.

When her skirts were bunched around her hips, high-cut white panties revealed her buttocks. She rocked a little from side to side and reached back to seek him, but he opened his mouth wide on her taut muscle and she cried out, grabbed to brace herself once more.

"We ought to go in." Chloe panted now, and she was wet—Steven felt how wet she was and employed what it took to make her legs sag while she helplessly sank onto his probing fingers.

"Still think we ought to take time to go in?" The delicate puffs of breath he sent into the swollen folds between her legs maddened her enough to make him grin. But he needed more. He found her center and stroked, stroked with increasing pressure and speed. "Let go, my love. I've got you. Let me take you."

"I want you," she murmured urgently. "Come to me, please."

"But—"

"*Come* to me."

Blindly, he pushed to his feet, ducked to find the entrance to her body, and, gently at first, eased into her from behind. She cried out and pushed away from the tree with both arms as he bent at the waist.

He couldn't hold back.

Chloe felt him fill her, withdraw, fill her higher, deeper, wider. With each lunge, tension built. "Yes," she said, not knowing for sure why. This couldn't be her, Chloe Dunn—Chloe Early, now—little Chloe the librarian. Standing in the woods with Steven making love to her. Behind her, making love to her. Steven naked while she wore all her clothes. He hadn't even taken off her panties. She had the disjointed thought that they would be shredded. Then she saw the vision of the two of them against the tree, the abandoned image she must make—the amazing, erotic picture of his penis penetrating her beneath the white dress, of her deliberately enticing garter belt, the parts of her that were exposed, yet adorned just enough to arouse.

Her feet were torn from the ground. With a large hand fondling each of her breasts through the dress, Steven swung her around and tipped her further forward until she gripped his hips with her thighs and absorbed the violence of his release, the echoing ripple of her own. And the onward echoes that trembled through them but died even as she wished they would never cease.

Beneath her dress she wore a thin chemise and no bra. She didn't need one and she'd wanted nothing to spoil the smooth lines of the gown.

Her husband's sensitive fingertips—her lover's hands—caressed the tips of her tingling nipples. She jerked against him and cried, "No," but laughed. "I can't stand it, you sadist. It's too much."

Steven laughed with her, and collapsed. He went to his knees with Chloe straddling his thighs. "Your stockings are never going to be the same."

"I don't care."

"I've ruined your panties."

"If I put on some more will you do that again, please? All of it? And again?"

He buried his face in her neck. "Don't you ever change. I love you just the way you are."

"Does that mean, yes, you will do it again?"

"Could I have time to recover? Just a few minutes maybe? You wouldn't want to kill me on our wedding day."

Carefully, she managed to clamber to her feet and straighten her dress. Steven promptly slipped his hands up her legs once more, threw her skirts over his head and shoulders, and sought her pouting clitoris with his tongue. Clever Steven—his tongue was inspired. He sucked, then blew again. Each breath whipped her to the breaking point.

Chloe batted at the back of his hidden neck. "Enough! Come out at once."

"Come out . . . Come out wherever you are." His muffled voice reached her between his deliberate and irresistible torment.

He managed to push his hands upward beneath her chemise and the bodice of the dress to claim her breasts. Another climax broke over her. This time he barely caught her.

Chloe rallied quickly. He'd scarcely lowered her in front of him before she made a dive and dealt him return attention he didn't attempt to fight. His release came very quickly.

Entwined in each other, they lay, panting, on a bed made of Steven's clothes and clumps of moss. He gazed into her eyes, kissed the tip of her nose. "You'll have to stop doing this to me."

"*Me!* Steven—" She gripped his shoulders and

strained to hear a sound that came, faintly at first, from somewhere that might be near, or far.

A familiar yowl joined strains of music and Merlin bounded into the clearing. He landed on Steven's chest.

"Music," Steven said, apparently oblivious to the cat walking over his face. "It can't be. Chloe, it isn't, is it? You don't hear music?"

"I do," she told him.

Merlin returned to Steven's chest, sat and raised a hind leg to begin a thorough wash.

" 'Masquerade,' " Steven whispered. Gently, he lifted Merlin to the ground and sat up. His rumpled slacks were more or less intact and he pulled them on, then his shoes, but no socks.

"It's getting louder," Chloe said, alarmed. She looked toward the sky, expecting to see the caposphere racing down.

Merlin dropped low to the ground and crept forward, his tail flicking. He made for the rock pool, leaped on top, and disappeared behind.

"Stay here," Steven told Chloe. "I'll get Merlin. Then we'll get out of here."

She let him get a few steps away, then followed.

"Masquerade" grew louder and louder.

The cat's tail showed above the rock. Steven went close and bent to see what Merlin had found. Chloe did the same.

Something silver glinted through the fronds of a fern. Steven moved the greenery aside and lifted a silver box. On top of the box rested a tiny green ball that pulsed with the musical notes.

Steven turned to Chloe. "You think they left this?"

"Who else?" She went to pick up the ball, but Steven stopped her. "The music's coming from that thing, not the box," she pointed out.

"I think we were supposed to come and find it."

Chloe glanced skyward again. "They know we're here."

"They're probably a million miles away by now. How could they know?"

"They did before. They connected with our minds and came here. I think they connected with our minds again just now—while we were making love."

He looked at her. His ruffled black hair turned him from Steven Early, physics teacher, to Steven Early, untamed lover. Perspiration still glistened on his shoulders and in the hair on his chest. The blue of his eyes was almost navy.

"Maybe this is a wedding gift," she told him.

He shook his head. "A sealing gift, you mean."

The music had softened to a faint chorus. Steven picked up the ball, that is, tried to pick it up. The instant his fingers met the surface, it crumbled. Tiny flecks of green sparkled and flew away in the breeze.

"S, and C," Steven said, brushing the lid of the box. "Our initials."

"They left it for us," Chloe said. "I feel sad. Isn't that stupid? I feel sad because they've gone, but they scared me when they were here. In a way." She opened the box and gasped. "Oh, my goodness."

Inside the box nestled the red crystal Steven had taken from the drawer in the chamber aboard the caposphere.

"Wow." He rested a single finger on its beautiful surface. "Who knows what it is, but it's great."

"Great proof," Chloe commented.

Steven rested his forehead on hers. "For you and me."

"Of course for you and me. If I ever want to get you locked away, I'll get you to try to make someone else believe that we were kidnapped by a couple of Sardines."

They laughed together and Steven looked at his watch. "Still time to be in bed before noon. Let's run."

"Run? You've got to be kidding."

"Would I kid my new bride? We've got to see how many times we can make love before we collapse."

"Steven!" she complained as he took her hand and pulled her along behind him. "We've got all day. All night. The rest of our lives."

"Sure we do, but I believe in living for the moment. And this is my time of day. I always was a morning kind of guy."

Dear Reader,

I hope you've enjoyed EARLY IN THE MORNING. I loved writing about these two and their battle of wills.

Some stories are not so lighthearted, and that would be the core difference between this tale and my next novel, TELL ME WHY, which Kensington will publish in hardcover this month. Here's an excerpt from that book, and I hope, after reading it, that you will want to know what happens next.

Cheers and best wishes,
Stella

"Ladies and gentlemen," Brandy Snopes said, tossing back her luxurious auburn hair and wetting carmine lips. "I give you—Carolee Burns!"

Applause broke out and Carolee entered from Brandy's office at Bistro Brandy on Kirkland's Lake Street. The full skirt of her black silk dress flipped about her calves. Her bare shoulders and the décolletage at the neck of the backless halter top were luminously pale.

Wearing a stretchy strapless dress of turquoise sequins, Brandy kissed and hugged Carolee, then backed away, clapping as she went.

Max Wolfe sat at a small round table to the right of the baby grand piano. To the right and with one table closer to, but not blocking, the makeshift space where Carolee performed.

He knew that she and Brandy were old friends—that they'd known each other since grade school. Max and Brandy had met more recently—four years ago when they'd had a brief fling and been lucky enough to realize they weren't meant for each other but that they liked the friendship.

It was Brandy who let Max know each time Carolee was going to play at the bistro. He didn't like feeling disappointed that this would be her last night here for more than a month.

When she sat down, the black dress swirled around slim ankles and drew attention to high, very sexy sandals.

She played, and Max sipped a glass of red wine. He didn't know the names of her pieces, but every one of them turned him on. A feeling that he wouldn't be anywhere else but watching her rattled him. Max Wolfe, the man no woman had managed to tame, had a bad case. Even though he'd been smitten by someone whose complicated life was public knowledge, including the fact that she wasn't interested in a new man, he wasn't finding a way to switch off his feelings. He lowered his eyes. If his history was repeating, the challenge she presented could add to her appeal.

He wasn't looking for a way to stop the feelings.

She looked at him.

Max smiled, just a little, and rolled the bowl of his glass between his hands.

Carolee seemed to keep looking at him but he couldn't be sure she actually saw him. When she played, her whole body moved. She wasn't thin and he liked that. He also liked the way she wore her thick, dark hair rolled away from her face and caught loosely at the back of her head. Her face was heart-shaped, her chin pointed. There was nothing typical about her. She'd been described as interesting but not conventionally good-looking. Max had spent more than one solitary evening enjoying visions of her, and wishing he could figure out how to spend a lot more time looking at her unconventional face.

"You again, huh?"

Max jumped and glanced up at a white-haired guy who was probably seventy, even if his light eyes could pierce a man.

"Have we met, sir?" Politeness to older males had been an obsession Max's father passed on.

"No," the man said. "I'm Sam. You expecting company?"

Max shook his head no, and Sam promptly commandeered the second chair at the table.

"What d'you think of this place?" Sam asked. "Hokey, huh? Faux Italian."

Max smiled and glanced around at rough-plastered terra cotta walls and silk grapevines draped along pink beams. "I don't know," he said. Bunches of purple plastic grapes dripped from the vines. "Have you been to Italy?"

"Nah. Why would I go somewhere foreign when I live in the best country in the world."

"I went there a couple of times," Max said. "I liked it. Beautiful country. Nice people. This place isn't so far off some of the ones I ate in there."

Sam snorted. "I guess that puts me in my place. Did you have dinner yet?"

"Nope."

"You gonna eat?"

"No," Max said. "Just stopping in for a drink. Can I buy you one? Or are you hungry. Don't let me put you off."

"Just coffee," the man said. "I'm not hungry and I abused the other privilege a long time ago. Now I don't need it."

Max signaled a waiter and ordered coffee.

"I saw you here before," Sam said. "Several times. You must be a real music lover." His sharp eyes skewered Max again.

"Depends on the music. I like this. I heard her play in New York once. She's got a supper club there. Or she did."

"Still does." The guy cleared his throat. "At least, that's what I'm told."

"Nice place. Burns Near Broadway. Good food. But I've got to confess I went for her, not the food. She's phenomenal. I don't guess she gets to New York much now."

Sam shrugged and cleared his throat. "You live around here?"

"Uh-huh. A condo. Here in Kirkland."

"I wish these bozos would quit talking and eating," Sam said of diners at the bistro.

Max didn't point out that Sam hadn't stopped talking since he sat down. "They do quiet down while she plays," he pointed out. "They know they're in on something special. I keep expecting the word to spread so much it'll be impossible to get in here, but this is mostly regulars and Brandy doesn't advertise."

"Carolee wouldn't come if things got out of hand."

Max noted Sam's confidence when he made statements about Carolee Burns, but made no comment.

She ran her fingers over the keys, and those who continued to eat did so discreetly. Sam's coffee was delivered but he ignored it. He bent forward over a bright yellow tablecloth, his eyes fixed on the pianist, and Max frowned. For Sam to have seen him here before meant the other man had also been present.

"What do you think of her?" Sam leaned close and whispered. "She's something, huh?"

"Yes, something." Her fingers skimmed across the keyboard and she sang in a husky voice, a slow, husky voice. Her eyelids closed and he could see her eyes moving beneath. "Gutsy, too. I like that."

"I know who you are, y'know," Sam said. "I bet everyone here does. Must be hard to hide when you're bigger than anyone else around."

"It might be if I was trying to hide." Max didn't want to talk about himself. "She shouldn't be shut away in this backwater. She's a woman who needs to be free and that doesn't make her a bad wife—ex-wife—or mother. She got a bum rap."

The unwavering attention that comment brought him wasn't too comfortable. "You ever been married?" Sam asked.

"No."

"Are you involved?"

"No." Max raised his eyebrows.

"I know, I know," Sam said. "Nosy old bastard, aren't I? Just wondered. What d'you do now you can't play football anymore?"

The waiter put a basket of warm bread on the table and Max tore off a piece. He made a diversion of gathering crumbs into a small pile. "I own a software company," he said finally. "And I help out with high school football for The Lakes. I'm kind of a visiting motivator who gives pointers."

"Must have been a helluva shock. The accident. Trapped under a pickup like that. Then watching your best buddy get your job had to hurt."

"I'm a grown-up. I got over it." More or less. "And Rob Mead is still the best friend a man could have. He couldn't help what happened to me." Max didn't want to talk about this anymore. Avoiding comments on what people liked to call his "tragedy" could keep him at home for long periods.

"Do you like kids?"

Startled, Max looked at him quizzically. He thought for a moment. "Yes, I guess I do. I don't think I'd have wanted to get involved with a high school team if I didn't."

"Ever think about having your own?"

"My own?" Max was having difficulty listening to Carolee Burns and understanding Sam's oblique questions.

"Your own kids."

He gave that some thought, too. "With the right woman, sure." Carolee was looking in his direction again and he smiled, making sure his expression was open and friendly. She smiled back but he still didn't think she was really aware of him.

"She's a charmer," Sam said. "Never saw a woman with so much to offer who had so little confidence in herself."

"Maybe you're right, but I like her just the way she is."

"You do, huh?"

"Well . . ." Max drank more wine and followed it with a bite of bread. "Well, I don't know her, do I. But I think I'd like her a lot if I did."

Sam sipped at his coffee and grimaced. "Swill," he said. "This stuff never saw a coffee bean. Do you ride."

"I'm sorry?" Max set his glass down on top of the wet circle that had already formed on the cloth.

"Horses," Sam said. "I'm getting a couple out at my place for when my granddaughter visits. I'm too old to keep up with exercising 'em."

"I grew up riding on my folks' farm. And if that's an invitation, thank you. I might take you up on the offer one of these days."

"That's good." The man's broad grin disconcerted Max.

"Do you know what this piece she's playing is called?" Max asked to change the subject.

Sam considered, then said, " 'I Know You in the Dark.' Strange she never wrote any words."

"Do you know if she wrote the music?"

"Sure, she wrote it. When she was married to that moron, the guy she was supposed to have taken advantage of. I ask you, does she look like she could take advantage of anyone?"

Good old Sam knew a great deal about Carolee Burns and Max intended to find out why. "She looks intense to me, intense but gentle."

"And she's beautiful if you like a face that's all eyes."

Max grinned. "She is beautiful."

"You must be pretty well fixed," Sam said offhandedly. "All that money from playing in the pros, and now your own software company."

"I can pay my bills."

The piece of music Carolee played didn't need any words. Just knowing the title conjured images of heat and damp skin that caused Max to ache in places where he enjoyed the sensation. She was really sexy, he hadn't noticed just how sexy before. Now and again she ran her tongue over her full lower lip and she kept her eyes closed almost all the time she played, only to open them with a vaguely startled expression, as if she was surprised to discover she wasn't alone.

He could watch her and imagine she was playing for him, telling him she'd know him in the dark.

She didn't know it, but they had things in common. The losses were different, but they had both lost. First her marriage had failed and her child had been all but taken from her. Then she'd chosen to walk away from a dynamic career. She could go back to the career. He didn't have that choice. He'd been a wide receiver with the Broncos. Speed and his teammates' confidence in his reliability went with the job. After the accident he'd brought himself back to excellent physical shape, but the metal plates in his legs meant he wouldn't play again. Carolee obviously wasn't sure exactly what she wanted for the rest of her life. Neither was he.

He'd just like to talk to her—alone. She might turn out to be vapid, but he didn't think so, and he couldn't shake the feeling that they'd have plenty to say to each other.

Sam didn't talk anymore, and soon the only sounds in the restaurant came from the piano and from Carolee singing. Her mood changed with the mood of each piece, but Max couldn't get that one melody out of his head. "I Know You in the Dark." He wanted to know her in the dark, and in the sunlight or the rain.

He'd been alone too long. It was time he found a new lady.

THE BRASS RING

Lisa Jackson

One

The old merry-go-round picked up speed, ancient gears grinding as black smoke spewed from the diesel engine and clouded the summer-blue Oregon sky.

Shawna McGuire clung to the neck of her wooden mount and glanced over her shoulder. Her heart swelled at the sight of Parker Harrison. Tall, with the broad shoulders of a natural athlete and brown hair streaked gold by the sun, he sat astride a glossy striped tiger. His blue eyes were gazing possessively at her and a camera swung from his neck.

Shawna grinned shamelessly. Tomorrow morning she and Parker would be married!

The carousel spun faster. Colors of pink, blue, and yellow blurred together.

"Reach, Shawna! Come on, you can do it!" Parker yelled, his deep voice difficult to hear above the piped music of the calliope and the sputtering engine.

Grinning, her honey-gold hair billowing away from her face, she saw him wink at her, then focus his camera and aim.

"Go for it, *Doctor!*" he called.

The challenge was on and Shawna glanced forward again, her green eyes fixed on the brass ring with fluttering pastel ribbons, the prize that hung precariously near the speeding carousel. She stretched her fingers, grabbed as she passed the ring and swiped into the air, coming up with nothing and nearly falling off her painted white stallion in the bargain. She heard Parker's laughter and looked back just in time to see him snatch the prize. A big, gloating smile spread easily across his square jaw and the look he sent her made her heart pound wildly.

She thought about her plans for the wedding the following morning. It was almost too good to be true. In less than twenty-four hours, under the rose arbor at Pioneer Church, she'd become Mrs. Parker Harrison and they would be bound for a week-long honeymoon in the Caribbean! No busy hospital schedules, no double shifts, no phones or patients—just Parker.

She glimpsed Parker stuffing the ring and ribbons into the front pocket of his jeans as the merry-go-round slowed.

"That's how it's done," he said, cupping his hands over his mouth so that she could hear him.

"Insufferable, arrogant—" she muttered, but a dimple creased her cheek and she laughed gaily, clasping her fingers around the post supporting her mount and tossing back her head. Her long hair brushed against her shoulders and she could hear the warm sound of Parker's laughter. She was young and in love—nothing could be more perfect.

When the ride ended she climbed off her glazed white horse and felt Parker's strong arms surround her. "That was a feeble attempt if I ever saw one," he whispered into her ear as he lifted her to the ground.

"We all can't be professional athletes," she teased, looking up at him through gold-tipped lashes. "Some of us have to set goals, you know, to achieve higher intellectual and humanistic rewards."

"Bull!"

"Bull?" she repeated, arching a golden brow.

"Save that for someone who'll believe it, Doctor. I won and you're burned."

"Well, maybe just a little," she admitted, her eyes

shining. "But it is comforting to know that should I ever quit my practice, and if you gave up completely on tennis, we could depend on your income as a professional ring-grabber."

"I'll get you for that one, Dr. McGuire," he promised, squeezing her small waist, his hand catching in the cotton folds of her sundress. "And my vengeance will be swift and powerful and drop you to your knees!"

"Promises, promises!" she quipped, dashing away from him and winding quickly through the crowd. Dry grass brushed against her ankles and several times her sandals caught on an exposed pebble, but she finally reached a refreshment booth with Parker right on her heels. "A bag of buttered popcorn and a sack of peanuts," she said to the vendor standing under the striped awnings. She felt out of breath and flushed, and her eyes glimmered mischievously. "And this guy," she motioned to Parker as he approached, "will foot the bill."

"Henpecked already," Parker muttered, delving into his wallet and handing a five-dollar bill to the vendor. Someday—" he said, blue eyes dancing as he shucked open a peanut and tossed the nut into his mouth.

"Someday what?" she challenged, her pulse leaping when his eyes fixed on her lips. For a minute she thought he was going to kiss her right there in the middle of the crowd. If he did, she wouldn't stop him. She couldn't. She loved him too much.

"Just you wait, lady—" he warned, his voice low and throaty, the vein in the side of his neck pulsing.

Shawna's heart began to thud crazily.

"For what?"

A couple of giggling teenage girls approached, breaking the magical spell. "Mr. Harrison?" the taller, red-haired girl asked, while her friend in braces blushed.

Parker looked over his shoulder and twisted around. "Yes?"

"I told you it was him!" the girl in braces said, nearly jumping up and down in her excitement. Her brown eyes gleamed in anticipation.

"Could we, uh, would you mind—" the redhead fumbled in her purse "—could we get your autograph?"

"Sure," Parker said, taking the scraps of paper and pen that had been shoved into his hand and scribbling out his name.

"I'm Sara and this is Kelly. Uh—Sara without an 'h.' "

"Got it!" Parker finished writing.

"Is, um, Brad here?"

" 'Fraid not," Parker admitted, the corner of his mouth lifting as he snapped the cap back onto the pen.

"Too bad," Sara murmured, obviously disappointed as she tucked her pen and paper into her purse.

But Kelly smiled widely, displaying the wires covering her teeth. "Gee, thanks!"

The two girls waved and took off, giggling to themselves.

"The price of fame," Parker said teasingly.

"Not too bad for a has-been," Shawna commented dryly, unable to hide the pride in her voice. "But it didn't hurt that you're Brad Lomax's coach. He's the star now, you know."

Parker grinned crookedly. "Admit it, McGuire, you're still sore 'cause you didn't get the ring." Draping his arm possessively around her shoulders, he hugged her close.

"Maybe just a little," she said with a happy sigh. The day had been perfect despite the humidity. High overhead, the boughs of tall firs swayed in the sultry summer breeze and dark clouds drifted in from the west.

Shawna's feet barely hit the ground as they walked through the "Fair from Yesteryear." Sprawled over several acres of farmland in the foothills of the Cascade Mountains, the dun-colored tents, flashy rides, and booths were backdropped by spectacular mountains.

Muted calliope music filled the summer air, and barkers, hawking their wares and games, shouted over the noise of the crowd. The smells of horses, sawdust, popcorn, and caramel wafted through the crowded, tent-lined fields that served as fairgrounds.

"Want to test your strength?" Shawna asked, glancing up at Parker and pointing to a lumberjack who was hoisting a heavy mallet over his head. Swinging the hammer with all of his might, the brawny man grunted loudly. The mallet crashed against a springboard and hurled a hearty weight halfway up a tall pole.

Parker's lips curved cynically. "I'll pass. Don't want to ruin my tennis arm, you know."

"Sure."

Parker ran his fingers through his sun-streaked hair. "There is another reason," he admitted.

She arched an eyebrow quizzically. "Which is?"

"I think I'll save my strength for tomorrow night." His voice lowered and his eyes darkened mysteriously. "There's this certain lady who's expecting all of my attention and physical prowess."

"Is that right?" She popped a piece of popcorn into his mouth and grinned. "Then you'd better not disappoint her."

"I won't," he promised, his gaze shifting to her mouth.

Shawna swallowed with difficulty. Whenever he looked at her that way, so sensual and determined, her heart always started beating a rapid double-time. She had to glance away, over his shoulder to a short, plump woman who was standing in front of a tent.

Catching Shawna's eye, the woman called, "How about I read your fortune?" With bright scarves wrapped around her head, painted fingernails, and dangling hooped earrings, she waved Shawna and Parker inside.

"I don't know—"

"Why not?" Parker argued, propelling her into the

darkened tent. Smelling of sawdust and cloying perfume, the tent was dark and close. Shawna sat on a dusty pillow near a small table and wondered what had possessed her to enter. The floor was covered with sawdust and straw, the only illumination coming from a slit in the top of the canvas. The place gave her the creeps.

Placing a five-dollar bill on the corner of the table, Parker sat next to Shawna, one arm still draped casually over her shoulders, his long legs crossed Indian style.

The money quickly disappeared into the voluminous folds of the Gypsy woman's skirt as she settled onto a mound of pillows on the other side of the table. "You first?" she asked, flashing Shawna a friendly, gold-capped smile.

Shrugging, Shawna glanced at Parker before meeting the Gypsy woman's gaze. "Sure. Why not?"

"Good!" Lady Fate clapped her wrinkled palms together. "Now, let me read your palm." Taking Shawna's hand in hers, she gently stroked the smooth skin, tracing the lines of Shawna's palm with her long fingers.

"I see you have worked long and hard in your job."

That much was true, Shawna thought wryly. She'd spent more hours than she wanted to count as a bartender while going to college and medical school. It had been years of grueling work, late shifts, and early morning classes, but finally, just this past year, she'd become a full-fledged internist. Even now, juggling time between her clinic and the hospital, she was working harder than she'd ever expected.

"And you have a happy family."

"Yes," Shawna admitted proudly. "A brother and my parents."

The woman nodded, as if she saw their faces in Shawna's palm. "You will live a long and fruitful life," she said thickly and then her fingers moved and she traced another line on Shawna's hand, only to stop short. Her face clouded, her old lips pursed and she dropped Shawna's wrist as quickly as she had taken it earlier. "Your time is over," she said gently, kindness sparking in her old brown eyes.

"What?"

"Next," Lady Fate said, calling toward the flap used as a door.

"That's all?" Shawna repeated, surprised. She didn't know much about fortune-telling, but she'd just begun to enjoy the game and some of her five-dollar future was missing.

"Yes. I've told you everything. Now, if you'll excuse me—"

"Wait a minute. What about my love life?" Glancing at Parker in the shadowed room, Shawna winked.

Lady Fate hesitated.

"I thought you could see everything," Shawna said. "That's what your sign says."

"There are some things better left unknown," the woman whispered softly as she started to stand.

"I can handle it," Shawna said, but felt a little uneasy.

"Really, you don't want to know," Lady Fortune declared, pursing her red lips and starting to stand.

"Of course I do," Shawna insisted. Though she didn't really believe in any of this mumbo jumbo, she wanted to get her money's worth. "I want to know everything." Shawna thrust her open palm back to the woman.

"She's very stubborn," Parker interjected.

"So I see." The fortune teller slowly sat down on her pillows as she closed Shawna's fingers, staring straight into her eyes. "I see there is a very important man in your life—you love him dearly, too much, perhaps."

"And?" Shawna asked, disgusted with herself when she felt the hairs on the back of her neck prickle with dread.

"And you will lose him," the woman said sadly,

glancing at Parker and then standing to brush some of the straw from her skirt. "Now go."

"Come on," Parker said, his eyes glinting mischievously. "It's time you got rid of that love of your life and started concentrating on me." He took Shawna by the hand and pulled her from the dark tent.

Outside, the air was hot and muggy but a refreshing change from the sticky interior of the tiny canvas booth. "You set her up to that, didn't you?" Shawna accused, still uneasy as she glanced back at the fortune-teller's tent.

"No way! Don't tell me you believed all of that baloney she tried to peddle you!"

"Of course not, but it was kind of creepy." Shuddering, she rubbed her bare arms despite the heat.

"And way off base." Laughing, he tugged on her hand and led her through a thicket of fir trees, away from the crowd and the circus atmosphere of the fair.

The heavy boughs offered a little shade and privacy and cooled the sweat beading on the back of Shawna's neck.

"You didn't believe her, did you?" he asked, his eyes delving deep into hers.

"No, but—"

"Just wait 'til the medical board gets wind of this!"

She couldn't help but smile as she twisted her hair into a loose rope and held it over her head, and off her neck. "You're laughing at me."

"Maybe a little." Stepping closer, he pinned her back against the rough bark of a Douglas fir, his arms resting lightly on her shoulders. "You deserve it, too, after all that guff you gave me about that damned brass ring."

"Guilty as charged," she admitted. She let her hair fall free and wrapped her hands around his lean, hard waist. Even beneath his light shirt, she could feel the ripple of his muscles as he shifted.

"Good." Taking the brass ring from his pocket, he

slipped the oversized band onto her finger. "With this ring, I thee wed," he said quietly, watching the ribbons flutter over her arm.

Shawna had to blink back some stupid tears of happiness that wet her lashes. "I can't wait," she murmured "for the real thing."

"Neither can I." Placing his forehead against hers, he stared at the dimpled smile playing on her lips.

Shawna's pulse leaped. His warm breath fanned her face, his fingers twined lazily in a long strand of her honey-gold hair and his mouth curved upward in a sardonic smile. "And now, Dr. McGuire, prepare yourself. I intend to have my way with you!" he said menacingly.

"Right here?" she asked innocently.

"For starters." He brushed his lips slowly over hers and Shawna sighed into his mouth.

She felt warm all over and weak in the knees. He kissed her eyelids and throat and she moaned, parting her lips expectantly. His hands felt strong and powerful and she knew that Parker would always take care of her and protect her. Deep inside, fires of desire that only he could spark ignited.

"I love you," she whispered, the wind carrying her words away as it lifted her hair away from her face.

"And I love you." Raising his head, he stared into her passion-glazed eyes. "And tomorrow night, I'm going to show you just how much."

"Do we really have to wait?" she whispered, disappointment pouting her lips.

"Not much longer—but we had a deal, remember?"

"It was stupid."

"Probably," he agreed. "And it's been hell." His angular features grew taut. "But weren't you the one who said, 'Everything meaningful is worth the wait'?"

"That's a butchered version of it, but yes," she said. "And we've made it this far."

"It's been agony," she admitted. "The next time I

have such lofty, idealistic and stupid ideas, go ahead and shoot me."

Grinning, he placed a kiss on her forehead. "I suppose this means that I'll have to give up my mistress."

"Your *what!*" she sputtered, knowing that he was teasing. *His mistress!* This mystery woman—a pure fantasy—had always been a joke between them, a joke that hurt more than it should have. "Oooh, you're absolutely the most arrogant, self-centered, egotistical—"

Capturing her wrists, he held them high over her head with one hand. "Go on," he urged, eyes slowly inching down her body, past her flashing green eyes and pursed lips, to the hollow of her throat where her pulse was fluttering rapidly, then lower still, to the soft mounds of her breasts, pushed proudly forward against apricot-colored cotton, rising and falling with each of her shallow breaths.

"—self-important, presumptuous, insolent bastard I've ever met!"

Lowering his head, he kissed the sensitive circle of bones at the base of her throat and she felt liquid inside. "Leave anything out?" he asked, his breath warm against her already overheated skin.

"A million things!"

"Such as?"

"Mistress," she repeated and then sucked in a sharp breath when she felt his moist tongue touch her throat. "Stop it," she said weakly, wanting to protest but unable.

"Aren't you the woman who was just begging for more a few minutes ago?"

"Parker—"

Then he cut off her protest with his mouth slanting swiftly over hers, his body pressed urgently against her. He kissed her with the passion that she'd seen burning in him ever since the first time they'd met. Her back was pinned to the trunk of the tree, her hands twined anxiously around his neck, wanton desire flowing from his lips to hers.

His hips were thrust against hers and she could feel the intensity of his passion, his heat radiating against her. "Please—" she whispered and he groaned.

His tongue rimmed her lips and then tasted of the sweetness within her open mouth.

"Parker—" She closed her eyes and moaned softly.

Suddenly every muscle in his body tensed and he released her as quickly as he'd captured her. Swearing, he stepped away from her. "You're dangerous, you know that, don't you?" His hands were shaking when he pushed the hair from his eyes. "I—I think we'd better go," he said thickly, clearly trying to quell the desire pounding in his brain.

Swallowing hard, she nodded. She could feel a hot flush staining her cheeks, knew her heart was racing out of control, and had trouble catching her breath. "But tomorrow, Mr. Harrison—you're not going to get away so easily."

"Don't tease me," he warned, his mouth a thin line of self-control.

"Never," she promised, forest-green eyes serious.

Linking his fingers with hers, he pulled her toward the parking lot. "I think we'd better get out of here. If I remember correctly, we have a wedding rehearsal and a dinner to get through tonight."

"That's right," she groaned, combing her tangled hair with her fingers, as they threaded their way through the cars parked in uneven rows. "You know, I should have listened to you when you wanted to elope."

"Next time, you'll know."

"There won't be a next time," she vowed as he opened the door of his Jeep and she slid into the sweltering interior. "You're going to be stuck with me for life!"

"I wouldn't have it any other way." Once behind

the wheel, he cranked open the windows and turned on the ignition.

"Even if you have to give up your mistress?"

Coughing, he glanced at her. One corner of his mouth lifted cynically as he maneuvered the car out of the bumpy, cracked field that served as a parking lot. "The things I do for love," he muttered and then switched on the radio and shifted gears.

Shawna stared out the window at the passing countryside. In the distance, dark clouds had begun to gather around the rugged slopes of Mount Hood. Shadows lengthened across the hilly, dry farmland. Dry, golden pastures turned dark as the wind picked up. Grazing cattle lifted their heads at the scent of the approaching storm and weeds and wildflowers along the fencerows bent double in the muggy breeze.

"Looks like a storm brewing." Parker glanced at the hard, dry ground and frowned. "I guess we could use a little rain."

"But not tonight or tomorrow," Shawna said. "Not on our wedding day." *Tomorrow,* she thought with a smile. She tried to ignore the Gypsy woman's grim prediction and the promise of rain. "Tomorrow will be perfect!"

" . . . and may you have all the happiness you deserve. To the bride and groom!" Jake said, casting a smile at his sister and holding his wineglass high in the air.

Hoisting her glass, Shawna beamed, watching her dark-haired brother through adoring eyes.

"Here, here," the rest of the guests chimed in, glasses clinking, laughter and cheery conversation filling the large banquet room of the Edwardian Hotel in downtown Portland. The room was crowded with family and friends, all members of the wedding party.

After a rehearsal marred by only a few hitches, and a lovely veal dinner, the wine, toasts and fellowship were flowing freely in the elegant room.

"How was that?" Jake asked, taking his chair.

"Eloquent," Shawna admitted, smiling at her brother. "I didn't know you had it in you."

"That's because you never listened to me," he quipped, and then, setting his elbows on the table, winked at Parker. "I hope you have better luck keeping her in line."

"I will," Parker predicted, loosening his tie.

"Hey, wait a minute," Shawna protested, but laughed and sipped from a glass of cold Chablis.

"I can't wait until tomorrow," Gerri, Shawna's best friend, said with a smile. "I never thought I'd see this day, when someone actually convinced the good doctor to walk down the aisle." Shaking her auburn hair, Gerri leaned back and lit a cigarette, clicking her lighter shut to add emphasis to her words.

"I'm not married to my work," Shawna protested.

"Not anymore. But you were. Back in those days when you were in med school, you were no fun. I repeat: *No fun!*"

Parker hugged his bride-to-be. "I intend to change all that, starting tomorrow!"

"Oh, you do, do you?" Shawna said, her gaze narrowing on him. "I'll have you know, Mr. Harrison, that *you'll* be the one toeing the line."

"This should be good," Jake decided. "Parker Harrison under a woman's thumb."

"I'll drink to that!" Brad Lomax, Parker's most famous student, leaned over Shawna's shoulder, spilling some of his drink on the linen tablecloth. His black hair was mussed, his tie already lost, and the smell of bourbon was heavy on his breath. He'd been in a bad mood all evening and had chosen to drown whatever problems he had in a bottle.

"Maybe you should slow down a little," Parker suggested, as the boy swayed over the table.

"What? In the middle of this celebration? No way, man!" To add emphasis to his words, he downed his drink and signaled to the waiter for another.

Parker's eyes grew serious. "Really, Brad, you've had enough."

"Never enough!" He grabbed a glass of champagne from a passing waiter. "Put it on his tab!" Brad said, cocking his thumb at Parker. "This is his las' night of freedom! Helluva waste if ya ask me!"

Jake glanced from Parker to Brad and back again. "Maybe I should take him home," he suggested.

But Brad reached into his pocket, fumbled around and finally withdrew his keys. "I can do it myself," he said testily.

"Brad—"

"I'll go when I'm damned good and ready." Leaning forward, he placed one arm around Parker, the other around Shawna. "You know, I jus' might end up married myself," he decided, grinning sloppily.

"I'd like to be there on the day some girl gets her hooks into you," Parker said. "It'll never happen."

Brad laughed, splashing his drink again. "Guess again," he said, slumping against Shawna.

"Why don't you tell me about it on the way home?" Parker suggested. He helped Brad back to his feet.

"But the party's not over—"

"It is for us. We've got a pretty full schedule tomorrow. I don't want you so hung over that you miss the ceremony."

"I won't be!"

"Right. 'Cause I'm taking you home right now." He set Brad's drink on the table and took the keys from his hand. Then, leaning close to Shawna, he kissed her forehead. "I'll see you in the morning, okay?"

"Eleven o'clock, sharp," she replied, looking up at him, her eyes shining.

"Wouldn't miss it for the world."

"Me neither," Brad agreed, his arm still slung over Parker's broad shoulders as they headed for the door. " 'Sides, I need to talk to you, need some advice," he added confidentially to Parker.

"So what else is new?"

"Be careful," Jake suggested. "It's raining cats and dogs out there—the first time in a couple months. The roads are bound to be slick."

"Will do," Parker agreed.

Jake watched them leave, his eyes narrowing on Parker's broad shoulders. "I don't see why Parker puts up with Brad," he said, frowning into his drink.

Shawna lifted a shoulder. "You know Brad is Parker's star student, supposedly seeded ninth in the country. Parker expects him to follow in his footsteps, make it to the top—win the grand slam. The whole nine yards, so to speak."

"That's football, Sis. Not tennis."

"You know what I mean."

"He's that good?" Obviously, Jake didn't believe it, and Shawna understood why. As a psychiatrist, he'd seen more than his share of kids who'd gotten too much too fast and couldn't handle the fame or money.

Leaning back in her chair, Shawna quoted, "The best natural athlete that Parker's ever seen."

Jake shook his head, glancing again at the door through which Parker and Brad had disappeared. "Maybe so, but the kid's got a temper and a chip on his shoulder the size of the Rock of Gibraltar."

"Thank you for your professional opinion, Dr. McGuire."

"Is that a nice way of saying 'butt out'?" Jake asked.

Shawna shook her head. "No, it's a nice way of saying, let's keep the conversation light—no heavy stuff, okay? I'm getting married tomorrow."

"How could I forget?" Clicking the rim of his glass to hers, he whispered, "And I wish you all the luck in the world." He took a sip of his wine. "You know what the best part of this marriage is, don't you?"

"Living with Parker?"

"Nope. The fact that this is the last day there will be two Dr. McGuires working at Columbia Memorial. No more mixed-up messages or calls."

"That's right. From now on, I'll be Dr. Harrison." She wrinkled her nose a bit. "Doesn't have the same ring to it, does it?"

"Sounds great to me."

"Me, too," she admitted, looking into her wineglass and smiling at the clear liquid within. "Me, too."

She felt a light tap on her shoulder and looked up. Her father was standing behind her chair. A tall, rotund man, he was dressed in his best suit, and a sad smile curved his lips. "How about a dance with my favorite girl?" he asked.

"You've got it," she said, pushing back her chair and taking his hand. "But after that, I'm going home."

"Tired?"

"Uh-huh, and I want to look my best tomorrow."

"Don't worry. You'll be the prettiest bride ever to walk down that aisle."

"The wedding's going to be in the rose garden, remember?" She laughed, and her father's face pulled together.

"I don't suppose I can talk you into saying your vows in front of the altar?"

"Nope. Outside," she said, glancing out the window into the dark night. Rain shimmered on the window panes. "I don't care if this blasted rain keeps falling, we're going to be married under the arbor in the rose garden of the church."

"You always were stubborn," he muttered, twirling her around the floor. "Just like your mother."

"Some people say I'm a chip off the old block, and they aren't talking about Mom."

Malcolm McGuire laughed as he waltzed his daughter around the room. "I know this is the eleventh hour, but sometimes I wonder if you're rushing things a bit. You haven't known Parker all that long."

"Too late, Dad. If you wanted to talk me out of this, you shouldn't have waited this long," she pointed out.

"Don't get me wrong; I like Parker."

"Good, because you're stuck with him as a son-in-law."

"I just hope you're not taking on too much," he said thoughtfully. "You're barely out of med school and you have a new practice. Now you're taking on the responsibilities of becoming a wife—"

"And a mother?" she teased.

Malcolm's eyebrows quirked. "I know you want children, but that can come later."

"I'm already twenty-eight!"

"That's not ancient, Shawna. You and Parker, you're both young."

"And in love. So quit worrying," she admonished with a fond grin. "I'm a big girl now. I can take care of myself. And if I can't, Parker will."

"He'd better," her father said, winking broadly. "Or he'll have to answer to me!"

When the strains of the waltz drifted away, he patted Shawna's arm and escorted her back to her chair. He glanced around the room as she slipped her arms through the sleeves of her coat. "So where is that husband-to-be of yours? Don't tell me he already skipped out."

"Very funny." She lifted her hair out of the collar of her raincoat and said, "He took Brad Lomax home a little earlier. But don't worry, Dad, he'll be there tomorrow. I'll see you then."

Tucking her purse under her arm, she hurried down the stairs, unwilling to wait for the elevator. On the first floor, she dashed through the lobby of the old Victorian hotel, and shouldered open the heavy wood door. The rain was coming down in sheets and thunder rumbled through the sky. Just a summer storm, she told herself, nothing to worry about. Everything will be clean and fresh tomorrow and the roses in the garden will still have dewy drops of moisture on their petals. It will be perfect! Nothing will ruin the wedding. Nothing can.

Two

Shawna stared at her reflection as her mother adjusted the cream-colored lace of her veil. "How's that?" Doris McGuire asked as she met her daughter's gaze in the mirror.

"Fine, Mom. Really—" But Shawna's forehead was drawn into creases and her green eyes were dark with worry. *Where was Parker?*

Doris stepped back to take a better look and Shawna saw herself as her mother did. Ivory lace stood high on her throat, and creamy silk billowed softly from a tucked-in waist to a long train that was now slung over her arm. Wisps of honey-colored hair peeked from beneath her veil. The vision was complete, except for her clouded gaze. "Parker isn't here yet?" Shawna asked.

"Relax. Jake said he'd let us know the minute he arrived." She smoothed a crease from her dress and forced a smile.

"But he was supposed to meet with Reverend Smith half an hour ago."

Doris waved aside Shawna's worries. "Maybe he got caught in traffic. You know how bad it's been ever since the storm last night. Parker will be here. Just you wait. Before you know it, you'll be Mrs. Parker Harrison and Caribbean-bound."

"I hope so," Shawna said, telling herself not to worry. So Parker was a few minutes late; certainly that wasn't something to be alarmed about. Or was it?

Parker had never been late once in the six weeks she'd known him.

Glancing through the window to the gray day beyond, Shawna watched the yellow ribbons woven into the white slats of the arbor in the church garden. They danced wildly over the roses of the outdoor altar as heavy purple clouds stole silently across the sky.

Doris checked her watch and sighed. "We still have time to move the ceremony inside," she said quietly. "I'm sure none of the guests would mind."

"No!" Shawna shook her head and her veil threatened to come loose. She heard the harsh sound of her voice and saw her mother stiffen. "Look, Mom, I'm sorry, I didn't mean to snap."

"It's okay—just the wedding-day jitters. But try to calm down," her mother suggested, touching her arm. "Parker will be here soon." But Doris's voice faltered and Shawna saw the concern etched in the corner of her mother's mouth.

"I hope you're right," she whispered, unconvinced. The first drops of rain fell from the sky and ran down the windowpanes. Glancing again out the window to the parking lot, Shawna hoped to see Parker's red Jeep wheel into the lot. Instead, she saw Jake drive up, water splashing from under the wheels of his car as he ground to a stop.

"Where did Jake go?" she asked. "I thought he was in the rose garden . . ." Her voice drifted off as she watched her brother dash through the guests who were moving into the church.

"Shawna!" Jake's voice boomed through the door and he pounded on the wood panels. "Shawna!"

The ghost of fear swept over her.

"For God's sake, come in," Doris said, opening the door.

Jake burst into the room. His hair was wet, plastered to his head, his tuxedo was rumpled, and his face was colorless. "I just heard—there was an accident last night."

"An accident?" Shawna repeated, seeing the horror in his gaze. "No—"

"Parker and Brad were in a terrible crash. They weren't found until a few hours ago. Right now they're at Mercy Hospital—"

"There must be some mistake!" Shawna cried, her entire world falling apart. Parker couldn't be hurt! Just yesterday they were at the fair, laughing, kissing, touching . . .

"No mistake."

"Jake—" Doris reproached, but Jake was at Shawna's side, taking hold of her arm, as if he were afraid she would swoon.

"It's serious, Sis."

Disbelieving, Shawna pinned him with wide eyes. "If this is true—"

"Damn it, Shawna, do you think I'd run in here with this kind of a story if I hadn't checked it out?" he asked, his voice cracking.

The last of her hopes fled and she clung to him, curling her fingers over his arm as fear grew in her heart. "Why didn't anyone tell me? I'm a doctor, for God's sake—"

"But not at Mercy Hospital. No one there knew who he was."

"But he's famous—"

"It didn't matter," Jake said soberly. His eyes told it all and for the first time Shawna realized that Parker, her beloved Parker, might die.

"Oh, my God," she whispered, wanting to fall to pieces, but not giving in to the horror that was coldly starting to grip her, wrenching at her insides. "I've got to go to him!"

"But you can't," her mother protested weakly. "Not now—"

"Of course I can!" Flinging off her veil, she gathered her skirts and ran to the side door of the church.

"Wait, Shawna!" Jake called after her, running to catch up. "I'll drive you—

But she didn't listen. She found her purse with the car keys, jumped into her little hatchback, and plunged the keys into the ignition. The car roared to life. Shawna rammed it into gear and tore out of the parking lot, the car wheels screeching around the curves as she entered the highway. She drove wildly, her every thought centered on Parker as she prayed that he was still alive.

Jake hadn't said it, but it had been written in his eyes. *Parker might die!* "Please God, no," she whispered, her voice faltering, her chin thrust forward in determination. "You can't let him die! You can't!"

She shifted down, rounding a curve and nearly swerving out of her lane as the car climbed a steep street. Fir trees and church spires, skyscrapers and sharp ravines, a view of the Willamette River and the hazy mountains beyond were lost to her in a blur of rainwashed streets and fear.

Twice her car slid on the slick pavement but she finally drove into the parking lot of the hospital and ignored a sign reserving the first spot she saw for staff members. Her heart hammering with dread, she cut the engine, yanked on the brake and ran toward the glass doors, oblivious to the fact that her dress was dragging through mud puddles and grime.

As she ran to the desk in the emergency room, she wiped the water from her face. "I need to see Parker Harrison," she said breathlessly to a calm-looking young woman at the desk. "I'm Dr. McGuire, Columbia Memorial Hospital." Flashing credentials in the surprised woman's face, she didn't wait for a response. "I'm also Mr. Harrison's personal physician. He was brought in here early this morning and I have to see him!"

"He's in surgery now—"

"Surgery!" Shawna said, incredulous. "Who's the doctor in charge?"

"Dr. Lowery."

"Then let me see Lowery." Shawna's eyes glittered with authority and determination, though inside she was dying. She knew her requests were unreasonable, against all hospital procedures, but she didn't care. Parker was in this hospital, somewhere, possibly fighting for his life, and come hell or high water, she was going to see him!

"You'll have to wait," the nurse said, glancing at Shawna's wet hair, her bedraggled wedding dress, the fire in her gaze.

"I want to see him. Now."

"I'm sorry, Dr. McGuire. If you'd like, you could wait in the doctors' lounge and I'll tell Dr. Lowery you're here."

Seeing no other option, Shawna clamped her teeth together. "Then, please, tell me how serious he is. Exactly what are his injuries? How serious?"

"I can't give out that information."

Shawna didn't move. Her gaze was fixed on the smaller woman's face. "Then have someone who can give it out find me."

"If you'll wait."

Swallowing back the urge to shake information out of the young woman, Shawna exhaled a deep breath and tried to get a grip on her self-control. "Okay—but, please, send someone up to the lounge. I need to know about him, as his physician and as his fiancée."

The young nurse's face softened. "You were waiting for him, weren't you?" she asked quietly, as she glanced again at Shawna's soiled silk gown.

"Yes," Shawna admitted, her throat suddenly tight and tears springing to her eyes. She reached across the counter, took the nurse's hand in her own. "You understand—I have to see him."

"I'll send someone up as soon as I can," the girl promised.

"Thank you." Releasing her grip, Shawna suddenly felt the eyes of everyone in the waiting room boring into her back. For the first time she noticed the group of people assembled on the molded-plastic couches as they waited to be examined. Small children whined and cuddled against their mothers and older people, faces set and white, sat stiffly in the chairs, their eyes taking in Shawna's disheveled appearance.

Turning back to the young nurse, she forced her voice to remain steady. "Please, I want to know if there's any change in his condition." *Whatever that is,* she added silently.

"Will do, Dr. McGuire. The doctors' lounge is just to the left of the elevator on the second floor."

"Thank you," Shawna said, scooping up her skirts and squaring her shoulders as she started down the hall. The heels of her soaked satin pumps clicked on the tile floor.

"Shawna! Wait!" Jake's voice echoed through the corridor. In a few swift strides he was next to her, oblivious to the eyes of all the people in the waiting room. Still dressed in his tuxedo, his wet hair curling around his face, he looked as frantic as she felt. "What did you find out?" he asked softly.

"Not much. I'm on my way to the lounge on the second floor. Supposedly they'll send someone up to give me the news."

"If not, I'll check around—I've got connections here," Jake reminded her, glancing at all the pairs of interested eyes.

"You what?"

"Sometimes I consult here, at Mercy, in the psychiatric wing. I know quite a few of the staff. Come on," he urged, taking her elbow and propelling her toward the elevators. "You can change in the women's washroom on the second floor."

"Change?" she asked, realizing for the first time that he was carrying her smallest nylon suitcase, one of the suitcases she'd packed for her honeymoon. Numb inside, she took the suitcase from his outstretched hand. "Thanks," she murmured. "I owe you one."

"One of many. I'll add it to your list," he said, but the joke fell flat. "Look, Mom went through that," he gestured at the bag, "and thought you could find something more suitable than what you're wearing." Frowning, he touched her dirty gown.

The sympathy in Jake's eyes reached out to her and she felt suddenly weak. Her throat was hot, burning with tears she couldn't shed. "Oh, Jake. Why is this happening?" she asked, just as the elevator doors whispered open and they stepped inside.

"I wish I knew."

"I just want to know that Parker will be all right."

"I'll find out," he promised as the elevator groaned to a stop and Shawna stepped onto the second floor. Pushing a button on the control panel, Jake held the doors open and pointed down the hallway. "The lounge is right there, around the corner, and the washroom—I don't know where *that* is, but it must be nearby. I'll meet you back in the lounge as soon as I find Tom Handleman—he's usually in charge of ER—and then I'll be back to fill you in."

"Thanks," she whispered. The brackets around Jake's mouth deepened as he grimaced. "Let's just hope Parker and Brad are okay."

"They will be! They have to be!"

"I hope so. For your sake."

Then he was gone and Shawna, despite the fact that she was shaking from head to foot, found the washroom. Trying to calm herself, she sluiced cold water over her face and hardly recognized her reflection in the mirror over the sink. Two hours before she'd been a beaming bride, primping in front of a full-length mirror. Now, she looked as if she'd aged ten years.

Eyes red, mouth surrounded by lines of strain, skin
pale, she stripped off her wedding dress, unable to
wear it another minute. Then she changed into a pair
of white slacks, a cotton sweater, and a pair of running
shoes, the clothes she had thought she would wear
while holding hands with Parker and running along
the gleaming white beach at Martinique.

Parker. Her heart wrenched painfully.

Quickly folding her dress as best she could and stuffing it into the little bag, she told herself to be strong
and professional. Parker would be all right. He had to
be.

Quickly, she found the lounge. With trembling
hands, she poured herself a cup of coffee. Groups of
doctors and nurses were clustered at round tables chattering, laughing, not seeming to care that Parker, her
Parker, was somewhere in this labyrinthine building
clinging to his very life. Forcing herself to remain calm,
she took a chair in a corner near a planter filled with
spiky leafed greenery. From there she could watch the
door.

Doctors came and went, some with two days' growth
of beard and red-rimmed eyes, others in crisply pressed
lab coats and bright smiles. Each time the door opened,
Shawna's gaze froze expectantly on the doorway, hoping that Jake would come barging into the room to tell
her the entire nightmare was a hellish mistake; that
Parker was fine; that nothing had changed; that later
this afternoon they would step on a plane bound for
white sand, hot sun, and aquamarine water . . .

"Come on, Jake," she whispered to herself, watching
the clock as the second hand swept around the face,
the minutes ticking by so slowly the waiting had become excruciating. She eavesdropped, listening to the
conversations buzzing around her, dreading to over-
hear that Parker was dead, hoping to hear that his
injuries were only superficial. But nothing was said.

Please, let him be all right! Please.

Somehow she finished her coffee and was shredding her cup when Jake pushed open the door and headed straight for her. Another young man was with him—tall and lean, with bushy salt and pepper hair, wire-rimmed glasses, and a sober expression. "Dr. McGuire?" he asked.

Bracing herself for the worst, Shawna met the young man's eyes.

"This is Tom Handleman, Shawna. He was just in ER with Parker," Jake explained.

"And?" she asked softly, her hands balling into fists.

"And he'll live," Tom said. "He was pinned in the car a long time, but his injuries weren't as bad as we'd expected."

"Thank God," she breathed, her voice breaking as relief drove aside her fears.

"He has several cracked ribs, a ruptured spleen, a concussion and a fractured patella, including torn cartilage and ripped ligaments. Besides which, there are facial lacerations and contusions—"

"And you don't think that's serious!" she cut in, the blood draining from her face.

Jake met her worried eyes. "Shawna, please, listen to him."

"I didn't say his condition wasn't serious," Tom replied. "But Mr. Harrison's injuries are no longer life-threatening."

"Concussion," she repeated, "ruptured spleen—"

"Right, but we've controlled the hemorrhaging and his condition has stabilized. As I said, his concussion wasn't as bad as Lowery and I had originally thought."

"No brain damage?" she asked.

"Not that we can tell. But he'll have to have knee surgery as soon as his body's well enough for the additional trauma."

She ran a shaking hand over her forehead. *Parker was going to be all right!* She felt weak with relief. "Can I see him?"

"Not yet. He's still in recovery," Tom said quietly. "But in a few hours, once he's conscious again—then you can see him."

"Was he conscious when he was brought in?"

"No." Dr. Handleman shook his head. "But we expect him to wake up as soon as the anesthetic wears off."

Jake placed his hand on Shawna's shoulder. "There's something else," he said quietly.

His grim expression and the fingers gripping her shoulder warned her. For the first time, she thought about the other man in Parker's car. "Brad?" she whispered, knowing for certain that Parker's star pupil and friend was dead.

"Brad Lomax was DOA," Tom said softly.

"Dead on arrival?" she repeated, the joy she'd felt so fleetingly stripped away.

"He was thrown from the car and his neck was broken."

"No!" she cried.

Jake's fingers tightened over her shoulders as she tried to stand and deny everything Tom was saying. She could see heads swing in her direction, eyes widen in interest as doctors at nearby tables heard her protest.

"I'm sorry," Tom said. "There was nothing we could do."

"But he was only twenty-two!"

"Shawna—" Jake's fingers relaxed.

Tears flooded her eyes. "I don't believe it!"

"You're a doctor, Miss McGuire," Tom pointed out, his eyes softening with sympathy. "You know as well as I do that these things happen. Not fair, I know, but just the way it is."

Sniffing back her tears, Shawna pushed Jake's restraining hands from her shoulders. Still grieving deep in her heart, she forced her professionalism to surface. "Thank you, Doctor," she murmured, extending her hand though part of her wanted to crumple into a miserable heap. As a doctor, she was used to dealing with death, but it was never easy, especially at a time like this, when the person who had lost his life was someone she'd known, someone Parker had loved.

Tom shook her hand. "I'll let you know when Mr. Harrison is awake and in his room. Why don't you go and rest for a couple of hours?"

"No—I, uh, I couldn't," she said.

"Your choice. Whatever I can do to help," he replied before turning and leaving the room.

"Oh, Jake," she said, feeling the security of her brother's arm wrap around her as he led her from the lounge. "I just can't believe that Brad's gone—"

"It's hard, I know, but you've got to listen to me," he urged, handing her the nylon suitcase he'd picked up and helping her to the elevator. "What you'll have to do now is be strong, for Parker. When he wakes up and finds out that Brad is dead, he's going to feel guilty as hell—"

"But it wasn't his fault. It couldn't have been."

"I know," he whispered. "But Parker won't see the accident that way—not at first. The trauma of the accident combined with an overwhelming sense of guilt over Brad's death might be devastating for Parker. It would be for anyone." He squeezed her and offered a tight smile. "You'll have to be his rock, someone he can hold on to, and it won't be easy."

She met his gaze and determination shone in her eyes. "I'll do everything I can for him," she promised.

One side of Jake's mouth lifted upward. "I know it, Sis."

"The only thing that matters is that Parker gets well."

"And the two of you get married."

Her fingers clenched around the handle of her suitcase and she shook a wayward strand of hair from her eyes. "That's not even important right now," she said, steadfastly pushing all thoughts of her future with Parker aside. "I just have to see that he gets through this. And I will. No matter what!"

The next four hours were torture. She walked the halls of the hospital, trying to get rid of the nervous tension that twisted her stomach and made her glance at the clock every five minutes.

Jake had gone back to the church to explain what had happened to the guests and her parents, but she'd refused to give up her vigil.

"Dr. McGuire?"

Turning, she saw Dr. Handleman walking briskly to her.

"What's happened?" she asked. "I thought Parker was supposed to be put in a private room two hours ago."

"I know," he agreed, his face drawn, "but things changed. Unfortunately Mr. Harrison hasn't regained consciousness. We've done tests, the anesthesia has worn off, but he's still asleep."

Dread climbed up her spine. "Meaning?"

"Probably that he'll come to in the next twenty-four hours."

"And if he doesn't?" she asked, already knowing the answer, panic sending her heart slamming against her rib cage.

"Then we'll just have to wait."

"You're saying he's in a coma."

Tom pushed his glasses up his nose and frowned. "It looks that way."

"How long?"

"We can't guess."

"How long?" she repeated, jaw clenched, fear taking hold of her.

"Come on, *Dr.* McGuire, you understand what I'm

talking about," he reminded her as gently as possible. "There's no way of knowing. Maybe just a few hours—"

"But maybe indefinitely," she finished, biting back the urge to scream.

"That's unlikely."

"But not out of the question."

He forced a tired smile. "Prolonged coma, especially after a particularly traumatic experience, is always a possibility."

"What about his knee?"

"It'll wait, but not too long. We can't let the bones start to knit improperly, otherwise we might have more problems than we already do."

"He's a tennis pro," she whispered.

"We'll take care of him," he said. "Now, if you want, you can see him. He's in room four-twelve."

"Thank you." Without a backward glance, she hurried to the elevator, hoping to stamp down the panic that tore at her. On the fourth floor, she strode briskly down the corridor, past rattling gurneys, clattering food trays, and the soft conversation of the nurses at their station as she made her way to Parker's room.

"Excuse me, miss," one nurse said as Shawna reached the door to room four-twelve. "But Mr. Harrison isn't allowed any visitors."

Shawna faced the younger woman and squared her shoulders, hoping to sound more authoritative than she felt. "I'm Dr. McGuire. I work at Columbia Memorial Hospital. Dr. Harrison is my patient and Dr. Handleman said I could wait for the patient to regain consciousness."

"It's all right," another nurse said. "I took the call from Dr. Handleman. Dr. McGuire has all privileges of a visiting physician."

"Thank you," Shawna said, entering the darkened room and seeing Parker's inert form on the bed. Draped in crisp, white sheets, lying flat on his back, with an IV tube running from his arm and a swath of bandages over his head, he was barely recognizable. "Oh, Parker," she whispered, throat clogged, eyes suddenly burning.

She watched the slow rise and fall of his chest, saw the washed-out color of his skin, the small cuts over his face, noticed the bandages surrounding his chest and kneecap, and she wondered if he'd ever be the same, wonderful man she'd known. "I love you," she vowed, twining her fingers in his.

Thinking of the day before, the hot sultry air, the brass ring, and the Gypsy woman's grim fortune, she closed her eyes.

You love him too much—you will lose him, the fortune-teller had predicted.

"Never," Shawna declared. Shivering, she took a chair near the bed, whispering words of endearment and telling herself that she would do everything in her power as a doctor and a woman to make him well.

Three

A breakfast cart rattled past the doorway and Shawna started, her eyelids flying open. She'd spent all day and night at Parker's bedside, watching, waiting, and praying.

Now, as she rubbed the kinks from her neck and stretched her aching shoulder muscles, she looked down at Parker's motionless form, hardly believing that their life together had changed so drastically.

"Come on, Parker," she whispered, running gentle fingers across his forehead, silently hoping that his eyelids would flutter open. "You can do it."

A quiet cough caught her attention and she looked up to the doorway, where her brother lounged against the door frame. "How's it going?" Jake asked.

She lifted a shoulder. "About the same."

He raked his fingers through his hair and sighed. "How about if I buy you a cup of coffee?"

Shaking her head, Shawna glanced back at Parker. "I don't think I could—"

"Have you eaten anything since you've been here?"

"No, but—"

"That's right, no buts about it. I'm buying you breakfast. You're not doing Parker any good by starving yourself, are you, Doctor?"

"All right." Climbing reluctantly to her feet, she stretched again as she twisted open the blinds. The morning rays of late summer sun glimmered on the puddles outside. Deep in her heart, Shawna hoped the sunlight would wake Parker. She glanced back at him, her teeth sinking into her lower lip as she watched the steady rise and fall of his chest, noticed the bandage partially covering his head. But he didn't move.

"Come on," Jake said softly.

Without protest, she left the room. As she walked with Jake to the cafeteria, she was oblivious to the hospital routine: the nurses and orderlies carrying medication, the incessant pages from the intercom echoing down the corridors, the charts and files, and the ringing phones that normally sounded so familiar.

Jake pushed open the double doors to the dining room. Trays and silverware were clattering, and the smell of frying bacon, sizzling sausages, maple syrup, and coffee filled the air. Despite her despondency, Shawna's stomach grumbled and she let Jake buy her a platter of eggs, bacon, and toast.

Taking a seat at a scarred Formica table, she sat across from her brother and tried to eat. But she couldn't help overhearing the gossip filtering her way. Two nurses at a nearby table were speaking in a loud whisper and Shawna could barely concentrate on her breakfast.

"It's a shame, really," a heavyset nurse was saying, clucking her tongue. "Parker Harrison of all people! You know, I used to watch his matches on TV."

"You and the rest of the country," her companion agreed.

Shawna's hands began to shake.

"And on his wedding day!" the first woman said. "And think about that boy and his family!"

"The boy?"

"Brad Lomax. DOA. There was nothing Lowery could do."

Shawna felt every muscle in her body tense. She was chewing a piece of toast, but it stuck in her throat.

"That explains the reporters crowded around the front door," the smaller woman replied.

"For sure. And that's not all of it. His fiancée is here, too. From what I hear she's a doctor over at Columbia Memorial. Been with him ever since the accident. She came charging over here in her wedding dress, demanding to see him."

"Poor thing."

Shawna dropped her fork and her fists curled in anger. *How dare they gossip about Parker!*

"Right. And now he's comatose. No telling when he'll wake up."

"Or if."

Shawna's shoulders stiffened and she was about to say something, but Jake held up his hand and shook his head. "Don't bother," he suggested. "It's just small talk."

"About Parker and me!"

"He's a famous guy. So was Brad Lomax. Loosen up, Shawna, you've heard hospital gossip before."

"Not about Parker," she muttered, her appetite waning again as she managed to control her temper. The two nurses carried their trays back to the counter and Shawna tried to relax. Of course Parker's accident had created a stir and people were only people. Jake was right. She had to expect curiosity and rumors.

"I know this is hard. But it's not going to get much better, at least for a while." He finished his stack of pancakes and pushed his plate to one side. "You may as well know that the reporters have already started calling. There were several recordings on your phone machine this morning."

"You were at my apartment?"

"I took back your bag and I gave the wedding dress to Mom. She's going to have it cleaned, but isn't sure that it will look the same."

"It doesn't matter," Shawna said. She wondered if

she'd ever wear the gown again. "How're Mom and Dad?"

"They're worried about you and Parker."

"I'll bet," she whispered, grateful for her parents and their strength. Whereas Parker was strong because he'd grown up alone, never knowing his parents, Shawna had gotten her strength from the support and security of her family.

"Mom's decided to keep a low profile."

"And Dad?"

"He wants to tear down the walls of this hospital."

"It figures."

"But Mom has convinced him that if you need them, you'll call."

"Or you'll tell them, if I don't," Shawna guessed.

Smiling slightly, he said. "They're just trying to give you some space—but you might want to call them."

"I will. Later. After Parker wakes up."

Jake raised one brow skeptically, but if he had any doubts, he kept them to himself. "Okay, I'll give them the message."

She quit pretending interest in her food and picked up her tray. She'd been away from Parker for nearly half an hour and she had to get back.

"There's something you should remember," Jake said as they made their way through the tightly packed Formica tables, setting their trays on the counter.

"And what's that?"

"When you leave the hospital, you might want to go out a back entrance, unless you're up to answering a lot of personal questions from reporters."

"I understand. Thanks for the warning."

She turned toward the elevator, but Jake caught her elbow.

"There is one other thing. Brad Lomax's funeral is the day after tomorrow. Mom already arranged to send a spray of flowers from you and Parker."

Shawna winced at the mention of Brad's name. His

death was still difficult to accept. And then there was the matter of Parker and how he would feel when he found out what had happened to his protegé. "Mom's an angel," Shawna decided, "but I think I'd better put in an appearance."

"The funeral's for family only," Jake told her. "Don't think about it."

Relieved, Shawna said, "I'll try not to. I'll see you later." Waving, she dashed to the stairwell, unable to wait for the elevator. She had to get back to Parker and make sure she was the one who broke the news.

Parker felt as if his head would explode. Slowly he opened an eye, ignoring the pain that shot through his brain. He tried to lift a hand to his head, but his cramped muscles wouldn't move and his struggling fingers felt nothing save cold metal bars.

Where am I? he wondered, trying to focus. There was a bad taste in his mouth and pain ripped up one side of his body and down the other. His throat worked, but no sound escaped.

"He's waking up!" a woman whispered, her voice heavy with relief. The voice was vaguely familiar, but he couldn't place it. "Call Dr. Handleman or Dr. Lowery! Tell them Parker Harrison is waking up!"

What the hell for? And who are Lowery and Handleman? Doctors? Is that what she said?

"Parker? Can you hear me? Parker, love?"

He blinked rapidly, focusing on the face pressed close to his. It was a beautiful face, with even features, pink-tinged cheeks, and worried green eyes. Long, slightly wavy honey-colored hair fell over her shoulders to brush against his neck.

"Oh, God, I'm so glad you're awake," she said, her voice thick with emotion. Tears starred her lashes and for the first time he noticed the small lines of strain near her mouth and the hollows of her cheeks.

She's crying! This beautiful young woman was actually shedding tears. He was amazed as he watched her tears drizzle down her cheeks and one by one drop onto the bed sheets. She was crying for him! But why?

Her hands were on his shoulders and she buried her face into the crook of his neck. Her tenderness seemed right, somehow, but for the life of him, he couldn't understand why. "I've been so worried! It's been three days! Thank God, you're back!"

His gaze darted around the small room, to the television, the rails on the bed, the dripping IV hanging over his head, and the baskets and baskets of flowers sitting on every available space in the room. It slowly dawned on him that he was in a hospital. The pain in his head wasn't imagined, this wasn't all a bad dream. Somehow he'd landed in a hospital bed, completely immobilized!

"Good morning, Mr. Harrison!" a gruff male voice called.

The woman straightened and quickly brushed aside her tears.

Shifting his gaze, Parker saw a man he didn't recognize walk up to the bed and smile down at him. A doctor. Dressed in a white lab coat, with an identification tag that Parker couldn't make out, the man stared down at Parker from behind thick, wire-framed glasses. Taking Parker's wrist in one hand, he glanced at his watch. "I'm Dr. Handleman. You're a patient here in Mercy Hospital and have been for the past three days."

Three days? What in God's name was this man talking about? Partial images, horrible and vague, teased his mind, though he couldn't remember what they meant.

Drawing his brows together in concentration, Parker tried to think, strained to remember, but his entire life was a blur of disjointed pieces that were colorless and dreamlike. He had absolutely no idea who these people were or why he was here.

"You're a very lucky man," the doctor continued, releasing his wrist. "Not many people could have survived that accident."

Parker blinked, trying to find his voice. "Accident?" he rasped, the sound of his own voice unfamiliar and raw.

"You don't remember?" The doctor's expression clouded.

"Wh-what am I doing here?" Parker whispered hoarsely. His eyes traveled past the doctor to the woman. She was leaning against the wall, as if for support. Wearing a white lab coat and a stethoscope, she had to be a member of the staff. *So why the tears?* "Who are you?" he asked, his bruised face clouding as he tried to concentrate. He heard her muted protest and saw the slump of her shoulders. "Do I know you?"

Four

Shawna's heart nearly stopped. "Parker?" she whispered, struggling to keep her voice steady as she took his bandaged hand in hers. "Don't you remember me?"

His gaze skated over her face and he squinted, as if trying to remember something hazy, but no flash of recognition flickered in his eyes.

"I'm Shawna," she said slowly, hoping to hide the tremble of her lips. "Shawna McGuire."

"A doctor?" he guessed, and Shawna wanted to die.

"Yes—but more than that."

Tom Handleman caught her eye, warning her not to push Parker too hard, but Shawna ignored him. This was important. Parker had to remember! He couldn't forget—not about the love they'd shared, the way they had felt and cared about each other.

"We were supposed to be married," she said quietly, watching his thick brows pull together in consternation. "The day after your accident, at Pioneer Church, in the rose arbor . . . I waited for you."

He didn't say a word, just stared at her as if she were a complete stranger.

"That's enough for now," Tom Handleman said, stepping closer to the bed, snapping on his penlight, trying to end the emotional scene. "Let's take a look at you, Mr. Harrison."

But before Tom could shine his penlight into

Parker's eyes, Parker grabbed the doctor's wrist. The crisp sheets slid from one side of the bed, exposing his bare leg and the bandages, still streaked with dried blood. "What the hell's going on?" he demanded, his voice gruff and nearly unrecognizable. "What happened to me? What's she talking about?" He glanced back to Shawna. "What marriage? I've never even been engaged—" Then his eyes dropped to Shawna's left hand and the winking diamond on her ring finger.

"Mr. Harrison, please—"

"Just what the hell happened to me?" Parker repeated, trying to sit up, only to blanch in pain.

"Parker, please," Shawna whispered, restraining him with her hands. She could feel his shoulder muscles, hard and coiled, flexing as he attempted to sit upright. "Just calm down. We'll straighten this all out. You'll remember, I promise." But she had to fight the catch in her throat and her professionalism drained away from her. She couldn't be cool or detached with Parker. "Dr. Handleman's your physician."

"I don't *know* any Handleman. Where's Jack Pederson?"

"Who?" Handleman asked, writing quickly on Parker's chart.

Shawna glanced nervously to the doctor. "Jack was Parker's trainer."

"Was?" Parker repeated, his features taut from pain and the effort of trying to remember those tiny pieces of his past that teased him, rising just to the surface of his mind only to sink deeper into murky oblivion. "Was?"

"That was a couple of years ago," Shawna said quickly.

"What're you talking about? Just last Saturday, Jack and I—" But he didn't finish and his features slackened suddenly as he turned bewildered blue eyes on Handleman. "No, it wasn't Saturday," he whispered, running one hand through his hair and feeling, for the first time, the bandages surrounding his head. Involuntarily his jaw tightened. "Maybe you'd better fill me in," he said, dropping his hand and pinning Tom Handleman with his gaze. "What the hell happened to me?"

"You were in an accident. Several days ago."

Parker closed his eyes, trying vainly to remember.

"From what the police tell me, a truck swerved into your lane, your Jeep crashed through the guard rail, and you were pinned inside the vehicle for several hours. They brought you in here, we performed surgery, and you've been unconscious ever since."

Parker seemed about to protest, but didn't. Instead he listened in stony silence as Tom described his injuries and prognosis.

"So, now that you're awake and the swelling in your leg has gone down, we'll do surgery on that knee. It will all take a little time. You'll be in physical therapy for awhile, then you'll be good as new—or almost."

"How long is 'awhile'?"

"That depends upon you and how everything heals."

"Just give me an educated guess."

Handleman crossed his arms over his chest, folding Parker's chart against his lab coat. "I'll be straight with you, Mr. Harrison."

"I'd appreciate that—and call me Parker."

"Fair enough, Parker. It could take anywhere from three months to a year of physical therapy before you can play tennis again. But, if you set your mind to it, work hard, I'll bet you'll be walking without crutches in six months."

Parker's jaw was rock hard and his eyes, clouded, moved from Tom's face to Shawna's. "Okay. That answers one question. Now, tell me about the driver of the truck—is he okay?"

"Not a scratch," Tom replied. "You missed him completely, even though he was all over the road. He was too drunk to report the accident."

A muscle jerked in Parker's jaw as he tried to remember. Horrifying images taunted him, but he couldn't quite make them out. Nonetheless his heart began to beat unsteadily and his hands, beneath bandages, had started to sweat. "There's something else, though," he said, rubbing his eyes. "Something—I can't remember. Something . . . important." *God, what is it?*

Shawna cleared her throat. Though she tried to appear calm, Parker read the hint of panic in the way she glanced at Handleman and toyed with the strand of pearls at her neck. "Maybe that's enough for you right now," she said.

"You know something, both of you. Something you're keeping from me."

Shawna, feeling the urge to protect him, to lie if she had to, to do anything to keep him from the horrid truth, touched his arm. "Just rest now."

"Is that your professional advice?" Parker asked. "Or are you trying to put me off?"

"Professional," Tom said, quickly, rescuing Shawna. "A nurse will be in to take your temperature and order you some lunch—"

"Wait a minute." Parker's voice was stern. "Something's wrong here, I can feel it. There's something you're not telling me about the accident." *What the hell is it?* Then he knew. "Someone else was involved," he said flatly. "Who?"

Shawna's shoulders stiffened a bit and her fingers found his on the cold metal railing.

Handleman offered a professional smile. "Right now all you have to worry about is—"

Parker sat bolt upright, tearing the IV tubing from the rail of the bed and ignoring the jab of pain in his knee. He kicked off the sheets and tried to climb out of bed. "What I have to worry about is who was with me. Where is he—or she?" Fire flared in his eyes as

Handleman tried to restrain him. "I have the right to know!"

"Whoa—Parker, settle down," Handleman said.

"Who, dammit!"

"Brad Lomax," Shawna whispered, unable to meet the confused torture in his eyes.

"Lomax?"

"He was in the car with you. He drank too much at our wedding rehearsal dinner and you were taking him home."

"But I don't remember—" He swallowed then, his eyes clouding. Somewhere deep in his mind he remembered the squeal of tires, the shatter of glass, felt his muscles wrench as he jerked hard on the steering wheel, heard a terrifying scream. "Oh, God," he rasped. "Who is he?"

"A tennis pro. Your student." Shawna felt her eyes grow moist as she watched the skin over his cheekbones turn white and taut.

"I was driving," he said slowly, as if measuring each agonizing word. "Lomax. How is he?"

"I'm afraid he didn't make it," Tom replied, exchanging glances with Shawna.

"He was killed in the wreck?" Parker's voice was sharp and fierce with self-loathing. "I killed him?"

"It was an accident," Shawna said quickly. "An unfortunate one—his seat belt malfunctioned and he was pinned under the Jeep."

Parker blinked several times, then lay back on the pillows as he struggled with his past. This couldn't be happening—he didn't even know these people! Maybe if he just went back to sleep he'd wake up and this hellish dream with the beautiful woman and clouded jags of memory would go away. "Does Lomax have any family?"

Just you, Shawna thought, but shook her head. "Only an uncle and a couple of cousins, I think."

"I think you'd better get some rest now," Tom advised, motioning to a nurse standing by the door. "I want Mr. Harrison sedated—"

"No!" Parker's eyes flew open.

"This has all been such a shock—"

"I can handle it," Parker said tightly, his face grim and stern. "No sedative, no pain killers. Got it?"

"But—"

"Got it?" he repeated, some of his old fire returning. "And don't try slipping anything into this!" He lifted his fist with the IV tubes attached.

Handleman's mouth became a thin white line. "Lie back down, Mr. Harrison," he said sternly, waiting until Parker reluctantly obeyed. "Now, it's my job to see that you're taken care of—that you rest. But I'll need your help. Either you contain yourself or I'll have the nurse sedate you."

Muscles rigid, eyes bright with repressed fury, Parker stared at the ceiling.

"Good. Just let me know if you change your mind about the sedatives or the pain killers. Now, Shawna, I think Mr. Harrison needs his rest."

"Wait a minute," Parker insisted, reaching for Shawna's hand again. "I want to talk to you. Alone." His gaze drilled past Handleman's thick glasses, and fortunately, the doctor got the message. With a nod of his head, he tucked his clipboard under his arm, left the room, and closed the door.

"Tell me," he said, forcing himself to be calm, though his fingers clenched tightly over hers.

"About what?"

"Everything."

Shawna sighed and sagged against the bed. How could she begin to explain the whirlwind fantasy that had been their relationship? How could she recount how Parker had seen the potential in a streetwise juvenile delinquent and had turned him into one of the finest young tennis players in the nation—a boy who had become a younger brother to him?

"Tell me," he insisted, hungry for knowledge of himself.

"First things first. What do you remember?"

"Not enough!" he said sharply, then took a deep breath. "Not nearly enough."

"I'll tell you what I can," she said, "but you've got to promise to stay calm."

"I don't know if that's possible," he admitted.

"Then we haven't got a deal, have we?"

Swearing under his breath, he forced a grin he obviously didn't feel. "Okay," he said. "Deal."

"Good."

"Something tells me I should remember you."

"Most definitely," she agreed, feeling better than she had since the accident and grinning as she blinked back tears. Then, as all her bravado crumbled, she touched him gently on his forehead. "Oh, Parker, I've missed you—God, how I've missed you." Without thinking, she leaned forward and kissed him, brushing her lips suggestively over his and tasting the salt from her own tears.

But Parker didn't respond, just stared at her with perplexed blue eyes.

Shawna cleared her throat. "Fortunately, that part— the loneliness—is over now," she said, quickly sniffing back her tears. "And once you're out of here, we'll get married, and go to the Bahamas, have a ton of children, and live happily ever after!"

"Hey, whoa. Slow down," he whispered. Rubbing one hand over his jaw, he said, "Tell me about Brad Lomax."

Shawna realized he wouldn't give up. Though she felt the urge to protect him, she decided he had to face the truth sooner or later. She wanted to soften the blow, but she had to be honest with him. "Brad Lomax," she said uneasily, "was a hellion, and he was a terror on the tennis courts, and you saw something in him. You recognized his raw talent and took him under your wing. You and he were very close," she admitted, seeing the pain in his eyes. "You knew him a lot longer than you've known me."

"How close?" Parker asked, his voice low.

"You were his mentor—kind of a big brother. He looked up to you. That night, the night of the accident, he'd had too much to drink and wanted to talk to you. You offered to take him home."

A muscle worked in his jaw. "Why did he want to talk to me?"

Shawna lifted a shoulder. "I don't know. No one does. I suppose now that no one ever will."

"I killed him," Parker said quietly.

"No, Parker. It was an accident!" she said vehemently.

"How old was he?"

"Don't do this to yourself."

"How old was he?" His eyes drilled into hers.

"Twenty-two," she whispered.

"Oh, God." With a shudder, he closed his eyes. "I should have been the one who died, you know."

Shawna resisted the overpowering urge to cradle his head to her breast and comfort him. The torture twisting his features cut her to the bone. "Don't do this, Parker. It's not fair."

Parker stared up at her with simmering blue eyes. His expression was a mixture of anguish and awe, and his hand reached upward, his fingers slipping beneath her hair to caress her nape.

She trembled at his touch, saw the torment in his gaze.

"I don't remember where I met you. Or how. Or even who you are," he admitted, his voice husky, the lines near his mouth softening as he stared up at her. "But I do know that I'm one lucky son of a bitch if you were planning to marry me."

"Am—as in present tense," she corrected, her throat hot with unshed tears. "I still intend to march down the aisle with you, Parker Harrison, whether you're in a cast, on crutches, or in a wheelchair."

She felt his fingers flex as he drew her head to his, and he hesitated only slightly before touching his lips to hers. "I will remember you," he promised, eyes dusky blue. "No matter what it takes!"

Her heart soared. All they needed was a little time!

Tom Handleman, his expression stern behind his wire-rimmed glasses, poked his head into the room. "Doctor?"

"That's my cue," Shawna whispered, brushing her lips against Parker's hair. "I'll be back."

"I'm counting on it."

She forced herself out of the room, feeling more lighthearted than she had in days. So what if Parker didn't remember her? What did it matter that he had a slight case of amnesia? The important consideration was his health, and physically he seemed to be gaining strength. Although mentally he still faced some tough hurdles, she was confident that with her help, Parker would surmount any obstacle fate cast his way. It was only a matter of time before he was back on his feet again and they could take up where they'd left off.

Jake was waiting for her in the hallway. Slouched into one of the waiting-room chairs, his tie askew, his shirtsleeves rolled over his forearms, he groaned as he stretched to his feet and fell into step with her. "Good news," he guessed, a wide grin spreading across his beard-stubbled jaw.

"The best!" Shawna couldn't contain herself. "He's awake!"

"About time!" Jake winked at her. "So, when's the wedding?"

Shawna chuckled. "I think Parker and I have a few bridges to cross first."

"Meaning Brad's death?"

"For one," she said, linking her arm through her

brother's and pushing the elevator button. "You can buy me lunch and I'll explain about the rest of them."

"There's more?"

"A lot more," she said as they squeezed into the crowded elevator and she lowered her voice. "He doesn't remember me—or much else for that matter."

Jake let out a long, low whistle.

"You're used to dealing with this, aren't you, in your practice?" she asked eagerly.

"I've seen a couple of cases."

"Then maybe you can work with him."

"Maybe," he said, his gray eyes growing thoughtful.

As the elevator opened at the hallway near the cafeteria, Shawna sent him a teasing glance, "Well, don't trip all over yourself to help."

"I'll do what I can," he said, massaging his neck muscles. "Unfortunately, you'll have to be patient, and that's not your strong suit."

"Patient?"

"You know as well as I do that amnesia can be tricky. He may remember everything tomorrow, or . . ."

"Or it may take weeks," she said with a sigh. "I can't even think about that. Not now. I'm just thanking my lucky stars that he's alive and he'll be all right."

Maybe, Jake thought, steering Shawna down the stainless steel counter and past cream pies, pudding, and fruit salad. Only time would tell.

Parker tried to roll off the bed, but a sharp pain in his knee and the IV tube stuck into his hand kept him flat on his back. He had a restless urge to get up, walk out of the hospital, and catch hold of the rest of his life—wherever it was.

He knew who he was. He could remember some things very clearly—the death of his parents in a boating accident, the brilliance of a trophy glinting gold in the sun. But try as he might, he couldn't conjure up Brad Lomax's face to save his soul.

And this Shawna woman with her honey-gold hair, soft lips, and intense green eyes. She was a doctor and they'd planned to be married? That didn't seem to fit. Nor did her description of his being some heroic do-gooder who had saved a boy from self-destruction while molding him into a tennis star.

No, her idealistic views of his life didn't make a helluva lot of sense. He remembered winning, playing to the crowd, enjoying being the best; he'd been ruthless and unerring on the court—the "ice man," incapable of emotion.

And yet she seemed to think him some sort of modern-day good Samaritan. No way!

Struggling for the memories locked just under the surface of his consciousness, he closed his eyes and clenched his fists in frustration. Why couldn't he remember? Why?

"Mr. Harrison?"

He opened one eye, then the other. A small nurse was standing just inside the door.

"Glad you're back with us," she said, rolling in a clattering tray of food—if that's what you'd call the unappetizing gray potatoes-and-gravy dish she set in front of him. "Can I get you anything else?"

"Nothing," he replied testily, his thoughts returning to the beautiful doctor and the boy whose face he couldn't remember. *I don't want anything but my past.* Sighing, the nurse left.

Parker shoved the tray angrily aside and closed his eyes, willing himself to remember, concentrating on that dark void that was his past. Shawna. Had he known her? How? Had he really planned to marry her?

Sleep overcame him in warm waves and bits of memory played with his mind. Dreaming, he saw himself dancing with a gorgeous woman in a mist-cloaked rose garden. Her face was veiled and she was dressed in ivory silk and lace, he in a stiff tuxedo. Her scent and laughter engulfed him as they stopped dancing to sip from crystal glasses of champagne. Sweeping her into his arms again, he spilled champagne on the front of her gown and she tossed back her head but her veil stayed in place, blocking his view of her eyes as he licked the frothy bubbles from the beaded lace covering her throat.

"I love you," she vowed, sighing. "Forever."

"And I love you."

Light-headed from the drink and the nearness of her, he captured her lips with his, tasting cool, effervescent wine on her warm lips. Her fingers toyed his bow tie, loosening it from his neck, teasing him, and he caught a glimpse of her dimpled smile before she slipped away from him. He tried to call out to her, but he didn't know her name and his voice was muted. Desperate not to lose her, he grasped at her dress but clutched only air. She was floating away from him, her face still a guarded mystery. . . .

Parker's eyes flew open and he took in a swift breath. His hand was clenched, but empty. The dream had been so real, so lifelike, as if he'd been in that garden with that beautiful woman. But now, in his darkened hospital room, he wondered if the dream had been part of his memory or only something he wanted so fervently he'd created the image.

Had the woman been Shawna McGuire?

Dear God, he hoped so. She was, without a doubt, the most intriguing woman he'd ever met.

The next evening, in her office at Columbia Memorial Hospital on the east side of the Willamette River, Shawna leaned back in her chair until it creaked in protest. Unpinning her hair, letting it fall past her shoulders in a shimmering gold curtain, she closed her eyes and imagined that Parker's memory was restored and they were getting married, just as they planned.

"Soon," she told herself as she stretched and flipped through the pages of her appointment book.

Because she couldn't stand the idea of spending hour upon hour with nothing to do, she had rescheduled her vacation—the time she had meant to use on her honeymoon—and today had been her first full day of work since the accident. She was dead tired. The digital clock on her desk blinked the time. It was eight-fifteen, and she hadn't eaten since breakfast.

She'd finished her rounds early, dictated patient diagnoses into the tiny black machine at her desk, answered some correspondence and phone calls, and somehow managed to talk to the amnesia specialist on staff at Columbia Memorial. Her ears still rang with his advice.

"Amnesia's not easy to predict," Pat Barrington had replied to her questions about Parker. A kindly neurosurgeon with a flushed red face and horn-rimmed glasses, he'd told Shawna nothing she hadn't really already known. "Parker's obviously reacting to the trauma, remembering nothing of the accident or the events leading up to it," Barrington had said, punching the call button for the elevator.

"So why doesn't he remember Brad Lomax or me?"

"Because you're both part of it, really. The accident occurred right after the rehearsal dinner. Subconsciously, he's denying everything leading up to the accident—even your engagement. Give him time, Shawna. He's not likely to forget you," Barrington had advised, clapping Shawna on her back.

Now, as Shawna leaned back in her chair, she sighed and stared out the window into the dark September night. "Time," she whispered. Was it her friend or enemy?

Five

Two weeks later, Shawna sipped from her teacup and stared through the kitchen window of her apartment at the late afternoon sky. Parker's condition hadn't changed, except that the surgery on his knee had been a success. He was already working in physical therapy to regain use of his leg, but his mind, as far as Shawna and the wedding were concerned, was a complete blank. Though Shawna visited him each day, hoping to help him break through the foggy wall surrounding him, he stared at her without a flicker of the warmth she'd always felt in his gaze.

Now, as she dashed the dregs of her tea into the sink, she decided she couldn't wait any longer. Somehow, she had to jog his memory. She ached to touch him again, feel his arms around her, have him talk to her as if she weren't a total stranger.

"You're losing it, McGuire," she told herself as she glanced around her kitchen. Usually bright and neat, the room was suffering badly from neglect. Dishes were stacked in the sink, the floor was dull, and there were half-filled boxes scattered on the counters and floor.

Before the wedding she'd packed most of her things, but now she'd lost all interest in moving from the cozy little one-bedroom apartment she'd called home for several years. Nonetheless, she had given her notice and would have to move at the end of the month.

Rather than consider the chore of moving, she stuffed two packets of snapshots into her purse and found her coat. Then, knowing she was gambling with her future, she grabbed her umbrella and dashed through the front door of her apartment.

Outside, the weather was gray and gloomy. Rain drizzled from the sky, ran in the gutters of the old turn-of-the-century building, and caught on the broad leaves of the rhododendron and azaleas flanking the cement paths.

"Dr. McGuire!" a crackly voice accosted her. "Wait up!"

Shawna glanced over her shoulder. Mrs. Swenson, her landlady, clad in a bright yellow raincoat, was walking briskly in her direction. Knowing what was to come, Shawna managed a smile she didn't feel. "Hi, Mrs. Swenson."

"I know you're on your way out," Mrs. Swenson announced, peering into the bushes near Shawna's front door and spying the lurking shadow of Maestro, Shawna's yellow tabby near the steps. Adjusting her plastic rain bonnet, Mrs. Swenson pursed her lips and peered up at Shawna with faded gold eyes. "But I thought we'd better talk about your apartment. I know about your troubles with Mr. Harrison and it's a darned shame, that's what it is—but I've got tenants who've planned to lease your place in about two weeks."

"I know, I know," Shawna said. If her life hadn't been shattered by the accident, she would already have moved into Parker's house on the Willamette River. But, of course, the accident had taken care of that. "Things just haven't exactly fallen into place."

"I know, I know," Mrs. Swenson said kindly, still glancing at the cat. "But, be that as it may, the Levertons plan to start moving in the weekend after next and your lease is up. Then there's the matter of having the place painted, the drapes cleaned, and whatnot. I hate to be pushy . . . but I really don't have much choice."

"I understand," Shawna admitted, thinking over her options for the dozenth time. "And I'll be out by Friday night. I promise."

"That's only four days away," Mrs. Swenson pointed out, her wrinkled face puckering pensively.

"I've already started packing." Well, not really, but she did have some things in boxes, things she'd stored when she and Parker had started making wedding plans. "I can store my things with my folks and live either with them or with Jake," she said. The truth of the matter was, deep down, she still intended to move into Parker's place, with or without a wedding ring. In the past few weeks since the accident, she'd discovered just how much she loved him, and that a certificate of marriage wasn't as important as being with him.

"And what're you planning to do about that?" the old woman asked, shaking a gnarled finger at Maestro as he nimbly jumped onto the window ledge. With his tail flicking anxiously, he glared in through the window to the cage where Mrs. Swenson's yellow parakeet ruffled his feathers and chirped loudly enough to be heard through the glass.

"He's not really mine—"

"You've been feeding him, haven't you?"

"Well, yes. But he just strayed—"

"Two years ago," Mrs. Swenson interjected. "And if he had his way my little Pickles would have been his dinner time and time again."

"I'll take him with me."

"Good. Saves me a trip to the animal shelter," Mrs. Swenson said. Shawna seriously doubted the old woman had the heart to do anything more dastardly than give Maestro a saucer of milk—probably warmed in the microwave. Though outwardly a curmudgeon, Myrna Swenson had a heart of gold buried beneath a crusty layer of complaining.

"I'll tell Eva Leverton she can start packing."

"Good!" Shawna climbed into her car and watched as Mrs. Swenson cooed to the bird in the window. She flicked on the engine, smothered a smile, and muttered, "Pickles is a dumb name for a bird!" Then slamming the car into gear, she drove away from the apartment complex.

More determined than ever to help Parker regain his memory, Shawna wheeled across the Ross Island bridge and up the steep grade of the west hills to Mercy Hospital.

Today Parker would remember her, she decided with a determined smile as she pulled on the emergency brake and threw open the car door. Sidestepping puddles of rain water, she hurried inside the old concrete and glass of Mercy Hospital.

She heard Parker before she saw him. Just as the elevator doors parted on the fourth floor, Parker's voice rang down the gray-carpeted hallway.

"Hey, watch out, you're killing me!" he barked and Shawna smothered a grin. One of the first signs of patient improvement was general irritability, and Parker sounded as if he was irritable in spades.

"Good morning," Shawna said, cautiously poking her head into the room.

"What's good about it?" Parker grumbled.

"I see our patient is improving," she commented to the orderly trying to adjust the bed.

"Not his temperament," the orderly confided.

"I heard that," Parker said, but couldn't help flashing Shawna a boyish grin—the same crooked grin she'd grown to love. Her heart did a stupid little leap, the way it always did when he rained his famous smile on her.

"Be kind, Parker," she warned, lifting some wilting roses from a ceramic vase and dropping the wet flowers into a nearby trash basket. "Otherwise he might tell the people in physical therapy to give you the 'torture treatment,' and I've heard it can be murder."

"Humph." He laughed despite his ill humor and the orderly ducked gratefully out the door.

"You're not making any friends here, you know," she said, sitting on the end of his bed and leaning back to study him. Her honey-colored hair fell loose behind her shoulders, and a small smile played on her lips.

"Am I supposed to be?"

"If you don't want your breakfast served cold, your temperature to be taken at four A.M., or your TV cable to be mysteriously tampered with."

"I'd pay someone to do it," Parker muttered. "Then maybe I wouldn't have to watch any more of that." He nodded in the direction of the overhead television. On the small screen, a wavy-haired reporter with a bright smile was sitting behind a huge desk while discussing the worldwide ranking of America's tennis professionals.

"*—and the tennis world is still reeling from the unfortunate death of Brad Lomax, perhaps the brightest star in professional tennis since his mentor, Parker Harrison's, meteoric burst onto the circuit in the midseventies.*"

A picture of Brad, one arm draped affectionately over Parker's broad shoulders, the other hand holding a winking brass trophy triumphantly overhead, was flashed onto the screen. Brad's dark hair was plastered to his head, sweat dripped down his face, and a fluffy white towel was slung around his neck. Parker, his chestnut hair glinting in the sun, his face tanned and unlined, his eyes shining with pride, stood beside his protégé.

Now, as she watched, Shawna's stomach tightened. Parker lay still, his face taut and white as the newscaster continued. "*Lomax, whose off-court escapades were as famous as his blistering serves, was killed just over two weeks ago when the vehicle Parker Harrison was driving swerved off the road and crashed down a hundred-foot embankment.*

"Harrison is still reported in stable condition, though there're rumors that he has no memory of the near-collision with a moving van which resulted in the—"

Ashen-faced, Shawna snapped the television off. "I don't know why you watch that stuff!"

Parker didn't answer, just glanced out the window to the rain-soaked day and the gloomy fir boughs visible through his fourth-floor window. "I'm just trying to figure out who I am."

"And I've told you—"

"But I don't want the romanticized version—just the facts," he said, his gaze swinging back to hers. "I want to remember—for myself. I want to remember *you.*"

"You will. I promise," she whispered.

He sighed in frustration, but touched her hand, his fingers covering hers. "For the past week people have been streaming in here—people I should know and don't. There have been friends, reporters, doctors, and even the mayor, for heaven's sake! They ask questions, wish me well, tell me to take it easy, and all the time I'm thinking, 'who the hell are you?' "

"Parker—" Leaning forward, she touched his cheek, hoping to break through the damming wall blocking his memory.

"Don't tell me to be patient," he said sharply, but his eyes were still warm as they searched her face. "Just take one look around this room, for crying out loud!" Everywhere there were piles of cards and letters, huge baskets of fruit, tins of cookies and vases of heavy-blossomed, fragrant flowers. "Who *are* these people?" he asked, utterly perplexed.

Shawna wanted to cry. "People who care, Parker," she said, her voice rough as her hands covered his, feeling the warmth of his palms against her skin. She treasured the comfort she felt as his fingers grazed her cheekbones. "People who care about us."

He swore under his breath. "And I can't remember half of them. Here I am with enough flowers to cover all the floats in the Rose Parade and enough damned fruit and banana bread to feed all the starving people in the world—"

"You're exaggerating," she charged.

"Well, maybe just a little," he admitted, his lips twisting into a wry grin.

"A lot!"

"Okay, a lot."

She stroked his brow, hoping to ease the furrows in his forehead. "Unfortunately neither of us can undo what's happened. Don't you think that I would change things if I could? That I would push back the hands of the clock so that I could have you back—all of you." She swallowed against a huge lump forming in her throat.

He rested his forehead against hers. His gaze took in every soft angle of her face, the way her lashes swept over her eyes, the tiny lines of concern etching the ivory-colored skin of her forehead, the feel of her breath, warm and enticing against his face. Old emotions, cloaked in that black recess of the past, stirred, but refused to emerge. "Oh, why can't I remember you?" His voice was so filled with torment and longing, she buried her face in his shoulder and twisted her fingers in the folds of his sheets.

"Try," she pleaded.

"I have—over and over again." His eyes were glazed as he stroked her chin. "If you believe anything, believe that I want to remember you . . . everything about you."

The ache within her burned, but before she could respond, his palms, still pressed against her cheeks, tilted her face upward. Slowly, he touched her lips with his. Warm and pliant, they promised a future together—she could feel it!

Shawna's heart began to race.

His lips moved slowly and cautiously at first, as if he were exploring and discovering her for the first time.

Tears welled unbidden to her eyes and she moaned, leaning closer to him, feeling her breath hot and constricted in her lungs.

Love me, she cried mutely. *Love me as you did.*

The kiss was so innocent, so full of wondering, she felt as flustered and confused as a schoolgirl. "I love you," she whispered, her fingers gripping his shoulders as she clung to him and felt hot tears slide down her cheeks. "Oh, Parker, I love you!"

His arms surrounded her, drawing her downward until she was half lying across him, listening to the beat of his heart and feeling the hard muscles of his chest.

The sheets wrinkled between them as Parker's lips sought hers, anxious and moist, pressing first against her mouth and then lower, to the length of her throat as his hands twined in the golden sun-bleached strands of her hair. "I have the feeling I don't deserve you," he murmured into her ear, desire flaring in his brilliant blue eyes.

From the hallway, Jake cleared his throat. Shawna glanced up to see her brother, shifting restlessly from one foot to the other as he stood just outside the door.

"I, uh, hope I'm not disturbing anything," he said, grinning from one ear to the other, his hands stuffed into the pockets of his cords as he sauntered into the small room.

Shawna hurriedly wiped her cheeks. "Your timing leaves a lot to be desired."

"So I've been told," he replied, before glancing at Parker. "So, how's the patient?"

"Grumpy," Shawna pronounced.

"He didn't look too grumpy to me." Jake snatched a shiny red apple from a fruit basket and polished it against his tweed sports jacket.

"You didn't see him barking at the orderly."

One side of Jake's mouth curved cynically as he

glanced at Parker. "Not you, not the 'ice man.' " Still grinning, he bit into the apple.

"This place doesn't exactly bring out the best in me," Parker said, eyeing the man who had almost become his brother-in-law.

"Obviously," Shawna replied. "But if everything goes well in physical therapy today and tomorrow, and you don't get on Dr. Handleman's bad side again, you'll be out of here by the end of the week, only doing physical therapy on an outpatient basis."

"No wonder he's in a bad mood," Jake said, taking another huge bite from the apple. "Outpatient physical therapy sounds as bad as the seventh level of hell, if you ask me."

"No one did," Shawna reminded him, but smiled at her brother anyway. Jake had a way of helping her find humor in even the most trying times. Even as children, she could count on him and his cockeyed sense of humor to lift her spirits even on her worst days.

Jake tossed his apple core deftly into a trash can. "Two points—or was that three?" he asked. When neither Parker nor Shawna answered, he shoved his fingers through his hair. "Boy, you guys are sure a cheery group."

"Sorry," Shawna said. "As I told you, Grumpy isn't in a great mood."

Jake glanced from Shawna to Parker. "So, what can we do to get you back on your feet?"

"You're the psychiatrist," Parker replied stonily. "You tell me."

Shawna reached into her purse. "Maybe I can help." Ignoring her brother's questioning gaze, she reached into her purse and withdrew a thick packet of photographs. "I thought these might do the trick."

Her hands were shaking as one by one, she handed him the snapshots of the fair. Her heart stuck in her throat as she saw the pictures of herself, her long

blond hair caught in the breeze, her green eyes filled
with mischief as she clung to the neck of that white
wooden stallion on the carousel and stretched forward,
reaching and missing the brass ring with the fluttering
ribbons.

Other photos, of Parker trying to catch a peanut in
his mouth, of Parker flaunting his prized brass ring,
and of the dark-eyed fortune-teller, beckoning them
inside her ragtag tent, brought back her memories of
the fair. Now, in the hospital room, only a little over
two weeks later, the old-time fair seemed ages past, and
the fortune-teller's prediction loomed over Shawna like
a black cloak.

Parker studied each picture, his eyes narrowed on
the images in the still shots. His brow furrowed in concentration.

Shawna held her breath. Couldn't he see the ado-
ration shining in her eyes as she gazed into the camera? Or the loving way he had captured her on film?
And what about the pictures of him, grinning and care-
free? Wasn't it obvious that they had been two people
hopelessly head over heels in love?

For a minute, she thought he reacted, that there
was a flicker of recognition in his gaze, but as suddenly
as it had appeared, it was gone.

"Nothing?" she asked, bracing herself.

He closed his eyes. "No—not nothing," he said, his
voice dry and distant. "But what we shared—what was
there at the fair—it's . . . gone."

"Just misplaced," Jake said quickly as if feeling the
searing wound deep in Shawna's soul. "You'll find it
again."

"I'd like to think so," Parker admitted but he still
seemed vexed, his thick brows knitted, his chin set to
one side, as if he were searching for a black hole in
the tapestry her pictures had woven.

"Look, I've got to run," Jake said quickly, looking

at his sister meaningfully. "Mom and Dad are expecting you for dinner tonight."

"But I can't," she said, unable to leave Parker. She felt that if she were given just a few more minutes, she could cause the breakthrough in Parker's memory.

"Don't stay on my account," Parker cut in, glaring angrily at the pictures spread across his bed.

Shawna saw them then as he did, pictures of a young couple in love, their future bright and untarnished, and she cringed inside, knowing instinctively what he felt—the anger and the resentment, the pain and the blackness of a time he couldn't remember.

"Maybe I shouldn't have brought these," she said hurriedly, scooping the photographs into the purse.

He snatched one out of her hands, the photo of her with her face flushed, her long hair billowing over the neck of the glossy white carousel horse. "I'll keep this one," he said, his features softening a little, "if you don't mind."

"You're sure?"

"Positive."

"Let's go." Jake suggested. "You can come back later. But right now, Mom and Dad are waiting."

Shawna felt her brother's hand over her arm, but she twisted her neck, craning to stare at Parker who didn't move, just studied the photograph in his hands. Impatiently, Jake half dragged her through the building.

"That was a stupid move!" Jake nearly shouted, once they were outside the hospital. "He's not ready for pictures of the past, can't you see that?" Jake's expression turned dark as he opened the car door for her, then slid behind the wheel and shoved the Porsche into gear.

"You can't just skip into his room and hand him pictures of a rose-colored future that could have been, you know. It takes time! Think about him, not just yourself! Where's your professionalism, *Doctor*?"

"Back in my medical bag, I guess," Shawna said, staring blindly out the windows. "I'm sorry."

"It's not me you have to apologize to." He let out a long, disgusted breath, then patted her shoulder. "Just hang in there. Try to think of Parker as another patient—not your fiancé, okay?"

"I will, but it's hard."

"I know," he said, "but he needs all your strength now—and your patience." Jake turned off the main highway and veered down the elm-lined driveway of his parents' house. "Okay, Sis. Show's on. Stiff upper lip for Mom and Dad," he teased, reaching across her and pushing open the car door.

As Shawna walked up the flagstone path, she steadfastly shoved all her doubts aside. Tomorrow she'd see Parker again and when she did, she wouldn't push too hard. She'd be patient and wait until the walls blocking his memory eroded—even if it killed her.

Long after Shawna left his room, Parker stared at the small photograph in his hand. Without a doubt, Dr. Shawna McGuire was the most fascinating, beautiful, and stubborn woman he'd ever met.

He knew now why he'd fallen in love with her. Though he was loath to admit it and despite all the problems he now faced, he was falling in love with her again. The depth of his feelings was a surprise. She aroused him sensually as well as intellectually. Doctor McGuire, though she professed her love, was a challenge. Just being near her, smelling her perfume, seeing the glimmer of mystique in her intelligent green eyes, was enough to drive him to distraction and cause an uncomfortable heat to rise in his loins.

Unfortunately, he had to be careful. No longer was he a recent tennis star with a future bright as the sun, acting in commercials and coaching younger, up-coming athletes. Now his future was unsure.

He glanced down and the woman in the photograph smiled up at him. She swore she loved him and he believed her. And, if he let himself, he could easily get caught in her infectious enthusiasm. Several times, when he'd kissed her, he'd seen images in his mind—smelled the salty air of the beach, or fresh raindrops in her hair, heard the tinkle of her laughter, felt the driving beat of her heart. Reality mixed with sights and smells that were as elusive as a winking star—bright one minute, dim and clouded the next.

And now, lying in the hospital bed, with months, perhaps years of physical therapy staring him in the face, what could he offer her?

A big fat nothing. Because no matter how she deluded herself, Shawna was wrong about one thing: Parker would never be the man he was before the accident. His perception, with his memory, had changed.

Brad Lomax was gone, as was Parker's ability to coach and play tennis. The man Shawna McGuire had fallen in love with no longer existed and this new man—the one who couldn't even remember her—was a pale substitute. How long could she love a faded memory, he wondered. When would that love, so freely given, turn to duty?

Glancing again at the woman in the picture, Parker ached inside. Yes, he wanted her, maybe even loved her. But he wouldn't let her live a lie, sacrifice herself because she believed in a dream that didn't exist.

Gritting his teeth, Parker took the snapshot of Shawna and crushed it in his fist—then feeling immediately contrite, he tried to press the wrinkles from the photo and laid it, face down, in a book someone had left by his bed.

"Help me," he prayed, his voice echoing in the empty room. "Help me be whole again."

Six

Shawna snatched a patient's chart from the rack next to the door of the examination room. She was running late and had to force herself into gear. "Get a move on, doctor," she muttered under her breath as she glanced quickly over the patient information file. The patient, Melinda James, was new to the clinic, had an excellent health record, and was eighteen years old.

"Good afternoon," Shawna said, shoving open the door to find a beautiful black-haired girl with round eyes perched on the edge of the examination table. She looked scared as her fingers clamped nervously over a sheet she'd pulled over her shoulders, and Shawna felt as if the girl wanted to bolt. "I'm Dr. McGuire," she said calmly. "And you're Melinda?"

Melinda nodded and chewed nervously on her lip.

"So what can I do for you?"

"I, uh, saw your name in the paper," Melinda said quickly, glancing away. "You're the doctor who's engaged to Parker Harrison, right?"

Shawna's stomach tightened at the mention of Parker. Was Melinda a reporter, pretending to be a patient just to get an inside story on Parker, or was there something else?

"That's right, but I really don't see what that has to do with anything." She clamped the chart to her chest. "Do you know Parker?"

"He's got amnesia, doesn't he?"

Shawna tried to keep her tongue in check. Obviously the girl was nervous—maybe she was just making conversation. "I can't discuss Parker's condition. Now—" she glanced down at her chart. "Is there a reason you came to see me? A health reason?"

The girl sighed. "Yes I, uh, I've only been in Portland a few months so I don't have a doctor here. I went to a pediatrician in Cleveland," Melinda continued, "but I'm too old for a pediatrician now and I've got this problem, so I made an appointment with you."

"Fair enough." Shawna relaxed a little and took a pen from the pocket of her lab coat. "What was the pediatrician's name?"

Melinda seemed hesitant.

"I'll need this information in case we need to contact him for his files," Shawna explained, offering the girl an encouraging smile.

"Rankin, Harold Rankin," Melinda said quickly and Shawna scrawled the physician's name in the appropriate spot on the form. "Thanks." Pushing her suspicions aside, Shawna set the chart on a cabinet. "You said you had a problem. What kind of problem?"

Melinda twisted the sheet between her fingers. "I'm sick." Avoiding Shawna's eyes, she said in a rush, "I can't keep anything down and I'm not anoretic or whatever it's called. I don't understand what's wrong. I've had the flu for over a month and it just won't go away. I've never been sick for this long."

"The flu?" Shawna said, eyeing the girl's healthy skin color and clear eyes. "You're feverish? Your muscles ache?"

"No, not really. It's just that one minute I'm feeling great; the next I think I might throw up."

"And do you?"

"Sometimes—especially in the afternoon." Melinda wrung her hands anxiously together and sweat beaded her forehead. "And sometimes I get horrible cramps."

"Anything else? Sore throat?"

Shaking her short glossy hair, Melinda sighed. "I kept hoping I would get better, but—" She shrugged and the sheet almost slipped from her fingers.

"Well, let me take a look at you. Lie down." Shawna spent the next fifteen minutes examining Melinda carefully, as the girl nearly jumped off the examination table each time she was touched.

"When was the date of your last menstrual period?" Shawna finally asked, once the examination was over and Melinda was sitting, sheet draped over her on the table.

"I don't know. A couple of months ago, I guess."

"You *guess*?" Shawna repeated.

"I don't keep track—I'm real irregular."

"How irregular?"

"Well, not every month. I skip around a little."

"Could you be pregnant?"

Melinda's eyes widened and she licked her lips. "I— I don't get sick in the morning. Never in the morning."

Shawna smiled, trying to put the girl at ease. "It's different with everyone. I had a patient who only was sick at night."

Melinda chewed on her lower lip. "I—uh, it's possible, I guess," she whispered.

"Why don't we run a quick test and see?" Shawna asked.

"When will I know?"

"In a little while. I have a friend in the lab. The pregnancy test is relatively easy; but if there's something else, we won't know about it for a couple of days. Now, why don't you try to remember the date of your last period."

Melinda closed her eyes as Shawna drew a small vial of blood from her arm and had a nurse take the filled vial to the lab.

"I don't know. I think it was around the Fourth of July."

Shawna wasn't surprised. All of Melinda's symptoms pointed toward pregnancy. "This is nearly October," she pointed out.

Melinda's lower lip protruded defiantly. "I said I was irregular."

"Okay. No need to worry about it, until we know for sure." She checked her watch. "It's still early—the hospital lab can rush the results if I ask."

"Would you?"

"Sure. You can get dressed and meet me in my office in a few hours—say four o'clock?"

"Fine." Melinda grudgingly reached for her clothes and Shawna, feeling uneasy, left the room.

By the time Shawna returned to her office after seeing the rest of her patients and finished some paperwork, she was ready to call it a day. It was four o'clock and she was anxious to drive to Mercy Hospital to spend some time with Parker.

But first she had to deal with Melinda James.

"Well?" Melinda asked as she plopped into the chair opposite Shawna's desk.

Shawna scanned the report from the lab, then glanced at the anxious girl.

"Your test was positive, Melinda. You're going to have a baby."

Melinda let out a long sigh and ran her fingers through her hair. "I can't believe it," she whispered, but her voice lacked conviction and for the first time Shawna wondered if Melinda had been suspicious of her condition all along. "There's no chance that"—she pointed to the pink report—"is wrong."

"Afraid not."

"Great," Melinda mumbled, blinking back tears.

"I take it this isn't good news."

"The worst! My dad'll kill me!"

"Maybe you're underestimating your dad," Shawna suggested.

"No way!"

"What about the father of your child?" Shawna asked.

Tears flooded the girl's eyes. "The father?" she repeated, swallowing with difficulty and shaking her head.

"He has the right to know."

"He can't," Melinda said, her voice low and final, as if she had no choice in the matter.

"Give him a chance."

Melinda's eyes were bright with tears. "I can't tell him," she said. "He thinks this is all my responsibility. The last thing he wants is a baby."

"You don't know—"

"Oh, yes I do. He said so over and over again."

Shawna handed her a couple of tissues and Melinda dabbed her eyes but was unable to stem the flow of her tears.

"I—I was careful," she said, blinking rapidly. "But he'll blame me, I know he will!"

"Sometimes a man changes his mind when he's actually faced with the news that he's going to be a father."

"But he can't!" Melinda said harshly, obviously hurting deep inside.

Shawna walked around the desk and placed her arm around the young woman's shaking shoulders. "I don't want to pry," she said evenly. "What's going on between you and the father isn't any of my business—"

"If you only knew," Melinda whispered, glancing at Shawna with red-rimmed eyes, then shifting her gaze. Standing, she pushed away Shawna's arm. "This is my problem," she said succinctly. "I—I'll handle it."

"Try not to think of the baby as a problem, okay?" Shawna advised, reaching for a card from a small holder on her desk. "Take this card—it has Dr. Chambers's number. He's one of the best obstetricians in the city."

"What I need now is a shrink," Melinda said, still sniffing.

"My brother's a psychiatrist," Shawna said quietly, locating one of Jake's business cards. "Maybe you should talk with him—"

Melinda snatched the cards from Shawna's outstretched hand. "I—I'll think about it. After I talk with the father."

Shawna offered the girl an encouraging smile. "That's the first step."

"Just remember—this was *your* idea!"

"I'll take full responsibility," Shawna replied, but read the message in the young woman's eyes. More clearly than words, Melinda had told her Shawna didn't know what she was saying. Anger and defiance bright in her eyes, Melinda James walked briskly out the door.

Shawna watched her leave and felt the same nagging doubts she had when she'd first talked to the girl. "You can't win 'em all," she told herself thoughtfully as she hung her lab coat in the closet and quickly ran a brush through her hair. But she couldn't shake the feeling that Melinda, despite her vocal doubts, had known she was pregnant all along.

She reached for her purse and slung it over her shoulder, but stopped before slipping her arms through her jacket. Feeling a little guilty, she called directory assistance in Cleveland and asked for the number of Harold Rankin, Melinda's pediatrician.

"There are several H. Rankins listed," the operator told her.

"I'm looking for the pediatrician. He must have an office number." The operator paused. "I'm sorry. There is no Doctor Rankin listed in Cleveland."

"Unlisted? Look, I'm a doctor myself. I need to consult with him about a patient and I don't have his number," Shawna said, new suspicions gnawing at her.

The operator muttered something under her breath. "I really can't—"

"It's important!"

"Well, I guess I can tell you this much, there's no Dr. Harold Rankin listed or unlisted in Cleveland. Just a minute." For a few seconds all Shawna could hear was clicking noises. "I'm sorry—I checked the suburbs. No Dr. Harold Rankin."

"Thank you," Shawna whispered, replacing the receiver. So Melinda had lied—or the doctor had moved. But that was unlikely. Shawna remembered Melinda's first words. *"I saw your name in the paper. . . . You're the doctor who's engaged to Parker Harrison, aren't you? . . . He's got amnesia, right?"*

Without thinking about what she was doing, Shawna buttoned her jacket and half ran out the door of her office. She waved good-bye to the receptionist, but her mind was filled with Melinda's conversation and the girl's dark grudging glances. No, Melinda James wasn't a reporter, but she was hiding something. Shawna just couldn't figure out what it was. As she took the elevator down to the underground parking garage, she was alone, her keys gripped in one hand. What did a pregnant eighteen-year-old girl have to do with Parker? she asked herself, suddenly certain she wouldn't like the answer.

Parker's leg throbbed, rebelling against his weight as he attempted to walk the length of the physical therapy room. His hands slipped on the cold metal bars, but he kept himself upright, moving forward by sheer will. Every rigid, sweat-covered muscle in his body screamed with the strain of dragging his damned leg, but he kept working.

"That's it, just two more steps," a pert therapist with a cheery smile and upturned nose persuaded, trying to encourage him forward.

Gritting his teeth he tried again, the foot slowly lifting from the floor. Pain ripped through his knee and he bit his lower lip, tasting the salt of his sweat. *Come on, Harrison*, he said to himself, squeezing his eyes shut, *do it for Shawna, that beautiful lady doctor who's crazy enough to love you.*

In the past few weeks, he'd experienced flashes of memory, little teasing bits which had burned in his mind. He could remember being with her on a sailboat—her tanned body, taut and sleek. She'd been leaning against the boom as the boat skimmed across clear green water. Her blond hair had billowed around her head, shimmering gold in the late afternoon sun, and she'd laughed, a clear sound that rippled across the river.

Even now, as he struggled to the end of the parallel bars, he could remember the smell of fresh water and perfume, the taste of her skin and the feel of her body, warm and damp, as she'd lain with him on the sand of some secluded island.

Had they made love? That one delicious recollection escaped him, rising to the surface only to sink below the murky depths of his memory, as did so much of his life. Though he knew—he could sense—that he'd loved her, there was something else stopping him from believing everything she told him of their life together—something ugly and unnamed and a part of the Brad Lomax tragedy.

"Hey! You've done it!" the therapist cried as Parker took a final agonizing step.

While thinking of the enigma that was his relationship with Shawna, he hadn't realized that he'd finished his assigned task. "I'll be damned," he muttered.

"You know what this means, don't you?" the therapist asked, positioning a wheelchair near one of the contraptions that Parker decided were designed for the sole purpose of human torture.

"What?"

"You're a free man. This is the final test. Now, if your doctor agrees, you can go home and just come back here for our workouts."

Parker wiped the sweat from his eyes and grinned. He'd be glad to leave this place! Maybe once he was home he'd start to remember and he could pick up the pieces of his life with Shawna. Maybe then the dreams of a mystery woman that woke him each night would disappear, and the unknown past would become crystal clear again.

The therapist tossed him a white terry towel and a nurse appeared.

Parker wiped his face, then slung the towel around his neck.

Placing her hands on the handles of the wheelchair, the nurse said, "I'll just push you back to your room—"

"I'll handle that," Shawna said. She'd been standing in the doorway, one shoulder propped against the jamb as she watched Parker will himself through the therapy. She'd witnessed the rigid strength of his sweat-dampened shoulders and arms, seen the flinch of pain as he tried to walk, and recognized the glint of determination in his eyes as he inched those final steps to the end of the bars.

"If you're sure, Doctor—" the nurse responded, noting Shawna's identification tag.

"Very sure." Then she leaned over Parker's shoulder and whispered, "Your place or mine?"

He laughed then. Despite the throb of pain in his knee and his anguish of not being able to remember anything of his past, he laughed. "Get me out of here."

"Your wish is my command." Without further prompting, she rolled him across the polished floors of the basement hallway and into the waiting elevator, where the doors whispered closed. "Alone at last," she murmured.

"What did I do to deserve you?" he asked, glancing up at her, his eyes warm and vibrant.

Her heart constricted and impulsively she jabbed the stop button before leaning over and pressing her lips to his. "You have been, without a doubt, the best thing that ever happened to me," she said, swallowing back a thick lump in her throat. "You showed me there was more to life than medical files, patient charts, and trying to solve everyone else's problems."

"I can't believe—"

"Of course not," she said, laughing and guessing that he was going to argue with her again, tell her he didn't deserve her love. "You've been right all along, Parker," she confided. "Everything I've been telling you is a lie. You don't deserve me at all. It's just that I'm a weak, simple female and you're so strong and sexy and macho!"

"Is that so?" he asked, strong arms dragging her into his lap.

She kissed him again, lightly this time. "Well, isn't that what you wanted to hear?"

"Sounded good," he admitted.

Cocking her head to one side, her blond hair falling across his shoulder, she grinned slowly. "Well, the strong and sexy part is true."

"But somehow I don't quite see you as a 'weak, simple female.'"

"Thank heaven. So just believe that you're the best thing in my life, okay? And no matter what happens, I'm never going to take the chance of losing you again!"

"You won't," he murmured, pulling her closer, claiming her lips with a kiss so intense her head began to spin. She forgot the past and the future. She could only concentrate on the here and now, knowing in her heart the one glorious fact that Parker, her beloved

Parker, was holding her and kissing her as hungrily as he had before the accident—as if he did indeed love her all over again.

Her breath caught deep in her lungs and inside, she was warming, feeling liquid emotion rush through her veins. She felt his hands move over her, rustling the lining of her skirt to splay against her back, hold her in that special, possessive manner that bound them so intimately together. Delicious, wanton sensations whispered through her body and she tangled her hands in his hair.

"Oh, what you do to me," he whispered in a voice raw and raspy as his fingers found the hem of her sweater and moved upward to caress one swollen breast. Hot and demanding, his fingers touched the soft flesh and Shawna moaned softly as ripples of pleasure ran like wildfire through her blood.

"Parker, please—" She cradled his head against her, feeling the warmth of his breath touch her skin. His lips teased one throbbing peak, his tongue moist as it caressed the hard little button.

Shawna was melting inside. Rational thought ceased and she was only aware of him and the need he created.

"Oh, Shawna," he groaned, slowly releasing her, his eyes still glazed with passion as a painful memory sizzled through his desire. "You're doing it again," he whispered, rubbing his temple as if it throbbed. "Shawna—stop!"

She had trouble finding her breath. Her senses were still spinning out of control and she stung from his rejection. Why was he pulling away from her? "What are you talking about?"

Passion-drugged eyes drilled into hers. "I remember, Shawna."

Relieved, she smiled. Everything was going to be fine. She tried to stroke his cheek but he jerked away. "Then you know how much we loved each—"

"I remember that you teased me, pushed me to the limit in public places. Like this."

"Parker, what are you talking about?" she cried, devastated. What was he saying? If he remembered, then surely he'd know how much she cared.

"It's not all clear," he admitted, helping her to her feet. "But there were times, just like this, when you drove me out of my mind!" He reached up and slapped the control panel. The elevator started with a lurch and Shawna nearly lost her footing.

"I don't understand—" she whispered.

The muscles of his face tautened. "Remember the fair?" he said flatly. "At the fir tree?"

She gasped, recalling rough bark against her bare back, his hands holding her wrists, their conversation about his "mistress."

"It was only a game we played," she said weakly.

"Some game." His eyes, still smoldering with the embers of recent passion, avoided hers. "You know, somehow I had the impression that you and I loved each other before—that we were lovers. You let me think that." His eyes were as cold as the sea.

"We were," she said, then recognized the censure in the set of his jaw. "Well, almost. We'd decided to wait to get married before going to bed."

Arching a brow disdainfully, he said through clenched teeth, *"We* decided? You're a doctor. I'm a tennis pro. Neither one of us is a kid and you expect me to believe that we were playing the cat-and-mouse game of waiting 'til the wedding."

"You said you remembered," she whispered, but then realized his memory was fuzzy. Certain aspects of their relationship were still blurred.

"I said I remembered part of it." But the anger in his words sounded hollow and unsure, as if he were trying to find an excuse to deny the passion between them only moments before.

The elevator car jerked to a stop and the doors

opened on the fourth floor. Shawna, her breasts still aching, reached for the handles of the wheelchair, but Parker didn't wait for her. He was already pushing himself down the corridor.

In the room, she watched him shove the wheelchair angrily aside and flop onto the bed, his face white from the effort.

"You're memory is selective," she said, leaning over the bed, pushing her face so close to his that she could read the seductive glint in his blue eyes.

"Maybe," he admitted and stared at her lips, swallowing with difficulty.

"Then why won't you just try to give us a chance? We were good together, sex or no sex. Believe me." She heard him groan.

"Don't do this to me," he asked, the fire in his eyes rekindling.

"I'll do whatever I have to," she whispered, leaning closer, kissing him, brushing the tips of her breasts across his chest until he couldn't resist.

"You're making a big mistake." He pressed her close to him.

"Let me."

"I'm not the same man—"

"I don't care, damn it," she said, then sighed. "Just love me."

"That would be too easy," he admitted gruffly, then buried his face in her hair, drinking in the sweet feminine smell that teased at his mind every night. He held her so fiercely she could feel the heat of his body through her clothes. Clinging to him, she barely heard the shuffle of feet in the doorway until Parker dragged his lips from hers and stared over her shoulder.

Twisting, half expecting to find Jake with his lousy sense of timing, she saw a young black-haired girl standing nervously on one foot, then the other.

"Melinda?" Shawna asked, her throat dry. "Are you looking for me?"

INTRODUCING

Zebra Contemporary —

To start your membership, simply complete and return the Free Book Certificate. You'll receive your Introductory Shipment of FREE Zebra Contemporary Romances. Then, each month as long as your account is in good standing, you will receive the 3 newest Zebra Contemporary Romances. Each shipment will be yours to examine for 10 days. If you decide to keep the books, you'll pay the preferred book club member price of $15.95 – a savings of over 20% off the cover price! (plus $1.50 to offset the cost of shipping and handling.) If you want us to stop sending books, just say the word… it's that simple.

BOOK CERTIFICATE

CN091A

Yes! Please send me FREE Zebra Contemporary romance novels. I understand I am under no obligation to purchase any books, as explained on this card.

Name _____

Address _____ Apt. _____

City _____ State _____ Zip _____

Telephone (___) _____

Signature _____

(If under 18, parent or guardian must sign)

Offer limited to one per household and not valid to current subscribers. All orders subject to approval. Terms, offer, and price subject to change. Offer valid only in the U.S.

Thank You!

lll.,l..lll....lll.ll..ll.l..lll.l..ll..lll.ll..l

Zebra Contemporary Romance Book Club
Zebra Home Subscription Service, Inc.
P.O. Box 5214
Clifton , NJ 07015-5214

PLACE
STAMP
HERE

"No," Melinda James said quietly, her large, brown eyes lifting until they clashed with Parker's. "I came to see him, on your advice."

"My advice—what—?" But a dark doubt steadily grew in her heart and she gripped Parker's shoulders more tightly, as if by clinging to him, she could stop what was to come. "No—there must be some mistake," she heard herself saying, her voice distant, as if in a dream.

"You told me to talk to him and that's . . . that's why I'm here," Melinda said, her eyes round with fear, large tears collecting on her lashes. "You see, Parker Harrison is the father of my child."

Seven

"He's what?" Shawna whispered, disbelieving.

"It's true."

"Wait a minute—" Parker stared at the girl, not one flicker of recognition in his eyes. "Who are you?"

Shawna wanted to tell him not to believe a word of Melinda's story, but she didn't. Instead she forced herself to watch his reaction as Melinda, hesitantly at first, then with more conviction, claimed she and Parker had been seeing each other for several months, long before he'd started dating Shawna, and that she'd become pregnant with his child.

Parker blanched, his mouth drawing into a tight line.

"This is absurd," Shawna finally said, praying that Parker would back her up.

"How old are you?" he asked, eyes studying the dark-haired girl.

"Eighteen."

"Eighteen?" he repeated, stunned. His eyes narrowed and he forced himself to stand. "And you're saying that you and I—"

"—were lovers," Melinda clarified.

Shawna couldn't stand it a minute more. "This is all a lie. Parker, this girl came into my office, asked all sort of questions about you and your amnesia, and then had me examine her."

"And?"

"And she *is* pregnant. That much is true. But . . . but . . . she's lying . . . you couldn't have been with her. *I* would have known." But even though her words rang with faith, she couldn't help remembering all the times Parker had taunted her by pretending to have a mistress. *I suppose I'll have to give up my mistress,* he'd said at the fair, teasing her, but wounding her just the same. Her old doubts twisted her heart. Was it possible that he'd actually been seeing someone and that the person he'd been with had been this girl?

"You don't remember me?" Melinda asked.

Parker closed his eyes, flinching a bit.

"I saw you the night of the accident," she prodded. "You . . . you were with Brad and he was drunk."

Parker's eyes flew open and pain, deep and tragic, showed in their vibrant blue depths.

"You stopped by my apartment and Brad became violent, so you hauled him back to the car."

"She's making this up," Shawna said. "She must have read about it in the papers or heard it on the news." But her voice faltered as she saw Parker wrestling with a memory.

"I've met her before," he said slowly. "I was at her apartment."

"No!" Shawna cried. She wouldn't believe a word of Melinda's lies—she couldn't! Parker would never betray her! She'd almost lost Parker once and she wasn't about to lose him again, not to this girl, not to anyone. "Parker, you don't honestly believe—"

"I don't know *what* to believe!" he snapped.

"But we've been through so much together . . ." Then she turned her eyes on Melinda and all of her professionalism and medical training flew out the window. No longer was Melinda her patient, but just a brash young woman trying to tarnish the one man Shawna loved. "Look," she said, her voice as ragged as her emotions. "I don't really know who you are or why you're here torturing him or even how you got into this room, but I want you out, now!"

"Stop it, Shawna," Parker said.

But Shawna ignored him. "I'll call the guards if I have to, but you have no right to come in here and upset any of the patients—"

"I'm *your* patient," Melinda said, satisfaction briefly gleaming in her eyes.

"I referred you to—"

"He's the father of my child, dammit!" Melinda cried, wilting against the wall and sobbing like the girl she was.

"She can stay," Parker pronounced as Tom Handleman, his lab coat flapping behind him, marched into the room. "What the devil's going on here?" he demanded, eyeing Shawna. "Who's she?" He pointed an accusing finger at the huddled figure of Melinda.

"A friend of mine," Parker said, his voice ringing with quiet authority.

"Parker, no!" Shawna whispered, ignoring Tom. "She lied to me this morning—told me the name of her previous physician in Cleveland. I tried to call him—there is no Dr. Harold Rankin in the area."

"Then he moved," Melinda said, stronger because of Parker's defense. "It's—it's been years."

"She has to leave," Shawna decided, turning to Tom, desperation contorting her face.

"Maybe she can help," Tom suggested.

"Help?" Shawna murmured. "She's in here accusing him, lying to him, lying to me—"

Melinda stood, squaring her shoulders and meeting Parker's clouded gaze. "I—I understand why you feel betrayed, Dr. McGuire. First Parker lied to you and then I had to lie this morning. But I just wanted to find out that he was all right. No one would let me in here. Then *you* convinced me that I had to tell him about the baby—"

"*Baby?*" Handleman asked, his face ashen.

"—and I decided you were right. Every father has the right to know about his child whether he wants to claim him or not."

"For cryin' out loud!" Tom whispered. "Look, Miss—"

"James," Melinda supplied.

"Let her stay," Parker said.

"You remember me," she said.

Shawna wanted to die as they stared at each other.

"I've met you," Parker admitted, his face muscles taut. "And I don't mean to insult you, Miss James—"

"Melinda. You called me Linnie. Don't you remember?" Her chin trembled and she fought against tears that slid from her eyes.

"I'm sorry—"

"You have to remember!" she cried. "All those nights by the river—all those promises—"

Good Lord, what was she saying? Shawna's throat closed up. "Parker and I were—are—going to be married, and neither one of us believes that he's the father of your child. This is obviously just some way for you and your boyfriend to take advantage—"

"No!" Melinda whispered. "I don't care what *you* believe, but Parker loves me! He—he—" her eyes darted quickly around the room and she blinked. "Oh, please, Parker. Remember," she begged.

Parker gripped the arms of his wheelchair. "Melinda," he said softly. Was it Shawna's imagination or did his voice caress the younger woman's name? "I don't remember ever sleeping with you."

"You deny the baby?"

He glanced at Shawna, his eyes seeming haunted. She could only stare back at him. "Not the baby. I'm just not sure it's mine."

Shawna shook her head. "No—"

"Then maybe you'd want a simple paternity test," Melinda suggested.

"Hey—hold the phone," Tom Handleman cut in.

"Let's all just calm down. Right now, Miss James, I'm asking you to leave." Then he glanced at Shawna. "You, too, Dr. McGuire. This has been a strain on Parker. Let's all just give it a rest."

"I'm afraid I can't do that," Melinda said staunchly, seeming to draw from an inner reserve of strength. "Don't get me wrong, Parker. I'm not interested in ruining your reputation or trying to damage your professional image, but my baby needs his father."

"So you want money," Parker said cynically.

"Money isn't what I'm after," Melinda said, and Shawna felt a chill as cold as a December wind cut through her. "I want to give my baby a name and I want him to know who his father is. If it takes a paternity test to convince you or a lawsuit, I don't care." Swallowing back a fresh onslaught of tears, she walked unsteadily out of the room.

Shawna turned a tortured gaze to Parker. "You remember her?"

He nodded and let his forehead drop to his hand. "A little."

Dying inside, Shawna leaned against the bed. After all these weeks, Parker still barely admitted to remembering her—only disjointed pieces of their relationship. And yet within fifteen minutes of meeting Melinda James he conceded that he recognized her. Dread settled over her.

Sick inside, she wondered if Melinda's ridiculous accusations could possibly be true. Did Parker remember Melinda because they had slept together? Was her face so indelibly etched in his mind because of their intimacy? But that was ridiculous—she knew it and deep down, so did he!

She felt that everything she'd believed in was slowly being shredded into tiny pieces.

"You—you and Brad. You saw her that night?" she asked, her voice barely audible over the sounds of the hospital.

He nodded, his jaw extending. "Yes."

"And you remember?"

"Not everything."

"Maybe she was Brad's girl. Maybe the baby is his."

Parker's eyes narrowed. "Maybe. I don't know."

Tom placed his hand over Shawna's arm and guided her to the door. "Don't torture yourself," he said in a concerned whisper. "Go home, think things through. I guarantee you Parker will do the same. Then tomorrow, come back and take him home."

"Home?" she repeated dully.

"Yes, I'm releasing him tomorrow." He glanced over his shoulder to Parker. "That is, unless Miss James's visit sets him back."

"I hope not," Shawna said, staring at Parker with new eyes, trying to smile and failing miserably. "Look, I really need to talk to him. Just a few minutes, okay?"

"I guess it won't hurt," Tom decided, "but keep it short. He's had one helluva shock today."

"Haven't we all?" Shawna said as Tom closed the door behind him.

Parker didn't look at her. He scowled through the window to the gray day beyond.

Had he betrayed her? Shawna couldn't believe it. Melinda had to be lying. But why? And why had Parker gone to visit the young girl before taking Brad home? Was it to call off their affair? Or had he needed to see her just one more time before the wedding? Shawna's stomach churned at the thought of them lying together, kissing—

"So much for the knight in shining armor, huh?" he mocked.

"I don't believe a word of her lies. And I really don't think you do, either."

"That's the tricky part," he admitted, staring up at the ceiling. "I know I've seen her—been with her, but—"

"—But you don't remember." Tossing her hair over her shoulder, she leaned against the bed.

"She has no reason to lie."

"Neither do I, Parker. I don't know anything about that girl, but I know what we shared and we didn't cheat or lie or betray one another."

"You're sure of that?"

"Positive," she whispered, wishing that awful shadow of doubt would disappear from her mind. "I only wish I could prove it."

Parker watched her blink back tears, saw her fine jaw jut in determination, and loved her for all of her pride and faith in him. Her blond hair draped across her shoulder to curl at her breast, and her eyes, fierce with indignation and bright with unshed tears, were as green as a night-darkened forest. How he loved her. Even lying here, charged with fathering another woman's child, he loved Shawna McGuire. But not because of any memories that had surfaced in his mind. No, this love was new, borne from just being near her. Never had he met any woman so proud and free-spirited, so filled with giving and fighting for what she believed in. And what she believed in was him.

"Do you think you're the father of Melinda's baby?" she finally asked, so close he could touch her.

"I don't know."

She blanched, as if in severe pain. Without thinking he took her hand in his and pulled her gently forward, so that she was leaning over him.

"But I do know that if I ever did anything that would hurt you this much, I have to be the worst bastard that ever walked the earth."

She swallowed. "You . . . you wouldn't."

"I hope to God you're right." His throat felt dry, and though the last thing he intended to do was kiss her again, he couldn't stop himself. He held her close, tilting her chin up with one finger and molding his mouth possessively over hers. "I don't want to ever hurt you, Shawna," he rasped hoarsely. "Don't let me."

"You won't." She felt the promise of his tongue as it gently parted her lips, then heard the sound of voices in the hall. She couldn't think when he held her, and she needed time alone to recover from the shock of Melinda James's announcement. Besides, she'd promised Dr. Handleman she wouldn't upset Parker. "Look, I don't want to, but I've got to go. Doctor's orders."

"To hell with doctor's orders," he muttered, his arms flexing around her, thwarting her attempts at escape.

"Don't mess with the medical profession," she warned, but the lilt she tried for didn't materialize in her voice.

"Not the whole profession," he said slowly, "just one very beautiful lady doctor."

Oh, Parker! Her throat thickened. "Later," she promised, kissing him lightly on the tip of the nose and hearing him moan in response.

"You're doing it again," he whispered.

"What?"

"Driving me crazy." His gaze slid down her body and stupidly, like a schoolgirl, she blushed and ran for the door.

As she drove home, her thoughts were tangled in a web of doubt and despair. Was it possible? Could Melinda's story be true?

"Don't be absurd," she told herself as she maneuvered her little car through the twisted streets of Sellwood. Maple and alder trees had begun to drop their leaves, splashing the wet streets with clumps of gold, brown, and orange.

As Shawna climbed out of the car, a cold autumn breeze lifted her hair from her face, cooled the heat in her cheeks.

"Hey, about time you showed up!" Jake accosted

her as he climbed out of a battered old Chevy pickup. "I thought you'd be home half an hour ago."

She'd forgotten all about him, and the fact that he'd offered to help her move. "I—I'm sorry. Uh, something came up," she said, trying to concentrate.

"Oh, yeah?" Jake's brows raised expectantly. "Don't tell me the coach is gonna be released."

"Tomorrow," Shawna said, her voice catching before her brother saw the pain in her eyes.

"Hey—whoa. What happened?" Jake grabbed both her shoulders, then forced her chin upward with one finger and stared down at her.

"You wouldn't believe it."

"Try me." One arm over her shoulders, Jake walked her to the front door and unlocked the dead bolt. The apartment was a mess. Boxes and bags were scattered all over the living-room floor, piled together with pictures, furniture, and clothes.

Shawna flopped in the nearest corner and told Jake everything, from the moment Melinda James had walked into her office until the time when she'd dropped the bomb about Parker being the father of her unborn child.

"And you bought that cockamamy story?" Jake asked, flabbergasted.

"Of course not." Shawna felt close to tears again.

"I hope not! It's ridiculous."

"But Parker did."

"*What?*"

"He claims to remember her, and admits that he visited her the night Brad was killed!"

Stricken, Jake sat on a rolled carpet. His eyes narrowed thoughtfully. "I don't believe it."

"Neither did I, but you should have been there." Outside, Maestro meowed loudly. "I'm coming," Shawna called, every muscle in her body suddenly slack as she tried to stand and couldn't.

"I'll let him in." Jake opened the door and the bedraggled yellow tabby, wet from the rain, dashed into the house and made a beeline for Shawna. He cried until she petted him. "At least I can trust you," she said, her spirits lifting a little as the tabby washed his face and started to purr noisily.

"You can trust Parker, too," Jake said. "You and I both know it. That guy's crazy about you."

"Tell him," she said.

Jake frowned at his sister. "Okay, so this lunatic girl has made some crazy claims and Parker can't remember enough to know that she's lying. It's not the end of the world." He caught her glance and sighed. "Well, almost the end," he admitted, and even Shawna had to smile. "Now, come on. What's your next step?"

"You're not going to like it," Shawna said, opening a can of cat food for the cat.

"Try me."

"When the movers come tomorrow, I'm going to have them take my things to Parker's."

"His house?" Jake asked, his brows shooting up. "Does he know about this?"

"Nope." She straightened and her gaze narrowed on her brother. "And don't you tell him about it."

"I wouldn't dare," Jake said with obvious respect for Parker's volatile temper. "What about Mom and Dad?"

"I'll explain."

"Good luck. That's one dogfight I don't want any part of."

"I don't blame you." Why was this happening, and why now? She couldn't help thinking back to the Gypsy fortune-teller and her grim prediction.

"Shawna?" Jake asked, concern creasing his brow. "Are you okay?"

She nodded, her chin inching upward proudly. "I'm fine," she said. "I just have to stick by Parker 'til all of this is resolved one way or the other."

"Can I help?"

"Would you mind taking care of Maestro, just for a few days?"

Jake eyed the tabby dubiously. As if understanding he was the center of attention, Maestro leaped to the counter and arched his back as he rubbed up against the windowsill.

"I'm allergic to cats."

"He's outside most of the time."

"Bruno will eat him alive."

Shawna couldn't help but laugh. Bruno was a large mutt who was afraid of his own shadow. "Bruno will stick his big tail between his legs and run in the other direction."

"Okay."

"By the way," she said, feeling better. "You should work on that dog's obvious case of paranoia!"

"Maybe I should work on yours," Jake said, clapping her on the back. "You and I both know that Parker wasn't unfaithful to you."

"But he doesn't know it," Shawna replied, her convictions crumbling a little.

"You'll just have to convince him."

"I'm trying. Believe me." She pushed her hair from her eyes and rested the back of her head against the wall. "But that's not the only problem. What about Melinda and her baby? Why is she lying? How does Parker know her? As much as this mess angers me, I can't forget that Melinda is only eighteen, unmarried, and pregnant."

"Does she have any family?"

"I don't know." Shawna blew a strand of hair from her eyes. "All she said was that her dad would kill her when he found out. I think she was just using a turn of phrase. At least I hope so."

"But you're not sure."

"That's one of the most frustrating things about all of this. I don't know a thing about her. I've never even heard her name before and now she claims to be carrying my fiancé's child."

"Maybe there's something I could do."

"Such as?"

"I don't know, but *something.*"

"Not this time," she decided, grateful for his offer. "But thanks. This one I've got to handle by myself."

"I don't believe it!" Doris McGuire exclaimed. Sitting on her antique sofa, she stared across the room at her daughter. "Parker, and some, some girl?"

"That's what she claims," Shawna said.

"She's lying!"

"Who is?" Malcolm McGuire opened the front door and shook the rain from his hat, then tossed the worn fedora over the arm of an oak hall tree in the foyer. "Who's lying?" he repeated as he strode into the den and kissed Shawna's cheek. "You're not talking about Parker, are you?"

"Indirectly," Shawna admitted.

"Some young girl claims she's pregnant with Parker's child!" Doris said, her mouth pursed, her eyes bright with indignation. "Can you believe it?"

"Hey, slow down a minute," Malcolm said. "Let's start at the beginning."

As Shawna explained everything that had happened since she'd first met Melinda, Malcolm splashed a stiff shot of Scotch into a glass, thought twice about it, and poured two more drinks, which he handed to his daughter and wife.

"You don't believe it, do you?" he finally asked, searching Shawna's face.

"Of course not."

"But you've got doubts."

"Wouldn't you?"

"Never!" Doris declared. Malcolm's face whitened a bit.

"Sometimes a man can make a mistake, you know," he said.

"He was *engaged* to Shawna, for goodness sake!"

"But not married to her," Malcolm said slowly.

"Dad?" Did he know something? She studied the lines of her father's face as he finished his drink and sat heavily on the edge of the couch.

"I have no idea what Parker was up to," Malcolm said. "But I warned you that we didn't know all that much about him, didn't I? Maybe he had another girl-friend, I don't know. I would never have believed it before, but now? Why would she lie?"

Why indeed?

"But let's not judge him too harshly," Malcolm said. "Not until all the facts are in."

"I don't think you understand the gravity of the situation," Doris replied.

"Of course I do. Now, tell me about Parker. What does he have to say?"

"Not much." Shawna told her parents about the scene in the hospital room.

Malcolm cradled his empty glass in both hands and frowned into it. Doris shook her head and sighed loudly, though her back was ramrod stiff. "He'll just have to submit to a paternity test—prove the child isn't his and then get on with his life."

"Maybe it's not that simple," Malcolm said quietly. "He has a career to think of. All this adverse publicity might affect it."

"We're talking about the man Shawna plans to marry," Doris cut in, simmering with fury, "and here you are defending his actions—if, indeed, he was in-volved with that . . . that *woman!*"

"She's barely more than a girl," Shawna said.

"Eighteen is old enough to know better!"

Malcolm held up his hand to calm his wife. "I'm just saying we should all keep a level head."

Now that she'd said what she had to say, Shawna snatched her jacket from the back of a wing chair. "I think Dad's right—we should just low-key this for now."

"The girl is pregnant!"

"I know, I know. But I've decided that what I'm going to do is try and help Parker through this. It's got to be as hard on him as it is on me. That's one of the reasons I've decided to move in with him."

"Do what?" Doris was horrified. She nearly dropped her drink and her pretty face fell.

"He's being released from the hospital tomorrow. And I'm taking him home—to his house—with me."

"But you can't—you're not married. And now, with that girl's ridiculous accusations—"

"All the more reason to try and help jog his memory." Shawna saw the protests forming on her mother's lips and waved them off.

"Look, I've already made up my mind. If things had turned out differently, I'd already be married to him and living in that house. He and I would still have to deal with Melinda—unless this is all a convenient story of hers just because he's lost his memory. So, I'm going to stand by him. I just wanted you to know how to get in touch with me."

"But—"

"Mom, I love him." Shawna touched her mother's shoulder. It felt stiff and rigid under Doris's cotton sweater. "I'll call you in a couple of days."

Then, before her mother or father could try to change her mind, she walked out of the room, swept her purse off an end table, and opened the front door. She was glad to drive away from her parents' house because she needed time alone, time to think and clear her head. Tomorrow she'd have the battle of her life with Parker. He'd already told her he didn't want her

tied to him as a cripple, that they couldn't marry until
he was strong enough to support them both. Now, after
Melinda's allegations, he'd be more adamant than
ever.

Well, that was just too damned bad. Shawna intended to stand by him no matter what, and if he never
walked again, she still intended to marry him. All she
had to do was convince him that she was right. Involuntarily, she crossed her fingers.

Parker shoved the dinner tray aside. He wasn't hungry and didn't feel like trying to force food down his
throat. With a groan, he reached for the crutches near
his bed.

Dr. Handleman and the idiot down in physical therapy didn't think he was ready for crutches, but he'd
begged them off a candy striper. Tomorrow he was going home and he wasn't about to be wheeled down
the hall like a helpless invalid.

Gritting his teeth against a stab of pain in his knee,
he slid off the bed and shoved the crutches under his
arms. Then, slowly, he moved across the room, ignoring the throbbing in his knee and the erratic pounding
of his heart. Finally he fell against the far wall, sweating
but proud that he'd accomplished the small feat of
walking across the room.

Breathing hard, he glanced out the window to the
parking lot below. Security lamps glowed blue, reflecting on the puddles from a recent shower. Parker had
a vague recollection of another storm. . . .

Rain had been drizzling down a windshield, wipers
slapping the sheeting water aside as he had driven up
a twisting mountain road. Someone—was it Brad?—
had been slumped in the passenger seat. The passenger had fallen against Parker just as the Jeep had
rounded a corner and there, right in the middle of

the road, a huge truck with bright glaring headlights was barreling toward them, out of control. The truck driver blasted his horn, brakes squealed and locked, and Parker, reacting by instinct alone, had wrenched hard on the wheel, steering the Jeep out of the path of the oncoming truck and through the guardrail into the black void beyond.

Now, as he stood with his head pressed to the glass, Parker squeezed his eyes shut tight, trying to dredge up the memories, put the ill-fitting pieces of his past into some order.

He remembered Melinda—he'd seen her that night. But she was just a girl. Surely he wouldn't have slept with her!

Impatient with his blank mind, he swore and knocked over one of his crutches. It fell against the table, knocking over a water glass and a book. From the pages of the book fluttered a picture—the single snapshot of Shawna on the carousel.

In the photograph, her cheeks were rosy and flushed, her eyes bright, her hair tossed wildly around her face. He'd been in love with her then. He could feel it, see it in her expression. And now, he'd fallen in love with her again and this time, he suspected, his feelings ran much deeper.

Despite the searing pain in his knee, he bent down, but the picture was just out of reach, in the thin layer of dust under the bed, and he couldn't coax the snapshot back to him, not even with the aid of his crutch.

He frowned at the irony. He couldn't reach the picture just as he couldn't have her, wouldn't chain her to a future so clouded and unsure. She deserved better than a man who might never walk without a cane—a man who couldn't even remember if he'd betrayed her.

Eight

Bracing herself, knowing full well that she was in for the fight of her life, Shawna walked into Parker's hospital room. "Ready?" she asked brightly.

"For what?" Parker was standing near his bed, fully dressed in gray cords and a cream-colored sweater, and balancing precariously on crutches.

"To go home." She picked up his duffel bag and tossed it over her shoulder, overlooking the storm gathering in his eyes. "Hurry up, I'm double-parked."

"I'll call a cab," he said quietly.

"No reason. Your house is on my way."

"To where?"

"The rest of my life."

Taking in a swift breath, he shoved one hand through his hair and shook his head. "You're unbelievable," he muttered.

"So you've said. Come on."

"Mr. Harrison?" A nurse pushed a wheelchair into his room and Parker swore under his breath.

"I don't need *that*."

"Hospital regulations."

"Change them," he said, jaw tight.

"Come on, Parker, don't buck the system now," Shawna said, grabbing the handles of the wheelchair from the nurse. "Everyone has to use these chairs in order to get out."

Muttering to himself he slid into the chair and grumbled all the way along the corridor.

"I see we're in good spirits today," Shawna commented drily.

"Don't start in with that hospital 'we' talk, okay? I'm sick to death of it."

"My mistake. But don't worry. I'll probably make a few more before the day is over." She wheeled him into the elevator and didn't say a word until they were through the emergency room doors—the same door she'd run through weeks ago in her soggy wedding dress. That day felt like a lifetime ago.

Once they were in the car and through the parking lot, Shawna drove south, down the steep fir-cloaked hills of west Portland toward Lake Oswego and Parker's rambling Tudor house on the cliffs.

He stared out the window in silence, his eyes traveling over the familiar landscape. Leaves of the maple and oak trees had turned vibrant orange and brown, swirling in the wind and hanging tenaciously to black branches as Shawna drove toward the river. She glanced at Parker and noticed the tight pinch at the corners of his mouth and the lines of strain on his forehead as his stone house loomed into view.

Rising a full three stories, with a sharply gabled roof and dormers, the Tudor stood high on the cliffs overlooking the green waters of the Willamette. Trees and shrubbery flanked a broad, pillared porch and leaded glass windows winked in the pink rays from a setting sun.

Shawna cut the engine in front of the garage. She was reaching for the handle of her door when his voice stopped her.

"Aren't you going to ask me about Melinda?"

She froze and her stomach twisted painfully. Inadvertently she'd been avoiding the subject. "Is there something you want to tell me?"

Swallowing, he glanced away, then stared straight

into her eyes. "I—I'm starting to remember," he admitted, weighing his words. "Part of the past is getting a little more clear."

She knew what was coming and died a bit inside, her fingers wrapping around the steering wheel as she leaned back in her seat. "The part with Melinda," she guessed, fingers clenched tight over the wheel.

"Yes."

"You . . . remember being with her?"

"Partly."

"Sleeping with her?"

She saw him hesitate, then shake his head. "No, but there's something . . . something about her. If only I could figure it out."

Licking her lips nervously, she forced her gaze to meet his. "I don't believe you betrayed me, Parker," she admitted, her voice rough. "I just can't."

"Maybe it would be easier if you did," he whispered.

"Why?"

"Because I feel—this tremendous responsibility."

She touched him then, her fingers light on his sweater, beneath which she could feel the coiled tension in his shoulders. "Give it time."

"I think we're running out." Then, as quickly as he'd brought up the subject, he jerked on the door handle and shoved the car door open. Cool wind invaded the interior as he gripped the frame and tried to struggle to his feet.

"Hey—wait!" She threw open her door and ran around the car just as he extracted himself from his seat and balanced on one leg, his face white with strain. "What do you think you're doing?" she demanded.

"Standing on my own," he said succinctly.

She caught his meaning, but refused to acknowledge it. "Sure, but you were almost flat on your face," she chastised. "How do you think Dr. Handleman would like it if you twisted that knee again and undid all his work?"

"I don't really give a damn what he does or doesn't like."

"Back to your charming sweet self, I see," she said, though her heart was pounding a rapid double-time. "Personally I'd hate to see you back in that hospital bed—in traction or worse—all because of your stupid, bullheaded male pride." She opened the hatchback of her car and wrestled with the collapsible wheelchair, noting that he'd paled slightly at the mention of the hospital. Good! He needed to think that one over. "So, quit being a child and enjoy being pampered."

"Pampered by whom?"

"Me." She locked the wheelchair and rolled it toward his side of the car.

"I don't want to be pampered."

"Oh, I think you will. Think of it as a reward for all those grueling hours you'll be spending with the physical therapist. I already hired him—he starts tomorrow."

"You did *what?*" Parker was livid, the fire in his eyes bright with rage. "I'm not going to—"

"Sure you are. And you're going to get off this self-reliant-male ego kick right now!"

She pushed the wheelchair next to him, but he held up a hand, spreading his fingers in her face. "Hold on, just one minute. I may not remember a lot about my past, but I know one thing, I never let any woman—even a lady doctor—push me around."

"Not even Melinda James?" Shawna snapped, instantly regretting her words when she saw his face slacken and guilt converge over his honed features.

"I'll deal with Melinda," he said, his voice ringing with authority, "in my own way." Then, ignoring the wheelchair, he reached down and tugged on the crutches she'd wedged into the car.

"You can't—"

"I can damned well do as I please, Dr. McGuire," he said cuttingly. "I'm not in a hospital any longer. You're not the boss." He slammed the crutches under his arms and swung forward, landing on his good leg with a jarring thud as he started up the flagstone path leading to the back door.

"You'll be back in the hospital before you know it if you don't watch out," she warned. Walking rapidly, she caught up with him.

"You can go home now, Shawna," he advised.

"I am."

Cocking his head to one side, he asked testily, "You're what?"

"Home."

"What?" he roared, twisting to look at her, his crutch wedging in the chipped mortar to wrench out from under him. He pitched forward, grabbing frantically at the lowest branches of a nearby willow tree and landing with a thud on the wet grass.

"Parker!" Shawna knelt beside him. "I'm sorry—"

"Wasn't your fault." But he winced in pain, skin tight over his cheeks. "Now, tell me I heard wrong."

"I moved in this morning," she said, but her eyes were on his leg and without asking she pushed up his pant leg, to make sure that the stitches in his knee hadn't ruptured.

"I'm all right." He caught her wrist. "You are *not* my doctor. And you're not moving in here."

"Too late," she said, reaching into her pocket with her free hand and extracting a key ring from which dangled the keys to his house, car, and garage. "You gave these to me—for better or for worse, remember."

"We didn't get married."

"Doesn't matter. I'm committed to you, so you'd better get used to it!" She met his gaze steadily, her green eyes bright with defiance and pride. His fingers were still circling her wrist, warm against her skin, and her breathing, already labored, caught in her throat

as his eyes moved from hers to the base of her neck
and lower still. "Whether the ceremony happened or
not, I consider myself your wife, and it will take an act
of God for you to get rid of me."

"What about another woman's child?"

Her heart constricted. "We'll just have to deal with
that together, won't we?" Nervously, she licked her lips,
her self-confidence slowly drifting away.

He studied her mouth. "Maybe I need to stand
alone before I can stand with someone," he said, sun
glinting off the burnished strands of his hair.

"Are you telling me you won't let me live here?"
She could barely concentrate. Her thoughts centered
on her wrist and the provocative movement of his fingers against her skin. And his eyes, blue as the sea,
stared into hers, smoldering with desire, yet bewildered.

"I just don't think we—you and I—can act like this
accident didn't happen, pretending that Melinda
James doesn't exist, that our lives will mesh in some
sort of fairy-tale happy ending, when there are so many
things pulling us apart." He glanced down at her lips
and then to her hair, shining a radiant gold in the
afternoon sunlight.

"Please, Parker, just give me a chance. I—I don't
mean to come on like gangbusters, but we need time
alone together, to work things out."

He pulled her close, kissing her as passionately as
she'd ever been kissed, his lips possessive and strong
with a fire she knew burned bright in his soul.

Responding, she cradled his head to hers, feeling
the texture of his hair, and the warmth of his breath.

He shifted, more of his weight falling across her, his
arms strong as they circled her waist.

"Parker, please—just love me," she whispered
against his ear. He groaned a response. "Let me help
you—help us." She placed both of her hands on his

cheeks and held his head between her palms. "I can't let go, Melinda or no Melinda. Baby or no baby."

Before he could respond, Shawna heard the back door swing open and there, standing on the porch, her eyes dark with unspoken accusation, was Melinda James.

"What the devil?" Parker whispered. "How'd you—? Don't even answer! It doesn't matter."

Shawna realized that he'd probably given her a set of keys, too, long before he'd met Shawna, and the wound she'd tried so hard to bind opened again, fresh and raw.

"Remind me to have my locks changed," Parker muttered.

Shawna dusted off her skirt and tried to help him to his feet, but he pushed her hands aside, determined to stand by himself.

"I—I didn't know she would be here," Melinda said quietly, but her dark eyes darted quickly from Shawna to Parker and back again.

"I live here," Shawna said.

Melinda nearly dropped her purse. "You what?"

Parker's brows shot up. "Hold on a minute. I live here. Me. Alone."

"Not any more," Shawna said, cringing at how brash she sounded. Two months ago she would never have been so bold, but now, with her back against the wall and Parker's physical and mental health at stake, she'd fight tooth and nail to help him.

"You invited her?" Melinda asked, surveying Parker with huge, wounded eyes.

"She invited herself." He forced himself upright and started propelling himself forward.

"Are—are you all right?" Melinda asked.

"Just dandy," he snapped, unable to keep the cynicism from his voice. "I think we'd all better go into the house, and straighten out a few things." He glanced over his shoulder to Shawna, who was attempting to comb the tangles from her hair with her fingers. "Coming, Doctor?"

"Wouldn't miss it for the world," she quipped back, managing a smile though her insides were shredding. What would she do if he threw her out, insisted that he cared about Melinda, that the child was his?

"One step at a time," she reminded herself, following him inside.

Melinda was already halfway down the hall to the den. "I don't like this," Shawna confided in Parker as she caught up with him.

"Neither do I." His gaze wandered to her face and she could feel his eyes taking in the determined slant of her mouth. "But then there's a lot of things I don't like—things I'm not sure about."

"Such as?"

Before she could walk down the two steps to the den, he leaned forward, balanced on his crutches, and touched her shoulder. "Such as you," he admitted, eyes dark and tormented. "It would be easy to fall in love with you, Shawna—too easy. I must have been one helluva lucky guy—"

"You still are."

"—but now, things have changed. Look at me! I still can't walk. I may never walk without these infernal things!" He shook one crutch angrily, his expression changing to violent anger and frustration. "And then there's Melinda. I can't say her story isn't true. I don't know! I can't remember."

"I'll help you."

He let out a weary sigh and rested his forehead against hers. Involuntarily her fingers caught in the thick threads of his sweater. So desperately, she wanted him to understand, remember, recapture that fleeting love they'd shared.

One of his hands stroked her cheek, as if he couldn't quite believe she was real. "You—you've got a medical practice—a future, and you're a gorgeous, intelligent woman. Any man would count himself lucky if you just looked sideways at him."

"I'm not interested in 'any man,' " she pointed out. "Just one."

"Oh, Shawna," he moaned, his voice as low as the wind rustling through the rafters of the old house. Against her cheek, his fingers trembled.

A hot lump filled her throat. "How come I feel like you're trying to push me away?"

"Because I am. I have to. I can't tie you down to this!" He gestured to his legs, furious that they wouldn't obey his commands.

"Let me make that decision." Tears filled her eyes, but she smiled bravely just the same. "I'll decide if you're so horrible that any sane woman wouldn't be interested in you."

From the doorway to the den, Melinda coughed. She glanced guiltily away, as if she didn't mean to eavesdrop, but hadn't been able to stop herself from witnessing the tender scene between Parker and Shawna. "If you want me to, I'll leave," she said, chin quivering.

"Not yet." Straightening, Parker rubbed one hand around his shoulders, as if to relieve a coiled tension in his muscles. "Not yet." He swung his crutches forward and hobbled down the two steps into the den.

Steeling herself, Shawna followed, only to find that Melinda had already lit a fire in the grate and had placed a carafe of coffee on the table. "You've been here a while."

Melinda shrugged but resentment smoldered in her large brown eyes. "I, um, didn't expect you."

Parker met the questions in Melinda's gaze. "I think we'd better set a few ground rules. First of all, I don't remember you, not in the way you think I should," he said to Melinda. "But, if that child is really mine, I'll do right by you."

"That's all I'd expect," Melinda replied quickly. "I'm just concerned for my baby."

Shawna's hands shook. Just thinking that Parker might have a child with someone else, even a child conceived before they had met, tore at her soul. I can handle this, she told herself over and over again, trying to convince herself.

"Okay, so how did we meet?" Parker said, leaning forward and cringing a little when a jab of pain shot through him.

"I—I was a friend of Brad's. I, uh, used to watch him play and you coached him. Brad—he introduced us."

"How did you know Brad?"

Melinda looked down at her hands. "We went to school together in Cleveland, before he dropped out," she explained. "We, uh, used to date."

"But then you met Parker," Shawna prodded.

"Yes, and, well, Brad was seeing someone else, Parker and I hit it off, and then," she licked her lips. "We fell in love. Until you came along."

Shawna exhaled slowly. How much of Melinda's story was fact and how much fantasy? If only Parker could remember! She wanted to hate the girl but couldn't. Melinda was afraid of something, or someone; it was written all over her downcast face.

"Do you have any family?" Parker asked.

"Not around here. My dad's a widower."

"Does he know that you're pregnant?"

"I didn't know until I saw her yesterday," Melinda said, then her shoulders slumped. "Though I guess I kinda expected it. But Dad, even if he did know, he wouldn't care. I haven't lived at home for a couple of years."

"I thought you said he'd kill you," Shawna whispered.

"I guess I was wrong. Melinda swallowed hard and Shawna almost felt sorry for her. "Look, I made a mistake. It's no big deal," she said, her temper flaring. "The thing is I'm in trouble, okay? And it's *his* fault. You know I'm not lying, you're the one who did the test."

Shawna slowly counted to ten. She couldn't lose her self-control. Not now. "Fine. Let's start over."

"I didn't come here to talk to you."

"This involves all of us," Parker said.

Shawna asked, "Did you finish high school?"

"Yep." Melinda flopped onto one of the cushions of the leather couch and stared at the ceiling. "I was going to be a model. Until I met Parker."

"After Brad."

"Right."

Shawna wondered how much, if any, of the girl's story were true. "And then you were swept off your feet?"

"That's about it," Melinda said, her smile faltering.

Parker's expression was unreadable. He stared at Melinda, his lips pressed together, as if he, too, were trying to find flaws in her words, some key to what had really happened. "Then you won't mind if I have a friend of mine look up your father, just to verify a few things," Parker said slowly.

Beneath her tan, Melinda blanched, but said, "Do what you have to do. It won't change anything, and at least then maybe she'll believe me." Disturbed, she slung her purse over her shoulder and left, the heels of her boots echoing loudly on the tiles of the foyer. A few seconds later Shawna heard the front door slam.

"Does anything she said sound true?" she asked.

"I don't know." Parker sighed heavily and, groaning, pushed himself to his feet. "I just don't know." Leaning one shoulder against the stones of the fireplace, he stared into the glowing red embers of the fire. "But she seemed pretty sure of herself. That seems to be a trait of the women I knew."

The firelight flickered on his face, causing uneven

red shadows to highlight the hard angle of his jaw. He added, "You know you can't stay here."

"I have to."

"You don't owe me any debts, if that's what you think."

"You need someone to look after you."

"Like hell!" he muttered, his eyes blazing with the reflection of the coals. "What I don't need is anyone who thinks they owe me."

"You just don't understand, do you?" she whispered, so furious she was beginning to shake again. "You just don't understand how much I love you."

"Loved. Past tense."

Standing, she tossed her hair away from her face and met his fierce, uncompromising stare. "One accident doesn't change the depth of my feelings, Parker. Nor does it, in any way, shape or form, alter the fact that I love you for life, no matter what. Legally, I suppose, you can force me out of here. Or, you could make my life here so intolerable that I'd eventually throw in the towel and move. But you can't, *can't* destroy the simple fact that I love you and always will." Into the silence that followed, she said, "I've made up the guest room for you so you won't have to hassle with the stairs. I've moved all of your clothes and things down here."

"And you—where do you intend to sleep?"

"Upstairs—for now. Just until this Melinda thing is straightened out."

"And then?"

"Then, I hope, you'll want me to sleep with you."

"As man and wife?"

"Yes. If I can ever get it through that thick skull of yours that we belong together! So," she added fiercely, "if we're finished arguing, I'll make dinner." Leaving him speechless, she marched out of the room, fingers crossed, hoping that somehow, some way, she could help him remember everything.

Parker stared after her in amazement. Nothing was going as he'd planned. Ever since she'd bulldozed her way back into his life, he seemed to have lost control— not only of his past, but of his future.

Unfortunately he admired her grit and determination, and even smiled to himself when he remembered how emphatic she'd become when she'd told him she intended to sleep with him. Any other man would jump at the chance of making love to her—but then any other man could jump and make love. So far he hadn't done either since the accident. He was sure he couldn't do one. As for the other, he hoped that he was experiencing only a temporary setback. He smiled a little. Earlier, when he'd fallen on the ground and he'd kissed Shawna, he'd felt the faintest of stirrings deep within.

Now, he found his crutches and pushed himself down the hallway toward the kitchen. Shawna was so passionate, so full of life. Why would he betray her with a woman who was barely out of childhood?

He leaned one shoulder against the wall and watched Shawna working in the kitchen. She'd tied a towel over her wool skirt, clipped her hair loosely away from her face, and kicked her shoes into a corner. In stocking feet and reading glasses, she sliced vegetables near the sink. She was humming—actually humming—as she worked, and she seemed completely at home and comfortable in his house, as though their argument and Melinda's baby didn't exist.

Watching her furtively, listening to the soft sound of her voice, seeing the smile playing upon her lips, he couldn't help feeling as lighthearted as she. She was a beautiful, intriguing woman—a woman with determination and courage—and she gave her love to him so completely.

So how could he have betrayed her? Deep inside, he knew he wouldn't have cheated on her. Yet he couldn't dismiss the fact that he vaguely remembered Melinda James.

She glanced up sharply, as if sensing him for the first time, and she blushed. "I didn't hear you."

"It's okay, I was just watching."

"Well, come in and take a center seat. No reason to hide in the hall," she teased.

Parker grinned and hobbled into the kitchen where he half fell into one of the caned chairs. "Don't let me disturb you," he said.

"Wouldn't dream of it!" She pushed her glasses onto the bridge of her nose and continued reading a recipe card. "You're in for the thrill of your life," she declared. *"Coq au vin* à la Shawna. This is going to be great."

"I know," he admitted, folding his arms over his chest, propping his bad leg on a nearby chair, and grinning to himself. Great it would be, but he wasn't thinking about the chicken in wine.

Nine

Shawna eyed the dining room table critically. It gleamed with a fresh coat of wax and reflected the tiny flames of two creamy white candles. She'd polished the brass candlesticks and placed a fresh bouquet of roses and baby's breath between the flickering candles.

Tonight, whether Parker was agreeable or not, they were going to celebrate. She'd been living with him for over three weeks in a tentative truce. Fortunately, Melinda hadn't intruded, though Parker had spoken with her on the phone several times.

"Buck up," she told herself, as she thought about the girl. Melinda was pregnant and they couldn't ignore her. Even though neither she nor Parker had brought up the subject of Melinda's baby, it was always in the air, an invisible barrier between them.

In the past weeks, Parker had spent his days in physical therapy, either at Mercy Hospital or here, at the house.

Shawna rearranged one drooping flower and frowned. As a doctor, she knew that Parker was pushing himself to the limit, forcing muscles and ligaments to work, as if regaining full use of his leg would somehow trip his memory. Though Shawna had begged him to slow down, he'd refused to listen, mule-headedly driving himself into a state of utter exhaustion.

Finally, at the end of the third week, he'd improved

to the point that he was walking with only the aid of a cane.

To celebrate, she'd taken the afternoon off and had been waiting for him, cooking and cleaning and feeling nearly as if she belonged in his house—almost as if she were his wife.

She heard his car in the drive. Smiling, she hurried into the kitchen to add the last touches to the beef stroganoff simmering on the stove.

Parker opened the back door and collapsed into one of the kitchen chairs. His hair was dark with sweat and his face was gaunt and strained as he hung his cane over the back of his chair. He winced as he lifted his bad leg and propped it on a stool. Glancing up, he forced a tired smile. "Hi."

Shawna leaned over the counter separating kitchen from nook. "Hi, yourself."

"I thought you had the late shift."

"I traded so that we could have dinner together," she said.

"Sounds good." But he really wasn't listening. He was massaging his knee, his lips tightening as his fingers touched a particularly sensitive spot.

"You've been pushing yourself too hard again," she said softly, worried that he would do himself more damage than good.

"I don't think so."

"I'm a doctor."

He rolled his eyes. "Don't I know it?"

"Parker, please," she said, kneeling in front of him and placing a kiss on his sweat-dampened forehead. "Take it easy."

"I can't."

"There's plenty of time—"

"Do you really believe that?" He was staring at her suspiciously, as if he thought she was lying to him.

"You've got the rest of your—"

"Easy for you to say, *doctor*," he snapped. "You're

not facing the rest of your life with this!" He lifted his cane, then, furious with the damned thing, hurled it angrily across the room. It skidded on the blue tiles and smashed into a far wall.

Shawna wanted to lecture him, but didn't. Instead she straightened and pretended interest in the simmering sauce. "I, uh, take it the session wasn't the best."

"You take it right, doctor. But then you know everything, don't you?" He gestured toward the stove. "What I should eat, where I should sleep, how fast I should improve—all on your neat little schedule!"

His words stung and she gasped, before stiffening her back and pretending he hadn't wounded her. The tension between them had been mounting for weeks. He was disappointed, she told herself.

But he must have recognized her pain. He made a feeble gesture of apology with his hand, then, bracing his palms on the table, forced himself upright.

"I wish things were different," he finally said, gripping the counter with both hands, "but they're not. You're a good woman, Shawna—better than I deserve. Do yourself a favor and forget about me. Find yourself a whole man."

"I have," she whispered, her throat swollen tight. "He's just too pigheaded to know it."

"I mean it—"

"And so do I," she whispered. "I love you, Parker. I always will. That's just the way it is."

He stared at her in amazement, then leaned back, propping his head against the wall. "Oh, God," he groaned, covering his face with his hands. "You live in such a romantic dream world." When he dropped his hands, his expression had changed to a mask of indifference.

"If I live in a dream world," she said quietly, "it's a world that you created."

"Then it's over," he decided, straightening. "It's just . . . gone. It vanished that night."

Shawna ignored the stab of pain in her heart. "I don't believe you and I won't. Until you're completely well and have regained all of your memory, I won't give up."

"Shawna—"

"Remember that 'for better or worse' line?"

"We didn't get married."

Yet, she thought wildly. "Doesn't matter. In my heart I'm committed to you, and only when you tell me that you remember everything we shared and it means nothing to you—then I'll give up!"

"I just don't want to hurt you," he admitted, "ever again."

"You won't." The lie almost caught on her tongue.

"I wish I was as sure as you."

Her heart squeezed as she studied him, his body drenched in sweat, his shoulder balanced precariously against the wall.

As if reading the pity in her eyes, he swore, anger darkening his face. Casting her a disbelieving glance, he limped down the hall to his room and slammed the door so hard that the sound echoed through the old house.

Shawna stared after him. Why couldn't he remember how strong their love had been? *Why?* Feeling the need to break down and cry like a baby, she steeled herself. In frustration, she reached for the phone, hoping to call her brother or her friend Gerri or anyone to whom she could vent her frustrations. But when she placed the receiver to her ear, she heard Parker on the bedroom extension.

"That's right . . . everything you can find out about her. The name's James—Melinda James. I don't know her middle name. She claims to have been living in Cleveland and that she grew up with Brad Lomax."

Quietly, Shawna replaced the receiver. It seemed that no matter where she turned or how fiercely she clung to the ashes of the love she and Parker had once shared, the winds of fate blew them from her fingers. Dying a little inside, she wondered if he was right. Maybe the flames of their love couldn't be rekindled.

"Give him time," she told herself, but she knew their time was running out. She glanced around the old Tudor house, the home she'd planned to share with him. She'd moved in, but they were both living a lie. He didn't love her.

Swallowing against the dryness in her throat, she turned toward the sink and ran water over the spinach leaves in a colander. She ignored the tears that threatened to form in the corners of her eyes. *Don't give up!* part of her insisted, while the other, more reasonable side of her nature whispered, *Let him go.*

So intent was she on tearing spinach, cutting egg, and crumbling bacon that she didn't hear the uneven tread of his footsteps in the hall, didn't feel his gaze on her back as she worked, still muttering and arguing with herself.

Her first indication that he was in the room with her was the feel of his hands on her waist. She nearly dropped her knife as he bent his head and rested his chin on her shoulder.

"I'm not much good at apologies," he said softly.

"Neither am I."

"Oh, Shawna." His breath fanned her hair, warm and enticing, and her heart took flight. He'd come back! "I know you're doing what you think is best," he said huskily. "And I appreciate your help."

She dropped the knife and the tears she'd been fighting filled her eyes. "I've done it because I want to."

His fingers spanned her waist. "I just don't understand," he admitted, "why you want to put up with me."

She wanted to explain, but he cut her off, his arms encircling her waist, her body drawn to his. His breath was hot on the back of her head and delicious shivers darted along her spine as he pulled her close, so close that her back was pressed against the taut muscles of his chest. A spreading warmth radiated to her most outer limbs as his lips found her nape.

"I—I love you, Parker."

His muscles flexed and she silently prayed he would return those three simple words.

"That's why I'm working so hard," he conceded, his voice rough with emotion. "I want to be able to remember everything."

"I can wait," she said.

"But I can't! I want my life back—all of it. The way it was before the accident. Before—"

He didn't say it, but she knew. *Before Brad was killed, before Melinda James shattered our lives.*

"Maybe we should eat," she said, hoping to divert him from the guilt that ran rampant every time he thought about Brad.

"You've worked hard, haven't you?"

"It's a—well, it was a celebration."

"Oh?"

"Because you're off crutches and out of the brace," she said.

"I've still got that." He pointed to where the cane still lay on the floor.

"I know, but it's the final step."

"Except for my memory."

"It'll come back," she predicted, sounding more hopeful than she felt. "Come on, now," she urged. "Make yourself useful. Pour the wine before I ruin dinner and the candles burn out."

During dinner Shawna felt more lighthearted than she had in weeks. At the end of the meal, when Parker leaned forward and brushed his lips over hers, she thought fleetingly that together they could face anything.

"Thanks," he whispered, "for putting up with me."

"I wouldn't have it any other way." She could feel

her eyes shining in the candlelight, knew her cheeks were tinged with the blush of happiness.

"Let's finish this—" he said, holding the wine bottle by its neck, "—in the gazebo."

A dimple creased her cheek. "The gazebo?" she repeated, and grinned from ear to ear as she picked up their wineglasses and dashed to the hallway where her down coat hung. Her heart was pounding with excitement. Just two months earlier, Parker had proposed in the gazebo.

Hand in hand, they walked down a flagstone path that led to the river. The sound of water rushing over stones filled the night air and a breeze fresh with the scent of the Willamette lifted Shawna's hair.

The sky was clear and black. A ribbon of silver moonlight rippled across the dark water to illuminate the bleached wood and smooth white rocks at the river's edge. On the east bank, lights from neighboring houses glittered and reflected on the water.

Shawna, with Parker's help, stepped into the gazebo. The slatted wood building was built on the edge of Parker's property, on the ridge overlooking the Willamette. The gazebo was flanked by lilac bushes, no longer fragrant, their dry leaves rustling in the wind.

As Shawna stared across the water, she felt Parker's arms slip around her waist, his breath warm against her head, the heat from his body flowing into hers.

"Do—do you remember the last time we were here?" she whispered, her throat swollen with the beautiful memory.

He didn't say anything.

"You proposed," she prodded.

"Did I?"

"Yes." She turned in his arms, facing him. "Late in the summer."

Squinting his eyes, fighting the darkness shrouding his brain, he struggled, but nothing surfaced. "I'm sorry," he whispered, his night-darkened eyes searching hers.

"Don't apologize," she whispered. Moonlight shifted across his face, shadowing the sharp angles as he lowered his head and touched his lips to hers.

Gently, his fingers twined in her hair. "Sometimes I get caught up in your fantasies," he admitted, his lips twisting cynically.

"This isn't a fantasy," she said, seeing her reflection in his eyes. "Just trust me."

He leaned forward again, brushing his lips suggestively over hers. "That's the trouble. I do." He took the wine and glasses and set them on the bench. Placing his palms on her cheeks, he stared into her eyes before kissing her again. Eagerly she responded, her heart pulsing wildly at his touch, her mouth opening willingly to the erotic pressure of his tongue on her lips.

She felt his hands quiver as they slid downward to rest near her neck, gently massaging her nape, before pushing the coat from her shoulders. The night air surrounded her, but she wasn't cold.

Together, they slid slowly to the weathered floorboards and Parker adjusted her down coat, using its softness as a mattress. Then, still kissing her, he found the buttons of her blouse and loosened them, slipping the soft fabric down her shoulders.

Slowly he bent and pressed his moist lips against the base of her throat.

In response, she warmed deep within, stretching her arms around him, holding him tight, drinking in the smell and feel of him.

"Shawna," he whispered.

"Oh, Parker, love," she murmured.

"Tell me to stop."

"Don't ever stop," she cried.

He shuddered, as if trying to restrain himself, then, in one glorious minute, he crushed his lips to hers and kissed her more passionately than ever before. His hands caressed her skin, tearing at her blouse and the clasp of her bra, baring her breasts to the shifting moonlight. Slowly he lowered his head and touched each proud nipple with his lips, teasing the dark peaks to impatient attention.

"Ooh," she whispered, caught up in the warm, rolling sensations of his lips and tongue as he touched her, stoking fires that scorched as they raced through her blood and burned wantonly in her brain.

Reckless desire chased all rational thought away.

Her breath tangled with his and his hands touched her, sweeping off her skirt until she was naked in the night. Her skin was as white as alabaster in the darkness. Despite the cool river-kissed wind, she was warm deep inside, as she throbbed with need for this one special man.

His moist lips moved over her, caressing her, arousing her, stealing over her skin and causing her mind to scream with the want of him.

She found the hem of his sweater and pushed the offending garment over his head. He groaned in response and she unsnapped his jeans, her fingers sliding down the length of his legs as she removed the faded denim until, at last, they lay naked in the tiny gazebo—his body gleaming with a dewy coat of sweat, hers rosy with the blush of desire.

"I will always love you," she promised as he lowered himself over her, twisting his fingers in her hair, his eyes blue lusting flames.

"And I'll always love you," he vowed into her open mouth as his hands closed over her breasts, gently kneading the soft, proud nipples, still wet from his kiss.

Her fingers moved slowly down his back, touching firm smooth muscles and the gentle cleft of his spine.

Though her eyes wanted to close, she willed them open, staring up at him, watching the bittersweet torment on his face as he delved inside, burying himself in her only to withdraw again and again. Her heart slamming wildly, her blood running molten hot, she arched upward, moved by a primitive force and whispering words of love.

Caught in her own storm of emotion and the powerful force of his love, she lost herself to him, surrendering to the vibrant spinning world that was theirs alone. She felt the splendor of his hands, heard him cry out her name.

In one glorious moment he stiffened, his voice reverberating through the gazebo and out across the river, and Shawna, too, convulsed against his sweat-glistened body.

His breath was rapid and hot in her ear. "This . . . could be dangerous," he whispered hoarsely, running a shaking hand through his hair.

Still wrapped in the wonder and glow of passion, she held him close, pressed her lips to his sweat-soaked chest. "Don't talk. For just tonight, let's pretend that it's only you and me, and our love."

"I'm not much good at pretending." Glancing down at her plump breasts, he sighed, then reached past her to a glass on the bench. Swirling wine in the goblet, he said, "I don't think we should let this happen again."

"I don't think we have a choice."

"Oh, Shawna," he whispered, drinking his wine and setting the empty glass on the floor before he reached behind her, to wrap the coat over her suddenly chilled shoulders before holding her close. "This isn't a question of love," he said.

Crushed, she couldn't answer.

"I just think we both need time."

"Because of Melinda's baby."

"The baby has something to do with it," he admitted, propping himself against the bench. He drew her draped body next to his and whispered against her neck. "But there's more. I don't want to tie you down."

"But you're not—"

"Shh. Just listen. I'm not the man you were in love with before the accident. Too much has changed for us to be so naive to think that everything will be just as we'd planned, which, for the record, I still can't remember."

"You will," she said, though she felt a gaping hole in her heart.

Parker slid from behind her and reached for his clothes. He'd never intended to make love to her, to admit that he loved her, for crying out loud, but there it was—the plain simple truth: He loved her and he couldn't keep his hands off her.

"I think I'll go for a drive," he said, yanking his sweater over his head and sliding with difficulty into his jeans.

"Now?"

"I need time to think, Shawna. We both do," he said abruptly. Seeing the wounded look in her eyes he touched her cheek. "You know I care about you," he admitted, stroking her hair. "But I need a little space, just to work things out. I don't want either of us to make a mistake we'll regret later."

"Maybe we already have," she said, clutching her coat over her full breasts. She lifted her chin bravely, though deep inside, she was wounded to the core. Just minutes before he was loving her, now he was walking away!

"Maybe," he groaned, then straightened and hobbled to the door.

Shawna watched him amble up the path and shuddered when she heard the garage door slam behind him. He was gone. It was that simple. Right after making love to her for the first time, he'd walked away. The pain in her heart throbbed horribly, though she tried to believe that his words of love, sworn in the throes of passion, were the only real truth.

* * *

Brittle night wind raced through the car as Parker drove, his foot on the throttle, the windows rolled down. He pushed the speed limit, needing the cold night air to cool the passion deep in his soul. He was rocked to his very core by the depth of his feelings for Shawna. Never would he have believed himself capable of such all-consuming physical and mental torture. He wanted her—forever. He'd been on the verge of asking her to marry him back in the gazebo and damning the consequences.

"You're a fool," he chastised, shifting down, the car squealing around a curve in the road. Lights in the opposite lane dazzled and blinded him, bore down on him. "A damned fool."

The car in the oncoming lane passed, and memories crashed through the walls of his blocked mind. One by one they streamed into his consciousness. He remembered Brad, passed out and unconscious, and Melinda crying softly, clinging to Parker's shoulder. And Shawna—Lord, he remembered her, but not as he saw her now. Yes, he'd loved her because she was a beautiful, intelligent woman, but in the past, he hadn't felt this overpowering awe and voracious need that now consumed him.

He strained to remember everything, but couldn't. "Give it time," he said impatiently, but his fingers tightened over the wheel and he felt a desperate desire to know everything.

"Come on, come on," he urged, then realized that he was speeding, as if running from the black hole that was his past.

With difficulty, he eased up on the throttle and drove more cautiously, his hot blood finally cooled. Making love to Shawna had been a mistake, he decided, though a smile of satisfaction still hovered over his lips at the thought of her ivory-white body stretched sensually in the gazebo, her green eyes luminous with desire.

"Forget it," he muttered, palms suddenly damp. Until he remembered everything and knew she loved the man he was today, not the person she'd planned to marry before the accident, he couldn't risk making love to her again.

And that, he thought, his lips twisting wryly, was a crying shame.

Ten

"He's pushing too hard," Bob Killingsworth, Parker's physical therapist, admitted to Shawna one afternoon. She had taken the day off and had intended to spend it with Parker, but he was still in his indoor pool, swimming, using the strength of his arms to pull himself through the water. Though one muscular leg kicked easily, the other, the knee that had been crushed, was stiff and inflexible and dragged noticeably.

"That's it!" Bob called, cupping his hands around his mouth and shouting at Parker.

Parker stood in the shallow end and rubbed the water from his face. "Just a couple more laps."

Glancing at his watch, Bob frowned. "I've got to get to the hospital—"

"I don't need a keeper," Parker reminded him.

"It's all right," Shawna whispered, "I'll stay with him."

"Are you sure?"

"I *am* a doctor."

"I know, but—" Bob shrugged his big shoulders. "Whatever you say."

As Bob left, Shawna kicked off her shoes.

"Joining me?" Parker mocked.

"I just might." The tension between them crackled. Since he'd left her the night they had made love, they had barely spoken. With an impish grin, she slid quickly out of her panty hose and sat on the edge of the pool near the diving board, her legs dangling into the water.

"That looks dangerous, Doctor," Parker predicted from the shallow end.

"I doubt it."

"Oh?" Smothering a devilish grin, Parker swam rapidly toward her, his muscular body knifing through the water. She watched with pride. In two weeks, he'd made incredible strides, physically if not mentally.

He'd always been an athlete and his muscles were strident and powerful. His shoulders were wide, his chest broad and corded. His abdomen was flat as it disappeared inside his swimming trunks to emerge again in the form of lean hips and strong legs—well, at least one strong leg. His right knee was still ablaze with angry red scars.

As he reached the deep end of the pool, he surfaced and his incredible blue eyes danced mischievously. He tossed his hair from his face and water sprayed on her blouse.

"What's on your mind?" she asked, grinning.

"I thought you were coming in."

"And I thought I'd change first."

"Did you?" One side of his mouth lifted into a crafty grin.

"Oh, Parker, no—" she said, just as she felt strong hands wrap over her ankles. "You wouldn't—"

But he did. Over her protests, he gently started swimming backward, pulling her off her bottom and into the pool, wool skirt, silk blouse, and all.

"You're despicable!" she sputtered, surfacing, her hair drenched.

"Probably."

"And cruel and . . . and heartless . . . and—"

"Adorable," he cut in, laughing so loudly the rich sound echoed on the rafters over the pool. His hands had moved upward over her legs, to rest at her hips as she hung by the tips of her fingers at the edge of the pool.

"That, too," she admitted, lost in his eyes as he studied her. Heart pounding erratically, she could barely breathe as his head lowered and his lips brushed erotically over hers.

"So are you." One strong arm gripped her tighter, so fierce and possessive that her breath was trapped somewhere between her throat and lungs, while he clung to the side of the pool with his free hand. "Oh, so are you."

Knowing she was playing with proverbial fire, she warned herself to leave, but she was too caught up in the wonder of being held by him, the feel of his wet body pressed against hers, to consider why his feelings had changed. She didn't care that her clothes were ruined. She'd waited too long for this glorious moment—to have him hold her and want her again.

His tongue rimmed her mouth before parting her lips insistently. Moaning her surrender she felt his mouth crush against hers, his tongue touch and glide with hers, delving delicately then flicking away as she ached for more. Her blood raced uncontrollably, and her heart hammered crazily against her ribs.

She didn't know why he had chosen this moment to love her again. She could only hope that he'd somehow experienced a breakthrough with his memory and could remember everything—especially how much they had loved each other.

His warm lips slid lower on her neck to the base of her throat and the white skin exposed between the lapels of her soggy blouse. The wet silk clung to her, and her nipples, proudly erect, were visible beneath the thin layer of silk and lace, sweetly enticing just above the lapping water.

Lazily, as if he had all the time in the world, his tongue touched her breast, hot as it pressed against her skin. She cried out, couldn't help herself, as he slowly placed his mouth against her, nuzzling her, sending white-hot rivulets of desire through her veins.

She could only cling to him, holding his head against her breast, feeling the warmth within her start to glow and a dull ache begin to throb deep at her center.

She didn't resist as with one hand he undid the buttons of her blouse, baring her shoulders, and letting the sodden piece of silk drift downward into the clear depths of the pool. Her bra, a flimsy scrap of lace, followed.

She was bare from the waist up, her breasts straining and full beneath his gaze as clear water lapped against her white skin.

"You are so beautiful," he groaned, as if her beauty were a curse. He gently reached forward, softly stroking her skin, watching in fascination as her nipple tightened, his eyes devouring every naked inch of her skin. "This is crazy, absolutely crazy," he whispered. Then, almost angrily, he lifted her up and took one bare nipple into his mouth, feasting hungrily on the soft white globe, his hand against her back, causing goose bumps to rise on her skin.

"Love me," she cried, aching to be filled with his spirit and soul. Her hands tangled in the hair of his chest and her eyes glazed as she whispered, "Please, Parker, make love to me."

"Right here?" he asked, lifting his head, short of breath.

"I don't care . . . anywhere."

His lips found hers again and as he kissed her, feeling her warm body in the cool water, a jagged piece of memory pricked his mind. Hadn't there been another time, another place, when Shawna—or had it been another woman—had pleaded with him to make love to her?

The sun had been hot and heat shimmered in vibrant waves over the river. They were lying in a canoe, the boat rocking quietly as he'd kissed her, his heart pounding in his ears, her suntanned body molded against his. She'd whispered his name, her voice rough with longing, then . . .

Just as suddenly as the memory had appeared, it slipped away again.

"Parker?"

He blinked, finding himself in the pool with Shawna, her green eyes fixed on his, her white skin turning blue in the suddenly cold water.

"What is it?"

"I don't know," he admitted, frustrated all over again. If only he could remember! If only he could fill the holes in his life! He released her and swam to the edge of the pool. "I think maybe you'd better get dressed," he decided, hoisting his wet body out of the water and reaching for a towel. "I—I'm sorry about your clothes."

"No—"

But he was already limping toward the door.

Dumbfounded, she dived for her blouse and bra, struggled into them, and surfaced at the shallow end. "You've got a lot of nerve," she said, breathing rapidly, her pride shattered as she climbed, dripping out of the pool. "What was *that*?" Gesturing angrily, she encompassed the entire high-ceilinged room to include the intimacy they'd just shared.

"A mistake," he said, wincing a little. Snatching his cane from a towel rack, he turned to the door.

"Mistake?" she yelled. "Mistake?" Boiling, her female ego trampled upon one too many times, she caught up to him and placed herself, with her skirt and blouse still dripping huge puddles on the concrete, squarely in his path. "Just like the other night was a mistake?"

His gaze softened. "I told you—we need time."

But she wasn't listening. "I know what you're doing," she said, pointing an accusing finger at him. "You're trying to shame me into leaving!"

"That's ridiculous!"

"Is it? Then explain what that scene in the pool was all about! We nearly made love, for crying out loud, and now you're walking out of here as if nothing happened. Just like the other night! That's it, isn't it? You're trying to mortify me!" All her pent-up emotions exploded, and without thinking she slapped him, her palm smacking as it connected with his jaw. The sound reverberated through the room.

"Thank you, Dr. McGuire," he muttered, his temper erupting. "Once again your bedside manner is at its finest!" Without another word he strode past her, limping slightly as he yanked open the door and slammed it shut behind him.

Shawna slumped against the brick wall. She felt as miserable and bedraggled as she looked in her wet clothes. Stung by his bitterness and the cruelty she'd seen in his gaze, she closed her eyes, feeling the cold of the bricks permeate her damp clothes. Had he set her up on purpose? Her head fell to her hands. Had he planned to make love to her only to throw her aside, in order to wound her and get her out of his life? "Bastard!" she cursed, flinging her wet hair over her shoulder.

Maybe she should leave. Maybe there was no chance of ever recovering what they had lost. Maybe, just maybe, their love affair was truly over. Sick at heart, she sank down against the wall and huddled in a puddle of water near the door.

Then her fists clenched tightly and she took a long, steadying breath. She wouldn't give up—not yet, because she believed in their love. She just had to get him to see things her way!

* * *

Parker slammed his bedroom door and uttered a quick oath. What had he been thinking about back there in the pool? Why had he let her get to him that way? He yanked off his wet swim trunks and threw them into a corner.

Muttering to himself, he started to struggle into a pair of old jeans when the door to his room swung open and Shawna, managing to hold her head high though her clothes were wet and dripping and her hair hung lankily around her face, said, "You've got company."

"I don't want—"

"Too late. She's here."

"She?" he repeated, seeing the pain in her eyes.

"Melinda. She's waiting in the den."

Parker zipped up his jeans, aware of her gaze following his movements. He didn't care, he told himself, didn't give one damn what she thought. Grabbing a T-shirt and yanking it over his head, he frowned and made a sound of disgust. "What's she doing here?" he finally asked, holding onto the rails of the bed as he hobbled toward the door.

"Your guess is as good as mine, but I don't think I'll stick around to find out. You know the old saying, three's a crowd."

He watched as she marched stiffly upstairs. He could hear her slamming drawers and he cringed as he made his way to the den.

Melinda was there all right. Standing next to the windows, she straightened as he entered. "So Shawna's still here," she said without any trace of inflection.

"So far."

"And she's staying?" Melinda asked, not meeting his eyes.

"That remains to be seen." He flinched as he heard Shawna stomping overhead. A light fixture rattled in the ceiling. Cocking his head toward an old rocker, he said, "Have a seat."

"No. I'm not staying long. I just came to find out what you intend to do—about the baby, I mean. You do remember, don't you? About the baby?"

Sighing wearily, he stretched his bad leg in front of him and half fell onto the raised hearth of the fire-place. The stones were cold and dusty with ash, but he couldn't have cared less. "What do you want to do?" he asked.

"I don't know." Her chin quivered a little and she chewed on her lower lip. "I suppose you want me to have an abortion."

His skin paled and he felt as if she'd just kicked him in the stomach. "No way. There are lots of alternatives. Abortion isn't one."

She closed her eyes. "Good," she whispered, obvi-ously relieved as she wrapped her arms around herself. "So what about us?"

"Us?"

"Yes—you and me."

He heard Shawna stomp down the stairs and slam the front door shut behind her. Glancing out the win-dow, he saw her, head bent against the wind as she ran to her car. Suddenly he felt as cold as the foggy day.

"Parker?"

He'd almost forgotten Melinda and he glanced up swiftly. She stared at him with wounded eyes and it was hard for him to believe she was lying—yet he couldn't remember ever loving her.

"We have a baby on the way." Swallowing hard, she fought tears that began to drizzle down her face and lowered her head, her black hair glossy as it fell over her face. "You still don't believe me," she accused, her voice breaking.

"I don't know what to believe," he admitted. Lean-ing his head back against the stones, he strained for images of that night. His head began to throb with the effort. Dark pieces emerged. He remembered seeing her that rainy night, thought she'd held him and cried into the crook of his neck. Had he stroked her hair, comforted her? God, if he could only remember!

"You're falling in love with her again," she charged, sniffing, lifting her head. When he didn't answer, she wiped at her eyes and crossed the room. "Don't be fooled, Parker. She'll lie to you, try to make you doubt me. But this," she patted her abdomen, "is proof of our love."

"If it's mine," he said slowly, watching for any sign that she might be lying. A shadow flickered in her gaze—but only for an instant—then her face was set again with rock-solid resolve.

"Just think long and hard about the night before you were supposed to get married, Parker. Where were you before the accident? In whose bed?"

His skin tightened. Surely he hadn't— Eyes narrowing, he stared up at her. "If I was in your bed, where was Brad?" he asked, as memory after painful memory pricked at his conscience only to escape before he could really latch on to anything solid.

"Passed out on the couch," she said bitterly, hiking the strap of her purse over her shoulder. "He'd drunk too much."

He almost believed her. Something about what she was saying was true. He could sense it. "So," he said slowly, "if I'd planned to stay with you that night, why didn't I take Brad home first?"

She paled a bit, then blinked back sudden tears. "Beats me. Look, I'm not trying to hassle you or Shawna. I just took her advice by giving you all the facts."

"And what do you expect to get out of it?" he asked, studying the tilt of her chin.

"Hey, don't get the wrong idea, you don't *have* to marry me—we never had that kind of a deal, but I do want my son to know his father and I would expect you to . . ." She lifted one shoulder. "You know . . . take care of us."

"Financially?"

She nodded, some of her hard edge dissipating. "What happened—the accident and you losing your memory—isn't really fair to the baby, is it?"

"Maybe nothing's fair," he said, then raked his fingers through his hair. He'd never let anyone manipulate him and he had the distinct feeling that Melinda James was doing just that. Scowling, he felt cornered, and he wanted to put her in her place. But he couldn't. No matter what the truth of the matter was, her unborn child hadn't asked to be brought into a world with a teenager for a mother and no father to care for him.

When the phone rang, she stood. "Think about it," she advised, swinging her purse over her shoulder and heading toward the door.

Closing his eyes, he dropped his face into his hands and tried to think, tried to remember sleeping with Melinda, making love to her.

But he couldn't remember anything. Though he strained to concentrate on the dark-haired young woman who claimed to be carrying his child, the image that swam in front of his eyes was the flushed and laughing face of Shawna McGuire as she clung to the neck of a white carousel stallion.

Once again he saw her laughing, her blond hair billowing behind her as she reached, grabbing blindly for a ribboned brass ring. Or was the image caused by looking too long at photographs of that fateful day?

Think, Harrison, think!

A fortune-teller with voluminous skirts sat by a small table in a foul-smelling tent as she held Shawna's palm. Gray clouds gathered overhead, rain began to pepper the ground, the road was dark and wet, and Brad was screaming. . . .

Parker gritted his teeth, concentrating so much his

entire head throbbed. He had to remember. He had to!

The phone rang again, for the fourth or fifth time, and he reached to answer it just in time to hear the smooth voice of Lon Saxon, a friend and private detective. "That you, Parker?"

"Right here," Parker replied.

"Good. I've got some of the information you wanted on Melinda James."

Parker's guts wrenched. Here it was. The story. "Okay, tell me all about her."

Shawna's fingers were clammy on the wheel as she turned into the drive of Parker's house. After driving aimlessly through the damp streets of Portland, she decided she had to return and confront him. She couldn't run from him and Melinda's baby like some wounded animal.

Silently praying that Melinda had already left, Shawna was relieved to see that the girl's tiny convertible wasn't parked in the drive.

"Remember that he loves you," she told herself as she flicked off the engine and picked up the white bags of hamburgers she'd bought at a local fast-food restaurant. "Just give him time."

Inside, the house was quiet, and for a heartstopping minute, Shawna thought Parker had left with Melinda. The den was dark and cold, the living room empty. Then she noticed a shaft of light streaming from under the door of his bedroom.

She knocked lightly on the panels, then poked her head inside.

He was still dressed in the old jeans but his shirt was hanging limply from a post on the bed, and his chest was stripped bare. His head was propped by huge pillows and he stared straight at her as if he'd never seen her before.

"Truce?" she asked, holding up two white bags of food.

He didn't move, except to shift his gaze to the bags.

"Was it bad? With Melinda?"

"Did you expect it to be good?"

Hanging on to her emotions, she walked into the room and sat on the bed next to him. The mattress sagged a little, but still he didn't move.

Though her hands were trembling, she opened one bag and held out a paper-wrapped burger. When he ignored the offering she set it, along with the white sacks, on the nightstand. "I didn't expect anything. Every day has a new set of surprises," she admitted, tossing her hair over her shoulders and staring straight at him, refusing to flinch. "Look, let's be completely honest with each other."

"Haven't we been?"

"I don't know," she admitted. "I—I just don't know where I stand with you any more."

"Then maybe you should move out."

"Maybe," she said slowly, and saw a streak of pain darken his eyes. "Is that what you want?"

"Honesty? Isn't that what you said?"

"Yes." She braced herself for the worst.

His jaw grew rock hard. "Then, *honestly*, I want to do the right thing. If the baby's mine—"

"It isn't," she said.

The look he gave her cut straight through her heart. "Do you know something I don't?"

"No, but—*Yes*. I do know something—something you don't remember—that we loved each other, that we would never have betrayed each other, that Melinda's baby *can't* be yours."

"I remember her," he said softly.

She gave a weak sound of protest.

His throat worked. "And I remember being with her that night—holding her. She was crying and—"

"No! This is all part of her lies!" Shawna screamed, her stomach twisting painfully, her breath constricted and tight. She wanted to lash out and hit anyone or anything that stood in her way. "You're lying to me!"

"Listen to me, damn it!" he said, grabbing her wrist and pulling her forward so that she fell across his chest, her hair spilling over his shoulders. "I remember being with her that night. Everything's not clear, I'll grant you that. But I was in her apartment!"

"Oh, no," she whispered.

"And there's more."

"Parker, please—"

"You were the one who wanted honesty, remember?" His words were harsh, but there wasn't any trace of mockery in his eyes, just blue, searing torment.

"No—"

"Her story checks out, at least part of it. I had a private detective in Cleveland do some digging. Her mother's dead. Her father is an unemployed steelworker who hasn't held a job in ten years! Melinda supported him while she went to high school. He was furious with her when he found out she was pregnant."

Shawna's fingers clenched over the sheets. "That doesn't mean—"

"It means she's not a chronic liar and she obviously has some sense of right and wrong."

"Then we'll just have to wait, won't we?" she asked dully, her entire world black. "Until you regain your memory or the baby's born and paternity tests can be run."

"I don't think so," he said thoughtfully. She didn't move, dread mounting in her heart, knowing the axe was about to fall. "She told me she wants me to recognize the baby as mine and provide support."

"She wants you to marry her, doesn't she? She expects it?"

"No—" he let his voice drop off.

"But you're considering it!" Shawna gasped, all her hopes dashed as the realization struck her. Parker was going to do the noble deed and marry a girl he didn't know! Cold to the bone, she tried to scramble away, but he held her fast. "This is crazy—you *can't* marry her. You don't even remember her!"

"I remember enough," he said, his voice oddly hollow.

For the first time Shawna considered the horrid fact that he might be the baby's father, that he might have betrayed her the week and night before their wedding, had one last fling with a young girl. "I . . . I don't think I want to hear this," she whispered.

"You wanted the truth, Shawna. So here it is: I'm responsible for Melinda's predicament and I can't ignore that responsibility or pretend it doesn't exist, much as I might want to." His eyes searched her face and she recognized his pain—the bare, glaring fact that he still loved her. She could smell the maleness of him, hear the beating of his heart, feel the warmth of his skin, and yet he was pushing her away.

"Please, Parker, don't do this—"

"I have no choice."

"You're claiming the baby," she whispered, eyes moist, insides raw and bleeding.

"Yes." His jaw was tight, every muscle in his body rigid as he took in a long, shaky breath. "So—I think it would be better for everyone involved if you moved out."

She closed her eyes as her world began spinning away from her. All her hopes and dreams were just out of reach. She felt his grip slacken. Without a word, she walked to the door. "I—I'll start packing in the morning," she whispered.

"Good."

Then, numb from head to foot, she closed the door behind her. As she slowly mounted the stairs, she thought she heard him swear and then there was a huge crash against one of the walls, as if a fist or object had collided with plaster. But she didn't pay any attention. All she could think about was the horrid emptiness that was her future—a future barren and bleak without Parker.

Eleven

Tossing off the covers, Shawna rolled over and stared at the clock. Three A.M. and the room was pitch black except for the green digital numbers. Tomorrow she was leaving, giving up on Parker.

Before a single tear slid down her cheek, she searched in the darkness for her robe. Her fingers curled in the soft terry fabric and she fought the urge to scream. How could he do this? Why couldn't he remember?

Angry with herself, Parker, and the world in general, she yanked open the door to her room and padded silently along the hall and down the stairs, her fingers trailing on the banister as she moved quietly in the darkness. She didn't want to wake Parker, though she didn't really know why. The thought that he was sleeping peacefully while she was ripped to ribbons inside was infuriating.

In the kitchen she rattled around for a mug, the powdered chocolate, and a carton of milk. Then, while her cocoa was heating in the microwave, she felt a wild need to escape, to run away from the house that trapped her with its painful memories.

Without really thinking she unlocked the French doors of the dining room and walked outside to the balcony overlooking the dark Willamette. The air was fresh and bracing, the sound of the river soothing as it flowed steadily toward the Columbia.

Clouds scudded across a full moon, filtering thin beams of moonlight which battled to illuminate the night and cast shadows on the river. Leaves, caught in the wind, swirled and drifted to the ground.

Shivering, Shawna tightened her belt and leaned forward over the rail, her fingers curling possessively around the painted wood. This house was to have been hers, but losing the house didn't matter. Losing Parker was what destroyed her. She would gladly have lived in a shack with him, if only he could have found his way back to her. But now it was over. Forever.

She heard the microwave beep. Reluctantly she turned, her breath catching in her throat when she found Parker staring at her, one shoulder propped against the open French door.

"Couldn't sleep either?" he asked, his night-darkened gaze caressing her face.

"No." She lifted her chin upward, unaware that moonlight shimmered silver in her hair and reflected in her eyes. "Can I get you a cup?" she asked, motioning toward the kitchen. "Hot chocolate's supposed to do the trick."

"Is that your professional opinion?" For once there was no sarcasm in his voice.

"Well, you know me," she said, laughing bitterly at the irony. "At least you did. But maybe you don't remember that I don't put too much stock in prescriptions—sleeping pills and the like. Some of the old-fashioned cures are still the best. So, if you want, I'll fix you a cup."

"I don't think so."

Knowing she should leave, just brush past him, grab her damned cocoa and hightail it upstairs, she stood, mesmerized, realizing that this might be their last moment alone. She couldn't help staring pointedly at his bare chest, at his muscles rigid and strident, his jeans riding low over his hips. Nor could she ignore his brooding and thoughtful expression. His angular features were dark and his eyes, what she could see of them, were focused on her face and neck. As his gaze drifted lower to linger at the cleft of her breasts and the wisp of white lace from her nightgown, she swallowed against her suddenly dry throat.

"I thought you should have this," he said quietly as he walked across the balcony, reached into the pocket of his jeans, and extracted the brass ring he'd won at the fair. Even in the darkness she recognized the circle of metal and the ribbons fluttering in the breeze. "You should have caught this that day."

"You remember?" she asked quickly as her fingers touched the cold metal ring.

"Pieces."

Hope sprang exuberantly in her heart. "Then—"

"It doesn't change anything."

"But—"

His hand closed over hers, warm and comforting, as his fingers forced hers to curl over the ring. "Take it."

"Parker, please, talk to me!" Desperate, she pleaded with him. "If you remember—then you know the baby—"

His jaw grew rock hard. "I don't know for sure, but you have to accept that the baby is mine," he said, his eyes growing distant. He turned then, limping across the balcony and through the kitchen.

For a few minutes Shawna just stared at the damned ring in her hands as memory after painful memory surfaced. Then, unable to stop herself from trying one last time, she practically flew into the house and down the hall, her bare feet slapping against the wooden floors. "Parker, wait!"

She caught up with him in his bedroom. "Leave it, Shawna," he warned.

"But you remember!" Breathless, her heart hammering, she faced him. "You know what we meant to each other!"

"What I remember," he said coldly, though his gaze said differently, "is that you wouldn't sleep with me."

"We had an agreement," she said weakly, clasping the post of his bed for support. "Maybe it was stupid, but—"

"And you teased me—"

"I what?" But she'd heard the words before. Stricken, she could only whisper, "It was a joke between us. You used to laugh!"

"I told you then you'd drive me to a mistress," he said, his brows pulling down sharply over his eyes.

"You're doing this on purpose," she accused him. "You're forcing yourself to be cruel—just to push me away! All that business about having a mistress . . . you were kidding . . . it was just a little game . . . oh, God." She swayed against the post. Had she really been so blind? Had Parker and Melinda—? Numb inside she stumbled backward. Before she could say or do anything to further degrade herself, she scrambled out of the room.

"Shawna—"

She heard him call, but didn't listen.

"I didn't mean to—"

But she was already up the stairs, slamming the door shut, embarrassed to tears as she flipped on the light and jerked her suitcases from the closet to fling them open on the bed.

"Damn it, Shawna! Come down here."

No way! She couldn't trust herself, not around him. She wouldn't. She felt close to tears but wouldn't give into them. Instead she flung clothes—dresses, sweaters, underwear, slacks—anything she could find into the first suitcase and slammed it shut.

"Listen to me—"

Dear God, his voice was closer! He was actually struggling up the stairs! What if he fell? What if he lost his balance and stumbled backward! "Leave me alone, Parker!" she shouted, snapping the second suitcase shut. She found her purse, slung the strap over her shoulder, slipped into her shoes, and hauled both bags to the landing.

He was there. His face was red from the exertion of the climb, and his eyes were blazing angrily. "Look," he said, reaching for her, but she spun out of his grasp and he nearly fell backward down the steep stairs.

"Stop it!" she cried, worried sick that he would stumble. "Just stop it!"

"I didn't mean to hurt you—"

"Too late! But it doesn't matter. Not any more. It's over. I'm leaving you alone. That's what you want, isn't it? It's what you've been telling me to do all along. You've got your wish."

"Please—"

Her traitorous heart told her to stay, but this time, damnit, she was going to think with her head. "Good luck, Parker," she choked out. "I mean it, really. I—I wish you the best." Then she ran down the stairs, feeling the tears filling her eyes as she fled through the front door.

The night wind tore at her robe and hair as she raced down the brick path to the garage and the safety of her little hatchback. Gratefully she slid behind the steering wheel and with trembling fingers flicked on the ignition. The engine roared to life just as Parker opened the kitchen door and snapped on the overhead light in the garage.

Shawna sent up a silent prayer of thanks that he'd made it safely downstairs. Then she shoved the gearshift into reverse and the little car squealed out of the garage.

Driving crazily along the empty highway toward Lake Oswego, she could barely breathe. She had to fight to keep from sobbing hysterically as she sought the only safe refuge she knew. Jake—her brother—she could stay with him.

Slow down, she warned herself, as she guided the car

toward the south side of the lake where Jake lived in a small bungalow. *Please be home,* she thought as she parked, grabbed her suitcases, and trudged up the front steps to the porch.

The door opened before she could knock and Jake, his dark hair falling in wild locks over his forehead, his jaw stubbled, his eyes bleary, grabbed the heaviest bag. "Come on in, Sis," he said, eyeing her gravely.

"You knew?"

"Parker called. He was worried about you."

She let out a disgusted sound, but when Jake kicked the door shut and wrapped one strong arm around her, she fell apart, letting out the painful sobs that ripped at her soul.

"It's okay," he whispered.

"I wonder if it will ever be," Shawna said, before emitting a long, shuddering sigh and shivering from the cold.

"Come on," Jake suggested, propelling her to the tiny alcove that was his kitchen. "Tell me what happened."

"I don't think I can."

"You don't have much choice. You talk and I'll cook. The best omelet in town."

Shawna's stomach wrenched at the thought of food. "I'm not hungry."

"Well, I am," he said, plopping her down in one of the creaky kitchen chairs and opening the refrigerator, "So, come on, spill it. Just what the hell happened between you and Parker tonight?"

Swallowing hard, Shawna clasped her hands on the table and started at the beginning.

Parker could have kicked himself. Angry with himself, the world, and one lying Melinda James, he ignored the fact that it was the middle of the night and dialed his lawyer.

The phone rang five times before he heard Martin Calloway's groggy voice. "Hello?" he mumbled.

"Hello. This is—"

"I know who it is, Harrison. Do you have any idea what time it is?"

"Vaguely."

"And whatever's on your mind couldn't wait 'til morning?"

"That's about the size of it," Parker said, his gaze roving around the dark, empty kitchen. Damn, but the house felt cold without Shawna. "I want you to draw up some papers."

"Some papers," Martin repeated dryly. "Any particular kind?"

"Adoption," Parker replied flatly, "and post-date them by about six or seven months."

"Wait a minute—what the hell's going on?"

"I've had a breakthrough," Parker said, his entire life crystal clear since his argument with Shawna. "Something happened tonight that brought everything back and now I need to straighten out a few things."

"By adopting a child that isn't born yet?"

"For starters—I don't care how you handle it—I just want to make sure the adoption will be legal and binding."

"I'll need the mother's signature."

"I don't think that will be a problem," Parker said. "Oh—and just one other thing. I want to keep the fact that I'm remembering again a secret."

"Any particular reason?"

"There's someone I have to tell—after we get whatever letters of intent for adoption or whatever it's called signed."

"I'll work on it in the morning."

"Great."

Parker hung up and walked restlessly to his bedroom. He thought about chasing Shawna down at Jake's and admitting that he remembered his past, but decided to wait until everything was settled. This time, he wasn't going to let anything come between them!

If Shawna had known the torment she was letting herself in for, she might have thought twice about leaving Parker so abruptly. Nearly a week had dragged by, one day slipping into the next in a simple routine of patients, hospitals, and sleepless nights. Though Shawna fought depression, it clung to her like a heavy black cloak, weighing down her shoulders and stealing her appetite.

"You can't go on like this," Jake said one morning, as Shawna, dressed in a skirt and blouse, sipped a cup of coffee and scanned the newspaper without interest.

"Or *you* can't?" Shawna replied.

Jake's dog, Bruno, was lying under the table. With one brown eye and one blue, he stared at Maestro and growled as the precocious tabby hopped onto the window ledge. Crouching behind a broad-leafed plant, his tail twitching, Maestro glared longingly past the glass panes to the hanging bird feeder where several snowbirds pecked at seeds.

Jake refused to be distracted. "If you don't believe that you're moping around here, take a look in the mirror, for Pete's sake."

"No, thank you."

"Shawna, you're killing yourself," Jake accused, sitting angrily in the chair directly across from hers.

"I'm leaving, just as soon as I find a place."

"I don't care about that, for crying out loud."

"I'm not 'moping' or 'killing myself' so don't you dare try to psychoanalyze me," she warned, raising her eyes to stare at him over the rim of her cup. He didn't have to remind her that she looked bad, for heaven's sake. She could feel it.

"Someone's got to," Jake grumbled. "You and Parker are so damned bullheaded."

Her heartbeat quickened at the sound of his name. If only he'd missed her!

"He looks twice as bad as you do."

"That's encouraging," she muttered, but hated the sound of her voice. Deep down, she wanted Parker to be happy and well.

"Talk to him."

"No."

"He's called twice."

Frowning, Shawna set her cup on the table. "It's over, Jake. That's the way he wanted it, and I'm tired of being treated as if my emotions don't mean a damned thing. Whether he meant to or not, he found my heart, threw it to the ground, and then stomped all over it."

"So now you don't care?"

"I didn't say that! And you're doing it again. Don't talk to me like you're my shrink, for Pete's sake."

Jake wouldn't be silenced. "Okay, so I'll talk like your brother. You're making one helluva mistake here."

"Not the first."

"Cut the bull, Shawna. I know you. You're hurting and you still love him even if you think he's a bastard. Isn't it worth just one more chance?"

She thought of the brass ring, still tucked secretly in the pocket of her robe. "Take a chance," Parker had told her at the fair that day. Dear Lord, it seemed ages ago.

"I'm out of chances."

Jake leaned over the table, his gaze fastened on her. "I've never thought you were stupid, Shawna. Don't change my mind, okay?" Glancing at the clock over the stove, he swore, grabbing his suit jacket from the

back of a chair. "Do yourself a favor. Call him back."
With this last bit of brotherly advice, Jake swung out
the door, then returned, his face flushed. "And move
your car, okay? Some of us have to work today."

She felt like sticking her tongue out at him, but instead she grabbed her purse and keys and swung her
coat over her shoulders. The beginning of a plan had
begun to form in her mind—and if Jake was right
about Parker . . .

"You don't have to leave," Jake said as they walked
down the frost-crusted path to the garage. "Just move
that miserable little car of yours."

"I think I'd better get started."

"Doing what?" he asked. "You have the next couple
of days off, don't you?"

She grabbed the handle of her car door and flashed
him a secretive smile as she climbed inside, "Maybe
you're right. Maybe I should do more than mope
around here."

"What's that supposed to mean?" he asked suspiciously.

"I'm not sure. But I'll let you know." Waving with
one hand, she rammed her car into gear and backed
out of his driveway. With only the barest idea of what
she was planning, she parked in front of the house
and waited until Jake had roared out of sight.

Spurred into action, she hurried back inside Jake's
house, called her friend Gerri, and threw some clothes
into a bag.

Her heart was in her throat as she climbed back
into her car. She could barely believe the plan that
had formed in her mind. Ignoring the screaming protests in her mind, she drove through the fog, heading
north until she slammed on the brakes at the street
leading toward the Willamette River and Parker's
house.

Her hands were damp. What if he wasn't home? Or
worse yet, what if he had company? Perhaps Melinda?

Well, that would be too damned bad. Because it's now or never!

Her muscles were so rigid they ached as she drove, her jaw firm with determination as Parker's huge house loomed to the side of the road. Without hesitation, she cranked the wheel, coasted along the long asphalt drive and parked near the brick path leading to the front door.

Then, with all the confidence she could gather, she marched up the path and rang the bell.

Twelve

Shawna held her breath as the door swung inward, and Parker, dressed in cords and a soft sweater, stared at her. Her heart started knocking against her rib cage as she looked into his eyes.

"Well, if this isn't a surprise," he drawled, not moving from the door. His face was unreadable. Not an emotion flickered in his eyes.

"I had a few things to sort out," she said.

"And are they sorted out?"

Nervously, she licked her lips. "Just about. I thought maybe we should talk, and I'm sorry I didn't return your calls."

Still suspicious, he pushed open the door. "Fair enough."

"Not here," she said quickly. "Someplace where we won't be disturbed."

"Such as?"

Shawna forced a friendly smile. "For starters, let's just drive."

He hesitated a minute, then shrugged, as if it didn't matter what she wanted to discuss—nothing would change. Yanking his fleece-lined jacket off the hall tree, he eyed his cane hanging on a hook but left it.

Striding back to the car, Shawna held her breath and felt his eyes bore into her back as he walked unsteadily after her and slid into the passenger side of the hatchback.

Without a word, she climbed behind the wheel and started out the drive. A surge of self-doubts assailed her. If he had any idea that she planned to kidnap him for the weekend, he'd be furious. She might have ruined any chance they had of ever getting back together again.

But it was a risk she had to take. The longer they were apart, she felt, the more likely stubborn pride would get in their way.

She put the little car through its paces, heading west amidst the fog still clinging to the upper reaches of the west hills. "So talk," Parker suggested, his arms crossed over his chest, his jean jacket stretched tight over his shoulders.

"I've had a lot of time to think," she said, gambling, not really knowing what to say now that he was sitting in the seat next to hers, his legs stretched close, his shoulder nearly touching hers. "And I think I acted rashly."

"We both behaved like children," he said, staring straight ahead as the city gave way to suburbs. Parker looked around, as if noticing for the first time that they'd left Portland far behind. Ahead the blue-gray mountains of the coast range loomed into view. "Where're we going?" he asked, suddenly apprehensive.

"To the beach." She didn't dare glance at him, afraid her emotions were mirrored in her eyes.

"The *beach*?" he repeated, stunned. "Why?"

"I think more clearly when I'm near the ocean." That, at least, wasn't a lie.

"But it's already afternoon. We won't be back until after dark."

"Is that a problem?"

"I guess not."

"Good. I know this great candy store in Cannon Beach—"

He groaned, and Shawna, glimpsing him from the

corner of her eye, felt a growing sense of satisfaction.
So he did remember—she could see it in his gaze.
Earlier in the summer they'd visited Cannon Beach
and eaten saltwater taffy until their stomachs ached.
So just how much did he recall? Everything? What
about Melinda? Shawna felt dread in her heart but
steadfastly tamped it down. Tonight she'd face the
truth—all of it. And so would Parker!

Once at the tiny coastal town, with its weathered
buildings and cottages, they found a quaint restaurant
high on the cliffs overlooking the sea. The beach was
nearly deserted. Only a few hardy souls braved the
sand and wind to stroll near the water's ragged edge.
Gray-and-white seagulls swooped from a steely sky, and
rolling whitecapped waves crashed against jagged black
rocks as Shawna and Parker finished a meal of crab
and crusty French bread.

"Want to take a walk?" Shawna asked.

Deep lines grooved around his mouth. "Didn't
bring my wheelchair," he drawled, his lips thinning.

She said softly, "You can lean on me."

"I don't think so. I really should get back." His eyes
touched hers for a moment and then he glanced away,
through the window and toward the sea.

"Melinda's expecting you?"

His jaw worked. "Actually, it's a case of my lawyer
wants to meet with her attorney. That sort of thing."

She braced herself for the showdown. "Then we'd
better get going," she said as if she had every intention
of driving him back to Portland. "I wouldn't want to
keep her waiting."

Parker paid the check, then ambled slowly toward
the car. Shawna pointed across the street to a mom-
and-pop grocery and deli. "I'll just be a minute. I want
to pick up a few things," she said, jaywalking across
the street.

"Can't you get whatever it is you need in Portland?"

Flashing him a mischievous smile, she shook her

head. He noticed the luxuriant honey-blond waves that swept the back of her suede jacket. "Not fresh crab. Just give me a minute."

Rather than protest, he slid into the hatchback and Shawna joined him a few minutes later. She swallowed back her fear. Until this moment, she'd been fairly honest with him. But now, if she had the courage, she was going to lie through her teeth.

"It's almost sunset," she said, easing the car into the empty street.

The sun, a fiery luminous ball, was dropping slowly to the sea. The sky was tinged rosy hues of orange and lavender. "I'd noticed."

"Do you mind if I take the scenic route home, through Astoria?"

Frowning, Parker rubbed the back of his neck and shrugged. "I guess not. I'm late already."

So far, so good. She drove north along the rugged coastline, following the curving road that wound along the crest of the cliffs overlooking the sea. Contorted pines and beach grass, gilded by the sun's final rays, flanked the asphalt. Parker closed his eyes and Shawna crossed her fingers. Maybe, just maybe, her plan would work.

"Here we are," Shawna said, pulling up the hand brake as the little car rolled to a stop.

Parker awakened slowly. He hadn't meant to doze, but he'd been exhausted for days. Ever since Shawna had moved out of his house, he'd spent sleepless nights in restless dreams filled with her, only to wake up drenched with sweat and hot with desire. His days, when he wasn't consulting his lawyer about Melinda's child, had been filled with physical therapy and swimming, and he could finally feel his body starting to respond. The pain in his injured leg had slowly less-

ened and his torn muscles had grudgingly started
working again. For the first time since the accident,
he'd felt a glimmer of hope that he would eventually
walk unassisted again. That knowledge was his driving
force, though it was a small comfort against the fact
that he'd given up Shawna.

But only temporarily, he reminded himself, knowing
that one way or another he would make her love him,
not for what he once was, but for the man he'd become. But first, there was the matter of Melinda's baby,
a matter which should have been completed this afternoon. If he'd had any brains at all, he never would
have agreed to drive to the beach with Shawna, but
he hadn't been able to stop himself.

When he had opened the door and found her, smiling and radiant on his doorstep, he hadn't been able
to resist spending a few hours with her.

Now, he blinked a couple of times, though he knew
he wasn't dreaming. "Where?" In front of her car was
a tiny, weathered run-down excuse of a cabin, behind
which was the vibrantly sun-streaked ocean.

"Gerri's cabin."

"Gerri?"

"My friend. Remember?" She laughed a little nervously. "Come on, I bet you do. You seem to be remembering a lot lately. More than you're letting on."

But Parker still wasn't thinking straight. His gaze was
glued to the gray shack with paned windows and a
sagging porch. "What're we doing here?" Was he missing something?

She pocketed her keys, then faced him. "We're
spending the weekend together. Here. Alone. No
phone. No intrusions. Just you and me."

He smiled until he saw that she wasn't kidding. Her
emerald eyes sparkled with determination. "Hey—wait
a minute—"

But she wasn't listening. She climbed out of the car
and grabbed the grocery bag.

"Shawna!" He wrenched open the door, watching in disbelief as she mounted the steps, searched with her fingers along the ledge over the porch, then, glancing back with a cat-who-ate-the-canary smile, held up a rusted key. *She wasn't joking!* "You can't do this—I've got to be back in Portland tonight!" Ignoring the pain in his knee, he followed after her, limping into the dark, musty interior of the cabin.

She was just lighting a kerosene lantern in the kitchen. "Romantic, don't you think?"

"What does romance have to do with the fact that you shanghaied me here?"

"Everything." She breezed past him and he couldn't help but notice the way her jeans fit snugly over her hips, or the scent of her hair, as she passed.

"I have a meeting—"

"It'll wait."

His blood was boiling. Just who the hell did she think she was—kidnapping him and then flirting with him so outrageously? If only she'd waited one more day! "Give me your keys," he demanded.

She laughed, a merry tinkling sound that bounced over the dusty rafters and echoed in the corners as she knelt on the hearth of a river-rock fireplace and opened the damper.

"I'm serious," Parker said.

"So am I. You're not getting the keys." She crumpled up a yellowed piece of newspaper, plunked two thick pieces of oak onto the grate, and lit a fire. Immediately flames crackled and leaped, climbing hungrily over the dry wood.

"Then I'll walk to the road and hitchhike."

"Guess again. It's nearly a mile. You're still recovering, remember?"

"Shawna—"

"Face it, Parker. This time, you're mine." Dusting her hands, she turned to face him and her expression had changed from playful and bright to sober. "And this time, I'm not letting you go. Not until we settle things once and for all."

Damn the woman! She had him and she knew it! And deep in his heart he was glad, even though he worried about his meeting with Melinda James and her attorney. He glanced around the room, past the sheet-draped furniture and rolled carpets to the windows and the view of the sea beyond. The sky was painted with lavender and magenta and the ocean, shimmering and restless, blazed gold. Worried that he might be blowing the delicate negotiations with Melinda, Parker shoved his hands into the pockets of his cords and waited. Protesting was getting him nowhere. "I'll have to make a call."

"Too bad."

He swore under his breath. "Who knows we're here?"

"Just Gerri. She owns this place."

Since Gerri was Shawna's best friend, he didn't doubt that she'd keep her mouth shut. "What about Jake or your folks?"

She shook her head and rolled out the carpet. "As I said, it's just you, me, the ocean, and the wind. And maybe, if you're lucky, white wine and grilled salmon."

"I'm afraid you'll live to regret this," he said, groaning inwardly as he deliberately advanced on her. Firelight caught in her hair and eyes, and a provocative dimple creased her cheek. The very essence of her seemed to fill the empty cracks and darkest corners of the cabin. He hadn't realized just how much he'd missed her until now. "We probably both will."

"I guess that's a chance we'll just have to take." She met his gaze then, her eyes filled with a love so pure, so intense, he felt guilty for not admitting that he remembered everything—that he, at this moment, had he been in Portland, would be planning for their future together. Reaching forward, he captured her wrist in his hand, felt her quivering pulse. "I want you to trust me," he said, his guts twisting when he recognized the pain in her eyes.

"I do," she whispered. "Why do you think I kidnapped you?"

"God only knows," he whispered, but his gaze centered on her softly parted lips and he felt a warm urgency invade his blood. "You know," he said, his voice turning silky, "I might just mete out my revenge for this little stunt."

He was close to her now, so close she could see the flecks of blue fire in his eyes. "Try me."

Would she never give up? He felt an incredible surge of pride that this gorgeous, intelligent woman loved him so tenaciously she would fight impossible odds to save their relationship. A vein throbbed in his temple, his thoughts filled with desire, and he gave in to the overpowering urge to forget about the past, the present, and the future as he gazed hungrily into her eyes. "I do love you. . . ." he whispered, sweeping her into his arms.

Shawna's heart soared, though she didn't have time to catch her breath. The kiss was hard, nearly brutal, and filled with a fierce passion that caused her heart to beat shamelessly.

She moaned in response, twining her arms around his neck, her breasts crushed against his chest, her blood hot with desire. He pulled her closer still, holding her so tight she could barely breathe as his tongue pressed against her teeth. Willingly her lips parted and she felt him explore the velvety recesses of her mouth.

"God, I've missed you," he whispered, his voice rough as his lips found her throat and moved slowly downward.

She didn't stop him when he pushed her jacket off her shoulders, nor did she protest when he undid the buttons of her blouse. Her eyes were bright when he kissed her lips again.

The fire glowed red and yellow and the sound of

the sea crashing against rocks far below drifted through the open window as she helped him out of his clothes.

"Shawna—are you sure?" he asked, and groaned when she kissed his chest.

"I've always been sure," she whispered. "With you." Tasting the salt on his skin, feeling the ripple of his muscles, she breathed against him, wanton with pleasure when he sucked in his abdomen, his eyes glazing over.

"You're incredible," he murmured, moving suggestively against her, his arousal evident as her fingers played with his waistband, dipping lower and teasing him.

"So are you."

"If you don't stop me now—"

"Never," she replied and was rewarded with his wet lips pressing hard against hers. All control fled, and he pushed her to the carpet, his hands deftly removing her clothes and caressing her all over until she ached for more. Blood thundered in her ears, her heart slammed wildly in her chest, and she could only think of Parker and the desire throbbing hot in her veins. "I love you, Parker," she said, tears filling her eyes at the wonder of him.

Firelight gleamed on his skin as he lowered himself over her, touching the tip of her breasts with his tongue before taking one firm mound possessively with his mouth and suckling hungrily. His hand was on her back, spread wide over her skin, drawing her near as he rubbed against her, anxious and aroused.

"I should tell you—"

"Shh—" Twining her fingers in the hair of his nape, she drew his head down to hers and kissed him, moving her body erotically against his. She pushed his cords over his hips, her fingers inching down his muscular buttocks and thighs, a warm, primal need swirling deep within her. His clothes discarded, she ran her fingers over his skin and turned anxious lips to his.

If he wanted to stop, he couldn't. His muscles, glistening with sweat and reflecting the golden light from the fire, strained for one second before he parted her legs with one knee and thrust deep into her.

"Shawna," he cried, his hand on her breasts, his mouth raining kisses on her face. "Love me."

"I do!" Hot inside, and liquid, she captured him with her legs, arching against him and holding close, as if afraid he would disappear with the coming night.

With each of his long strokes, she felt as if she were on that carousel again, turning faster and faster, spinning wildly, crazily out of control.

Tangled in his passion, she shuddered, and the lights of the merry-go-round crackled and burst into brilliant blue and gold flames. Parker cried out, deeply and lustily, and it echoed with her own shriek of pleasure. Tears filled her eyes with each hot wave of pleasure that spread to her limbs.

Parker kissed the dewy perspiration from her forehead, then took an old blanket from the couch and wrapped it over them.

"My darling, I love you," he murmured, his voice cracking.

"You don't have to say anything," she whispered, but her heart fairly burst with love.

"Why lie?" Levering himself on one elbow, he brushed the honey-streaked strands of hair from her face and stared down at her. "You wouldn't believe me anyway. You've always insisted that I loved you." He kissed her gently on the cheek. "You just have no idea how much." His gaze lowered again, to the fullness of her breasts, the pinch of her waist, the length of her legs. "I love you more than any sane man should love a woman," he admitted, his voice thick with emotion.

"Now, we can forget about everything except each other," she whispered, winding her arms around his neck. "I love you, Parker Harrison. And I want you.

And if all I can have of you is this one weekend—then I'll take it."

"Not good enough, Doctor," he said, his smile white and sensual as it slashed across his jaw. "With you, it has to be forever."

"Forever it is," she whispered, her voice breaking as she tilted her face eagerly to his.

Gathering her into his arms, he made love to her all night long.

Thirteen

Shawna stretched lazily on the bed, smiling to herself as she reached for Parker again. But her fingers rubbed only cold sheets. Her eyes flew open. "Parker?" she called, glancing around the tiny bedroom. Where was he?

Morning light streamed into the room and the old lace curtains fluttered in the breeze.

"Parker?" she called again, rubbing her eyes before scrambling for her robe. The little cabin was cold and she didn't hear any sounds of life from the other room. There was a chance he'd hobbled down to the beach, but she doubted he would climb down the steep stairs of the cliff face. Worried, she crossed the small living room to peer out a side window, and her fears were confirmed. Her hatchback was gone. He'd left. After a night of intense lovemaking, he'd gone.

Maybe he's just gone to the store, or to find a phone booth, she told herself, but she knew better, even before she found a hastily scrawled note on the table. Her hands shook as she picked up a small scrap of paper and read:

Had to run home for a while. I'll be back or send someone for you. Trust me. I do love you.

She crumpled the note in her hand and shoved it into the pocket of her robe. Her fingers grazed the cold metal of the brass ring he'd won at the fair all those weeks ago and she dropped into one of the old, dilapidated chairs. Why had he returned to Portland?

To settle things with Melinda.

And after that?

Who knows?

Her head fell to her hands, but she tried to think positively. He did love her. He had admitted it over and over again the night before while making love, and again in the note. So why leave? Why take off and abandon her now?

"Serves you right," she muttered, thinking how she'd shanghaied him to this cabin.

She had two options: she could walk into town and call her brother, or trust Parker and wait it out. This time, she decided to give Parker the benefit of the doubt.

To pass the time, she cleaned the house, stacked wood, even started lamb stew simmering on the stove before changing into clean clothes. But at five-thirty, when he hadn't shown up again, she couldn't buoy her deflated spirits. The longer he was away, the more uncertain she was of the words of love he had whispered in the night.

"He'll be back," she told herself, knowing he wouldn't leave her stranded, not even to pay her back for tricking him. Nonetheless, she slipped into her shoes and jacket and walked outside.

The air was cool and as the sun set, fog collected over the waves. A salty breeze caught and tangled in her hair as she threaded her way along an overgrown path to the stairs. Brambles and skeletal berry vines clung to her clothes and dry beach grass rubbed against her jeans before she reached the weathered steps that zigzagged back and forth along the cliff face and eventually led to the beach. She hurried down, her shoes catching on the uneven boards and exposed nails, to the deserted crescent-shaped strip of white sand. Seagulls cried over the roar of the surf and foamy waves crashed against barnacle-riddled shoals. Far to the north a solitary lighthouse knifed upward, no light shining from its gleaming white tower.

Shawna stuffed her hands in her pockets and walked along the water's edge, eyeing the lavender sky and a few stars winking through tattered wisps of fog. She walked aimlessly, her thoughts as turbulent as the restless waves.

Why hadn't Parker returned? Why? Why? Why?

She kicked at an agate and turned back toward the stairs, her eyes following the ridge. Then she saw him, standing at the top of the cliff, balanced on the weather-beaten stairs. His hair ruffling in the wind, Parker was staring down at her.

He'd come back!

Her heart took flight and she started running along the water's edge. All her doubts were washed away with the tide. He waved, then started down the stairs.

"Parker, no! Wait!" she called, her breath short. The steps were uneven, and because of his leg, she was afraid he might fall. Fear curled over her heart as she saw him stumble and catch himself. "Parker—don't—"

But her words were caught in the wind and drowned by the roar of the sea. Adrenaline spurred her on, her gaze fastened on the stairs. He was slowly inching his way down, his hands gripping the rail, but she was still worried.

Her legs felt like lead as she raced across the dry sand toward the stairs, her heart hammering, slamming against her ribs, as his eyes locked with hers. He grinned and stepped down, only to miss the final sunbleached stairs.

"No!" she cried, as he scrambled against the rail, swore, then pitched forward. In an awful instant, she watched as he fell onto the sand, his strong outstretched arms breaking his fall. But his jeans caught on a nail, the fabric ripped, and his bad leg wrenched.

He cried out as he landed on the sand.

"Parker!" Shawna flew to his side, dropping to her knees in the sand, touching his face, her hands tracing the familiar line of his jaw as his eyes blinked open.

"You—you were supposed to catch me," he joked, but the lines near his mouth were white with pain.

"And you weren't supposed to fall! Are you all right?" She cradled his head to her breast, her eyes glancing down to his leg.

"Better now," he admitted, still grimacing a little, but his blue gaze tangled in hers.

"Let me see—"

Ignoring his protests, she ripped his pant leg further and probed gently at his knee.

He inhaled swiftly.

"Well, you didn't do it any good, but you'll live," she thought aloud, relieved that nothing seemed to have torn. "But you'll have to have it looked at when we get back." She tossed her hair over her shoulder and glared at him. "That was a stupid move, Harrison—" she said, noticing for the first time a crisp white envelope in the sand. "What's this?"

"The adoption papers," he replied, stretching his leg and grimacing.

"Adoption—?" Her eyes flew to his.

"Melinda's agreed to let me adopt the baby."

"You—?"

"Yep." Forcing himself to a standing position, he steadied himself on the rail as Shawna scanned the legal forms. "It didn't even take much convincing. I agreed to send her to school and take care of the baby. That's all she really wanted."

Shawna eyed him suspiciously and dusted off her hands to stand next to him. "Are you sure you're okay?"

His eyes darkened with the night. "I'm fine, now that everything's worked out. You know the baby isn't really mine. Melinda was Brad's girlfriend. I just couldn't remember the connection for a while."

She couldn't believe her ears. "What triggered your memory?"

"You did," he said affectionately. "You literally jarred me to my senses when you moved out."

Dumbstruck, she felt her mouth open and close—then her eyes glimmered furiously. "That was days ago!"

"I called."

Trying to hold onto her indignation, she placed her hands on her hips. "You could have said something last night!"

"I was busy last night," he said and her heart began to pound. "So, do you want to know what happened?"

"Of course."

"The night of the wedding rehearsal, I drove Brad to Melinda's apartment and they had a knock-down-drag-out about her pregnancy. He didn't want to be tied down to a wife and kid—thought it would interfere with his career." Parker whitened at the memory. "Melinda was so upset she slapped him and he passed out on the couch. That's why I remembered her, because I held her, told her everything would work out, and tried to talk some sense into her. Later, I intended to give Brad the lecture of his life. But," he sighed, "I didn't get the chance."

"So why did she claim the baby was yours?"

"Because she blamed me for Brad's death. It was a scheme she and her father cooked up when they read in the papers that I had amnesia. But she couldn't go through with it."

"Because you remembered."

"No, because she finally realized she had to do what was best for the baby. Nothing else mattered."

"That's a little hard to believe," Shawna whispered.

He shrugged. "I guess the maternal instinct is stronger than either of us suspected. Anyway, I told her I'd help her through school, but I want full custody of the child." His eyes narrowed on the sea and now, as if to shake off the past, he struggled to stand. "It's the least I can do for Brad."

"Be careful," she instructed as she brushed the sand from her jeans. She, too, was reeling. Parker was going to be a father!

Wincing a little, he tried his leg, then slung his arm over Shawna's shoulders. "I guess I'll just have to lean on you, he whispered, "if you'll let me."

"You think I wouldn't?"

Shrugging he squeezed her shoulder. "I've been kind of an ass," he admitted.

"That's for sure," she agreed, but she grinned up at him as they walked toward the ocean. "But I can handle you."

"Can you? How about a baby?"

She stopped dead in her tracks. "What are you saying, Parker?" They were at the water's edge, the tide lapping around her feet.

"I'm asking you to marry me, Shawna," he whispered, his gaze delving deep into hers. "I'm asking you to help me raise Brad's baby, as if it were ours, and I'm begging you to love me for who I am, not the man I was," he said, stripping his soul bare, his eyes dark with conviction.

"But I do—"

"I'm not the same man you planned to marry before," he pointed out, giving her one last door to walk through, though his fingers tightened possessively around her shoulders.

"Of course you are. Don't you know that no matter what happens in our lives, what tragedy strikes, I'll never leave you—and not just out of some sense of duty," she explained, "but because I love you."

She saw the tears gather in his eyes, noticed the quivering of his chin. "You're sure about this?"

"I haven't been chasing you down for weeks, bull-dozing my way into your life just because I thought it was the right thing to do, Parker."

"I know, but—"

" 'I know but' nothing. I love *you*—not some gilded memory!"

"All this time I thought—"

"That's the problem, Parker, you didn't think," she said, poking a finger into his broad chest and grinning.

"Oh how I love you," he said, his arms pulling her swiftly to him, his lips crashing down on hers, his hands twining in the long silky strands of her hair.

The kiss was filled with the wonder and promise of the future and her heart began to beat a wild cadence. "I'll never let you go now," he vowed.

"I don't want to."

"But if you ever decide to leave me," he warned, his eyes drilling into hers. "I'll hunt you down, Shawna, I swear it. And I'll make you love me again."

"You won't have to." She heard the driving beat of his heart over the thrashing sea, saw pulsating desire in his blue eyes, and melted against him. "I'll never leave." She tasted salt from his tears as she kissed him again.

"Good. Then maybe we can exchange this—" Reaching into his pocket, he withdrew the beribboned brass ring.

"Where did you get that?"

"In the cabin, where you were supposed to be."

"But what're you going to do?"

"We don't need this anymore." Grinning wickedly, he hurled the ring with its fluttering ribbons out to sea.

"Parker, no!" she cried.

But the ring was airborne, flying into the dusk before settling into the purple water.

"As I was saying, we'll exchange the brass ring for two gold bands."

She watched as pastel ribbons drifted beneath the foaming waves. When he tilted her face upward, her eyes were glistening with tears. Finally, Parker had come home. Nothing separated them.

"Will you marry me, Dr. McGuire?"

"Yes," she whispered, her voice catching as she flung her arms around his neck and pressed her eager lips to his. He loved her and he remembered! Finally, they would be together! "Yes, oh, yes!" Her green eyes shimmered in the deepening shadows, her hands urgent as desire and happiness swept through her.

"Slow down, Shawna," he whispered roughly. But even as he spoke, her weight was dragging them both down to the sea-kissed sand. "We've got the rest of our lives."

Dear Reader,

I can't tell you how thrilled I am that THE BRASS RING has been republished by Zebra Books. When I first wrote this book I didn't anticipate it becoming a "classic romance" or that my career would take the twists and turns it has to the point that I'm now writing mainstream romantic suspense.

THE BRASS RING really is a favorite of mine. I remember thinking as I wrote the story, What would happen if a woman who has it all, including the man of her dreams, loses everything right before her wedding? How would she react? Would her love survive? From there, the characters came to mind and the story was born! THE BRASS RING is a story of true love and I hope you liked it.

I also hope you'll look for my most recent novels of romantic suspense from Zebra Books: HOT BLOODED, which has just been published, and COLD BLOODED, which will be available in June 2002. Set in New Orleans, the stories are a blend of chilling suspense and hot romance. For a sneak peek of *Hot Blooded,* just turn the page!

Best,

Lisa Jackson

P.S. You can visit my website at www.lisajackson.com

The moon was blocked by thick, night-blackened clouds. Rain slanted from the sky, and the wind kicked up, causing whitecaps to foam on the usually calm surface of Lake Pontchartrain as the summer squall passed over. Ty Wheeler's sailboat bobbed wildly at the mercy of the wind, sails billowing, deck listing over dark, opaque water. He ignored the elements along with the certainty that he was on a fool's mission—definitely in the wrong place at the wrong time. He should take down the sails and use the damned engine, but it wasn't reliable, and a part of him liked daring the fates.

The way he figured it, this was his chance, and he damned well was going to take it.

Bracing his feet on the rolling deck, he stood at the helm, legs apart, eyes squinting through the most powerful set of binoculars he could find. He focused the glasses on the back of the rambling old plantation-styled home Samantha Leeds now occupied.

Dr. Samantha Leeds, he reminded himself. P H damned D. Enough credentials to choke the proverbial horse and more than enough to allow the good doctor to hand out free advice over the airwaves. No matter who it harmed.

His jaw hardened, and he caught a hint of movement behind the filmy curtains. Then he saw her. His fingers clenched over the slick glasses as he watched, like a damned voyeur, as she walked unevenly through her house. He checked his watch. Three-fifteen in the morning.

And she was beautiful—just as she was in the publicity shots he'd seen—maybe even more so with her tousled red-brown hair and state of undress. Dr. Leeds wore a nightshirt buttoned loosely, its hem brushing the tops of her long, tanned thighs as she walked unevenly through a room lit by Tiffany lamps and adorned with a lot of old-looking furniture—probably antiques. He caught a glimpse of the cast that encased her left foot and half her calf. He'd heard about that, too. Some kind of boating accident in Mexico.

Lips compressed, he anchored the wheel with one hip and felt rain slide down the neck of his parka. The wind had snatched off his hood and tossed his hair around his eyes, but he kept the powerful glasses trained on the house nestled deep in a copse of live oaks. Spanish moss clung to the thick branches and drifted in the wind. Rain ran down off the dormers and down the gutters. An animal—cat, from the looks of it—crept through a square of light thrown from one window. It disappeared quickly into dripping bushes flanking the raised porch.

Ty concentrated on the interior of the house—through the windows. He lost sight of Samantha for a second, then found her again, bending down, reaching forward to pick up her crutch. The nightshirt rode upward, giving him a peek at lacy white panties stretched over round, tight buttocks.

His crotch tightened. Throbbed. He ground his back teeth together, but ignored his male response just as he disregarded the warm rain stinging his face blurring the lenses of his binoculars.

He wouldn't think of her as a woman.

He needed her. He intended to lie to her. To use her. And that's all there was to it.

But, God, she was beautiful. Those legs—

She straightened suddenly, as if she sensed him watching her.

Turning, she walked to the windows and stared out, green eyes wide, red hair tousled as if she'd just gotten out of bed, skin without a hint of makeup. His pulse jumped a notch. She squinted through the glass, her eyes narrowing. Maybe she saw the silhouette of the boat, his shadow at the helm. Eerily, as if she knew what he was thinking, she met his stare with distrustful eyes and a gaze that scoured his black soul.

Wrong.

She was too far away.

The night was dark as pitch.

His imagination was running wild.

There was a slight chance she could see his running lights or the white sails, and, if so, make out the image of a man on his boat, but without binoculars there was no way she'd be able to see his features, would never recognize him, and couldn't, not for a minute, guess what he was thinking, or his intentions.

Good.

There was time enough for meeting face-to-face later. For the lies he would have to spin to get what he wanted. For a half a second, he felt a twinge of remorse, gritted his teeth. No time for second-guessing. He was committed. Period. As he watched through the glasses, she reached up and snapped the shades of her window closed, cutting off his view.

Too bad. She wasn't hard on the eyes. Far from it.

And that might pose a problem.

In Ty's mind, Dr. Samantha Leeds was too pretty for her own damned good.

". . . so you're sure you're okay?" David asked for the fifth time in the span of ten minutes. Holding the cordless receiver to her ear, Sam walked to the window of her bedroom and looked into the gloomy afternoon. Lake Pontchartrain was a somber gray, the waters shifting as restlessly as the clouds overhead.

"I'm fine, really." Now she wished she hadn't confided in him about the caller, but when David had phoned, she decided that he would find out soon enough anyway. It was a matter of public record, and sooner or later the news would filter across state lines. "I've talked to the police, and I'm having all the locks changed. I'll be okay. Don't worry."

"I don't like the sounds of it, Samantha." She imagined the tightening of the corners of his mouth. "Maybe you should look at this as some kind of . . . warning . . . you know, a sign that you should turn your life in a different direction."

"A sign?" she repeated, her eyes narrowing as she stared at the lake stretching from her yard to the distant shore. "As in God is trying to talk to me? You mean like the burning bush or—"

"There's no reason to get sarcastic," he cut in.

"You're right. I'm sorry." She balanced her hips on the arm of a wing chair. "I guess I'm a little edgy. I didn't sleep well."

"I'll bet."

She didn't mention the boat; she was certain a sailboat had been drifting off her dock, that in the barest of light from the shore, she'd seen running lights and the reflection of giant sails with a man's contour against the backdrop. Or maybe it had been her imagination running wild. . . .

"So where are you, again?" she asked, reaching to the nightstand and retrieving a knitting needle she'd found in the closet, part of the personal items she'd inherited from her mother. Feeling a twinge of guilt, she slipped the needle between the cast and her leg and scratched. Her doctor would probably kill her if he knew, but then he was the crusty old guy down in

Mazatlan, the expatriot she'd never see again if she was lucky.

"I'm here in San Antonio, and it's a deluge. I'm standing at the window of my hotel room looking over the River Walk and it's like a wall of water—can't even see the restaurant across the river. The sky just opened up." He sighed and for a second his cell phone cut out, the connection was lost, only to return. " . . . wish you were here Samantha. I've got a room with a Jacuzzi and a fireplace. It could be cozy."

And it could be hell. She remembered Mexico. The way David had smothered her. The fights. He'd wanted her to move back to Houston, and when she'd refused, she'd witnessed a side of him she didn't like. His face had turned a deep scarlet and a small vein had throbbed over one eyebrow. His fists had even clenched as he'd told her that she was an idiot not to take him up on his offer. At that moment, she'd known she never would.

"I thought I made it clear how I felt," she said, watching a raindrop drizzle a zigzag course down the window. She gave up on the knitting needle and tossed it onto the bureau.

"I hoped you'd changed your mind."

"I haven't. David, it won't work. I know this sounds corny and trite, but I thought you and I, we could—"

"—just be friends," he finished for her, his voice flat.

"You don't have to put the 'just' in there. It's not like being friends isn't a good thing."

"I don't feel that way about you," he said, and she imagined his serious face. He was a good-looking man. Clean-cut. Athletic. Handsome enough to have done some print work while he was attending college, and he had the scrapbooks to prove it. Women were attracted to him. Sam had been, or thought she'd been, but in the two years they'd dated some of the luster had faded, and she'd never really fallen in love. Not that there was anything specifically wrong with him. Or nothing she could name. He was handsome, intelligent, the right age, and his job with Regal Hotels was certain to make him a millionaire several times over. They just didn't click.

"I'm sorry, David."

"Are you?" he asked with a bite. David Ross didn't like to lose.

"Yes." She meant it. She hadn't intended to lead him on; she'd just wanted to be careful, to make sure this time.

"Then I suppose you don't want me to be your escort at that benefit you've been talking about?"

"The auction for the Boucher Center," she said wincing when she remembered she'd brought it up to him months ago. "No, I think it would be best if I went alone."

He didn't immediately answer, as if he expected her to change her mind. She didn't and the tension on the line was nearly palpable.

"Well," he finally said. "I guess there's nothing more to say. Take care of yourself, Samantha."

"You too." Her heart twisted a bit. She hung up and told herself it was for the best. It was over, and that was that.

All of her friends thought she was nuts not to marry him. "If I were you, I'd set my hooks in him and reel him in faster'n you could say prenup," her friend Corky had confided over shrimp bisque less than a month ago. Corky's eyes had twinkled mischievously, almost as brightly as the three rings she wore on her right ring finger—prizes from previous relationships and marriages. "I don't know why you're so uptight about the whole thing."

"I've been married before, and I believe in the old once burned twice shy routine."

"I thought it was once bitten." Corky had broken off a chunk of bread as she glanced out the windows of the restaurant to the slow-flowing Mississippi, where a barge covered with gravel was chugging upstream.

"Samey-same."

"The point is you'll never find a better catch than David, believe you me." Corky had nodded, her short blond curls bobbing.

"Then you take him."

"I would. In a heartbeat. But he's in love with you."

"David's in love with David."

"Harsh words, Sam. Wait 'til you get back from Mexico, then you tell me," Corky had said with a naughty smile. As if hot sand, even hotter sun, and, she implied, far hotter sex, would change how Samantha felt. It hadn't. The sand had been warm, the sun hot, the sex nonexistent. It had been her problem, not his. The fact of the matter was that she just wasn't in love with the guy. Period. Something about him grated on her nerves. An only child, a brilliant scholar, David was used to having things his way. And he always wanted them to be perfect.

Life wasn't supposed to be messy, which, of course, it always was.

"All men are not Jeremy Leeds," Corky had said, wrinkling her pert nose as she mentioned Samantha's ex-husband.

"Thank God."

Corky had signaled to the waiter for another glass of Chardonnay, and Sam had absently stirred the soup while trying not to conjure up images of her ex-husband.

"Maybe you're still not over him."

"Jeremy?" Sam had rolled her eyes. "Get real."

"It's hard to get over that kind of rejection."

"I know about this," Sam had assured her. "I'm a professional, remember?"

"But—"

"Jeremy's flaw is he falls in love with his students and doesn't take his marriage vows very seriously."

"Okay, okay, so he's yesterday's news," Corky had said, waving the air as if she could push the subject of Jeremy Leeds out the window. "So what's wrong with David? Too good-looking?" She'd held up a finger. "No? Too eligible—never been married before, you know, so there's no baggage, no kids or ex-wife." She'd wiggled another digit. "Oh, I know, too rich . . . or too ambitious. Too great a job? Lord, what is he, CEO of Regal Hotels?"

"Executive vice president and director of sales for the eastern United States."

Corky had flopped back in her chair and thrown her hands over her head as if in surrender. "There you have it! The man's too perfect."

Hardly, Samantha had thought at the time. But then she and Corky, friends since second grade in LA had always had different views on boyfriends, courtship and marriage. One lunch hadn't changed anything, and the trip to Mexico had convinced her—David Ross wasn't the man for her, and that was just fine. She didn't need a man, didn't really want one right now. She shook herself out of her reverie and stared through the sweating windowpanes to the lake . . . where she'd imagined a mysterious man on the deck of his sailboat, binoculars trained on her house in the middle of the night, no less. She grinned at her folly. "You're jumping at shadows," she told herself, and with Charon trailing behind her, hitched her way to the bathroom, where she tied a plastic sack over her cast, sent up a prayer that the damned thing would be cut off soon, and climbed into the shower. She thought about David, about the man on the sailboat in the lake, about the seductive voice on the phone and about the mutilated picture of herself—the eyes gouged out.

Shivering, she turned the spray to hot and closed her eyes, letting the warm jets wash over her.

Summer Fantasy

Jill Marie Landis

One

I must be out of my mind.

Kylee Christopher tightened her hold on the steering wheel of the black Jeep Wrangler 4x4 and braced herself for a jolt. Leaning forward to wipe the fogged windshield, she pressed her palm against the cool glass and used her hand as a wiper blade. The smeared trail she left in the condensation did little to improve her vision.

The sly smile on the face of the clerk working the auto rental desk at Lihue Airport should have warned her something was up. When he heard she was staying up on Powerhouse Road, he immediately suggested she opt for a Jeep instead of a standard model vehicle.

Leave it to Sylvia to get her into this fix. Kylee swerved to avoid another puddle the size of a small lake and sighed. When her literary agent, Sylvia Greene, suggested she get away and then convincingly recommended a secluded vacation rental on the north shore of Kauai, Kylee had envisioned an elegant ocean-front condo, or at the very least a sprawling hillside retreat—not a trek into the uncharted reaches of a dense rain forest.

The rutted road narrowed and then curved sharply as it wound steadily uphill. Whenever she dared take her eyes off the smeared windshield, the dark emerald jungle appeared to be encroaching closer on both sides. Huge monstera vines sensuously wound themselves around the trunks of the trees close to the right side of the road. On her left, the jungle growth partially obscured the land where it fell away into a deep ravine. She couldn't see clearly enough to tell how far it was to the bottom.

Swinging her glance back to the road ahead of her, she saw an animal lumber into her path. Kylee cursed and stood on the brake. The Jeep swerved. The oversized tires ground into the gravelly mud. The car stopped short of a very fat, spotted dog.

Kylee leaned on the horn, expecting the animal to run off, but it didn't budge. Rain beat a steady tattoo on the roof. Her fingers began to echo the beat as she tapped on the steering wheel.

"There's no way I'm getting out to chase you off."

Kylee had mumbled aloud, but her voice was lost in the beat of the rain as she downshifted, intending to head the Jeep straight for the dog at a crawl and hope the creature gave way. She was releasing the clutch when a little Hawaiian boy no more than four years old careened into the road on a rusty, miniature dirt bike.

Kylee slammed on the brakes again.

"What next?" she yelled at the windshield, watching in awe as the dark-haired, nearly naked boy jumped off the bike and scurried over to the fat dog.

She opened the door, stood on the inside edge of the floorboard and ignored the rain that felt like ice when it hit her overheated skin. She blinked twice, then wiped the water out of her eyes and stared harder.

The dog was a pig. The biggest, ugliest, meanest looking pig she'd ever seen, not that she'd seen many pigs up close and personal. Even more amazing, the kid in the Batman underpants was tugging on the pig's ear, trying to get him to move.

The boy shouted something she couldn't understand and the pig finally got the message. It headed back up the steep, narrow drive to the right. The little boy jumped back on the rusted, muddy bike. Pedaling furiously, he rode straight through a puddle, nearly tipped over, then kept going without a backward glance.

Recovering from her surprise, Kylee leaned against the roof of the Jeep and yelled, "Wait!"

She could see the deep ruts going up the driveway on the hillside. The drive wound steeply uphill to a small, ramshackle island home. Dark green, the house blended into the dense growth and might not have even been discernable if it hadn't been for the yard filled with old cars, wandering rust-colored roosters, and a pack of dogs, that had to be related to each other, chained together.

The little boy didn't say a word. He sat there straddling his bike, staring back at her with a broad smile on his face.

"Do you know where *Hale Nanea* is?"

The child shrugged.

"Hale Nanea?" She yelled.

Finally, the boy pointed to the opposite side of the road.

"Hah-lay. Down dere," he hollered back.

Kylee squinted toward the opposite side of the road. All she saw was a smear of jungle. Amid the wild greenery along the road stood a row of tall gingers in full yellow bloom, but there was no sign of the vacation rental the brochure described as "The perfect island retreat in the peaceful Wainiha Valley."

"Where?" She turned back to question the child, but he had disappeared. The only sign of him was the abandoned bike lying in the yard.

"Damn," she whispered, ducking back into the Jeep. She shoved the stick shift into first gear and eased off on the clutch. On the passenger seat, her brand-new, woven straw bag was getting soaked, so she punched the window button, determined to head back down the cursed road as soon as she found a wide enough place to turn around. Once she reached the bottom of Powerhouse Road, she was going to head back to the five star hotel she had seen on the bluff at Princeville about ten miles back.

Just then, a flash of color caught her eye. Red, saffron, and royal blue against the tangle of green. Braking, she slowly backed up until the Jeep was directly across from a pretty, hand-painted sign decorated with a lei of orchids wound around the words, *Hale Nanea*.

Grumbling, Kylee scanned the bushes for some sign of a drive and finally found it. She would have to make a left turn into a steep incline without any notion of what might be waiting at the bottom. Checking to be sure she was in four-wheel drive, she shoved the gearshift into first and started down the hill.

Water was running off the main road in heavy rivulets on both sides of the rock-paved driveway, which had become a sea of mud. She gripped the wheel. The Jeep rolled down, reaching the end of the drive well before she expected it to, and she was forced to slam on the brakes. She took a look around. A small house stood just ahead of her. Behind it was a wall of thick growth. On the driver's side was a larger version of the cottage.

"Just wait, Sylvia," she mumbled to herself, thinking of her hare-brained agent and wondering how she ever let herself get talked into *this*. Living like Tarzan's Jane wasn't exactly what she needed right now.

She opened the car door and discovered the rain was beginning to lighten up. A wide wooden veranda fronted the large house beside her. It was crowded with comfortable looking wicker furniture. A plaque on the wall beside the wide double doors was a reduced version of the one on the road. *Hale Nanea*.

With a sigh of relief, Kylee reached for her purse and the carryall that held her essentials intent on heading for the shelter of the porch. She stepped out of the Jeep. Her new white tennis shoes sank into the red mud.

"What next?" Squashing her way to the veranda, she climbed two of the three low steps and stood on the edge of the porch.

"Hello?" she called out, looking for some sign of life. The inside doors were open, the screens closed. She could see through to a comfortable room with casual furniture upholstered in fabric with a palms and hibiscus motif, accessorized with island touches. Woven mats covered the floors.

The porch was unbelievably clean, especially since it was surrounded by a sea of mud. She could hear water rushing beyond the curtain of thick trees with shiny green leaves and fragile-looking yellow flowers that looked like they were made of crepe paper. The small house in back was connected to the larger but identical structure by a raised wooden walkway.

Just before she took a step onto the immaculate veranda, she saw a sign opposite the *Hale Nanea* plaque that read: ISLAND STYLE—PLEASE REMOVE YOUR SHOES.

She tossed her purse and the carryall toward the nearest chair without taking another step onto the porch. The skies were still gray, but the rain had momentarily stopped, so she decided to unload the car before the next deluge. Trudging back and forth to the Jeep, she carried up two suitcases, her laptop, printer, then a box of books and magazines. Luckily, she finished just before the rain started again.

Kylee paused to rest on the edge of the porch and wiped her brow with the back of her hand. The humidity was as thick as a flannel blanket. She was hungry, exhausted, and frustrated.

" '*Complete with all the amenities.*' Ha. Good joke, Sylvia. All the amenities except for a bellboy," she grumbled aloud.

"You're early."

At the sound of the deep, masculine voice behind her, she nearly jumped out of her skin. Kylee spun around and found herself face-to-face with a Polynesian god. Dressed in a faded tank top that sported a surfboard logo and shorts, he was over six feet tall with wide shoulders, a tapered waist, well-developed biceps, and legs that would make a weightlifter drool. His complexion was bronze; his shoulder-length, coal black hair was tied back in a ponytail. His dark eyes had an exotic, slight tilt at the corners. His lips were stunning, lush and full, framing a smile wide enough to reveal perfect teeth. He was definitely half-Hawaiian, if not more.

Kylee had to blink twice to break the spell. For the first time in her life, she knew what it meant to be rendered speechless. She took a step back. The mud on her shoes was beginning to stiffen.

"You must be Kylee Christopher. Welcome to *Hale Nanea.*" The god held out his hand.

Like a robot, Kylee offered hers. He shook it.

"I guess the rain on the roof kept me from hearing you drive in. I'm Rick Pau. P-a-u, not p-o-w. Houseboy, chef, caretaker, and gardener. Like the brochure says, I'm here to see to your every need."

Kylee didn't recall the brochure or Sylvia mentioning anything about a Hawaiian god being on hand to "see to her every need."

"Well, Mr. Pau, I wish you had been here to help me unload."

She watched him glance over to her pile of assorted bags and boxes and took the opportunity to study him closer. He was far too handsome for his own good. Probably used that killer smile to get him out of any jam.

"In fact," she went on, ignoring the sparkle in his eyes, "I wish you had put more detailed directions on that little brochure of yours. I was almost hopelessly lost in this jungle, and I nearly ran over a pig in the road. A *pig.* A big one. Not to mention a little boy on a dirt bike."

As he leaned back against the veranda railing, he folded his arms across his chest. The move emphasized all his muscular assets.

"You *are* having a bad day." He continued smiling for all the world as if he were trying to win the Mister Congeniality division of a Gorgeous Island Man contest. Then suddenly he straightened and pushed off the rail.

"Why don't you take off your shoes? Go on in and relax. I'll bring all your things in."

She wanted to be furious at him, she really did, but her conscience got the best of her. The rain wasn't his fault, nor did he have anything to do with the pig or the poor condition of the road. Deep down, she knew exactly what was *really* bothering her and it certainly wasn't Rick Pau.

It was the ever-mounting panic that her Emmy award–winning career as a television screenwriter was on the brink of disaster.

Rick stepped aside and watched the trim, leggy blonde walk into the house. Even drawn back in a severe ponytail, her hair was stunning, long and thick, shot through with golden highlights. She had sensuous curves in all the right places. It would be a long, long time before he forgot the impact she had on his senses when he rounded the corner of the lanai, or veranda, and found her standing there.

Like most tourists who came to the island, she was wearing brand-new clothes; what had once been pristine white shorts nicely revealed her shapely legs. Her pale peach sports shirt had a pricey logo riding over her left breast.

"This is like a movie set," she said while her bright, sea-blue eyes roamed over the interior of the main room. "Right out of *South Pacific.*"

"Did you know the movie was filmed on the island?" He easily hefted the bags and started toward the master suite.

The warm sound of her voice followed him into the other room. "How could I *not* know? It's in every article I ever read about Kauai."

Rick laughed. "The tourist bureau tries to get a lot of mileage out of the locations of film sights around the island. *Jurassic Park,* the remake of *King Kong, Raiders of the Lost Ark,* some scenes from *The Thorn Birds* were even shot here."

"I like these mats on the floor." Obviously not interested in movie trivia, she continued to prowl.

"They're called *lau hala.*" He set her suitcases down and led her back to the main room that opened onto front and rear verandas. He found Kylee standing at the huge window staring out at the picture-postcard view of the Wainiha River, water-filled taro fields, and the ocean beyond. Rick couldn't help but admire her profile as she stood there unaware that he had joined her again.

He walked over to the door and stacked her laptop on top of the box that appeared to hold a printer. "Would you like me to hook these up at the desk?"

"I can manage."

"I guess you plan on doing a little work while you're here."

It wasn't a question. One of his former guests from L.A., Sylvia Greene, had called to tell him that she was going to suggest *Hale Nanea* to one of the writers she represented, a woman who needed to get away. When Sylvia added that she wanted Rick to see that her client had a good time, he had expected someone a bit more . . . well, literary looking. Someone who might have a problem meeting people. Not a woman who didn't seem shy at all and who could hold her own in a beauty contest.

No, Kylee Christopher wasn't what he had expected.

Not at all. The effect she was having on him—both physical and mental—was something that hadn't happened to him around any other woman for a long, long time. There was something about her eyes, something deep down inside the blue depths that reflected a lost, tentative side of her, one that didn't mesh with the capable, confident air she had shown so far. She was a woman with secrets. He felt drawn to her, compelled to know her better. He wanted to be the one to help her find whatever it was she was missing in her life. If he wasn't careful, she just might turn his well-orchestrated life, not to mention his heart, upside down.

Rick walked over to a wide desk trimmed in bamboo and gently set down her things.

"I plan on doing a lot of work, not a little," she said in answer to his earlier question.

"On Kauai? You crazy?"

"No, I'm not crazy."

He couldn't help but notice that she didn't sound very certain as she continued to stare out at the steadily falling rain.

"Hopefully this weather will keep up. I won't even be tempted to go outside," she said.

"Oh, it'll rain some in the next three weeks, but just wait till the sun comes out," he said. The beauty of Kauai was almost the best-kept secret in the world.

Before he could stop himself, Rick took one quick perusal of her bare legs and damn, if she didn't turn around and catch him at it. She shot him an icy glare even as she self-consciously tugged on the hem of the white shorts that hit her mid-thigh. He felt as guilty as hell, but could he help it if he appreciated beauty in all its forms?

"Anything else you need before dinner?" He smiled and tried focusing on her eyes, which turned out to be an even bigger mistake. He was drawn to them the way he was drawn to the blue Pacific waters on a sunny day.

* * *

Fighting the urge to shiver despite the heat, Kylee ran her hands up and down her arms and turned away to avoid Rick Pau's heated stare.

"No, thank you. All I need is peace and quiet," she said.

She heard him moving across the room. When she turned around, expecting to watch him leave, she found he'd paused beside the door. Her cool dismissal hadn't diminished his smile in the least.

"I'll just leave your dinner on the table in the kitchen. That's my house in back. If you need anything, just call the number on the pad next to the phone in the kitchen or walk on over. The door's always open."

"Thank you," she said, watching him let himself out of the door. When the screen door closed behind him, she let out a sigh. She was alone at last with nothing but the sound of the rain on the metal roof for company. Aside from Rick Pau's sudden appearance, this was just what she wanted. Just what she needed to get her writing back on track. No more excuses.

She cast a wary glance at the laptop in its padded case and decided that after the five-hour flight from L.A. and then the quick, interisland commute and drive out, it wouldn't hurt to take a shower and slip into some clean, comfortable clothes. She'd been traveling a good nine hours. Waiting a few more minutes before she started working wouldn't hurt.

Hurrying toward the master bedroom, she left both bags on the floor, opened them flat, and then dug out a short, cool, lemon yellow summer shift and carried it toward the bathroom. Upon opening the door, Kylee stood there gaping at a bathroom complete with almost everything, right down to thick, fluffy towels with *Hale Hanea* embroidered on them—everything except exterior walls. Two sides of the room consisted of open air and the tangled jungle beyond.

She knew enough about exotic plants to recognize the ginger that bloomed profusely. The bushes covered with the crepe-textured yellow flowers grew there, too. A lava rock waterfall stood outside, a few feet from the varnished, wooden floor of the deck. Blooming orchids growing in woody coconut halves hung from the tree limbs, adding a touch of magic to the atmosphere. The shower was off to one side of the open lanai, the fixtures plumbed into more lava rock.

She glanced over at the toilet standing in the opposite corner, then at the sink and the sunken bathtub before she turned around and searched the house. There wasn't another bathroom in the entire place. She made a beeline for the kitchen phone.

Rick Pau answered on the first ring. *"Hale Hanea.* Can I help you?"

"There seems to be a little something missing in the bathroom."

"Ah. Miss Christopher. Didn't I put out fresh soap and towels?"

"No walls."

She could hear him laughing on the other end before he said, "No need."

"You don't expect me to shower or to . . . to . . . do *everything* right out in the *open* do you?" She hated hearing her voice rise on every word and tried to get a grip.

"Nobody can see you. The room's completely surrounded by thick *hau* bush and ginger, not to mention the hill behind it. In fact, that's the room that usually gets the most compliments."

"It's totally unacceptable."

"Give it a try." There was a long, pregnant pause.

"Well, if I stay here I guess I'll have to, won't I?"

"Trust me, it's totally private," he assured her.

Kylee simply sighed. She was from Los Angeles, for

heaven's sake, where nearly every house and car was fully armed and alarmed and this man expected her to strip down and shower out in the open? He *had* to be kidding.

"Is there anything else I can do?" He was obviously quite serious.

She wondered if anything ever got to Rick Pau and made a mental note to *never,* ever take one of Sylvia's vacation recommendations again.

"No. Thanks." She hung up before he could say another chipper thing and stalked back to the bathroom. Whipping a towel off the rack, she went back into the bedroom to strip off her mud-splattered, damp clothes and wrapped herself up in the towel.

With her lemon shift in hand, she trudged back to the bathroom and simply stood there for a good three minutes, silent, half-expecting to catch sight of someone creeping through the bushes. Birds were singing despite the falling rain that trailed off the metal roof in steady streams. The waterfall bubbled merrily; the hanging orchids swayed in the gentle breeze.

Kylee shrugged and walked over to the handles in the lava wall to turn on the water. *What the heck,* she thought with a shrug. *When in Rome . . .*

Rick put a mini loaf of freshly baked basil-sourdough bread into the basket he had filled with the rest of Kylee's dinner. A swatch of tropical print fabric lined the heavy wicker. He tucked the material around containers of chilled salmon flavored with dill, a green salad, and some assorted veggies he'd grilled earlier on the barbecue on his lanai. The addition of a chilled bottle of chardonnay and a container of rice pudding completed the task.

Staring down at the basket without really focusing

on its contents, he gave up trying and admitted he couldn't get his new houseguest out of his mind.

If the look in those clear blue eyes was any indication, Ms. Kylee Christopher's life wasn't as perfect as the cool, totally put together image she projected. There was something eating away at her that even her standoffish attitude couldn't hide. What he thought he had read in the depths of her eyes was fear—certainly not of him—but from some undefinable source, and for some curious reason, he found himself wanting to be the one to help remedy her situation.

The rain had stopped and the sky was beginning to clear as Rick picked up the basket and walked out of the kitchen of the house that backed up to the Wainiha River. Originally, he'd built the smaller cottage, a mirror image of the large structure, as the guest house, intending to move into the more spacious dwelling when it was complete. But after two years in the cottage, he found that he was so comfortable right next to the river that he decided to establish the main house as a vacation rental and share with others the solitude of the garden spot he had created.

Hale Hanea was usually a honeymooner's paradise, not often rented by singles, yet Kylee Christopher had come here alone, not to sightsee, but to work. It gave him one more facet of her life to think about, one more piece of the puzzle to toy with.

When he reached the wide double doors of the main house, he immediately saw Kylee seated at the desk that overlooked the taro patches in the field below the house. She had obviously dealt with the open-air shower, for her long hair was still damp. A wisp of a yellow dress showed off her bare shoulders to perfection. She had already plugged in her computer and was seated with her back to him, staring at the blinking cursor on a blank screen.

He shuffled his bare feet against the lanai floor and

cleared his throat so that he wouldn't startle her before he called out a greeting.

"I've got your dinner," he explained, opening the door for himself as he carried the basket inside.

"Set it in the kitchen," she told him, not turning around, her attention focused on the blank computer screen.

He carried the basket over to the tile counter that separated the living space from the kitchen appliances, opened the refrigerator, and unpacked the separate food containers.

"Ever been to Kauai before?" Rick asked as he straightened.

"No."

"Let me know when you'd like a guided tour of the north shore." *Nice going, Rick.* The offer was made before he could stop himself. If he wasn't careful, she would be gone before morning.

She made no comment, as she ran her hand through her hair.

"No extra charge," he added.

Her shoulders rose and fell on a sigh. Rick found the corkscrew and uncorked the wine, then shoved the cork back in and placed the bottle in the refrigerator. He straightened, still unable to take his eyes off of her.

"Plenty to see. Lots to do if you like the outdoors. Kauai can be pretty slow for some folks." He left the basket on the counter and walked around it into the main room.

Kylee turned around, her elbow propped on the desk, and pinned him with an icy stare.

"Thank you for your offer, but this is strictly a working vacation for me, Mr. Pau. I need *absolute* privacy. I don't intend to go anywhere or do anything, just work."

"Rick," he said.

"What?" She looked startled.

"The name's Rick. Mr. Pau always ends up sounding

like the name of a World Championship Wrestler when a haole says it. You know. Mr. *Pow!*"

"Haole?" She frowned.

"A stranger." Rick started toward the door. Something in the way she was hovering on the edge of the chair, every inch of her tensed and waiting for him to leave, prodded him to keep talking. He'd love to see her relax. "I left your dinner in the refrigerator. Tonight it's all alfresco. Salmon, vegetables, salad. Some wine."

"Thank you." She finally softened a bit and ran her hand through her hair again, shaking out the damp ends. "That sounds fine. I'm sorry if I was a bit abrupt, but I plan on spending the next three weeks working and really do need privacy."

"Working on . . . ?"

"I'm a television screenwriter."

"I kind of figured it was something like that," he said quickly, glancing at the blank computer screen again.

"I'm on a pretty tight deadline, so if you see my lights on late at night, don't worry. Time gets away from me."

"Working on anything exciting?" Expecting a brush-off, he was surprised at how easily she opened up to talk about her work.

"An M.O.W. Movie of the week. For Charese LaDonne. Something that'll have to go up against Monday night football. Something romantic aimed at the female audience that doesn't want to watch Neanderthals grunt and bash their heads together."

"Charese LaDonne?" He whistled, impressed. The middle-aged actress had been low profile for a while, but there weren't many people who wouldn't have recognized the name of the Oscar winner.

Kylee nodded. "Last year I won an Emmy for Movie-of-the-Week Original Screenplay. Charese loved the show. Her agent called mine and now I'm contracted to do a comeback script for her."

"Pretty scary stuff." He leaned back against the door frame and crossed his arms.

She looked surprised by his comment and then frowned, nodding in agreement. "Yeah. It is."

"Any ideas?"

"Some. I just can't seem to get started."

"Maybe you should take a few days off, see the sights and relax," he suggested. As suddenly as it had appeared, her candidness was replaced by a closed look and an icy tone.

"Are you a writer, Rick?"

Although she was no longer smiling, it pleased him to hear her use his first name. "I've dabbled some," he admitted.

"Then you don't really know what you're talking about. This script isn't going to get finished unless I keep my butt in this chair and write it."

He held his hands up in surrender. "Enough said. I'll get out of your hair."

He didn't want to dwell on her cute butt in or out of the chair. Besides, he couldn't help notice how vulnerable she looked sitting there with her bare feet curled around each other and that anxious, haunted look in her eyes. He would have loved to have crossed the room, to massage her neck and shoulders to try to ease away some of the tension that was so palpable. But he wouldn't dare make a move like that without invitation. Kylee looked volatile enough to pack up and leave at the least provocation and the last thing he wanted was to see her drive away.

As much as he was tempted to linger, when she turned away, Rick slipped out without a good-bye.

It was dark when Kylee gave up and shut down the computer. Frustrated beyond belief, she found she hadn't even been able to decide what to type for the page headers. Rummaging through the refrigerator, she filled a plate with some of the luscious goodies Rick had left, poured herself a glass of wine, and carried everything out to the lanai.

The jungle surrounding the house was pitch black. She set her plate down on a side table beside the wicker couch and lit three citronella buckets he had conveniently left there to keep the mosquitoes at bay. The flames flickered and, when coupled with the light streaming out through the windows, the wide veranda was enveloped in a soft, butter yellow glow.

Night intensified the rain forest sounds. Bullfrogs croaked out a deep, rumbling chorus. Small brown lizards with suction-cup toes clung to the corners of the windows where the bugs congregated. They chirped and clucked while patiently waiting to attack their next catch. Somewhere beyond the dense growth that lined the property, water rushed downstream toward the beach, singing against the river rock along the way. All in all, the sounds blended into a calming, lyrical melody. There was a serenity about the place that should have soothed and inspired her. Instead, the tranquil atmosphere was beginning to drive her crazy. There wasn't even a single, small screen black-and-white television in the place.

Kylee was forced to admit that she was used to the big city pace and noise; the sound of the nightly newscaster droning on the television with the latest doom and gloom statistics; murder and mayhem; the rush of traffic, not water. The smell of smog, not the scent of flowers. By the time she finished the delicious evening snack and set the plate aside, she had convinced herself that her hectic L.A. lifestyle stoked her well-honed competitive edge.

Obviously, coming to Kauai to work had been a big mistake.

"Clear your head. Get out of L.A. and you'll see, the script will come together."

Good old Sylvia and her advice. Usually her agent was right on with her suggestions, but this one had obviously materialized out of left field. Kylee started to stand up and call Sylvia to tell her that the getaway idea wasn't working until she realized it was already eleven o'clock in California, far too late to give her agent a piece of her mind.

Kylee leaned back against the plush sofa cushions and sighed, then she curled up her legs beneath her and stared off toward the small cottage at the back of the property. There was a light burning in Rick Pau's front window, but she saw no other sign of life. She wondered if he might have a television hidden away back there, then realized after the waspish way she'd reacted to him earlier, she didn't dare go asking any favors.

For a while she sat there staring out at the night while the lilting strains of guitar music accompanied by a man's voice singing in Hawaiian drifted on the breeze. The haunting, seductive sounds drew her, lured her into walking across the lanai until she stood against the railing and looked over at the small cottage. Rick Pau had obviously been blessed with talent and good looks.

While she admired the music as much as Rick's ability to make it, she wished she had learned to play an instrument, but having been raised in a series of foster homes, her only consistent childhood pastime had been reading.

Later, in her teens, writing had become her passion. Journalism classes, writing competitions, submissions to small presses and literary journals had filled her life and took the place of the family and love she never experienced.

Early on, she discovered she had a gift for screenwriting, for melding a concept into a storyline of action and dialogue. Without firsthand knowledge of a loving relationship, she became driven to write. Now, at twenty-five, her work took the place of a husband and children.

Writing filled the void. It was and had always been her life, which made her even more terrified to think that now, at the peak of her career, she might be blocked.

She *was* her work. It defined who and what she was. What would she do if she never wrote another word? What would she become? Pushing away from the rail, she warned herself not to think so negatively. This inability to come up with an idea, this lack of words, was just a phase.

Sylvia was right. She had just needed to get away, change her environment. Things would be all right tomorrow. She'd be right back at it again in the morning and before she knew it, the first draft of her screenplay would be stacked up on the desk beside the computer.

The night air was thick and humid, alive with mosquitoes. She moved back into range of the candle smoke that kept them at bay. One by one, she blew out the candles and then walked back into the house. Shutting off the lights, she made her way into the master suite and undressed in the dark. As she slipped between the crisp, clean sheets, she lay there listening to the sound of Rick Pau's soothing voice, wondering about the meaning behind the haunting sound of the Hawaiian words. The air was close and hot. She tossed and turned as geckoes chirped and mosquitoes whined against the screens. Kylee sighed and resigned herself to a long night.

What seemed like minutes later, she awoke to the sound of roosters crowing in the bush outside the bedroom window. With a groan, she rolled over and stared at the clock on the rattan table beside the bed: 5:00

A.M. Although it was overcast and drizzling outside, the weak daylight didn't seem to dampen the roosters' enthusiasm.

Extracting herself from the tangle of sheets, she stood up and realized the aroma of freshly brewed coffee was wafting through the house. She shoved her fingers through her hair, pulled on a pair of shorts and a black jogging bra. Bleary-eyed, she headed for the kitchen.

There was no sign of Rick Pau, but the table was set for one and a bright display of tropical blossoms in a pottery vase made a pretty centerpiece. A note printed in bold handwriting was taped to the coffeepot. She pulled it off and read as she reached for a ceramic mug.

Aloha kakahiaka. Good morning. Spinach quiche and croissants are in the oven. Hope you got lots of work done last night. Rick.

Kylee groaned again. *Work?* Who was he kidding? She poured her coffee, kept it black and reached for the phone. It was eight o'clock in California. Sylvia was a notorious late riser. *If she isn't up yet, she can wake up to the sound of my voice,* Kylee thought as she punched in her calling card numbers.

She was delighted when Sylvia Greene picked up the phone sounding groggy.

"Greene Literary Agency."

"It's Kylee. Very funny, Sylvia. You could have warned me."

Over the line came the sound of rustling bedclothes and the protesting mew of a cat. Kylee pictured Sylvia wrestling around, trying to sit up in bed.

"Kylee? Where are you? Did you find the place all right?"

Unable to stand still, Kylee carried the cordless phone out onto the lanai. Through the gauze of rain she could see Rick's cottage a few yards away. He was on his own wide veranda, doing sit-ups no less. She tried to turn away, but she was mesmerized by the sheen of sweat on his warm, honey brown skin and the way his abs flexed and unflexed with every curl. She tried to imagine what those muscles might feel like were she to run her hands over them—

"Kylee? I said, what do you think of the view?" Sylvia's voice jolted her back to reality.

"Oh, the view's just *great,*" Kylee said, slapping away a mosquito on her thigh before she turned around and padded back into the house. "I am beginning to have a sneaking suspicion that you set this whole thing up on purpose, Syl."

"Set *what* up?"

"I'm stuck out here in the mud with the devastatingly handsome houseboy that you so very slyly failed to mention."

"Houseboy?"

Kylee had to give the old gal credit. She actually managed to sound like she hadn't a clue.

"Rick Pau. You didn't tell me he was such a knockout and apparently single."

"Oh. Yeah, well. I guess I forgot." Sylvia yawned and didn't try to hide it. "I just loved the house. I really thought you would, too."

While Sylvia went on and on about how much she had enjoyed the place during her own stay, Kylee opened the oven door, reached for a warm croissant and bit into the flaky, buttery flavored bread. She munched away and then, when Sylvia paused to take a breath, she informed her, "There are no bathroom walls, Syl."

"So? It's in a jungle for god's sake."

"It hasn't stopped raining since I got here."

"So? We live in a desert. Soak it up for a while. It's good for your skin."

Kylee sighed.

"He *is* handsome, isn't he," Sylvia admitted, not bothering to clarify.

"Yeah, he is that," Kylee mused, polishing off the last of the croissant.

"Maybe a little injection of passion would do you good."

Kylee almost choked on a swig of coffee. *"Passion?"*

"You know, the stuff of which you write? Passion. Lust. Romance. Your script *is* for a movie of the week aimed at the women who want to avoid the NFL playoffs. Remember? It's *supposed* to be steamy, PG-rated erotic. A woman's fantasy. Why not do a little physical research while you're there?"

Kylee tensed. "I don't need a physical relationship. I don't need any relationship at all." She found herself drifting over to the door again and glancing over at Rick's lanai. He had flipped over and was doing push-ups now. Push-ups. The exercise helped her conjure up all sorts of images.

"Kylee? Kylee, are you still there?"

She spun away from the door, wiped the perspiration from her forehead with the back of her hand, and then held her hair up off the nape of her neck. She'd give anything for even a whisper of a breeze.

"I'm here."

"So how is it going? You're all settled in, ready to write? What time is it there? Six o'clock? What are you doing up so early?"

"Roosters." There was no way she was going to admit that she hadn't written word one on the script yet and didn't know if she was going to do any better today. "Listen, Sylvia, I've got to get going."

"Say hello to Rick for me," Sylvia trilled. Then, in her best old Hollywood style, she oozed, "Bye, bye, dahling."

Kylee hung up the phone, grabbed oven mitts and pulled the quiche out, then turned the oven off. When she straightened, there was a quick knock at the side door.

Rick Pau, his rippling abs thankfully covered in a faded, ripped tank top, stood watching her from the other side of the screen.

"Want to go for a jog? I was just on my way and thought you might like to join me."

"A *jog?*" She scooped her hair back off her face but it fell over one eye again. "I don't jog. Besides, it's raining."

"It's always raining."

"I noticed."

"How was breakfast?"

"Fine," she said, watching him through the screen. "Actually, I haven't had any of the quiche yet, but it looks delicious. Where'd you get it?"

He laughed. "I made it."

He cooks, too. Kylee was beginning to think he was too good to be true.

"How's your script coming along? I saw your light on late last night." He hunkered down to tie his running shoe.

A bout of anxiety made her head swim and her stomach lurch. "Fine," she managed. "It's coming along just fine." She knew a panic attack when it hit her, even though she'd never taken time to allow herself the luxury of one before.

Rick got to his feet and paused, watching her closely. Too closely.

"Are you all right?"

"Sure. I think . . . I . . . it's probably just jet lag."

He was out of his shoes before she could blink. Opening the screen, he stepped inside and walked over to her. Rick reached out and put his hand against her forehead.

"No fever."

"No kidding. I said I was all right."

He was so close she could study each of his lush

eyelashes. *It should be illegal for a man to have such beautiful eyes,* she found herself thinking. He continued to hover, watching her with concern and something more, something she didn't want to think about—a look that made her cheeks feel flushed and her pulse jumpy.

She swallowed, backed up a step, and found herself pressed up against the kitchen cabinet. "Sylvia said to say hello."

Rick smiled and leaned back against the round tabletop. "Now there's a lady who knows how to have fun."

"Meaning?"

Kylee didn't even want to imagine young, virile Rick Pau playing gigolo to her agent. Sylvia was tops in her field and a great friend in the bargain, but even a succession of Beverly Hills facelifts couldn't hide the fact that Syl had seen sixty up close and personal quite a few years back. Rick Pau didn't look a day over twenty-nine.

"Meaning, you might need to take time to get out in the fresh air, take a walk or a swim and clear your head."

"That's impossible. I'm on a deadline."

"How can you create if you're uptight? I think you need to relax and get into the beauty of the island. Slow down. This is Kauai, one of the most inspiring places in the world. You have to let the island work its magic."

"Do you have a degree in psychology?" Her tone was cool, her words clipped.

He assessed her for a long, quiet moment. Kylee dropped her gaze first.

"No, I don't, but it doesn't take an expert to see that you're pretty stressed out."

"Thank you so much. I feel a lot better now." With his dark brown eyes staring into hers the way they were, she could hardly think. Unfortunately, when she did, she recalled Sylvia's suggestion that she do a little physical research. What would it be like to kiss Rick Pau? Were his lips as conditioned as his stomach muscles?

As if he could read her mind, Rick abruptly shoved away from the table and cleared his throat. "Listen," he said, "I'm going to a luau tonight on the other side of the island. One of my cousin's kids is turning a year old. If you'd like to go with me, see the real thing instead of a tourist luau—"

"No thanks. Really." She tried to ignore the wave of loneliness that hit her. She had no idea what it would be like to have one cousin, let alone a number of them with children.

He shrugged off her refusal. "Just thought I'd ask. I'd better get going."

Thank god, Kylee thought.

As soon as the screen closed behind him, she let out an inaudible sigh of relief. Rick picked up his jogging shoes and carried them over to the steps where he sat down to put them on. Kylee turned away and began rummaging through the lower cabinets and drawers. The anxiety attack she had suffered earlier reminded her of a writer friend, one of Sylvia's other clients. Rita Mainville tended to suffer panic attacks near the end of every deadline and had plenty of suggestions for first aid remedies of all sorts.

In an end cupboard, Kylee located a neatly folded stack of paper bags. She chose a small one to set on the desk beside the computer in case she wound up hyperventilating.

Two

Three long, torturous days later, the rain finally stopped just as Kylee finished struggling through the first ten pages of her script. The day was half over. She was pacing the confines of the house when she decided it was the peace and quiet that was driving her stark raving mad. Carrying her work out onto the lanai, she began to read through it while seated in one of the comfy chairs. By the time she finished, she was certain the first draft was definitely nothing more than a pile of dog doo.

Frustrated, she tossed what little there was of the script onto the small bamboo end table beside her and then weighted it down with a citronella candle before she stood up and stretched. Glancing over at the cottage set against the trees, she wondered what in the world Rick Pau did to amuse himself during the long, rainy days. Complying with her wishes, he hadn't interrupted her at all in the last few days except to leave her meals in the kitchen. Once he had come by to ask if she needed anything special from Hanalei, the little town up the road.

She wanted to tell him to bring back a fresh idea.

As much as she would have liked to avoid thinking of him, she couldn't seem to get Rick out of her mind. The more he adhered to her wishes and stayed away, the more she found herself wondering what he was doing, listening for the sound of his pickup truck coming and going or the strains of guitar music that often came from his house.

She glanced over at his place again and thought it looked decidedly magical against the backdrop of green. All around the yard, crystal raindrops still clung to the leaves and blossoms on the thick foliage sparkling like rainbow-hued gems in the sunlight.

Just then, the sound of an automobile on Powerhouse Road drew her attention. Rick's beat-up pickup was parked in the carport beside his cottage, so she was surprised and curious when another truck came barreling down the steep drive and ground to a halt amid the mud and gravel. It came to a stop right in front of her lanai.

Inside the cab sat three middle-aged women who waved cheerfully at her as they hopped out and collected six-packs of sodas and beers from the back of the pickup. Kylee waved back and watched them hurry up the steps to the covered walkway that connected the two houses. The blonde woman leading the way called out, "Aloha, Rick!" and Kylee heard him respond in a deep, resonant voice, *"Komo mai!* Come in, come in. You're right on time.

Three-to-one odds, Kylee mused. Probably just what a man as handsome as Rick Pau was used to. Ignoring the sound of laughter and frivolity issuing from the cottage, Kylee stood up and stretched and wandered back inside, intent on reading through a stack of recent issues of *Variety* she'd packed along, that and pouring a glass of iced tea.

From her kitchen she could hear the sound of Rick singing in Hawaiian. Upon opening the refrigerator door, she discovered the light was out inside and glanced over at the microwave. Sure enough, the clock wasn't on. The electricity was probably out in the entire house. After removing the tall glass tea pitcher, she banged the refrigerator door closed and wondered at her bad humor.

"No way," she mumbled to herself when the thought struck her that she was actually feeling put out at the women having such uproarious fun in Rick's cottage. "No way," she mumbled. Surely she couldn't be jealous, she decided, quite appalled at the notion. His dark eyes and hair and his megawatt smile gave him looks any woman might swoon over, but even if she had been the swooning type, she didn't even know the man.

Besides, *she* certainly wasn't looking for any *Fantasy Island* romantic interlude.

Kylee poured the tea into a tall glass filled with ice and decided to take a stroll through the rest of the house to see if the electricity was out all over or if perhaps just the circuit breaker in the kitchen had blown. When none of the switches she hit in the living area or in the master bedroom worked either, she headed for the bathroom. Opening the door, she stepped in and got the shock of her life. There, right in the middle of the lava rock shower, nosing at the drain, was a pig as big as an overstuffed easy chair.

And if she wasn't mistaken, it was the same pig she'd nearly run down when she first arrived.

"Go away," she yelled, trying a shooing motion in the pig's direction. He merely turned beady eyes her way, stared for a minute or two, and then went back to snuffling at the drain.

"Okay, that's it." She marched out of the bathroom, slamming the door behind her, then walked back through the house and out onto the lanai.

Without even pausing to slip on her sandals, she hurried along the short platform walk that connected the cottages. As she drew near, she heard Rick call out, *"Lewa. Ami. Holoholo."*

His words were followed by a burst of laughter and then one of the women giggled, "Rick, show me *exactly* where to put my hands."

Kylee paused just outside the door when she heard

Rick reply softly, "The bosom. Remember, it's 'to my bosom I call you.'" His voice, strong and melodic, resonated even when he wasn't singing.

She tried to peer into the window beside the front doors, curious to see what was going on. As she drew closer, Kylee kicked over a basket filled with gardening tools. A small hand spade and a trowel clattered onto the wooden lanai floor.

Inside the house, all talk immediately stopped. Kylee was struck with a ridiculous urge to run, but instead she straightened, waiting while condensation dripped down the glass of iced tea in her hand. Almost immediately, Rick was at the door, smiling in welcome.

"Komo mai. Come in, Kylee. We'd love to have you join us." He glanced down at the garden tools and added, "I thought one of the cats from up the road was out here making mischief."

"I'm sorry. It was an accident." She found herself glancing around curiously at the tidy interior of his small house as she stepped past him over the threshold.

"Hey, Kylee, I'm glad you decided to take a break and stop by. It looks like that iced tea could be freshened up. Or how about a beer?"

"I'm not here to party," she assured him as he led her into the sparsely furnished, open-air house that was a more compact version of *Hale Hanea.* She was somewhat surprised to see an office set up with all manner of state-of-the-art computer equipment on the screened-in back lanai. There was even a copy machine and a fairly extensive library displayed in assorted plastic stacking crates.

At the bar in the living area, his three female guests were all hunched over open notebooks arguing about bosoms again. As Rick interrupted to introduce Kylee, they looked up in unison and waved just as they had upon arrival.

Rick's hand brushed hers as he reached for the iced

tea. When they touched, Kylee felt an instantaneous shock wave jolt her. Startled by her overwhelming physical reaction to him, she looked up and found Rick staring down at her, surprise mirrored in his own eyes.

It was a moment longer before he took a step back and said softly, "Let me see about getting you something to drink."

Feeling a sudden, intense need to put plenty of space between them, Rick hurried over to the kitchen and began offering her a list of drink options.

"I'll just have half a glass of wine," she decided.

He glanced over his shoulder at Kylee. It had certainly turned out to be a day full of surprises. First, not only had she shown up at his door looking like something out of a *California Girl* magazine in short white shorts and a lime green tank T-shirt, but then she agreed to stay a few minutes. Now she was even letting her hair down enough to accept half a glass of wine.

Most surprising of all was the jolt he'd received when he had touched her. Not since he had fallen out of love with Angela, his first wife, had any woman had the power to arouse him so intensely.

Noticing Kylee still standing awkwardly in the center of the room watching the others, Rick pulled himself together, walked around the bar, and handed her the wineglass half full of chardonnay.

She thanked him, took a sip, and continued to stand there, obviously uncomfortable. He stayed beside her and began to explain. "These ladies are old friends of mine."

"Not that *old*, Rick. You want to make us feel bad?" The shortest of the three women looked over at him and smiled.

"You know I don't," he laughed. "Uncle Raymond would have my head if I upset you ladies." Then he turned back to Kylee. "My uncle is a *kumu hula*, a hula teacher, as well as a singer at a local restaurant. A couple of times during the summer he goes fishing off the Big Island and I take over three of his hula classes. These ladies have been learning hula for years now."

"Sometimes I don't feel like we're getting any better," the thin, suntanned blonde quipped.

"You're doing the best you can for not being Hawaiian," Rick teased. Then he turned to Kylee and touched his heart. "Hula comes from here," he explained. She was listening intently. He liked that about her, that when he was talking to her she gave him her full attention. She took another sip of wine and nodded, her hypnotic, blue-eyed gaze locked on his.

He felt himself quicken and abruptly headed for the sofa where he had left his guitar, deciding he had better have something to hide behind before he let his traitorous body embarrass the hell out of him.

When he invited her to watch his uncle's students hula, Kylee nodded and finally sat down on a chair across the room. He knew that after the thirty-minute session and a beer or two, the older gals would be more than delighted to show off their skills—which were minimal at best—but they all had a good time.

Kylee seemed to relax and sat back to enjoy the dance. He began to play and sing the words to an old favorite, *"Ke Aloha,"* and watched her smile over the rim of her wineglass when he had to call out the English translation that keyed the dance steps. For a moment he was lost in the teaching, reminding the women to draw their hands into their bosoms. When they finished the dance, Kylee set her glass down to applaud and compliment them.

Much to Rick's embarrassment, all three women turned admiring eyes his way and proclaimed him as good a teacher as his uncle. He knew he wasn't anything of the sort and so did they, but Raymond Pau was almost seventy. Rick was sure the ladies didn't do half as much flirting during Uncle Raymond's lessons.

On their way out the door, the women invited him to join them for dinner, an offer he quickly declined so that he could get back to Kylee before she decided to leave. He was amazed to find that she hadn't moved, but had simply curled up in the big chair with one foot tucked beneath her. When he noticed her empty wineglass, he picked it up and headed for the kitchen before she could protest.

"They certainly have a good time," she said.

"They do at that. What a trio." He walked back into the sitting area and handed her the wine.

"If I drink this, I'm not going to get much done this evening." Kylee looked into the pale liquid, swirled it around the glass, and took a sip.

"How's the work going?"

She shrugged. "Could be better, but it's coming along. At least it's stopped raining." Her gaze lingered on the window. Anywhere but on him.

"There's a tropical depression off the islands." He felt himself break into a sweat. The sight of her sitting here just the way he'd pictured her so many times over the past three days had him acting like a teenager in heat instead of a thirty-year-old who should have known better than to let his body take control of his better judgment.

"I think *I'm* tropically depressed." She stretched forward to place the wineglass on the table in front of her. The innocent move gave him a quick glimpse down the front of her T-shirt.

Rick almost groaned aloud. He swallowed the sound and wiped his forehead.

"That's quite an electronic setup out there," she was saying. "What do you do with the latest in high-tech computer equipment?"

He forced himself to concentrate on what she was saying. She was looking at his office.

"I dabble some. In this and that. I just created a home page to advertise this place. And I put a business newsletter together. Television cable stops at Hanalei, so nearly everyone out here is on the Net. Brings the world right to the island. Sometimes I wonder if that's good or bad."

He watched her gaze drift back to him and hold on his eyes. For a moment that seemed like forever, yet at the same time far too brief, they stared into each other's eyes.

Kylee suddenly blinked and then quickly uncurled her legs until she was seated almost primly. "I almost forgot why I came over here."

Rick watched her sit up even straighter, a move that emphasized the high swell of her lovely breasts "Why's that?"

"The electricity is out." She slipped forward until she was perched on the edge of the chair as if ready to run.

"That happens a lot. The county is always working on the lines. It's probably back on by now." He couldn't keep his eyes from roaming over her face, along her throat, down to her breasts, and back to her eyes again.

"And there's a pig in the bathroom." She folded her arms and waited, obviously expecting him to be shocked.

"What did it look like?"

"What do you mean what did it *look* like? What can I say? It was fat. It was a pig. It was standing in the shower snorting down the drain, that's what."

"Around here, a pig isn't just a pig." He tried to keep from staring at her bare thighs, tried not to imagine what it would be like to run his hands up them. "There are wild pigs that have tusks and they can be very, very dangerous. If you ever see one of those, put something between you and it as fast as you can. Better yet, climb a tree. Then there are domestic pigs that usually end up as the center of attention at a luau. The family on the opposite side of the road has a pet pig named Kiko, which is Hawaiian for Spot."

"It had spots and no tusks. In fact, I almost ran over it the day I tried to find this place." She stood up, tugged on the hem of her shorts, and stared down at him.

"Kiko is a him."

"Whatever. He's in my shower."

"Probably gone by now."

"I hope so." She glanced at the door, then back." "I have to be going."

"Stay for dinner." The invitation was out before he could stop himself.

"I can't." She looked like she was going to sprint for the door.

"You have to eat." He sounded like his mother.

"I should get back. To work." She was decidedly nervous now, looking around as if she just realized how very alone they were.

"What are you afraid of Kylee?" He knew immediately that he had pushed the wrong button.

She tossed back her hair, obviously angry. "Is this your m.o., Rick? You play host to women looking for a summer fling? A thrill? A quick passionate tryst in paradise that'll get them through another year, give them a summer fantasy to cling to? I'm not interested."

"Whoa! Is that what you *think* I do? Sit out here in the country and prey on uptight mainland women looking to get laid? That's not why I invited you to dinner. I thought you might enjoy seeing four different walls for a change." His own fury had been ignited by the fact that he *had* been fantasizing about her.

"I'm sorry." She still looked too furious to be offering a sincere apology.

"You should be."

They stood there staring at each other as tension sizzled in the void between them.

Finally, Rick let out a pent-up breath and decided to try again. "So, do you like raw fish?"

Kylee didn't know what had come over her. All she was certain of at the moment was that Rick Pau had the ability to bring out the shrew in her and she had absolutely no idea why. She tried smiling.

"I like it," she admitted.

"I'm going to make some fresh *ahi sashimi*. You're welcome to join me." Then he added hastily, "No strings attached."

"I'm sorry for that comment," she apologized again. "I've been out of sorts lately. Probably this weather." It was hot and sticky now that the rain had stopped and the sun had spent the rest of the day drying out the soggy landscape. There wasn't a breath of air stirring the palm fronds.

Rick headed for the refrigerator and as she wandered over to the serving bar to watch, he pulled a white paper-wrapped package out of the refrigerator along with a head of cabbage and some soy sauce.

"I'd bet it's your script that's bothering you, not the weather," he said offhandedly as he began to unwrap a piece of dark red fish and set it on a cutting board.

Kylee grudgingly had to admit he was right. "It's been like pulling teeth to get the words on the page," she confessed. A tremor of anxiety hit her stomach and she set her wineglass aside.

"Want to talk about it?" He took a lethally sharp-looking knife out of a wooden block and headed back to the cutting board.

"I'd rather talk about anything else," she told him.

"How did you end up way out here running a bed and board?"

"I was born on Kauai. Over on the other side, in Hanapepe. My mom and dad worked for a big sugar company. Dad worked the mill. I went to the University of Hawaii. Majored in business. Sort of followed in the footsteps of one of my uncles in Honolulu. I've been lucky."

Kylee watched him execute a shrug, a casual move that drew her eye to his well-honed shoulder and upper arm. She had an instant visual image of him doing push-ups and looked away, concentrating on the interior of the cottage.

With what he made renting out the larger cottage, she figured he had enough to live comfortably, if not lavishly. Faded tank tops and running shorts seemed to be the uniform he lived in. There was little overhead with him doing all the work around the place himself and that rusted pickup couldn't have cost him more than a few hundred dollars. She envied anyone who could live without all the "stuff" most people, including her, thought they needed.

Although he had mentioned his family, there were no photos in the living area, no pictures of family, or children, old or young people, no one who might be a lover. Perhaps they had more in common than she thought. She thought she was the only person in the world without photographs from her past.

"You don't have any photos around." She tried to sound offhanded, casual.

"Lost 'em all in *Iniki*, the hurricane that hit the island back in '92."

So, unlike her, at least he once had photos and the memories that came with them. Curiosity got the best of her. "Have you ever been married?"

"Yeah. Once." The knife slipped easily through the firm, chilled fish as he cut it into a long row of even slices. "Have you?"

Married? How could she tell him that she had never had a chance to learn how to love? How could she tell him that she didn't know the first thing about love or commitment, for she had never been exposed to it in her young life. Then, later, she had never slowed down enough to let herself learn.

Kylee shook her head but all she said was, "No. Not even close."

He looked up, his dark eyes assessing her, before he turned his attention back to the fish and continued. "Why's that?"

"I . . . I've just been too busy." She was adept at changing that subject. "How did you meet your wife?"

"I met Angela at U. H.," he began. "She was a law student, driven, competitive. Determined to be successful. Her dream was to live on the mainland and run with a fast L.A. crowd, shop Rodeo Drive, rub shoulders with the rich and famous. I went along with it for a while, but my heart wasn't in that lifestyle and her heart wasn't in anything but work. She ended up with a big law firm, Tanner, Wilson and Warrenberg."

"Not the defense lawyers in the Ortega case?" Everyone in L.A. was familiar with the murder case which had garnered more than its share of news time over the past few months.

"Yeah. That's the firm. I guess she's got all she ever wanted now." He looked up and smiled. "Then again, I'm happy, too."

Kylee shifted on the bar stool, rolled the stem of the wineglass between her thumb and forefinger. Lost in thought, Kylee didn't comment. *Determined to be successful.* Rick's description of his first wife hit way too close to home. Kylee had never let herself make time for anything but writing, nor had she ever attempted to nurture any kind of a relationship with a man, lasting or otherwise.

While she watched Rick deftly chop cabbage and mix a soy and wasabi sauce to dip the fish into, she found an odd contentment settle over her. The sound of his voice soothed her frazzled nerves as effectively as a massage and an herbal wrap.

She discovered it was quite pleasant to let a handsome man wait on her, set the table, pour the wine. He lit a hurricane lamp and set it in the center of the table. After she sat down and spread the napkin across her lap, then picked up her chopsticks, Kylee looked up and found Rick staring at her over the rim of his wineglass. His sensuous dark eyes were enhanced by the lamplight. She felt a slow, melting warmth spread through her.

"Here's to getting that script finished," he toasted.

As Kylee lifted her glass, she watched Rick, hypnotized by his exotic dark looks, a perfect, utterly stunning mix of features. Even as she stared at him across the table, feeling the warm glow of the wine and the close, humid night air scented with ginger and night-blooming jasmine, a warning bell went off in the back of her mind. Rick Pau was intriguing, genuinely charming, killer handsome, and every woman's summer fantasy—exactly what she didn't need at this point in her life.

How in the world could she balance a love affair with the script opportunity of a lifetime? Besides that, she would be leaving the island in less than three weeks. Rick was a jack-of-all-trades who could obviously live on a shoestring. Except for the fact that he was divorced, she knew little else about him—which, she noticed with irritation, didn't keep her from wondering all kinds of things about him that had nothing to do with his background.

She watched him deftly ply the chopsticks as he dipped the *sashimi* into the sauce and carry the dripping, chilled slices to his lips. What would it be like to have him kiss her? To have him touch her with those same gentle hands that played the guitar with such emotion, hands that could coax a blossom into an arrangement or tuck a ginger flower into one of the baskets he left in her kitchen?

Forbidden curiosity, feelings she had so avidly avoided for so long, surged inside her like the water flowing in the streambed behind the house.

Somehow she was able to manage the chopsticks and eat the delicious *ahi*. Somehow she was able to keep from staring at Rick, at his lips, his hands, into his eyes. If someone asked her tomorrow what they had talked about, she was certain she wouldn't be able to say. She was functioning as if she were two entities, the Kylee that was smiling and eating and conversing on all manner of subjects, and the Kylee who could only think of one thing and that one thing involved Rick Pau and only Rick Pau.

Thankfully, she got through the meal without embarrassing herself. When he asked if she would stay awhile longer, she told him that she had to get back to her computer.

"I'll walk you back," Rick said, stacking the dishes on the counter and turning away from them.

"No, really, you don't have to." Her heart was hammering, her mouth suddenly dry. She didn't want to have to test her resolve out there alone in the dark with Rick. She didn't want him walking her home as if they were two adolescents on their first date.

"I'd like to make certain Kiko isn't lurking in your shower," he laughed.

"Oh, yes. That pig." She sighed, recalling for the first time all evening why she had ventured over to his cottage. She didn't want to walk into the bathroom and have to face half a ton of porker anymore than she wanted to be tempted by being alone with Rick in the dark.

Her fear of the pig won out.

* * *

Rick watched the sensuous sway of Kylee's walk all the way back to the rental house. The white shorts that molded her body stood out like a beacon in the dark.

When they reached the house, he stepped inside and turned on the lights, walked into the master bedroom and then the bath. Just as he'd suspected, Kiko the pig was long gone. Kylee was waiting for him in the living room, standing stiff as a sentry beside the door.

He paused a couple of feet away, reached out, and leaned one hand against the door frame, an uncalculated move that brought him within inches of her. As he stood there looking down into her deep blue eyes, he couldn't help thinking of the ocean again and found himself wanting to drown in her gaze.

It would be so easy to lean a little closer, to press his lips to hers. What would she do if he did? She seemed half-convinced he was nothing more than a gigolo, a *hapa*, or half-Hawaiian beachboy looking for a fling with a rich *haole* girl. Stealing a kiss was just what she expected of him. Trying to start something was what she had accused him of earlier. But looking down into the heated depths of her confused, wary eyes, he realized that he didn't want to risk offending her.

When he did kiss her, he wanted to do it right. He wanted her willing.

"I'm going snorkeling tomorrow." He kept his voice low and soft. He could see that she was nervous being alone with him, so much so that he was half-afraid she would rush out of the house. Her breath was coming rapidly and shallowly. Her cheeks were stained with color, not all of it from the wine.

"Let me know if you change your mind and want to come along," he finished.

"I . . . I have to work."

He wanted to touch her hair, to run his hands through it, wrap it around his fist and draw her into his arms. He wanted to tell her anyone could see that

she was pushing herself too hard. He wanted to save
her from herself. Instead he said, "It's supposed to be
hot and dry tomorrow."

He didn't know how he could feel any hotter.

"I don't think so," she mumbled, but this time she
sounded unsure. Her hesitation gave him hope.

"The offer stands." Finally, he pushed away from
the door and from her and opened the screen.

"Thanks for dinner," she said, as he stepped out
into the night.

Rick bid her good night and turned away, heading
back to his own place. He could feel her eyes following
him as he traveled the wooden walkway that connected
their lanais. It took all the strength of will he had not
to turn around and go back.

The next day dawned, bright and sunny. Up with
the roosters before dawn, Kylee worked until one in
the afternoon. Despite the thick, cloying humidity and
the sweat running between her breasts and into her
eyes, she had written eight fresh pages and had even
edited what she had finished the day before.

Confident she was back on track, grudgingly admitting to herself that Rick Pau might have been right
when he said she had needed to relax and let the story
come to her, she stood up and stretched and stared
out the window, concentrating on the taro patch and
the highway beyond.

The rumble of the old pickup's engine caused her
to start to make her way over to the front door. She
stepped out on the lanai and watched Rick toss a mesh
bag of snorkeling equipment into the back of the
pickup. The area beneath his house looked like a sec-
ondhand sporting goods store with racks of surfboards
of all shapes and sizes, windsurfing boards, rolled-up
sails, and long masts. There was a rusted mountain

bike and a shiny new racing bike with a helmet dangling from the handlebars.

It appeared what money he did manage to save he spent on toys. The man was obsessed with fun.

What would that be like, she wondered, not to be so caught up in work? To be able to take the time to learn not to hide behind writing?

She stood against the wooden railing and watched him back the truck out of the still-muddy gravel drive. When he looked over and noticed her standing there, he leaned out the open driver's side window. If the sun hadn't already been shining, the man's smile would surely have chased away the clouds.

"You sure you don't want to go?" he called out over the deep rattle of the pickup's engine.

Kylee started to tell him no, then a thrush called out from the *hau* bush, its song light and breezy, as if the orange-breasted bird was actually encouraging her to acquiesce. Her clothes were sticking to her; her hair was plastered to her temples and the back of her neck.

"I've never snorkeled before," she admitted.

"I'm a great teacher." No doubt about it, his electric smile could have coaxed the habit off a nun.

"Wait thirty seconds," she said, spinning around, hurrying to change into her swimsuit before rational thought could take hold of her.

In less than five minutes she'd slipped into her suit, tossed an oversized tank top over it, grabbed her sandals, and was riding on the bench seat in Rick's pickup with the window down, her hair unbound and blowing in the breeze. He negotiated the sharp curves on Kuhio Highway with such ease she suspected he could drive the road with his eyes closed. She relaxed and stared over the steep embankment, down into the crystal waters and the shore break that pounded the glistening sand.

"Congratulations." Rick downshifted and glanced

over at her, one hand on the wheel, the other arm
still draped over the edge of the window.

"For what?"

"For walking out on your computer to come with
me."

"I'm making headway. Finally." She caught herself
actually smiling. The world was looking brighter than
it had in weeks.

"Want to talk about the script?"

"No." *Not while it's still in the fragile, first draft stage,*
she thought. "Tell me about your island instead."

As they drove the few short miles to a place he called
Tunnels, Kylee listened as Rick pointed out the highlights of the North Shore as they drove past them.
While she was still staring up at the ebony lava cliff
face covered with fern, he pulled into a short, narrow
dirt road that ended on a bluff overlooking a beach
protected by a coral reef.

The sand was hot enough not only to fry an egg
but to blister the soft underside of her toes. Rick told
her to keep her sandals on and run for it, tossing her
a beach towel while he carried the bag of snorkel
equipment to the spot she chose.

"I think I'd be content to sit here and watch the
water." She stared at the mound of swim fins and fluo-
rescent-colored masks with long snorkels attached that
he'd dumped on a towel.

"No way." He tossed her a pair of medium-sized
fins, one at a time. "Carry them to the water," he told
her, "but put the mask and snorkel on here to be certain they fit."

Finally, she put everything on just the way Rick
wanted it. The water was cool and refreshing, the first
relief she'd had from the heat in days. Before she
could begin swimming, Kylee felt Rick's hand on her
shoulder.

"Wuuhaa?" It was impossible to talk with a rubber
mouthpiece between her teeth.

Looking like Neptune come to life, Rick stood in the shallow water with droplets beaded across the rippling muscles of his well-honed chest, his mask riding the crown of his head. When he reached for her and cupped her face with his hands, Kylee's breath caught in her throat.

"Let me adjust this for you," he said, gently pulling her mask up and brushing her hair away from the faceplate.

Her heart was pounding so hard she feared she was going to faint dead away and drown in three feet of water. Where his hands had touched her shoulders, her skin burned. Kylee blinked, trying to see Rick clearly through the water-spotted window of her mask.

Gently, he carefully tucked her hair behind her ears with his fingertips. She shivered. Her skin dimpled with goose bumps. He held on to her shoulders.

"Ready?"

Ready for what? It was disconcerting to realize that his touch could make her forget where she was and what she was doing. When he let her go, she experienced an odd sense of disappointment. Kylee couldn't take her eyes off Rick as he stretched out in the shallow water and began to swim a little ways away.

The minute she put her mask in the water she thrilled to the sight of a shimmering rainbow-hued collection of tropical fish gathered around her. As much as she enjoyed watching the fish, most of her concentration was centered on breathing through the rubber mouthpiece and praying the plastic tube would stay above the waterline.

She heard her heart beating in her ears. For the first few minutes they were in the water, they swam shoulder to shoulder. A shiver wriggled through her as they floated side by side in the warm water, skin to skin. Rick stayed beside her, touching her arm whenever he wanted to point out some underwater wonder.

Within no time at all, Kylee forgot about breathing

through the snorkel and began to move naturally through the water. The swim fins gave her the strength and confidence she needed and in no time at all she had left Rick's side to follow fluorescent fish over the dramatic underwater landscape without fear. Time ceased to exist as she floated above the magical underwater world, her mind going in countless directions and yet, at the same time, strangely focused.

While she stared at a little black fish with white spots and shaped something like a box with a tail, she began to envision a scene from her screenplay. Dialogue fell into place, the banter witty, the exchange between the character played by Charese LaDonne and the yet-unnamed male lead was complete from the beginning of the scene until the end.

As a parrot fish spit out a mouthful of sand, Kylee hoped she would remember every word when she was back at *Hale Nanea* staring at the computer again. A cloud passed in front of the sun and she actually felt chilled. Lifting her head, she scanned the surface for Rick but didn't see any sign of his blue snorkel tube or his fins kicking up water.

She swam around full circle, searching for him and, with relief, suddenly spotted him swimming a few yards away. Thinking it best to let him know she was heading to shore, she took two strokes in his direction and then stopped dead still. A scream lodged in her throat. There, a few feet below her in a deep crevice between the coral shelves, the dark sinister shape of a shark wove its way through the water.

She forgot to breathe. Blood rushed to her head, and for a split second, she was afraid she was going to black out.

Something told Rick that Kylee might be ready to get out of the water. Forty-five minutes was longer than he had anticipated her wanting to stay in, but each time he had looked up, she'd appeared to be swimming confidently over the reef. Now, as he closed in on her, he could see that she was lying perfectly still, floating on the surface of the water. Her long, fair hair was fanned out around her head as she stared downward.

Movement near the ocean floor caught his eye and he felt the hair on the back of his neck prickle. In a second he recognized the dorsal fin and knew why Kylee had frozen. A small sand shark was cruising in the depths beneath them. He knew the shark was harmless.

And he knew Kylee didn't know anything of the sort.

She wouldn't see him out of the side of her mask unless she moved, so he hesitated, not wanting to swim up to her without warning and frighten her anymore than she probably already was. He hovered to the side of her and waited for the slow-moving shark to swim on.

Eventually it did, but the few seconds it took seemed like hours. He could only imagine what Kylee was thinking. He saw her turn and head for the beach. In a few long strokes, he was close enough to reach out and touch her. Before he did, she looked over and pulled back with a start. A strangled squeal muffled by the mouthpiece escaped her.

They were near the shore, floating above a sand bottom. Rick put his feet down. His head and shoulders came up out of the water. He spit out his snorkel and raised his mask. Kylee did the same. The minute her mouth was clear, she started gasping for air.

"Are you all right?" He started to reach for her but she jerked away from his touch.

"Am I all right? Am I *all right*?"

"Kylee—"

"Shark bait, that's what I feel like. Shark bait. Did you *see* that shark out there? Go snorkeling, you said.

Nothing to it, you said. You'll see turtles and fish. You failed to mention *sharks*, Rick." She stopped long enough to take a breath.

A shiver shook her tempting frame. He told himself this was no time to notice, but there were just some things a man couldn't ignore.

"Are you actually *laughing* at me?" she shouted.

"No. Just smiling."

She turned away and tried striding through the waist-high water, but the swim fins unbalanced her. So did the shallow waves near the shore. She whipped around to face him again.

"Do you really think this is funny?"

"Not at all. It's just that you were never in a minute's danger. I would never had brought you out here if I thought you could get hurt."

She was trembling all over. Her mask was shoved up on the crown of her head; her snorkel dangled beside her cheek. Chicken skin peppered her sleek frame. Her breasts rose and fell, and the smooth swell above her suit drew his attention.

"Of all the nerve," she railed. "I'm standing here frightened to death and *you* stand there staring at my breasts! Take me back" she demanded. She pulled off the fins and went struggling through the shore break and up the steep, sandy bank.

"Kylee—"

She didn't stop until she reached their towels. Kylee whipped off her snorkel gear and tossed it on the mesh bag. Glancing up and down the nearly deserted section of the beach, she ignored him while she shook the sand out of her towel and whipped it around her shoulders.

Rick threw off his snorkel and mask and walked up beside her. "Kylee, I'm sorry you were frightened, but you were never out of my sight—"

"Ha. I looked up once and you were halfway down the beach."

"It just seemed that way. When you were watching that sand shark I was right behind you, a little to your right."

"*Watching* that shark? I was paralyzed with fear. Terrified."

"Kylee, it was a harmless sand shark."

"I don't care if it was *plastic*. It scared the hell out of me." She pulled the towel tighter. Her teeth were chattering now but the sun was blazing once more. He realized she had been more frightened than he could guess.

Disregarding the stubborn tilt of her chin, he closed the distance between them and wrapped her in his arms. She stiffened, but was trembling so hard that she couldn't fight back and quickly sagged against him. As he gently cupped her head and pressed her cheek against his shoulder, Rick closed his eyes and let out a deep sigh. Holding Kylee against him felt so right, so perfect, that he was shaken.

Rick held her, sharing his warmth, willing to stand there until she felt safe again. He looked down the beach, toward Makana Peak, the mountain dubbed Bali Hai after *South Pacific* was filmed. The water was clear, azure blue, the summer waves gentle as toddlers tumbling against the sand.

The beauty of Kauai was timeless and achingly lovely, much like the woman in his arms. Around him spread a stunning scene, one he'd gazed at countless times and would never grow tired of. While he stood there holding Kylee in his arms, Rick realized that everything around him was exactly the same as it had been before he touched her, but now his life was suddenly, irrevocably changed.

She needed him. Whether she knew it or not, she did. She needed him as much as he needed her. Although the sudden surety of the notion had been a shock, he was not a man to question fate.

Three

Early the next morning, Kylee couldn't stop thinking of Rick and the way she had behaved after he brought her back and dropped her off at the house yesterday afternoon. She turned off the water, stepped out of the shower, and wrapped one of the plush guest towels around her. She quickly scanned the landscape for signs of Kiko, the trespassing pig, but there wasn't so much as a snout print near the house. Kylee headed for the bedroom, her thoughts once more on her host.

Her anger had subsided, her fear of the shark replaced by a whole new threat—her mounting attraction to Rick. Lord help her, she didn't want to feel anything for him, didn't want to imagine what it would be like to let herself fall in love. She hated to admit it, but she was so attracted to him that she felt an aching need every time she thought of what making love to him might be like.

She had tried all night long, but even now she couldn't deny the way she had felt when he took her in his arms to comfort her on the beach.

After towel-drying her hair, she slipped into clean shorts and a tank top and walked into the kitchen. As usual, the coffee was already brewed. Hot cinnamon rolls were in the oven. As Kylee sat sipping a cup of rich Kona coffee, she marveled at the turn her life had taken in just a few days' time.

Last night, after she had calmed down enough to sit, she found herself working long into the night. She had thrown out the entire script, changed the setting to the tropics, and begun a love story in which the character that Charese LaDonne was going to portray slowly discovered she was in love with a devastatingly handsome man who lived alone in a jungle paradise.

The story flowed from her fingertips, the words and scenes inspired. She had twenty-one pages by the time she was through for the night. Afterward, she turned off the computer, went to bed, and lay in the dark, listening to the now-familiar night sounds of the geckoes and the bullfrogs, the water rushing in the river. Without a doubt, she knew that Rick had been right about getting out and experiencing life.

Her work had been inspired by the roller coaster of emotion she had been riding yesterday afternoon: her anger at Rick, the fear of the shark, the joy and wonder she had experienced when she first saw the universe beneath the surface of the ocean. For a few hours she had actually let go of the anxiety of not being able to produce. Instead of straining to come up with ideas, she had poured out page after page, experiencing all over again the emotion, the tension, and her own growing need in every line of dialogue and every scene.

The coffee mug was empty. She set it down and traced her finger around the rim and then, her mind made up, she pushed away from the table. She owed Rick Pau an apology. Not only that, but she actually wanted to see him again. Needed to see him again and couldn't wait any longer.

When he had dropped her off last night she was still fuming and she let him know it. Although, at that point, most of her anger had been fueled by her own reaction to him, not by the shark sighting. He had left his place shortly after they parted. Not until the wee hours of the night did she hear his pickup come rattling down the driveway again.

As she crossed the lanai and slipped on her sandals, she reminded herself it would be safer to stay put, get to work, and keep her distance from Rick Pau. It was bad enough that lately he haunted her every waking thought. Her heart had betrayed her last night, beating double-time when she heard the sound of his truck on the drive.

Closing the distance between the two houses, she told herself that she was only going to his place to set things straight. Even though she didn't want the rest of her stay to end on a sour note, she definitely didn't want him getting the idea there was the slightest chance of anything happening between them.

No indeed. Not at all. Not even if there were thousands of miles of Pacific Ocean and countless numbers of sharks between them when the affair was over.

Rick heard Kylee's footsteps on the lanai. He stood up and backed away from the computer, raised his arms and stretched. A glance at the clock told him it was almost ten in the morning. As it did whenever he was working, time had gotten away from him again.

The soft knock at the front door drew his attention. He left the screened-in porch, crossed the living room, and invited Kylee in.

She looked gorgeous standing there with the sun streaming in the open window behind her, highlighting her blonde hair like a halo. He didn't know how it was possible, but apparently just a few hours' exposure to the sun and salt water yesterday had already added new, lighter streaks of gold. Even without a touch of makeup except for a hint of lip gloss, she was naturally stunning. He couldn't help noticing she was also very ill at ease. She looked everywhere but at him.

"So, you doing better today?" He shoved his hands into the back pockets of his shorts for want of something to do.

"Yes. Actually, I am. I . . . I came over to apologize for the way I acted yesterday—"

"You don't know me well enough to know I'd never put your safety in jeopardy."

Kylee reached up and tucked her hair behind her ear. Finally she looked directly at him. "No, I guess I don't."

Rick took a deep breath. "Would you like to?"

"Like to what?"

"Get to know me better."

He could see the idea threw her off balance and inwardly cursed himself for not being able to keep his mouth shut. Kylee wasn't the type to be pushed. She glanced over his shoulder at his office, then looked down at her hands.

"The script is finally coming along," she said.

Rick felt a surge of relief. Maybe he was making some progress after all. Two days ago she would have taken his head off for making the offhanded suggestion that they get to know one another better.

"I'm glad. Can I get you anything to drink? A soda? Iced tea?"

He didn't know when he'd ever felt so awkward around a woman and hoped his reaction wasn't making her uncomfortable. After the way they had parted company yesterday, he had already convinced himself that she'd probably pack up and head out today.

"No, thanks." A half smile teased her lips. "I see you're working on the computer. Are you sure you're not a writer?"

He looked over his shoulder at the monitor and shook his head. "The newsletter keeps me pretty busy."

She shifted her stance, crossed her arms, then dropped them to her sides. "Listen, Rick, I came here to apologize, so I suppose I should quit stalling and

say I'm sorry for the way I acted at the beach yesterday."

"I told you I understood—"

"I overreacted. I had no right to carry on so long
after you apologized. I just wanted you to know I'm
sorry."

"Apology accepted."

"I also came over to tell you that you were absolutely
right about getting out of the house and away from
the computer. I guess my little adventure yesterday inspired me. I've already rewritten the first draft. Things
are moving right along."

"That's great."

"No 'I told you so'?"

He couldn't help smiling at the way she was watching him from beneath her lashes.

"Nope. I've got a suggestion though."

"What's that?"

"How about another inspiring adventure?"

Her brow gathered over her clear eyes. He felt himself quicken when she ran her tongue over her plump
bottom lip.

"Another adventure?"

"Why not? Think of your productivity."

"I'm thinking of that shark. What kind of an adventure? Is it on dry land?"

"Nope. Water, but it's—"

She held her hands up in front of her. "No way. I
don't think I'm up for another up-close-and-personal
encounter. Pigs are one thing, but—"

"River water. No snakes on the islands, no dangerous fish. Just a simple little kayak trip to a waterfall.
I'll throw in a picnic lunch." He glanced down at the
black Casio diving watch on his arm. "I'll have you
home before 3:30. Plenty of time to crank out a few
more pages before dinner and then you have the
whole night ahead of you to work. What do you say?"

"Kayak?"

"Perfectly safe. A monkey could do it. As long as the monkey swims," he quickly added. Rick watched her sigh and knew he had her. If she had been dead set against it, she would have flatly refused.

"Think of it as research. Think of your script."

"Actually, I am." She was still frowning, but he could see that she was considering the possibilities.

"Can you guarantee no sharks?"

"Absolutely."

"What time?" She looked at her sports watch.

"Change into a swimsuit and bring a towel. Give me thirty minutes to finish up here and throw a lunch together. I'll load the kayak in the truck and pick you up outside the door."

He couldn't believe his luck when she smiled and turned to let herself out. "I'll be ready. Watch out for the traffic on the way over."

He laughed at her joke and watched her bounce out the door with her hair swinging around her shoulders. Turning around, he headed back to the computer, saved the work on the screen, and switched off the machine. Trying to finish now would be a waste of time when all he could think of was Kylee, her smile, her lips, the feel of her satin-smooth skin beneath his fingertips.

He'd promised her there would be no danger from sharks. That meant he'd have to concentrate on keeping his hands to himself.

Kylee found Rick true to his word. Ignoring her own nagging conscience, she was in the pickup forty-five minutes later. A long, bright green kayak hung out of the truck bed as they rode up Kuhio Highway.

Less than five minutes from his home in Wainiha Valley, Rick was pointing out the Lumahai River when they almost drove past a woman using an emergency call box on the side of the road. At first glance, Kylee thought the woman looked the typical tourist in a T-shirt with I ♥ KAUAI emblazoned on the front, baggy white shorts, a floppy straw hat, and a camera dangling around her neck. But as Rick slammed on the brakes and pulled up alongside the frantic, middle-aged traveler, Kylee could see that the tourist was in great distress. The woman slammed down the emergency phone and ran over to the truck.

"My son's being washed out to sea!" The woman's hands clung to the open driver's window of the truck as she stared, panicked and helpless, at Rick. "Can you do something? I called the emergency number but I'm afraid by the time anyone gets here, Richie will be gone."

The woman choked back sobs and explained that her family was from Ohio and that her son had ridden a boogie board too far out and couldn't get back to shore. Kylee glanced up the highway. The road angled around a sharp curve at the top of a steep grade and disappeared. Aside from two nondescript rental cars coming toward them, there was no help in sight.

"Hang on," Rick told Kylee before he directed the tourist to step out of the way and run back across the highway. He whipped the steering wheel to the left and drove across to the ocean side of the road. Pulling up between tall, ironwood pines with wispy, thin needles, he set the emergency brake and was out of the car all in one swift move.

Kylee hopped out and ran around the front of the pickup. Panting and out of breath, the distraught mother came running with one hand atop the crown of the wide-brimmed straw hat while her camera banged against her breasts.

Kylee's heart went out to this woman who was too scared to cry. Rick quickly commandeered a surfboard from one of a group of young teens loitering by their cars. Kylee took the woman's hand and started across the wide sand beach toward the pounding shore break.

Rick jogged past them with the surfboard tucked beneath his arm as if running in the soft sand took absolutely no effort. After half a dozen steps, Kylee felt as if she were trudging through molasses. The trembling, overweight woman beside her was panting from overexertion. They were both winded by the time they reached the tide line, where the woman's husband and daughter were waving and shouting to a young boy clinging to his boogie board a good quarter mile out to sea.

"I just don't understand it," the midwesterner said as she held tightly to Kylee's hand. "He swims real good in the pool."

"He's caught in a riptide," Kylee told them. Having gone to the beach in Southern California all her life, she could easily spot the rippling current that was carrying the youth away from the island.

Kylee watched the waves suck away from the shore and then crash with a vengeance onto the sharply sloped sand. Lumahai Beach was nothing like the gentle, protected reef at Tunnels where Rick had taken her snorkeling. As she watched the pounding surf, she didn't know how the inexperienced youth had ever made it out through the rough shore break to begin with.

"I told him not to go in, but he never listens to me anymore." The boy's father was complaining aloud to no one in particular. The terror in his voice overrode his anger.

As Kylee and the family waited, standing in a tight knot of anxiety on the beach, she watched Rick time the waves before he jumped in and began paddling out through the current to get to the young teen. Her heart was in her throat until she realized Rick was stroking with what appeared to be effortless power, cutting swiftly through the water.

When he reached the boy, the two of them were not far from disappearing around an outcropping of rocks on the far side of a river mouth that emptied into the sea. Rick waved and Kylee instantly waved back. So did the tourists, as well as a few other beach-goers who had gathered to watch the unfolding drama.

Just then, the shrill scream of a siren cut the air. Kylee turned around and saw a red fire engine roar into the sandy parking area between the pines. The rescue crew climbed down. One of the men, outfitted in swim gear and carrying a buoy, came running across the sand.

"What's up?" The rescue swimmer ran up to the small crowd on the beach while he scanned the water.

"My son—" the woman from Ohio began.

"I think they're all right," the father cut in. "That man out there on the surfboard got to him in time. It looks like they're both headed back."

Relief shot through Kylee like a jolt of caffeine when she realized Rick was indeed on the way back, paddling and towing the boy and his boogie board behind him with the surfboard leash. Their progress was slow but steady toward the river mouth. Still holding the woman's hand, Kylee turned to the fireman closest to her.

"We were on our way to go kayaking when my friend saw this lady making an emergency call. He borrowed a board and went in after the boy. There wasn't time to wait."

"Is that Rick Pau?" The fireman was watching Rick's progress. The rescue swimmer stood by, waiting to see if he'd have to go in at all.

"Yes. That's him." Kylee couldn't keep the note of pride out of her voice any more than she could wipe the smile off of her face. Rick Pau, houseboy, chef, gardener, snorkeler, newsletter writer, and self-proclaimed dabbler had just added hero to his list of titles. She turned to the tall blonde man beside her. "Do you know him?"

"Sure. He used to paddle for the Hanalei Civic Hawaiian Canoe Club." The fireman called out to the crew. "No need to stay. Looks like Rick's got it under control. Call in and cancel the rescue 'copter." Then he turned back to Kylee and added in an undertone, "Lucky you two were driving by when you did. Unfortunately, we've lost so many tourists off this beach the locals have taken to calling it Luma-die instead of Lumahai."

Rick was so close now that Kylee could see his smile. His hair was wet, slicked back, and shining blue-black in the sunlight. Without thinking, she waved again. His smile widened when he recognized her and waved back. Her heart managed to trip over itself.

Three firefighters wandered back to the truck while the fourth took down information from the Ohio family. The fireman who had been appointed rescue swimmer stood by on the beach in case Rick needed help getting the boy into shore. Most of the onlookers had wandered back down the beach, one or two hunched over, searching for *puka* shells in the sand.

Finally, Rick was in and the boy was safe. The girl from Ohio volunteered to carry the surfboard back to the boys standing by the cars parked amid the tall pine tree trunks while the wayward Richie, none the worse for his close call, walked away between his parents, who alternately gave him an earful of admonishments and hugged him.

Kylee soaked up every word and nuance when Rick slipped easily into island pidgin English. She didn't mind standing by when he and the firemen exchanged handshakes and 'talked story,' for it gave her time to compare him to the firefighters on the beach. All of them were tall, tan, and fit, but it was disconcerting to notice that she found none of them could hold a candle to Rick Pau. As he laughed with the others, Rick moved up beside her, letting her know without words that he hadn't forgotten her. He didn't so much as touch a shoulder to hers, but he let her know that being with her was important to him. A gentle ache began in the vicinity of her heart.

Finally, the hubbub died down and they walked back to the truck alone.

"I hate to think what might have happened to that boy if you hadn't jumped in to save him," she told Rick.

"It was just luck we came by when we did and he had that boogie board. He would never have been able to stay afloat until the rescue swimmer got out here."

As they got back inside the pickup, Kylee slid onto the bench seat and waited for Rick to get in and close the door. "Don't discount what you did back there," she told him once he was inside the cab. "You saved that boy's life."

He turned the key in the ignition. "Any good swimmer would have done the same thing."

She guessed there had been a number of competent swimmers on the beach, but none of them had wanted to risk going after the tourists' son. Yet Rick had done so as confidently and effortlessly as he apparently did everything else.

Kylee settled back for the rest of the ride to the Kalihiwai River, intending to watch the breathtaking North Shore scenery unfold. It wasn't until she grudgingly admitted to herself that she was actually stealing glances at Rick Pau that she realized she was in real danger of losing her resolve, not to mention her vulnerable, inexperienced heart.

Rick had been up the Kalihiwai River so often that he knew every inch of the valley. Deciding to memorize everything about Kylee instead, he focused his attention on her. Seated in front of him in the double-occupant kayak, she alternately paddled the long paddle and exclaimed over new sights as they floated over the water. The sun was doing its best to make the noon ride up the river perfect. They had stripped off their T-shirts and then, garbed in swimsuits, slathered each other with sunscreen. It would be a long, long time before he forgot the sensation of her hands slicking the lotion over his shoulders and down his back. Nor would he easily forget the way her fair skin had felt like satin beneath his palms.

"What's that?" she whispered in awe as they drifted by a tall, white bird that reminded her of a small stork. It was perched on a *hau* branch that hung out over the water.

"An egret. They nest in the growth along the river."

Kylee watched the bird until the kayak turned the bend and headed beneath the huge concrete bridge that spanned the narrow valley. Rick watched Kylee, mesmerized by the way she moved. As her gold hair teased her bare shoulders, Rick knew that it would feel like heavy silk. What would she do if he were to reach out, to gently brush the hair away from the nape of her neck, lean forward, and kiss the vulnerable spot behind her ear?

His blood was running hot. He felt himself grow hard and decided to put his energy into paddling. The opaque green water had become more shallow and he knew that momentarily they would be able to see the riverbed beneath them. Not much farther ahead the water would be too shallow to navigate so they would beach the kayak and continue on foot to the falls.

Kylee shifted, drawing his eyes to her cute little bottom as she wriggled around on the wet seat. When the seductive coconut scent of her lotion wafted back to him, he almost groaned aloud.

"We're almost there," he said, fighting to hide the frustration in his tone. He needed to get his feet on solid ground and put some distance between them—fast.

"How much farther to the waterfall?"

"We'll have to walk about a quarter of a mile."

"That's not bad."

He glanced over at the tall grass growing in the field on the valley side of the river. "The field is pretty overgrown, and I don't want to risk running into any pigs or pig hunters, so we'll have to walk upstream through the water."

She immediately stopped negotiating her paddle and smiled over her shoulder. "You don't want to risk running into any pigs and yet you don't mind that I have to put up with one in my bathroom?"

He shrugged and laughed, enjoying the easy exchange. "I told you, there are two kinds of pigs around here."

Kylee laid her paddle down across her lap and continued to look back at him. Her blue eyes were bright, her cheeks flushed with sun and exhilaration. She was the perfect California calendar girl. And she was within arm's reach.

"You know what, Rick?"

"What, Kylee?" He gave up, stopped paddling, and decided to concentrate on her and really enjoy the view.

"I'll say it again. You were right. This is absolutely beautiful. Very inspiring."

It was the perfect opportunity, the perfect opening. He thought of reaching for her, of kissing her. Had it been any other woman, he would have done so and risked her ire, but with Kylee things were different somehow. He didn't want to risk losing her over a stolen kiss.

Instead, he forced himself not to touch her at all.

"You know what?" he asked. "You have a beautiful smile." Once the compliment was out, he expected that megawatt smile to shut down, but today she surprised him.

"Thank you. To tell you the truth, it's been a long time since I've even felt like smiling."

The bottom of the kayak was only a few inches above the smooth, round stones that covered the riverbed.

"Sit still," he said just before he put both hands on the rails of the craft and pushed up and out of his seat. He stepped over the side into the water. Using the nylon rope threaded through the nose of the kayak, Rick pulled it up onto the small area on the sandy shoreline and then reached down to help Kylee out.

She unfolded her long legs and groaned as she stood up. While she stretched out her stiff muscles, she gazed up the hillside that plunged down to the water's edge on the right. The land was covered with thick mango, guava, and umbrella trees, the ground beneath it dank and damp. There was no sound except for the rushing water and the song of a shama thrush hidden somewhere in the nearby trees.

"I can hear the waterfall up ahead," she said.

"Do you want to eat here or take the picnic up to the falls? It's no problem to carry it. I put everything in a backpack."

By the look in her eyes it was easy to guess her answer. He began digging the pack out of the storage bin in the front of the kayak.

"I've never been to a waterfall. Maybe it would be fun to eat up there."

"You got it." He slipped the straps over his shoulders and pointed up river in the direction of the falls. "After you.

Ten minutes later, Kylee wished she had never heard the word waterfall. Up to her ankles in river water, she was certain she was going to break her neck, or worse, one of her arms.

"You know, I have to get that script done and I won't be able to do it in a cast." Her buoyant mood evaporated when her foot slipped for what seemed like the hundredth time. Slowly, she cautiously picked her way over the slick, mossy stones that lined the river bottom. "How much farther is it?"

"Just around the next bend."

She stopped short and turned her frustration on him. The fact that he was smiling his usual killer smile didn't make things any better.

"You have no idea where the waterfall is, do you?"

"Yes, I do," he nodded. "Just ahead we cross the river and climb up the path."

"Climb up the path," she repeated. "Why do I think there's probably more to it than that?"

He shrugged. "Don't you trust me?"

Kylee stared up into his deep dark eyes, then at that smile that was so impossible to ignore, and shook her head. "Not even as far as I could throw you."

When he laughed, she turned around and started off again. They rounded the bend and, anxious to see the falls, she forgot to watch her footing. The moss was too much even for the rubber-soled water socks he'd given her to wear. Her foot slipped off the surface of a rock. Her arms went wide automatically as she fought to maintain her balance but it was too little too late. She started to topple over. Suddenly, Rick grabbed her arm just above the elbow.

Kylee threw herself at him to keep from falling. In a split second, she thought that they were both going to fall, but crashing into Rick was like hitting a lava rock wall. His arms went around her, but other than that he didn't budge. His legs were braced, his stance surefooted, even on the slippery rocks.

Disoriented, she stood there within the circle of his arms, her cheek pressed against his chest, listening to the strong, steady beat of his heart. Her own heart was racing, and an aching need began to throb deep within her. She nearly groaned aloud.

Pull away, she told herself. *Don't do this.* But she didn't budge. Time seemed to stop. Everything was so perfect: the sound of the river, the birds calling to one another; the balmy trade winds; the soothing, dense green forest all around. It felt so good to just let go, to let down her guard and let someone else be stronger for this one perfect moment.

When his hand slipped to the small of her back, she felt him press her, ever so slightly, closer. Kylee closed her eyes. He was so tempting. Everything a lover should be, but a temptation she definitely didn't need at this point in time.

When? The question instantly insinuated itself into her thoughts. *If not now, when?* Would there ever come a time when she wasn't running as fast as she could to stay in one place, to keep up with her work and her career? Would there ever be a time to learn to let herself love and be loved?

Rick had his hand on her chin. He tipped her face up to his and when he stared down into her eyes, she was powerless to move. He began to lower his head. She watched his full, sensuous lips as they came closer to her mouth. Her heart fluttered. Her mouth went dry. He was going to kiss her.

Kylee closed her eyes for a heartbeat and then quickly pushed away, forcing herself to stand on her own two feet. She took a deep, shaky breath and then tried to make light of the situation.

"That was a close call," she whispered.

Rick shifted the backpack. "Yeah. I guess so."

She wished he looked relieved, but he appeared pained more than anything else. She could read the truth in his eyes. He thought she was a tease.

"That was an accident, Rick. Not some ploy I used just to fall into your arms."

He looked over his shoulder, downriver. There was no sign of any other kayakers coming upstream. In fact, she thought, there was probably no one around for miles.

"I know that," he said. Still, the lightness which had threaded his tone all morning was gone. "You can rest assured I wasn't trying to take advantage of the situation, either. It's just that for a moment there, you seemed plenty content to be in my arms."

She felt herself blush and knew she deserved his anger. She had lingered in his embrace. It had felt so very right.

"I'm sorry you came to the wrong conclusion," she told him coolly.

He was no longer smiling. "Do you want to go back?"

She could take the coward's way out and say yes, but she hated to end the otherwise perfect outing with both of them acting like stubborn children. Someone had to budge. She shoved her hair back off her face and smiled.

"Not on your life. Not without seeing that damn waterfall."

It was just the light touch needed to dispel the tension. Rick's lips lifted in a half smile. His shoulders rose and fell as he took a deep breath. Then he held out his hand.

Kylee looked down at it for a moment, hesitating.

"The stones are slippery," he explained.

She reached out and put her hand in his.

The climb to the pool at the base of the waterfall was slow because the ground beneath the thick forest canopy was virtually untouched by sunlight and slick with moisture from the recent rains. As the afternoon heat intensified, the humidity against the rock wall that formed the base of the valley was stifling. Water thundered down from the pool above, the ceaseless cascade showering the rocks that broke the surface with a refreshing mist.

They climbed over the rocks and stood behind the cascade, then swam across the pool where they picnicked on sandwiches and sodas. When they finished, Rick was content to watch Kylee, seated on the black rock beside him.

"I can't stop staring up at the water as it pours over the ridge. It's hard to believe it never stops."

"You should see it when it rains. It's not safe to be up here then, but it's visible from the bridge. The water flows from upriver and turns red from all the mud it carries in it."

"I could sit here forever."

"Take all the time you want."

She turned to him then, her eyes shadowed with something he could feel but not read. Regret?

"I'd love nothing better than to sit here forever, but I can't run away from my life that easily. I have to get back and work this afternoon to make up for all this time off."

"You *have* to work? Is it worth it, if you love it so little?"

"I guess I put that the wrong way. I want to get back to the script because it's finally coming along. I don't want to lose my pace."

A sadness for her settled in his heart but did nothing to decrease his longing. He wanted to tell her that she was on a fast path to self-destruction if she didn't take time to live, to love, but he would be pushing it, he knew, to say anything of the sort. Especially after she had given in and taken the morning off.

He slipped the pack back on, stood up, and for the second time that afternoon, held out his hand to her. Instantly, she took it and he pulled her up without stepping back or away. Her nearness, her smiles were driving him crazy. As he looked down into her eyes, he made a split second decision.

Time was slipping away. In two weeks, she would be gone and he would be alone trying to figure out how he had let her slip away and wondering what might have been.

He was going to kiss her now and damn the consequences.

Four

Kylee knew what was about to happen before Rick pulled her into his arms. Even so, she was powerless to stop what had been building between them since they met. At first, when his lips touched hers, she refused to be seduced. Then, all too quickly, her will evaporated and she began to soften as he teased the seam of her lips with his tongue. Unable to resist her own hunger for him any longer, wanting more than a quick, stolen kiss, she opened her mouth and let him slip his tongue inside.

His strong arms were wrapped around her. His hands rested at the small of her back. She gasped against his mouth when he lifted her slightly and pressed her against his erection.

It was an instant before she realized she was kissing him back with pure abandon, but obviously Rick noticed, for he moaned low in his throat, slashed his mouth across hers, and deepened his kiss.

She raked her fingers through his long, thick hair and relished the feel of him, all hard planes and angles. The waterfall thundered behind them, just as it had for countless centuries. Locked in the moment, standing in the heat and the mist coming off the falls, Kylee almost wished they could slip back to a time when the island was raw and new and as primitive as the torrent of emotion seething inside her.

What this man's touch could do to her was terrifying. His kiss had the power to be her undoing. She felt his hand slip over her rib cage as he slowly slid it up to cup the underside of her breast through her swimsuit. Compelled, she lifted slightly, pressing her breast against his palm, and felt his fingers tighten, ever so slightly, over her fullness.

She almost cried aloud at the blessed pleasure-pain that blossomed inside her. His fingers closed around the nipple budded tightly beneath the clinging fabric of her swimsuit. For the first time in her life, she wanted more, wanted to feel his fingers strip the swimsuit straps off her shoulders. She wanted her breasts exposed to his warm hands, his teasing mouth. She wanted to feel him over her, around her. She wanted to take him inside her. She wanted to pleasure him, to let him give her the pleasure she had denied herself for so long.

She knew Rick Pau could make her blood sing. That made him dangerous to her—and to her career. Kylee let go of his hair. She drew her arms from around his neck, slipped her hands between them, and pushed against his well-muscled chest until he lifted his head.

They were breathing as hard as if they had scaled the rugged cliff face behind the falls. Shaken by the potency of their kiss, Kylee didn't know how long her trembling legs would hold her or if she could even stand alone. Thankfully, Rick kept her within the circle of his arms. It was a gentle cradling, nothing more.

"It would be so good between us, Kylee," Rick whispered against her ear.

Still too shaken to put her thoughts into words, she shook her head, trying to deny it. She had no experience, no idea how it would be, or should be.

"You know it would," he said, reaching down to tip her face up to meet his eyes. "Tell me you don't want me as much as I want you."

His words terrified her, because they were so true. "What I want and what's good for me are two different things. What about you, Rick? Do you actually think I'd be good for you? You told me about your wife, about how she put her career before everything and that eventually split up your marriage. Why do you think I'm here on Kauai alone with my computer for company? My work is my life, Rick. It always has been. You'd be making the same mistake all over again, unless you're only looking for a quick affair."

"I think you know me better than that by now."

"Not really," she said too quickly, even though right now she felt deep in her soul that she might have known this man forever.

His arms dropped away from her. Rick took a step back and glanced at the upper ledge of the falls. Kylee followed his gaze and caught a glimpse of brightly colored fabric. As she watched, three tourists with cameras at the ready strolled into view.

"How in the world did they get up there?" Her frustration made it sound as if she were furious at these people she had never laid eyes on.

"Horseback. The stable over the hill offers rides through the countryside to the waterfall." He studied the clouds overhead. "We'd better go. There's heavy rain coming."

Rick had already negotiated the boulders at the edge of the pool and was about to enter the path that wound back to the river through the thick vegetation. The sunshine had disappeared along with the light-hearted mood of the day. Thick gray clouds with trailing rain were gathering over the valley. She had no option but to follow.

They rode back to *Hale Nanea*, the sound of the rain against the roof of the pickup the only disruption of their cold silence. Rick pulled up at the front of the rental house and kept the engine running, his hands tight on the steering wheel. He turned his head to look at Kylee.

With one hand on the door handle, she stared out the window, watching the rain trickle slowly down the glass. Her hair was still damp from the rain that caught them while they paddled down the Kalihiwai River to the park on the bay. She looked so bedraggled and forlorn sitting there wrapped in a striped beach towel with her limp, wet hair dripping onto her shoulders that he wanted to pull her into his arms and hold her until he could coax a smile to her lovely mouth.

"Why don't you come over for dinner tonight and we'll talk about this like two adults?" It was all he could think of, short of locking her in the truck while he tried to convince her to take a chance on love.

"There is no *this* to talk about. You aren't going to change the way I feel," she said without looking over at him. "Besides, I have to work tonight." She pulled on the door handle to let herself out. "I can let myself in," she said when he started to open his own door.

"If not me, then who, Kylee? Are you ever going to let anyone love you? You can't run from your emotions forever. You can't spend your life storing them up just to put them on paper." He reached over and rested his palm on her thigh. Her skin was soft and warm. She didn't pull away. Instead, she turned around and looked into his eyes for a fleeting moment. Confusion, anxiety, intense longing were mirrored in blue before she quickly looked down at the hand he still held on her thigh.

"What's between us, if there is anything at all, is a purely physical attraction, Rick." She sounded uncertain, as if she needed convincing more than he did.

"Maybe that was true," he said slowly, choosing his words carefully, knowing this might be the last chance he had to win her trust. "I knew the moment I laid eyes on you that I wanted you, Kylee. But now it's more than that. I've gotten to know you over the past few days and I want to get to know you better. You've got a lot of love bottled up inside."

She shook her head. "How can you possibly know that when I don't?"

"You do," he said before she could protest. "I saw the way you stood by that poor woman, a stranger, on the beach today when she was terrified of losing her son. You were there for her—"

"Anyone would have done that."

"No, not everyone would have. If you'd just open up, take a chance, you'd find you have a lot of love to give, Kylee."

"And you want me to give it to you?"

He couldn't help but smile. She'd backed him into a corner.

"I'm not going to deny it. No matter what you might think, I'm not looking for a one night stand anymore than you are. It's been a long time since I've wanted to be with someone, Kylee. A long time. I don't want to blow it with you. All I'm asking is that you think about what I've said, think about what we might have together. If you'll take a step in that direction, I'll be there to meet you no matter how long it takes. Will you do that before it's too late? Will you at least think about it?"

Unshed tears shimmered in her eyes. She quickly blinked them back, trying to deny them just as she had her feelings. She took a deep breath.

"I'll think about it," she whispered.

He let go of her thigh and clamped his hand on the steering wheel again. "Promise?"

She nodded, then slid off the seat, stepped out of the truck, and closed the door behind her. In the rearview mirror, Rick watched her walk around the back of the pickup and run up the stairs. He smiled when she abruptly stopped at the top step to peel off her rubber shoes like a local before she stepped onto the lanai. At the door she paused and looked at him over her shoulder. Her eyes were wide, the confusion in them intensified. He waited until she disappeared inside before he pulled the truck the rest of the way up the drive.

He'd stated his case. All he could do now was wait.

Four days later the first draft of the screenplay was finished. Kylee had taken advantage of a deluge that hadn't let up since the day of the kayak trip. She welcomed the gray skies. They matched her mood. Just as Rick had accused her of doing, she had spent the days pouring her emotional turmoil into the script. By the time she wrote the last line of dialogue of the final, moving scene where Charese LaDonne was reunited with the hero of the tale, silent tears were sliding down her own cheeks.

Her burst of creative energy spent, Kylee changed into a clean top and then grabbed her purse and the keys to the Jeep. After staring at the taro patch beyond the window for four days, she was ready for a change of view and felt the need to clear her head. Within ten minutes she had reached the town of Hanalei where she stopped in at the crowded Village Variety for postcards. Without intending to, she ended up buying a piece of tropical print fabric that the clerk guaranteed could easily be tied and wrapped into fifteen different styles.

Then, beneath an umbrella-topped table, Kylee sipped an iced cafe mocha while she watched a new generation of hippies in tie-dyed tees and rubber sandals wander in and out of the Hanalei Health Food Store in the Ching Young Center.

Usually when she finished a first draft, she felt both excited and relieved. This time she felt neither. She knew the script was good, probably some of her best work—and knew she had Rick to thank for it.

Rick. Day and night, even as she worked, she thought of him. Of what he'd said. Of how right he had been about her wanting him. She wanted to know everything about him, what made him laugh, what he dreamed of. She wished she could get inside him for a day and learn everything there was to know of Rick Pau. The very idea that she wanted him so much terrified her. Why Rick? Why now? She had asked herself over and over. What was there that attracted two people from very different worlds?

A young couple walked by the table, arm in arm, wearing bright new sunburns over tender mainland skin. As she watched them stroll along, Kylee decided they must have driven over from the other side of the island or just arrived from Maui, because the sun hadn't shone on the north shore for four days. The couple was in their late teens or early twenties, newlyweds by the way the girl studied the bright solitaire on her left hand when her new husband wasn't looking.

Was there a chance that with Rick she might be able to experience something she had been certain would always elude her? Or was she fooling herself?

Finishing up the iced mocha, she picked up her package and left the shelter of the umbrella. She tossed the empty plastic cup into a recycle bin and made a run for the Jeep, but by the time she got the door open and hopped in, she was soaked.

The rain was coming down in steady sheets as she negotiated the curved highway back to Powerhouse Road. By the time she made it down the steep muddy driveway and parked at *Hale Nanea*, she was thankful she'd rented an all-terrain vehicle. She'd barely cleared the lanai steps when a black pickup truck came sliding down the drive. Her heart lodged in her throat as she watched the full-sized truck swerve around her rented Jeep before it skidded to a stop at her front door.

She'd only seen a flash of the driver as he slid by, a burly Hawaiian with arms the size of ham hocks and a smile as bright as a full moon. He revved the engine of the truck and shouted Rick's name. Two other Hawaiian men were riding in the truck bed, sheltered from the rain by a lumber rack covered with plywood sheets.

One of the men waved when he noticed Kylee standing on her lanai. She waved back, stepped into the house, and laid her package on the sofa. She wandered over to the desk and was about to pick up her script when the truck motor shut off and she heard Rick shout to the men.

She closed her eyes. Her hands tightened on the script. Just the sound of his voice could send a raw ache through her. She paused where she was, arrested by the lilt of his words as he spoke to one of the other men in island pidgin.

"You hear, Rick?"

"Yeah. I hear. Coming dis way, yeah?"

"Looks like, yeah. Plenty beeg, but nutting like *Iniki*, eh?"

"Nutting like *Iniki* evah come again, bra, you tink?"

Kylee couldn't fathom much of what they said, except for the word *Iniki*, powerful hurricane, as she recalled. She set the script down. Walking to the kitchen door, she steeled herself for her first glimpse of Rick in days. Standing just inside the door, she saw him clearly through the screen. He was leaning against the railing on his lanai, his arms spread, his strong brown hands gripping the white wooden rail. The breeze had strengthened enough to where it ruffled his long dark hair and lifted it off his shoulders.

Quiet power and strength emanated from him. She knew in a glance that here was a man who had an iron will. He would wait forever, just as he had said, until she made up her mind to meet him halfway.

It was hard to look at Rick and concentrate on what he and the pickup driver were talking about but she tried.

"Need wood?" the driver shouted.

"Nah. I got 'em. You take care." Rick raised his hand to give the *shaka* or hang loose salute as the truck driver started the pickup, gunned the engine, and threw it into reverse. The wheels spun, sending a shower of mud and gravel in the air before they caught and the driver maneuvered a U-turn in what looked like an impossible space. The truck disappeared up the drive.

Kylee took a deep breath, pushed the screen open, and stepped out onto the lanai. Rick was facing her door and saw her immediately. She watched him smile. Just knowing that smile was for her made her simmer down to her toes. What would it be like to wake up to *that* every morning?

Impossible. The answer came immediately after the question popped into her head. Impossible. Rick was an island boy, his way of life as simple as he could make it. His home was here in this serene valley. Her life was her work. L.A. Hollywood.

Impossible. Impossible.

The word echoed with every step that took her closer to where he stood waiting on his own lanai. As she drew nearer, she imagined walking straight into his arms. *What if she did it?* What if she let herself go to him?

She stopped an arm's length away.

"You went out for a while," he said.

"To Hanalei. Just to get outside. It's a nice little town."

"Everyone talking about the hurricane?"

"Hurricane? No . . . but now that you mention it, there were long lines at the Big Save. I'm so used to L.A., I thought that was normal." She had been too preoccupied with thoughts of him to pay much attention to what anyone around her was saying.

She looked away from him, scanning the thick tropical foliage surrounding the houses. The images of the aftermath of *Iniki* that she had seen on the newscasts in L.A. had been unforgettable. Even though she'd had no connection to the island at all, her heart had gone out to the residents of Kauai. Rick's homes were eclectic and charming. The garden was lovely, so tranquil and lush. She thought of the lost photos, of what it must have taken for him to return this place to its perfection. She hated to think of them being destroyed.

She swung around to face him. "What can we do?"

"Not panic." Again, that heart-melting smile. "Right now, they've issued a hurricane warning. If the storm progresses on course, it will hit within twelve hours. There's always a chance it will turn in another direction, or be downgraded to a tropical storm if it loses intensity."

"Your friends sounded worried."

He glanced up at the dense, gray cloud cover. There was no hint of blue, no patch of sunlit sky. "Everyone here is a little gun-shy of hurricanes, with good reason. What you can do is pack up your computer and printer and put them in the boxes you shipped them over in."

"That won't take me ten minutes. What else? What can I do to help you?"

"I'm going to keep checking the National Hurricane Center on the Net. They're tracking the storm. I've got plywood cut to fit over all the windows stored beneath the house. You can help me put them up, but I hope to God we won't need them."

He was so calm in the face of what might lie ahead that her heart went out to him. As she stood there, hesitant and awkward in the sudden silence, he leaned against the lanai railing. She knew he was waiting for her to make the next move.

"Rick, I—"

The phone in the guest house started ringing. Kylee glanced over her shoulder. No one had called her for ten days. No one but Sylvia knew she was here.

"You probably want to get that," he said, straightening away from the railing.

"It must be Sylvia," she mumbled, taking a step back as relief washed over her. Thank God for small favors, she thought. She had no idea how to put her thoughts into words.

"Tell her I said hello," Rick told her before Kylee turned to walk away.

Sylvia called to tell her that word of the mounting storm headed for the islands was on the news broadcasts in L.A. and then she breezily told Kylee not to worry.

Kylee wished she could have taken the advice to heart. For the next few hours she alternately paced the house and tried to skim her script. Everything that she would have hated to lose fit into two boxes, all of it work related. She'd brought no good jewelry, not that she owned that much, nor did she care about her clothing. It could be replaced far more easily than Rick could repair the fine wood floors, the stained glass windows, or the furnishings in the house.

She felt totally isolated. Without looking at the clock it was hard to tell what time it was by the dingy gray sky. A small pond had formed at the end of the driveway. She couldn't imagine what the valley would be like if the storm blew in with full fury.

Unwilling to wait any longer to find out what was going on, she was about to open the door when she nearly ran into Rick. He was only wearing shorts. His upper torso was soaked, his hair dripping wet and stuck to his shoulders. "I've been pulling out plywood to put on the windows of this house."

"You said I could help," she reminded him.

"That would be great, but you're liable to get pretty dirty."

If his own mud-streaked shorts were any indication, she knew he was right. "I don't care. Let's go."

She followed him outside and together they waded beneath the house where he began pulling window-sized sheets of precut plywood out from a rack. Her job was simply to prop them up until he could haul them out one by one, and then stand by and lend a hand while he hung them on preset hinges.

When they stooped over to walk into the four-feet-high space beneath the house, Kylee's nervousness in the face of the impending storm came out in giggles.

"What's so funny?" Rick looked down, inspecting the front of his pants, and then peered over his shoulder at the back of them.

His assumption that there was something odd about him only made her laugh harder. "I'm sorry," she finally managed. "It's just that standing here hunched over, ankle deep in mud under a house, waiting for a hurricane, isn't exactly the way I pictured the *serene respite in tranquil surroundings* described in your brochure."

She brushed her hair back off her face and grabbed one end of the last plywood sheet they would have to wrestle up the steps and hang. Much to her relief, Rick laughed, too. "Remind me to give you a refund."

"Oh no. I should pay you. Imagine the amount of fresh material I'll get out of this."

"Do you think I'd get more bookings if I threw in an adventure package?" He laughed.

Kylee found herself smiling at him across the plywood. "How do you do it, Rick?"

"Do what?"

"Keep laughing."

"What's the alternative?"

She thought about that for a moment and then admitted, "I never looked at it that way." Together they moved the last piece of wood and hung it over the picture window on the wall above the desk Kylee had been using. It was almost pitch dark inside the rental house, stuffy and eerie without windows. The rain beat down on the metal roof.

"I'm going to run up to the house across the road and make sure the Makais have enough drinking water and blankets."

Kylee thought of the fragile-looking structure on the opposite side of the hill. "Do you think they should come over here?"

"I'll ask, but they probably won't want to. During *Iniki* they chose to stay put. You gather up all the candles and hurricane lamps in this place and have them ready along with your boxes. When I come back, I'll move you into my house."

She hadn't thought past boarding up the house. The idea of sitting out the storm alone was terrifying enough, but to actually move into Rick's place—

"Kylee?"

"Yes? What?"

"My house is more sheltered in the trees. It weathered *Iniki* just fine, so I'm not going to board it up unless the predictions get worse. There's still time. If you have any reservations about staying alone with me—"

"I don't," she quickly assured him. How could she tell him it wasn't *his* behavior she was worried about anymore, but her own weakness? "I'll have everything ready."

"The storm is projected to hit in a few more hours. It was just barely upgraded to a hurricane, so we can always hope it'll be downgraded again." He started toward the door to leave and see about the family up the hill, then paused. "I'll be right back. Will you be all right alone?"

Kylee nodded. Then she forced herself to smile, stuck out her little finger and thumb and shook her hand, giving him the hang loose sign.

His laughter trailed behind him as he headed out the door.

Kylee sat on Rick's comfortable, deep cushioned sofa with her feet tucked up beneath her, content just to dwell in the flickering light of the hurricane lamps and listen as Rick strummed his guitar.

She glanced over at the dark hallway where Rick had tucked her boxes far from any doors or windows. It was where they would hide, Rick told her, if one of the windows blew, but he had added that there was little chance of that now.

At the last possible moment, hurricane 'Io, named for the Hawaiian hawk, had veered westward. NHC had predicted it would barely touch Kauai and the island would suffer no more damage than with any heavy tropical storm. It had already generated enough wind to knock out the power, but not until after they had worked together making omelets and hash browns on the electric stove.

As she rolled her head back and forth trying to ease the ache out of her shoulder muscles, Kylee surreptitiously watched Rick. He was intent on his music, seemingly oblivious to the havoc outside.

With most of the windows closed, the air inside the little house was sultry, thick with humidity, but not totally uncomfortable. The music and the lamplight created a romantic atmosphere that overrode the intense tropical storm. They sat like two turtles in the same shell. Despite the weather raging outside the boarded-up house, Kylee felt an inner peace and contentment, even though it left her puzzled.

Was this what it would be like to share a life with someone? Would there often be these comfortable, quiet moments of solitude? All her life she had been afraid she didn't have enough to give to both her work and a permanent relationship. She thought she needed to channel all of her emotion, all of her time and energy into her work if she was going to be the success she dreamed of. As a child, and then a teen, she had never lived with a foster family long enough to learn how a woman, a wife, could divide time between her work and a husband and family. Could she really be equally devoted to all of them?

As she sat there staring at Rick, soaking in the music, the tranquil atmosphere he'd created, she realized there was a solace here that, in and of itself, was rejuvenating. She had also gained contentment from the opportunity to be at ease and laugh with him as they hastily threw dinner together and playfully argued over who should wash and who should dry the dishes.

She had always feared that if she became too content, too settled, she would become complacent, that her work would lose its edge and her career would suffer for it. But that certainly wasn't the case if the new script she had written was any indication.

One thing she had always been blessed with was a clear insight into the quality of her own work and she *knew* that the LaDonne script was as good or better than the Emmy winner she had penned last year.

"You look like you're thinking much too hard. You aren't scared, are you?"

Kylee started and found Rick standing over her. She had been so lost in thought that she didn't know how long ago he had stopped playing, set aside his guitar, and crossed the room.

"Of course not. We're locked up tight as a drum in here." She started to smile, but just then something shuddered against the back of the house that made them both jump.

"Tree limb," Rick speculated.

"What'll we do?"

"Nothing right now, but I'll have plenty of yard work

tomorrow. You'll have to get back to your *serene respite in peaceful surroundings.*"

"This is actually the most peaceful hour I've ever spent with someone," she admitted, her voice barely audible.

He sat down on the other end of the sofa and draped his arm along the back. "In the middle of a hurricane you find peace. Care to explain?"

She didn't think she could put what she was feeling into words until she looked into his eyes. He was a man of his word. Somehow, like a disciplined warrior, he had tempered the passion he'd shown earlier. Like her own for him, it was still there. But he had given a promise and he was doing his damnedest to keep it. She could trust him with her innermost thoughts.

"Tonight is a first for me, Rick. I've never spent quiet hours alone with a man, never shared any household chores or just . . . well, sat around sharing quiet hours with a man."

"You've never lived with anyone?"

"I've never let any relationship go that far."

He was watching her closely, intent on what she said. She could almost see the wheels of his mind working and braced herself for the inevitable question.

"Are you still a virgin, Kylee?" His tone was laced with disbelief, as if he'd just stumbled across an archeological wonder and questioned having found it.

Her gaze dropped to where her hands were folded in her lap. "I'm twenty-five years old."

"That's not exactly an answer."

Her heart was in her throat. Her palms were sweating. In a moment of clarity, she thought of what a reflection on society it was that she felt ashamed having to admit it.

"Yes. I am." She crossed her arms beneath her breasts and then met his gaze directly. "I've dated plenty of men, but . . . I just never got around to . . . you know."

"That's nothing to be ashamed of."

"Then why do you look so astounded?"

A half smile slid across his lips and he shrugged. "A woman like you . . . I can't believe you've never been in love before."

"I give everything to my work, Rick. At least I have until now."

"And now?"

"This stay here on Kauai has made me think. I've been able to go out and play and still produce." She felt herself blushing when she thought of what she had just said. "I didn't mean play around, I meant the snorkeling, the—"

"I knew what you meant." He reached over and picked up a lock of her hair and rubbed it between his fingers. She was tempted to lean closer and brush her cheek against his knuckles.

"And tonight?"

"Tonight has been . . . well, nice, despite the storm. I've always thought that loving someone meant putting one hundred percent into nurturing the relationship." She paused, trying to find a way to make him understand.

He found the words for her. "A relationship can nurture you, too. It doesn't just take, but can give something back. Make you stronger." His voice had a mellow, hypnotic tone, as if he were speaking slowly and softly so as not to frighten her.

"Can it Rick? Can it make you stronger? What if it turns out like your marriage? Why take a chance?"

"The human race would end if people didn't take a chance on love and believe it would last."

"Despite all the odds?"

"Despite them all."

"Kiss me, Rick."

"Kiss *me*, Kylee. It's been harder than hell to keep my hands off you all day long. *You* kiss me. That way, you can set the limits."

Five

You kiss me.

For a moment she sat perfectly still. The riot of weather outside was nothing compared to what was going on inside her. Slowly, Kylee unfolded her legs and slid in closer, her gaze jumping from Rick's mouth to his eyes. Reaching up, she cupped the side of his face, paused a moment, then touched her lips to his.

All the pent-up desire, all the hunger and need raging inside her, took over. Kylee moaned and slipped her fingers through Rick's hair, pressing against him until her breasts were crushed against the hard wall of his chest. Her tongue slipped into his mouth, delved, tasted, explored. She shivered as their tongues touched, danced, circled.

With her eyes closed, she was lost in a heady whirl of sensation. She drank him in, the taste, the scent, the hard planes of his well-honed body. She held nothing back and for the first time in her life let her heart take over.

Rick was the first to pull back, to end the kiss. They were breathing as hard as racehorses. Kylee realized she still had his face imprisoned between her hands. She couldn't break contact with his dark-eyed gaze, for in the depths of his eyes lay the promise of fulfillment.

She had never felt so alive, as if every nerve ending were pulsing with life. She was quivering in anticipation. When a bead of perspiration trickled between her breasts, she felt every centimeter of its sensuous slide. Despite the heat in the closed-up house, she shivered. Leaning into Rick, she kissed him again, daring to move boldly against him. Her nipples ached. Deep in her throat, a moan voiced her need.

Rick felt that need, for it was echoed in his own heart. He slipped his hands up beneath her tank top, touched her naked breasts. Her nipples were pebble hard. When he traced his open palms over them, she cried out. Her fingers tightened in his hair.

"Let me love you, Kylee. Let me show you how good it will be between us," he whispered.

She sat up and his hands slipped away from her breasts, down her midriff. He lay his palms on her thighs below the hem of her shorts, watching her intently. She reached down and grabbed the hem of her tank top. Yanking it up over her head, Kylee tossed it over her shoulder. With her breasts exposed to his gaze, she sat there waiting, wanting, but not for very long.

Rick reached out and cupped her breasts gently, lifted them, gazed down at the perfection that was Kylee. He lowered his head to suck on her nipples, one and then the other, back and forth.

She threw her head back, her hands grasping the soft material of his worn T-shirt. She cried out, desperate for release as the incessant throb building in the bud at the apex of her thighs intensified. Burning with desire, her hands tore at Rick's T-shirt. The fabric was worn, thin from many washings. The material ripped away from the neckline with a rending tear.

Beyond control, she jerked the front of his shirt down to his waist, leaving his arms in the sleeves, the crew neck banding his throat. Kylee ran her fingers up and down his abs, just the way she had envisioned doing when she first saw him exercising. He was rock hard perfection.

Rick's hand went to the button at the waistband of

her shorts. After two tries at slipping it open, he gave up and pulled. The button popped and flew over the back of the sofa. Kylee squirmed around until he could lower her zipper and slid her shorts and panties to her hips.

In one deft move, he used his strength to hold her close as he slid them both off the sofa to the *lau hala* mat on the floor. Kylee stretched out full length and lay there looking up at him. Her blue eyes had darkened to the color of the midnight sky backlit by a full moon. He reached down and drew her shorts and panties the rest of the way over her hips and down her legs. She kicked them off and reached for him.

Before he moved into her arms, Rick shucked off his own shorts, pulled off the remnants of his T-shirt with a smile, and then raised himself to his knees. He was fully aroused.

Kylee stared up at Rick, the *lau hala* mat beneath her cool and slick. She gazed up in wonder at his erection. Despite her past, despite the wave of trepidation, she felt as she lay there watching him, she wanted Rick Pau, wanted him in ways she'd wanted no other man.

There was no rational explanation for the way she felt about him, other than that he had given her a glimpse into a world she had never known and never would know unless she took a chance.

"Are you sure this is what you want, Kylee?" His words came to her over the sound of the rain lashing the roof and the wind howling outside.

"Yes, yes it is." She reached up, slowly, like a child who has been warned against touching a rare treasure, and stroked him with her fingertip.

Still on his knees beside her, Rick closed his eyes, threw his head back, and let her explore him with her hand until he thought he would explode.

"Stop, Kylee," he whispered. When he had collected himself, he looked down at her again. Panic and confusion pained her expression.

"Did I do something wrong?"

"You are perfect. I'm going to leave you for a minute. I almost hate to give you time to change your mind, but I think we should play it safe."

"I won't change my mind," she told him. There was a confident certainty in her calm assurance.

Rick pushed up to his feet and left her staring up at the vaulted, open-beamed ceiling of the cottage. *Play it safe.* She shook her head in the semidarkness. Even though she might have lost all sense of reason, Rick was responsible enough to look out for both of them.

He was back in only seconds, but they seemed like hours. Once more he knelt beside her knees and sat back on his heels. Reaching down, he lifted her hair out from beneath her head and shoulders, spread it around her like a golden halo on the woven mat. Then he ran his hands over her face, traced her lips with his fingertips, continued down along her throat, trailed his hands over her collarbones.

Kylee closed her eyes and bit her lips together to keep from crying out. He was slowly, systematically charting his way down, all the way from her hairline. When he reached her breasts, stroking them slowly, then moving his fingers over her rib cage, she almost screamed with need.

He was molding his hands over her hips, along the outside of her thighs. Her knees, her calves, her ankles, and then her toes were kneaded and caressed in turn. Kylee was writhing now, her head thrashing from side to side.

His hands closed around her ankles. He opened her legs. He drew the left one over his knees until he was kneeling between her thighs.

Kylee's breath caught in her throat. She pressed her open palms on the mat on either side of her as Rick bent forward, lifted her legs, and draped them over his shoulders. He lowered his head and kissed her in that most intimate of places.

Out of control, as if she were being tossed on the waves of the stormy sea that surrounded the island, she bucked and moaned but he wouldn't stop, wouldn't lift his head or stop the intense, soul-shattering torture until she finally shuddered and came.

She could hear herself sobbing his name over and over, and yet was powerless to stop. He had given her the universe and she had yet to give him anything at all.

Rick gently drew her legs off his shoulders. When she lay there pliant and willing, he slid over her, took her in his arms and buried his face against the crook of her neck and felt her frantic pulse until it began to subside.

He reached down, slid his hand between their bodies, and slipped his fingers inside her. She was hot and wet and ready for him. Knowing this was her first time, he didn't want to hurt her. He wanted to take things slowly, to make it perfect for her, but he was ready to explode. Rick moved his fingers along her slippery flesh. She quivered and rose to follow the movement of his hand.

"Rick, oh Rick," she whispered.

"I'm going to come inside you, Kylee."

"Yes," she whispered, urging him on with her hands on his hips.

As she lay beneath him, relishing the feel of his smooth, hard body, Kylee was certain she could feel each and every inch of her skin. Flashing hot and cold, she was alive with sensation, pulsing with the need to have him fill her.

"Please, Rick," she urged, not caring how desperate she sounded, but she was desperate—for him, for his body, for the deep, resonating fulfillment to hit her again. But this time she wanted to share it with him.

Rick withdrew his hand and pressed closer as he positioned himself. He hoped and prayed she was as ready as she claimed. He wanted this to be a special night for her, a memory she would cherish no matter what the future held in store. With aching slowness he pressed into her, further, further until he heard her gasp. She froze, held still, and so did he.

His breath was coming, harsh and fast. Every muscle tensed as he strained to hold back while she accustomed herself to the fullness of having him inside her. She was tight, so very tight, so warm.

He eased in further. She clutched his shoulders and cried out, a sharp, keening sound that lasted only a split second. He plunged into her and withdrew partially.

"No! Don't stop," she urged.

It was all the encouragement he needed. Rick moved, rocking with her, holding back until he could feel her quiver and tighten around him. He carried her up, up and over the edge again. This time he was with her. This time when she called out his name, he threw back his head and let out a cry of his own when his release came.

The sound of their voices was lost in the moan of the wind and the tattoo of the falling rain.

Dawn came all too soon for Kylee, who woke up naked as a newborn in Rick's bed with one leg draped over his thigh. The bedroom was still dim, but daylight was trying to squeeze through the edges of the boarded-up windows. Kylee was content to lie with her hand on Rick's heart while he slept on. She could hear the roosters outside, crowing their little fowl hearts out and wondered how they had survived the wind. When she pictured them in the branches of the *hau* bush stripped naked of their feathers, she couldn't suppress a giggle.

Rick opened one eye and stared up at her. "What's so funny?"

"Naked roosters."

"I'm tempted to make a joke about naked cocks."

"Please don't," she groaned and buried her face against his neck.

They fell silent and he pulled her close. Kylee let her mind drift, lulled by the isolation they shared in the boarded-up house. Once they opened the doors to the new day, once the drapes were opened, they would have to face the sunlight and the world. Not to mention the ravages of the storm. She likened herself to a butterfly emerging from a cocoon, except she was far from certain that she had unfolded her wings.

Last night with Rick seemed like a dream now. She was almost afraid to think about what happened, about how far she had let herself go. Giving herself to this man, to any man for that matter, had been the furthest thing from her mind when she packed up her computer to come to Kauai. The holiday had been a last-ditch effort to hang on to her sanity and get her work moving again.

She had moved more than her work. She had been profoundly changed. Now, she was profoundly frightened. Who was this man she had given herself to? What magic had the sun and the sea, the jungle-like forest alive with birds and flowers, worked on her heart and soul?

She had been seduced by the island and the man. Seduced in such a casual, gentle way, almost as if she didn't know it was happening until she was under a spell.

"You're so quiet," he said.

Kylee started. She'd never woken up with a man before, never had a hard masculine body in bed beside her, never heard the sound of a deep, sensual voice in her ear at the break of day.

"I was thinking."

"About me?"

She could answer honestly. "Who else?"

"Kylee, I want to tell you something and I want you to listen well. I treasure what you gave me last night."

She closed her eyes and could almost feel his hands on her again. After they made love, he had picked her up and carried her into his room. Before the storm, he had filled the sunken tub in his bath with water to save in case they would be without it after the storm. After they made love, he had put her on the hardwood floor, washed her thighs with cool, clear water, wiped away all traces of her lost virginity.

"I feel like such an oddity. A twenty-five-year-old virgin." Nervousness made her laugh. "Sort of like finding the missing link, huh? I hope I wasn't too clumsy or anything."

"Are you embarrassed?" He put his hand beneath her chin, made her face him. "You might say I was as inexperienced as you last night. I've never slept with a virgin. Angela certainly wasn't one when we met. I hope I didn't hurt you."

"No. You didn't." Kylee shook her head, expecting to die of embarrassment within the next two minutes. The fear she had felt upon remembering was building. She wanted to think about anything but what they had done last night. Without a clue as to where to go from here, she looked over at the clock on the bedside table.

"Power's out," Rick said, stretching his arms wide over his head. His toes wriggled back and forth beneath the sheet. "Maybe we should forget the time and stay in bed all day."

"Maybe we should go outside and see if anything is damaged." She tried to slide out from beneath the sheet.

His hand grasped her upper arm. "Let's do stay here a little longer. What do you say?"

Kylee sat on the edge of the bed with her back to him. She stared at the light passing through the cracks around the boarded windows and then curled her bare toes. Once the sun flooded the house and the day was allowed inside, the magic of the night would end. She would have to think about what she had done and why and where she would go from here.

But for now, they were alone, closeted in the house, comfortably hidden away from the world. Kylee turned and slid back into bed.

Rick had recognized the fear in her eyes the minute they arose and he opened the doors and the screens. All through breakfast, he had kept up a steady stream of talk, outlining the cleanup plan he would undertake once they had the plywood off the windows and stacked away again. He asked her to help him, not so such because he needed it, but because he wanted to keep her beside him so that he could hold her fear at bay.

Making love with Kylee had been more than he had ever dreamed. He had suspected they would be good together, ever since that first day when he had found her standing there like a wet kitten on the lanai—but he had never imagined just how good. The haunting sensation that somehow she had been meant for him since the beginning of time had not lessened as the days passed and he got to know her. If anything, that feeling had grown stronger.

Now that they had made love, he wanted her more than he had ever wanted anything in his life—even more than life itself. Rick marveled at the depth of the feeling he had for this woman who, a little more than a week ago, had been a virtual stranger until he looked into her eyes.

She was fragile and uncertain. He was determined to help her through the next few hours and days, to stay close to her and yet give her enough space to work things through.

* * *

"Want a soda?"

Kylee heard Rick call out and watched him throw down the green rake he'd been wielding for far too long. He swiped his arm across his forehead, wiping off sweat. She stopped gathering broken branches from a tall, wild plum tree and piling them at the edge of the lot.

"I thought you'd never ask." She pushed her sunglasses up her nose and started walking across the yard. "I would have hated to see this place after the hurricane," she said, surveying the damage to the yard.

There were leaves and small branches everywhere, thick as a carpet in some spots. They had cleaned most of the debris away from the house, but there was more than a day's work to be done. If anyone had asked her before today if she might have actually enjoyed doing yard work after a storm, she would have said no. And she would have been wrong.

While she watched him rake up the leaves, she wondered what he would say if she told him flat out how much she needed him. It had been downright perverted of her to stop every few minutes and watch the play of the sunshine on his muscular upper arms or the way the sunlight tinted his dark hair with shimmering blue-black highlights as he bagged up leaves.

More than once as they worked together, she wished that he would stop and take her in his arms and kiss her. She felt too shy to initiate any love-play herself, too uncertain of what she was caught up in, or how to go on from here. Each minute that passed brought on more apprehension, gave her more time to wonder about what she had done last night.

On the lanai, Rick grabbed a couple of diet sodas out of the big cooler he'd packed full of ice before the storm, slammed the lid down tight, and then started back to where Kylee was waiting in the shade of a tulip tree.

"Here," he said, handing her a can and popping

the top on his own. He put the can to his lips and chugged down a good third of it before he looked over and found her watching.

"What?"

She smiled. "Nothing." She popped her own top and took a few sips, then licked her lips.

Rick stole a kiss the minute her tongue disappeared.

"What was that for?" she asked, surprised.

"Just saying thanks."

"This is slave labor," she sniffed.

"Not thanks for helping, I was thanking you for—"

Just then they heard a terrible commotion coming from behind his house, near the river. The cries sounded half-human. A cold chill of dread snaked down her spine.

Rick immediately started running toward the house. She followed on his heels. They put the sodas on the edge of the lanai as they raced by headed toward the river. The cries kept coming.

Rick ducked and picked his way through the bush, following the sound of high-pitched shouts mingled with loud squeals.

"What is it?" Kylee couldn't see what was up ahead. She forgot to dodge a low hanging branch, bumped her forehead, and cursed under her breath.

"Sounds like Kiko," he yelled back.

She heard someone distinctly call out in a high-pitched wail, "Help me!"

"Kiko can't *talk*," she reminded him.

Rick stopped short, staring at the edge of the stream. She came up behind him and peered over his shoulder. The Wainiha River, usually a clear running stream, was flowing deep and wild, carrying storm water down from the mountains. The water was no longer clear and bubbling as usual, but a madly thundering, muddy torrent.

They heard the shout again and plunged on to the right. Within ten yards she saw the little boy she'd talked to in the road clinging to a thick branch that hung out over the deadly stream. The child was shouting for help and each time he did, Kiko, happily mired in mud on the slippery bank nearby, would raise his dirt-encrusted snout and squeal in harmony.

"Oh my God, Rick. If he slips into the water—"

"This kid is always getting himself into scrapes. He'll be all right." Rick sounded calm and certain. Kylee wasn't as sure.

"Hang on, Zeb," Rick called out to the boy as he made his way down the last few feet of slick embankment. He grabbed the trunk of the nearest tree and used it to steady himself until he'd tested enough of the tangled undergrowth to find a sturdy branch to hold him.

"Don't come too far down the bank," Rick warned her over his shoulder. "You might slip and get swept under."

She didn't want to think about losing her footing or being tugged along over the rocks in the streambed.

"Help!" Zeb spied Rick and started crying. "I get plenty stuck ovah heah!"

"Hang on, Zeb. I'll get you down but you have to hold on until I get closer." Rick inched his way down the bank, hanging on limbs as he went. He was within arm's reach of the little boy who had shimmied out over the water and wrapped himself around the damp branch.

Kylee's heart was in her throat as she watched Rick work his way down the embankment. "Be careful," she warned.

Her tennis shoes were practically buried in mud. She clutched a dangling tree branch. Her thighs were streaked with dirt, her tank top clinging to her damp skin. At the sound of her voice, Kiko had left the water and was grunting his way over to her. Kylee tried to motion him away with one hand, her attention focused on Rick.

Rick called up to the child in the tree. "Wiggle out this way, Zeb." Patiently, keeping his voice calm, Rick slowly coaxed the child forward.

"Mo' bettah I stay heah." Zeb sounded as if he wasn't going anyplace.

"Mo' bettah you come dis side. I get you down. No mattah." Rick easily slipped into the island pidgin the boy was most familiar with. "Come."

There was a two-second contest of wills while Rick stared down the frightened little Hawaiian boy. Finally, inch by inch, Zeb slowly started crawling toward Rich's hand.

"What you doing deah anyway?" Rick tried to keep the child talking while he inched closer.

"I come get Kiko. Him by da wattah, I get scared. I go up tree, so can hit heem with da steek, den he run back." Zeb had stopped moving while he spoke.

"Keep crawling," Rick urged. The kid was almost close enough for him to grab.

"Did he say he was going to make a *steak* out of this thing?" Kylee asked. She was backed up against a rock, still trying to shoo Kiko back. The porker was obviously smitten with her.

"He said he was going to hit him with a 'steek,' a stick." Rick's hand closed over the little boy's T-shirt. He stretched and managed to get his arm locked around Zeb's waist.

Kylee held her breath.

Apparently, lifting the five-year-old adventurer took very little effort on Rick's part. Within seconds, he was holding Zeb on safe, if not dry, land.

Then he reached out for Kylee, who put her hand in his. Rick pulled her up the bank and Kiko followed, as tame as a kitten.

Kylee watched as Rick set the child down, cupped the boy's little chin in the palm of his hand, and looked down into Zeb's face. "Don't go by da wattah no more aftah a storm come tru'. You gotta be more *akamai* den dat."

"Okay, Reek."

"You family good?"

"Okay."

"Tell 'em hi. Bettah get home." Rick gave the child a gentle tap on the rear.

"Tanks, Reek!" Zeb called out with a wave and a holler as he scrambled through the foliage at the edge of the river, quickly heading for home.

"No problem," Rick called out before he smiled down at Kylee and pulled her into the shelter of his arm.

She leaned against him, thankful the boy was safe. Watching Rick's natural exchange with the wayward child had warmed her heart and started her thinking thoughts she had never before entertained.

"What did you tell him?"

"To be smarter next time."

They watched as Kiko snorted and then ran after the child, but the animal paused once to look back adoringly at Kylee before he pranced on. She and Rick both started laughing at once. It was the most light-hearted she had felt since they had opened the house and stepped out into the light of day.

"I know what he sees in me," she said.

"And what might that be?" Rick kept his arm around her shoulders as they headed back to the house.

"I'm sure *he* thinks all this mud's attractive," she motioned down at her dirty shorts and mud-streaked legs. She thought Rick might kiss her then, for he was staring into her eyes with a thoughtful look.

Instead, he took a step back and asked, "Why don't we quit for the day? We've been at it since breakfast. With any luck the power will be back on and I can hook your computer up for you. I'll come hose the leaves and mud out of your bathroom so you can shower."

Feeling the need to be alone, Kylee hosed down her own outdoor bathroom, taking pleasure and satisfaction from watching the lava rock turn from muddy brown to black as she worked. Finally, the job was finished and the place was back in order. She'd gathered up a set of clean towels from the closet in the hall, replaced the soap, and even found her shampoo container where it had blown off the lanai.

She stripped down and stepped in, lathered up and let the warm water soothe her aching muscles. Once the layer of mud was gone, she spread shampoo through her hair and let her mind wander.

"Kylee?"

She nearly choked on a mouthful of water when she jumped at the sound of Rick's voice and gasped beneath the shower spray. Blinking furiously, she looked over her shoulder and found him standing there in the doorway, watching her.

"What are you doing?" Her adrenaline was pumping from more than the fright he'd given her.

"Admiring the view." He was still filthy from the yard work, right down to his ankles where his shoes and socks had protected his feet from the mud. "Can I get in?"

"Here?"

"There."

She was still shy around him, uncomfortable with the fact that she was stark naked and his gaze was on her. Before she had a chance to say anything, he dug a condom out of his pocket, stripped off his shorts, and tossed them aside as he headed for the shower.

She turned around, hid her face in the stream of water while he readied himself. Then she stepped aside and let him have the full force of the shower spray, feeling awkward while he ducked his head beneath the jet and came up sputtering. He gave an audible sigh of relief once the water had begun to wash the mud off his skin.

Kylee was practically hugging the lava wall, at the same time taking care the rough rock surface didn't touch her.

Rick picked up a bar of soap. "Come here."

"What?"

"I'll wash your back for you."

"I—"

"It'll be nice, you'll see."

She stared at the oval bar of soap in his hand. Slowly, he lathered it until his hands were soapy, then motioned for her to turn around. Putting aside her reservations, she did and let him rub the ache out of her shoulders and back.

"That feels great," she sighed, closing her eyes as he worked his way down her back to her waist and then her hips. His hands on her skin were water slick, sliding like warm butter above the soap bubbles.

He hadn't said a word since he'd touched her. She didn't want to break the spell as she put aside the embarrassment of being naked in the shower with him and relaxed. Her weary muscles let go under his ministrations, so much so that she soon realized he'd pulled her up against him. She leaned back against his strong chest and felt his erection probing between her thighs.

Kylee stifled a moan and reached behind her to touch his water-slick thighs. He pressed against her again, seeking entrance.

Instinctively she reached out and put her hands against the rock wall to brace herself. Rick was nuzzling his face against her neck, gently nipping the sensitive spot near the base of her throat. His soapy hand cupped her buttocks and slipped between her legs.

This time she couldn't hold back a small cry of longing.

She pressed up against him again, took a step, and opened her legs, bracing herself for his entry.

"I want you, Kylee," he whispered against her neck, then kissed her temple.

The warm water sluiced down their bodies. He eased forward, slipped between her thighs and then, with his hands on her hips, tilted and lifted her until he could enter her from behind.

Kylee cried out again and threw her head back against his shoulder. It was maddening not to be able to touch him, and wonderful at the same time. He filled her, moved in and out of her, possessed her completely. His breath was coming ragged against her ear, his own throat caught on a low, animal-like growl.

Finally, when Kylee was certain she could not bear any more of the sweet ecstasy, he pushed upward, all the way to the mouth of her womb. She convulsed around him, unable to hold back a cry. He began moving faster, thrusting before he drew her closer. As they stood beneath the gentle pulse of the shower, she felt him shudder against her.

They were out of the shower, clean and dry. Rick looked over at Kylee where she stood on the open lanai, lost in thought as she combed out her long wet hair. He didn't want to spook her by making any more assumptions like the one he'd just made when he climbed into the shower with her. Had she ordered him out of there, he would have respected her choice even though he found himself wanting to spend every minute with her.

"I've moved your boxes back into the living room," he told her and watched as her gaze shot over to him. Her eyes were wide, blue, and unreadable. He couldn't tell if the idea thrilled her or not. All he knew was that she had cared enough for him to have given him something very precious, a treasure she had guarded her whole life, and he didn't want to lose her. He'd already decided the best way to insure that was to let her call the shots from here on out.

"I set up the computer on the desk."

She didn't respond at all. Rick waited for her to ask him to spend the night with her, but all she did was look at him. Her eyes were shadowed, haunted, and confused.

"Kylee?"

"Thanks," she said with a start after he prodded her. "I need to polish up a few scenes."

He knew she was confused; he'd seen it in her eyes all day and now that look had intensified. He wanted nothing more than to have her confident and self-assured again.

"Are you all right?"

She smiled, but it didn't reach her eyes. "I'm just tired."

Deciding to give her the time and space she needed, he said, "I'll bring your dinner over as soon as it's ready. It won't be fancy—"

"I'm not too hungry," she said, her gaze not on him, but on the leaves scattered all over the ground off the lanai.

He paused in the doorway, watching her for a moment longer before he headed back to his own house, determined that no matter how much it taxed his will, he was going to wait for her to come to him.

She never showed or called. He slept alone that night.

Six

Kylee's hands shook as she folded the last piece of clothing and tucked it into her suitcase. Tears slid down her cheeks as she told herself to calm down so that she would be packed and ready to go before Rick brought breakfast over.

During a sleepless night, she had come to a decision. Before dawn she had started packing. It took her no time at all to gather her paperwork and magazines, the computer and her clothes.

She had to leave, had to get away from Rick before the sight of him, the warmth of his touch, the sound of his voice could lure her into staying.

Yesterday, when he left her after making love to her in the shower, she had been in a state of shock, not at what they had done together, but at the power he had to make her respond to his touch. How could she have lost her heart and her control? How could this have happened to her so quickly?

Last night she prowled the house alone, not knowing whether to go to him or not. When he didn't show up at her door, she thought maybe he was reconsidering. Maybe he had realized everything had moved too far too quickly and he wanted to backtrack. Worse yet, maybe leaving her alone in the guest house had been his subtle way of saying he was through with her.

She had no idea what the protocol between lovers might be.

All night she had tossed and turned, trying to imagine where they would go from here. She was due back in L.A. in less than two weeks with script in hand. The first draft was finished. Editing it in L.A. would be no problem.

She would come to her senses once she put time and space between them.

While she was lying in bed last night, her heartbeat had been in tune with the hum of the insects outside, the rhythm of the surf, the rustle of palm fronds on the trade winds. By dawn, she was convinced she definitely had been seduced by the island, not to mention the man, and needed to get back to L.A. where she could clear her head and think about their relationship without Rick around to captivate her with his charm.

Now, in the bright light of a sunny new day, she glanced up and looked out over the taro patch. Her fingers tightened around the cotton sweater in her hands.

There was a sound behind her, the hush of bare feet against the *lau hala* mat. She turned, clutching the sweater against her heart. Rick moved into the doorway and stopped. His eyes narrowed as he took in the suitcase on the bed.

"What's up, Kylee?" The warmth she had come to know and expect was missing from his tone.

"I think you know." She looked away.

"You're leaving."

"Yes, I am, I—"

"Why?" He took a step into the room.

She took a step back. "I think you know why," she said. "I need some time alone, Rick."

"I'm willing to give you that. And space. That's why I left you alone last night. I'll give you all the room you need."

Her heart fluttered. So last night he had left her alone so that she could make the next move—and she had been too frightened by the power of her feelings to do anything but lie there in the dark, mired in confusion.

"I honestly don't know where we go from here," she said. "I've never done this before."

"You can't just walk away from what happened between us."

She shook her head. Turning around, she leaned over to lay the sweater in the suitcase. "But it's all happening too fast."

"Why did you do it?"

Kylee straightened. "Do what?"

"Let me make love to you. Now you want to just walk out as if nothing happened? I don't understand. Maybe you didn't take this as seriously as I did. Did you just want to change your status? Open up new possibilities when you get back to the mainland?"

"That's not true—"

"Then why are you running out and turning this into the very thing you were trying so hard to avoid?"

"What are you talking about?"

"A one night stand. A summer fling."

"I'm doing no such thing," she cried.

Rick began to pace, walking to the window and then halfway back. "Then what are you doing?"

"I don't know."

"Are you running because you can't admit you love me? I'm not afraid to say it, I love you, Kylee."

His profession of love startled and shocked her. She felt as if a mighty hand were squeezing her heart. He just said the three words she had longed to hear for a lifetime and all she felt was sheer panic. She had no idea how to respond.

She held her hands out before her, palms up, pleading. "How do you *know*, Rick? How can you be so sure? I've never been in love. I don't know what it's supposed to feel like."

His expression changed, softened. Now he looked

more sad than angry. "If you have to ask me that, then you really *don't* know whether or not you love me."

"I want to," she said softly. "I really *want* to love you. This is the very first time in my life I've ever gotten this close to anyone."

"Then why not stay and give this a chance to work?"

She closed her eyes and took a deep, shuddering breath as she clutched her hands. "I'm afraid," she whispered.

When she opened her eyes he was standing there before her, reaching out, about to take her in his arms.

She held up her hands. "No, Rick. Don't. Please. That won't solve anything. I'm going home to finish up the script and do some soul-searching by myself."

"I'm beginning to think that's how you like it, Kylee. By yourself." He ran his hand through his hair and sighed. "Forget I said that. You have about a week's time left here. I'll send you a refund." His tone was void of emotion.

"Oh, Rick . . . I never meant—"

He turned and walked out the door. Two minutes later, as Kylee sat numbly on the edge of the bed, she heard his truck roar out the driveway.

Two hours later, Rick sat on the top step of the lanai. Kiko lay beside him in a pool of sunlight. Kylee was gone when he got back. He'd gone bodysurfing to clear his head and cool his anger, unwilling to ruin any chance they might have had together.

He had hoped she would change her mind, but obviously, Kylee had been too scared to stay and talk things through. As he stared over at the empty guest house, he couldn't believe she was really gone. Rick reached over and scratched the pig behind the ears.

If Kylee needed time, he was going to give it to her, but he wasn't about to let her slip out of his life that easily and certainly not without a fight. He would give her time, but not enough to become wrapped up in her work again and lose herself in it.

Eventually, though, if he didn't hear from her, he was going after her. He'd enlist help if he had to.

Kylee sat across from Sylvia at a table on the patio of The Ivy, one of Beverly Hills' trendiest cafés. Sylvia lifted a tall fluted glass of champagne and smiled over the rim in salute.

"Here's to you, Kylee. *Through Her Own Eyes* is the best script you've ever written." The agent shivered dramatically and then declared, "I feel an Emmy coming on." She took a sip of the sparkling white wine and then nodded to two men who had just walked in, headed for indoor seating.

"Those two are in production at Paramount," Sylvia whispered. "By the way, I think you're ready to try your hand scripting a feature." Changing the subject again, she said, "Did I thank you for meeting me here on such short notice?"

"You know I'll always show up for a free meal. Is anything else up?" Kylee couldn't help noticing that her friend was more unfocused than usual.

Sylvia scanned the patio. "No . . . not really. I just felt like getting out and thought it would be great to see you. We haven't really had time to visit since you've been back."

Kylee settled back in her chair and looked around at the beautiful people who filled the restaurant, those who *were* somebody, those who *thought* they were somebody, those who *wanted* to be somebody, and those who were just there to ogle the rest.

As Sylvia went on and on about the way Charese LaDonne was gushing over the script and the "role of her career," Kylee made a mental tally of the Armani suits, the Gucci shoes, the Tag Heuer watches, Prada totes, Black Fly wraparounds, and Lunor shades and wondered if there was anything under the glittering surface of most of these people.

The entertainment industry was a game she didn't really want to play any more than she had to.

"Kylee? Don't you like your salad?"

Kylee glanced down at the plate filled with the very latest in designer food and picked up her fork. "It's great, Syl. I was just thinking."

"Tell me, tell me. What about? Got a new idea already?" Sylvia leaned forward, engrossed in the role of co-conspirator.

"I've got an idea, but it's not about a script. Charese loves the new one and so does the producer so I was thinking—"

"Love? Darling, they're *raving.*" Sylvia was not really looking at Kylee anymore, but over her shoulder. "Hi, Jerry." She nodded and waggled her fingers in the direction of the white picket fence that fronted the place. "What were you saying, dear?"

Kylee sighed. "Sylvia, if I'm to believe what everyone's saying about *Through Her Own Eyes,* I did my best work ever on Kauai."

"And it was *my* idea to send you over." Sylvia looked like the cat that ate more than a canary. "I just knew it would be inspirational, in more ways than one."

"What would you think if I told you I was moving there permanently?"

She should have waited until Sylvia had swallowed her champagne before she made the announcement. The champagne came spewing out again just before Sylvia fell into a coughing spasm.

"Should I do the Heimlich or call the waiter?" Kylee shifted in her chair and pushed her sunglasses up the bridge of her nose.

Sylvia pressed her napkin to her lips and shook her head.

"Kauai?" she said at last when she could finally draw a breath. "You are going to *move* to Kauai?"

Kylee took a deep breath and voiced aloud the conclusion she had reached weeks ago. "I fell in love with Rick Pau." She had realized it was true after the first miserable days away from Kauai. She waited for the terrible, wrenching pain to pass, hoped that the longing would fade, but instead, her need to see him again, to hear his voice, only intensified over the weeks they were apart. Yes, she admitted to herself, it was true. She loved him. Sylvia, her trusted agent and friend, deserved to know.

Her reaction wasn't exactly what Kylee expected.

Sylvia's hand flew to her throat. Kylee thought she was honestly choking this time and started to get up until Sylvia all but moaned, "Rick Pau? You fell in *love* with Rick Pau? I gave him strict instructions to make sure you had a good time but—"

Kylee's heart dropped to her knees. Her mouth went dry, her palms went damp. "It was a setup?" she whispered.

"Well, it wasn't supposed to be *that* big of a setup. All I wanted was for him to take you out a few times, make sure you got out and relaxed a little. I could see how uptight you were over this script. I've never seen you like that before. I wanted you to loosen up a bit."

"I'm afraid I might have loosened up a bit more than you intended."

Sylvia leaned forward and whispered, "You don't mean . . ."

Kylee nodded. "I'm afraid so. Don't forget it was your idea that I experience a little passion while I was there."

"But, my God, Kylee."

"I must have been crazy for even *thinking* about moving to Kauai. I must have been crazy period." The whole thing had been a setup from the start—a little ploy Sylvia had finagled to get her out of her funk.

"Yes." Sylvia blotted her lips with her napkin, then stared hard at Kylee. "Oh, don't look like that. Have some champagne. I suppose with today's technology, that damned hair-net highway or whatever it is that's bridging the gap to the twenty-first century, you can work anywhere." Sylvia's brow knit and her eyes scrunched, a sure sign that she was mulling over the idea. "Rick Pau is a great guy. I'd be the first to admit that. Besides, it's not as if you can't afford to fly back here whenever you need to. I hear there are quite a few famous writers and celebrities with homes on Kauai."

"I wouldn't know. I didn't get out much while I was there." Kylee was miserable. A few seconds ago, everything was so very clear, so simple. She thought she had figured out what she wanted. Now she knew Rick's undivided attention toward her had been set up by her well-meaning agent.

"Sylvia, what are you doing?" When she noticed the odd motions Sylvia was making, Kylee was tempted to turn around. Her agent was partially out of her chair, half-waving, half-patting her head with a white linen table napkin. "Are you signaling the waiter? What's wrong?"

"Nothing."

"Sylvia, you're the worst liar on the face of the earth. You're up to something. Now what gives?" Kylee turned around and looked over her shoulder. Her breath caught in her throat.

A striking, dark-haired, bronzed-skinned man in a stunning silk Hawaiian print shirt and linen pants was threading his way through the tables.

Rick.

Kylee watched, stunned, as he walked up to Sylvia. His exotic black eyes were hidden behind dark, reflective sunglasses. Kylee's heart stumbled just looking at him. For two months she had thought of nothing but this man and the magical time she had spent on Kauai.

The longer she was away from him and the island, the stronger the pull to go back became until, up to a few moments ago, she had been obsessed with returning.

Now, here he stood. Stunned speechless, all she could do was watch while he bent to give Sylvia a quick kiss on the cheek.

"Kiliwia, how are you?" Rick was smiling down at the agent.

Sylvia actually fluttered her lashes up at Rick. "You know how I *love* it when you say my name in Hawaiian. I'm wonderful. How else would I be when I'm with my two favorite people in all the world? Look, Kylee. What a surprise. Rick Pau of all people. Fancy meeting him here."

"Kylee." Rick nodded in her direction as the waiter slipped up to the table with another chair. Rick sat down, smiling at Kylee all the while.

"You look wonderful," he told her.

She didn't say it, but she thought that he looked better than wonderful. He looked absolutely good enough to eat sitting there amid the salon-tanned, carefully outfitted crowd. Neither the men nor the women seated around them bothered to hide the fact that they were trying to figure out who the hell he was.

When Kylee couldn't manage word one, Sylvia quickly began to fill the void. "Rick, we were just talking about you—"

"All good I hope." He turned to the waiter hovering at his elbow and ordered an iced tea.

Kylee refused to smile as she sat there studying her two companions, both partners in crime. "You two set me up again today, didn't you?"

Rick looked at Sylvia. Sylvia shrugged. "All right. I'll admit I went along with Rick when he called last night and asked if I'd have you here by 1:30. But I honestly had no idea things were so serious between you two."

"You told her that things were serious between us?" Rick asked, watching Kylee closely.

Kylee wanted to slide under the table. "That was before I knew she'd asked you to make sure I had a good time on Kauai."

"She just admitted that she was in love with you and that she's thinking of moving to Kauai." Sylvia lowered her voice to a mumble. "I wanted you to be nice to her, show her the sights, but I never expected, I never thought . . ."

Rick was staring hard at Kylee. The waiter came with the iced tea and left before either one of them moved.

Kylee looked back and forth at both of them. Without a word she slowly folded her napkin and set it on the table beside her untouched salad. Her champagne had gone flat.

"Kylee, I was only trying to help." Sylvia laughed.

"So you *were* in on this?" Kylee turned and stared at Rick. She couldn't trust herself to speak. He wasn't smiling now, but watching her closely.

"I think we need to go somewhere and talk. I'm staying at the Beverly Hills Hotel, but if you'd rather not go there, then—"

"I'd rather not go anywhere with you."

Just then, one of the Armani-suited execs walked out from inside the café and came over to the table.

"Hey, Rick. How's it going?" The man stood beside the table nervously jingling the change in his pocket.

"Great, Jimmy. Howzit with you?" Rick smiled a slow smile in Kylee's direction before he looked up at the newcomer.

"Good to see you again, Rick. How long are you in town?" He paused, obviously waiting for Rick to introduce Kylee and Sylvia, but the introduction never came.

"Just two days."

"Still content over there on Maui?" The man either

couldn't take a hint, or didn't care that Rick was barely making conversation.

"It's Kauai. Yeah. I'm staying put."

Jimmy nodded at Sylvia, stared a bit too long at Kylee, then said good-bye and made his way out.

"It seems like you still have some connections here," Kylee said, watching Rick as he held the tea glass up to his lips and took a long swallow. How many nights had she lain awake remembering the way his mouth felt against her skin? Was what he had said and done sincere, or had he merely been devoting his time to saving a mercy-case of Sylvia's?

Sylvia tried to fill the silence. "Rick inherited lots of property here in California. He owns the block of buildings where my office is located over on Robertson. He edits and publishes one of the biggest Internet investment bulletins, but then, I'm sure you already know all of that, seeing as how you two . . . well, I just can't believe it." Sylvia stopped abruptly, looking at each of them in turn. "Did I say something wrong?"

Rick was far kinder to her than Kylee felt like being at the moment. "No, Sylvia, you didn't. I never got around to telling Kylee any of that before she left Kauai."

"And just when *did* you intend to tell me you were a real estate magnate and investment wizard?" Kylee asked him.

"Would that have made a difference?" He was leaning forward, on his forearms, so closely she could see herself quite clearly in his mirrored glasses. She felt as if she were looking at the reflection of a fool.

"Of course not, but you have to admit it's a pretty whopping secret. Not telling all of the truth is the same as lying," she said.

Sylvia polished off her champagne and signalled the waiter, who hurried over to refill her glass.

Kylee and Rick ignored her. "You fell in love with me when you thought I was nothing but a beach bum who ran a bed and board. So now you know I have some income. I'd think you'd be happy, not furious."

"I'd think you'd have the decency to be just a little embarrassed about not telling me how close you and Sylvia really are and that you knew exactly who I was when I got there. How do you think I feel knowing I was a little mercy project for both of you?"

"I would think you'd be happy Sylvia loves you enough to sense you were in trouble, that she cared enough to want you to get some R-and-R and have a good time. Besides, from the minute I saw you standing there on the lanai, soaking wet, looking mad as a wet hen, you stopped being a duty to Sylvia." He tried to reach for her hand. "You were never a mercy case."

"What about today? You two set me up again."

Sylvia held up her hands in surrender. "I was *totally* innocent this time. Last night Rick called out of the blue and said he had to see you. He thought it would be best if I got you two together."

"I didn't even know if you'd take my call, Kylee. We didn't part on the best of terms and I haven't heard from you for two months," Rick reminded her.

Sipping champagne in the sun had given her a thunderous headache. "I've got to go." Kylee abruptly pushed herself out of her chair.

Rick stood. Sylvia blinked and looked around. "I'll get the check," she said to no one in particular before she drained another glass of champagne.

Kylee grabbed her purse and headed for the exit. She was conscious of how many heads turned while they walked across the patio. She whipped the valet ticket out of her pocket and handed it to the smiling young man waiting at the curb. Handsome enough to be a *GQ* model, he ran down the tree-lined street to get her car.

Totally aware of Rick standing at her side, she tried her damnedest not to react. "Don't do this, Kylee. Not again. Not after you admitted to Sylvia that you love me."

Finally, she looked up at him. A slight breeze played through his hair, ruffling the familiar ponytail.

"You're not the man I thought I fell in love with." She looked him up and down, from his dark glasses to the toes of his Italian loafers.

"You're not holding a grudge against me because I happen to have money, are you?"

She looked over her shoulder. There was no one close by, but she lowered her voice anyway. "Of course not. I'm upset. For the first time in my life I opened up enough to fall in love with someone and now I find out that person wasn't who or what I thought he was at all."

The valet came roaring up in her low slung, black Corvette, hopped out, and waited for Kylee beside the open door. The engine rumbled.

"I've got to go." Kylee was torn with confusion and anger, her bruised heart aching.

Rick grabbed her upper arm just as she started off the curb. "Kylee, wait."

"There's nothing left to say, Rick."

"There's this." He pulled her into his arms before she could protest. His lips covered hers in an almost fierce meeting, as if he were trying to bend her to his will with his kiss. Stunned, Kylee could do nothing but cling to him. Her purse cut into her right breast, one of her square-heeled mules nearly slipped off her foot. He held her so tightly there was no way she could break his hold, even if she had wanted to.

Just as she had feared, his deep, soul-wrenching kiss moved her more than words. As his tongue teased hers, as his embrace brought back the heady scents and sounds of the island, Kylee felt a rush of longing so deep she wanted to cry. His hands pressed her close as his lips moved against hers. She was clinging to his shirtfront, leaning into him. Drinking in the heady taste of him as chills ran down her spine despite the dry heat of the California summer afternoon.

He raised his head, put his hands on her arms, and set her on her feet. Behind them swelled a round of quick applause and laughter. Kylee glanced back at the café patrons, who were already dismissing the display and getting back to the business of power lunching.

The valet had already given up on his tip and ran to get another car. Rick was watching Kylee intently.

"I love you, Kylee. You love me. Anything else is irrelevant. I've come this far to find out how you feel and now that I know you love me, I'm not going home without you."

He opened the passenger door and stood there wait-'ng. She looked at Rick, then back at the restaurant. He didn't look as if he were going to budge.

"Get in, Kylee."

She didn't move.

"Please." There was nothing but rock-hard determination in his tone.

Kylee slipped into the car and Rick shut the door behind her. She sat without moving, waiting for him to walk around the front of the car and get in. When he did, she spared him a quick glance.

"Where are we going?" she wanted to know.

"Anywhere you say. Someplace we can talk."

Her eyes scanned the street, which was hemmed in by high walls formed by buildings on both sides. A ragged flash of memory came to her.

"Let's go to the beach."

He put the car in gear. The tires squealed as he headed away from the curb.

The contrast between staring out at the Pacific Ocean from the Santa Monica pier and watching waters off Kauai made it seem to Rick as if he were on another planet. The pier itself was covered with various food stands and amusement booths, a permanent carnival of sights, sounds, and activities.

He and Kylee walked to the end of the pier and stopped a few feet away from a group of fishermen. Bewitched by the sight of her, Rick couldn't take his eyes off of Kylee as she stood there leaning against the railing with her long hair blown back away from her face, exposing her long, slender neck and shoulders. The breeze off the water molded her black silk blouse against her breasts. Her troubled eyes were hidden behind dark glasses, her brow marred by a slight frown. Since it didn't appear that she was going to start any conversation whatsoever . . .

"Sylvia was worried enough about you when you came to Kauai to call me and ask for my help. Are you going to hold that against me?"

She turned slightly, enough to look at him. There was a slight, sad smile on her lips. "This isn't about holding anything against you, Rick. This is about trust."

"Kylee—"

"Let me finish." She took a deep breath. "When I was three, my mother deserted me. She was nineteen when she left me with a neighbor and simply walked out of my life. I never knew my father. As I moved through a series of foster homes, the one constant in my life became books and reading. Later I took up writing. I've never been exposed to a real family situation, never known what it would be like to have a brother or a sister who really cared, let alone a mom or a dad."

As she spoke, Rick thought of his own *ohana*, his extended family of aunts, uncles, cousins. Every month was marked by family celebrations, birthday luaus, anniversaries, holidays. Imagining life without his family was impossible. He wondered how she had survived.

"So," she went on, "my work became my family, my

stability. I threw myself into it. I dated some, but whenever I got close to anyone, I felt inept, uncertain." She shrugged. "Anytime anyone got too close, I was afraid that I'd be wanting when it came to sustaining a relationship. I don't know the first thing about day to day give and take."

Rick reached for her hand. He couldn't stand to see her so alone and vulnerable, pouring her heart out to him. She surprised him by accepting the gesture. He stepped closer, until they stood at the rail, shoulder to shoulder, their fingers entwined. For the first time that day, he felt a sweeping sense of relief. She had opened up to him.

"Sylvia is the closest thing to family I have—"

"Which is why she called me in June and wanted me to make sure you were okay," he told her. "That's what family does. They look out for one another."

She swallowed twice. The bittersweet smile crossed her lips again.

"Kylee, I can only tell you what I said before. From the moment I saw you, everything Sylvia said to me flew out the window. I wanted to get to know you. I wanted to show you Kauai. There was something in your eyes, in your smile, that told me you were the one I've been waiting for since my marriage ended. When I got to know you, I knew my intuition was right."

"But—"

He gently squeezed her hand. "Let me finish. I didn't tell you about the extent of my business ventures because I don't really see all of that as who I am. I've always wanted to keep that part of my life separate so that I could walk away from all of it tomorrow and be happy waiting tables in Hanalei. I don't define myself by what I have. As far as I'm concerned, money is just dirty paper that gets you through life. I wanted you to fall in love with me, Rick Pau, without all the trappings.

That way, if I ever did decide to drop out and walk away from it all, you wouldn't be disappointed."

"When were you planning to tell me?"

"You walked out on me, Kylee. I was waiting for you to come back. I can't wait any longer."

He could see her struggling. Finally, she shoved her sunglasses up onto her head and looked him in the eyes.

"I was confused. I didn't know if I was in love with you or the *idea* of you, the handsome, island lover, but every day I was away from you, I missed you more. I wanted to go back that first week I was here in L.A. again, but I made myself wait. There was the script to finish, then the meetings with Charese and the producers. I kept waiting for my feelings for you to cool. I kept thinking I would forget the way you make me feel, the way I need you, but it only got worse."

He let go of her hand to slip his arms around her shoulders and hold her close.

"No one told me love was supposed to hurt," she whispered.

"It only hurts when you deny it, Kylee, when you don't nourish it. You know what we had on Kauai, how great it was between us. You were able to write. I thought I knew what your work means to you, but I had no idea that it was all you had. It's your lifeline and I would never ask you to give that up. Not in a million years. All I'm asking is that you think about loving me as much as your writing. Think about what we had this summer and what it would be like to have that love last a lifetime."

With a glance over his shoulder, Rick dismissed the fishermen, tourists, and sightseers on the pier. Placing his hand beneath her chin, he tipped Kylee's face up to his and lowered his head to kiss her.

* * *

Kuiho Highway was packed with rental cars, and the humid September air was as thick as pea soup without the trade winds to cool the island. Bumper-to-bumper traffic lined the single-lane bridges that spanned the Wainiha River. Two weeks earlier than she'd planned on arriving on Kauai, Kylee drove with care. She snaked the rental Jeep forward until it was her turn to cross the bridges and then, a few yards farther, she turned left up Powerhouse Road. She laughed when the Jeep hit a deep pothole and mud flew up off the tires. The interior of the small car was packed with a duffle filled with clothing, boxes of computer equipment, a copy machine, a modem, and three phones.

The *Hale Hanea* sign appeared amid the foliage before she expected it. Kylee slammed on the brakes, put the gearshift into reverse, and then swung the Jeep across the road and down the steep drive. There were three cars in the drive already. As Kylee maneuvered to pull up in front of the rental house, a stunning young woman wrapped in a colorful sarong, her long dark hair hanging to her waist, walked across the lanai and waved.

Kylee felt her stomach lurch. The lighthearted euphoria she had been feeling since she boarded the plane that morning quickly dissolved. Rick had said she would know where to find him.

But she hadn't expected to find him with someone else.

Dazed, she sat there immobilized until she realized the brunette was waiting for her to roll down the window. Kylee hit the power button and the window slipped down.

"Hi, are you looking for Rick?" When the girl leaned against the lanai railing, Kylee couldn't help but notice she was very well endowed.

"I was," Kylee said, tempted to throw the still-idling Jeep into reverse, whip around, and head back up the

drive before Rick found out she was here and she suffered more humiliation.

"If you're in the hula class, they've already started."
The girl shook out her hair and let it dust her shoulders.

"No. I . . . I just came by to . . ." *To have my heart
broken into a thousand pieces.*

Just then, a short, paunchy, balding man with a
goatee walked out of the guest house, crossed the lanai, and slipped his arm around the girl's waist.

"Hi," he called out with a wave. "I'm Dave Thompson.
You a friend of Rick's?"

"I . . ." Kylee's heartbeat accelerated. "Yes," she
smiled. "I am. Are you two staying here?"

"Two weeks. We're from Seattle. On our honeymoon." Dave Thompson gave his new bride another
squeeze.

"Congratulations," Kylee called out as she popped
the door of the Jeep, swung out, and headed for the
house at a trot. As she drew near, she heard a recording of a Hawaiian song. Kiko came prancing out of
the bushes and froze when he saw her. She laughed
aloud when he came lumbering across the lawn, snorting out a greeting. She hurried up the steps, leaving
him behind, and kicked off her shoes when she
reached Rick's lanai.

Her bare feet made no sound as she crossed the
deck and stopped outside his door. She could see him
inside, dressed in his familiar tank top and swim
trunks, his back to her. For a moment she thought he
might be playing the guitar when she saw him sway,
then she noticed his arms moving in time to the music.
He was doing the hula. Beyond him, seated together
on the sofa, his *haole* students were watching intently,
mesmerized by the seductive lure of the sheer animal
magnetism of an expert male hula dancer.

Kylee slipped inside and stood there watching in excitement and anticipation until the recording ended

and so did Rick's dance. The ladies on the couch burst into enthusiastic applause.

Rick immediately turned around, as if he knew someone was watching. His gaze instantly locked with hers across the room.

"Komo mai," he said with a wide smile as he held his hand out to her. "Come in."

She crossed the cool, wood floor and took his hand. "I got away earlier than I expected and decided to surprise you, but you don't look very surprised."

"I knew you were here. I felt it when you walked in, just the way I knew we were meant to be together from the start." Rick reached for her, ran his hand up and down her bare arm. His smile widened. "It helps to have a cousin at the car rental booth in Lihue, too."

"It looks like I won't be able to get away with anything here on Kauai."

"You won't have any time to try," he said, pulling her close. "Not with all the aunties and uncles and cousins and new in-laws you are going to have in your life."

She felt a wave of anxiety and then drank in his smile, reassuring herself that Rick would help her adjust. Soon she would have all the family she'd ever wanted and more.

She couldn't resist kissing him, so she stood on tiptoe and pressed her lips to his. When Rick raised his head, he looked over at the women watching spellbound on the couch.

"Class dismissed, ladies. Go home and practice."

It took them a few minutes to gather their notebooks and hurry out the door. Kylee couldn't help noticing the touch of envy in their eyes as she said good-bye from the circle of Rick's arms.

Once they were out of the house and headed up the drive, she turned to Rick with a smile of her own.

"Speaking of practicing—"

"Just what I was thinking." Rick scooped her into

his arms. Kylee looped her arm around his neck and was about to smile up at him when someone knocked at the door.

Still holding her, Rick swung around and both of them burst out laughing at the sight of Kiko standing at the door with his nose pressed up against the screen as he made deep snorting sounds.

"Looks like I'm not the only one who's glad to have you back." Rick chuckled.

"I never thought I'd be so glad to see a pig again." Kylee laughed. An overwhelming peace settled over her as she nestled close to Rick's heart. Any last shred of doubt she might have had fled. He loved her. Together, they could see anything through.

His heart was in his eyes as he ignored Kiko's snorts of protest and guided Kylee toward the bedroom.

DO YOU HAVE THE
HOHL COLLECTION?